tormented
ROYAL

THE KNIGHTS OF ECHOES COVE - *BOOK ONE*

USA TODAY BESTSELLING AUTHOR
LILY WILDHART

Cover Designer: The Pretty Little Design Co
Editor: Christine George
Proofreader: Sassi's Editing Services
Interior Formatting & Design: Wild Elegance Formatting

Tormented Royal/Lily Wildhart – 1st ed.
ISBN-13 - 979-8-464060-44-9

I don't need you to light up my world.
Just sit with me in the dark.

-Unknown

Playlist

Most Girls - Hailee Steinfeld

Hailey - WRENN

Better Than Revenge - Taylor Swift

All the Fucking Time - Loote

Skin - Sabrina Carpenter

Fuck You - Don Vedda

STAY - The Kid LAROI & Justin Bieber

Hoodie - Hey Violet

Sex With Me - TRAMP STAMPS

Beautiful Way - You Me At Six

Good 4 u - Olivia Rodrigo

Last Night's Mascara - Brynn Cartelli

Fuck Being Sober - Annika Wells

She's So Gone - Naomi Scott

Karma - MOD SUN

Queen - Loren Gray

You Don't Own Me - SAY GRACE & G-Eazy

Say Your Prayer - Blithe

Don't Need A Man - Liv Grace Blue
Survivor - 2WEI & Edda Hayes
X Gon' Give It To Ya - DMX
Boss Bitch - Doja Cat
I Am Defiant - The Seige
I'd Rather Die - TRAMP STAMPS
Sociopath - Olivia O'Brien
Future Ex - Abigail Barlow & Ariza
Deal with it - Ashnikko & Kellis
S.L.U.T - Bea Miller
Kiss or Kill - Stela Cole
Intimidate You - Bloom Line & Brooke Alexx
Bitchcraft - Jax
Lost Without You - Freya Ridings
Unthinkable - Cloudy June
Only Be Mine - Arrows in Action
Never Ending Nightmare - Citizen Soldier & Kellin
Quinn
PSYCHOLOGICAL WAR - RORY
What the Stars See - Cassadee Pope
again&again - Against The Current
Just My Type - Taylor Bickett
You Oughta Know - Gabbie Hanna
Murder Party - NOT THE MAIN CHARACTERS

One

OCTAVIA

"Rise and shine, princess." The snicker makes me stir, but it's the icy water raining down on me that wakes me right the hell up.

"What the fuck?!" My shout comes out half choked as I struggle to breathe against the stream of freezing cold water raining down on my face.

"Welcome back to Echoes Cove, Octavia. You may be the nation's Princess to the rest of the world, but here, I'm the Queen. You better not forget it." My vapid bitch cousin, Blair, flicks her long, blonde hair over her shoulder before spinning and leaving the pool house I'm currently calling home.

I lie back down on the wet sheets, in a pool of icy water, and curse my dad for being so fucking selfish once again. Thanks to him, I'm trapped in Echoes Cove for senior year, and I am obviously not wanted around here, by anyone. Unfortunately for everyone involved, I'm trapped in this hellhole for at least ten more months until I graduate. My eighteenth birthday cannot get here fast enough, at least then I can move out of this house of horrors.

Taking a deep breath, I push myself up and out of bed, not caring about my wet hair or pajamas, and strip the bed. I know my aunt and uncle have staff for this sort of thing, but one, it's so not cool to leave this kind of mess for someone else; and two, I want the mattress to actually be dry when I go to sleep tonight. Luckily, the bed is in the middle of the room, so if I keep the curtains open it should heat up plenty and dry everything out.

The pool house, where I've been shoved like a toy no one wants to play with, is deceptively big. I have my own kitchenette—not that I can cook to save my life, but I keep the mini fridge stocked with peach iced tea, and all the things I need to bake red velvet cupcakes in the cupboards, should the urge hit me. The headboard of the bed sits against the counter, which is convenient when I want water but can't be bothered to get out of bed, and there's a small sofa to the left of it where there is a small living space. Two of the walls are basically just giant panes of glass, so it looks bigger than it is. Luckily, the curtains in here are all blackout, so I can get some half decent sleep.

Once I've wrestled the sheets into the hamper, I take

a deep breath and repeat the mantra that has gotten me through the past few weeks.

I can get through this. It's just under a year. I can survive this.

I pull my wet, chestnut-brown hair into a messy bun, pull on some dry yoga pants, pocket my earpods, and trudge over to the main house, wet t-shirt and all. I don't have any fucks left to give about what the people in there might think of me. Thankfully, the blistering summer heat means I won't be cold or wet for long.

"Good morning, Miss Royal. How are you this morning?" Pattie, my aunt and uncle's cook, cleaner, and well, general caretaker, smiles at me warmly as I enter the kitchen from the back of the house. Her smile drops when she takes in my appearance, but I shake my head.

"I'm fine." I give her a tight smile, and hope the shake of my head is enough to keep her from peppering me with questions as she has done every morning since I arrived. My father's death was originally ruled as suspicious, and everyone seems to have their own opinions on that. Despite my requests not to talk about it, everyone wants to tell me their theories, even though that ruling was overturned. It took two weeks before they deemed it a suicide, during which I stayed with Mac and the rest of the team. My found family. But after the cremation, and reading of the Will, child services dragged me here despite my protests.

Out of everyone in this place, Pattie's been the nicest since I arrived two weeks ago, though the bar here has been set pretty low. But she, at least, has treated me like an actual human being.

"If you're sure." She frowns as she looks me up and down again, but then forces a smile as I shift from foot to foot and try to look anywhere but directly at her friendly face. "Food is on the table in the breakfast room. If you need anything else, please let me know."

"Thank you, Pattie." I turn and head toward the breakfast room, trying not to laugh. Who the fuck has a room just for breakfast anyway? This McMansion is beyond insane, and for the umpteenth time, I can't help but be kind of glad I'm in the pool house. At least I can't get lost out there.

"Good morning, Octavia." My aunt's shrill voice makes me wince. Fuck ever having a hangover around her. Her voice is squeakier than a fucking dog toy. "I assume from your current state, you fell into the pool on your way to the house?"

Blair snickers from her chair, hiding it terribly as a cough, but my aunt and uncle are too busy scowling at me to notice. Though my aunt has had so much work done, it's hard to tell if she's frowning at me or if that's just how she looks now. Almost everything about her is devoid of life and emotion. Even her platinum hair hangs straight and dead.

My uncle brings his newspaper back in front of his potbelly and rounded face, his disapproval very much evident from the narrow-eyed look he gave me. Though his sparse hair doesn't exactly help the thinning look, his dark combover just makes me laugh. "In the future, I expect you to be dressed before you come for breakfast. I don't care how you lived when you were with your father. While you're living in our house, you'll follow our rules."

"Sure thing, Uncle Nate." I sigh as I slip into the spare chair opposite Blair. Her smug look is almost enough to make me lose my appetite, but I'm not about to give up the joy of food because of her.

"You need to go to the office when you get to the school," Aunt Vivienne starts, and I clench my jaw in preparation for the deluge of bullshit that's getting ready to spew from her lips. "The office administrator will have your schedule and locker designation for you. Your uniform is hanging in your closet, Pattie collected it for you on Friday... And before I forget, you haven't sent over your rent payment. I suggest speaking to your bank and having a regular payment set up so we don't have any issues while you're staying here."

"Yes, Aunt Vivienne," I grind out. Paying them rent is my penance for my father leaving everything he had to me, with no limitation and no guardian to watch my money until I turn eighteen. Well, so long as I graduate ECP with a 4.0 GPA, but that's beside the point. Hell, the only reason I'm staying here is because of the clause in my father's Will, stating I must actually reside with my guardian until I come of legal age. Stupid fucking clause if you ask me, since I'm financially independent, but what's a girl to do? "I thought I'd have to meet with the guidance counselor to pick my classes?"

She looks down her nose at me and tuts. "If you'd paid any attention to the brochures I put in the pool house, you'd know that isn't how things work at Echoes Cove Prep. Your classes are picked in advance so they can build the schedule. You were a late enrollment, so you should be thankful you have a spot there at all."

I nod and take a deep breath, pushing down all the spiteful comments that threaten to rise. I reach for a bagel, and Vivienne clucks, looking down her nose at me with a quirked eyebrow. Got to love the disapproval coming from her in waves.

"Carbs will do horrible things to your hips, Octavia," she scolds, and I roll my eyes, slathering the bagel in cream cheese and taking a bite anyway. I'll be damned if I'm letting these assholes dictate any more of my life to me than they already have power to. I'll eat whatever the hell I want.

"She's a lost cause, Mother. I mean, just look at her.

She's not going to fit in at school at all. I don't understand why she's coming to the prep anyway. I'm sure Octavia would feel much more comfortable at public school," Blair whines. She makes it out like she's doing me a favor, but if her little show this morning is anything to go by, she doesn't want me anywhere near her school. I have no idea why, though. The last thing on Earth I want is her perceived crown. She can keep it. Popularity contests don't interest me in the slightest. I'd rather have a small group of true friends than the masses kissing my feet just because they feel like they should. Life with my dad on the road taught me that much. Fake friends are not the way forward.

I finish my bagel, drowning out their inane drivel by slipping one of my ear pods from my pocket into my ear. If nothing else, I will always be a child of music. Music is my higher power—my soul needs it to survive. Once I finish my food, I push away from the table, not saying a word since no one is paying attention to their newest inconvenience anyway, and head back to the pool house to find my uniform. Maybe Echoes Cove Prep won't be worse than being here with a group of people who couldn't feel any less like a functional, loving family.

I snort. *Yeah right.* Here, at the house, there's only Blair. At school, there will be an entire fucking herd of mini-Blairs. Once upon a time, I went to school with most of these people, but that's before my mom split and my dad hit the big time with his music. Both of their families were richer than God, though after my mom left, they disowned us both. Thankfully Dad had his own money, so life wasn't turned upside down anymore than it already had been. When we went on the road, he had huge arguments with my grandparents, but I was never close to them. They died not long after we left... It feels like a lifetime ago now.

I'm not the same person I was back then, and I don't expect anyone else to be either. Life on the road, with my dad, his band, the roadies... They are my people. They helped shape me into the person I am today, and I'm glad. I think if I'd grown up here, I'd be just like Blair, and the thought alone makes me want to yeet myself through a plate glass window.

After going back to the pool house, I lock the doors from the inside, double checking them since I'm pretty sure I locked them last night and Blair still got in. Once I know it's secure, I head toward the shower. The bathroom is one of the only redeemable qualities about being forced to live here. The shower is legit becoming my fortress of solitude. I never want to leave. After living in hotels and on a tour bus for years, a good shower is something I've learned to appreciate.

I don't rush. It's just fucking school, and I've never really been a high maintenance kind of girl, so why be in a hurry? I smother my hair in my honey and vanilla shampoo that I discovered when I was in the UK, and I refuse to ever go back. When I put the conditioner on, I use my honey soap that I ship in from Marseille. It's to die for, and I just adore the smell. I enjoy the solace of my morning, knowing that once I leave here, my peace isn't likely to last.

I blow out my dark hair, which falls dead straight down to my waist, though the only real attention I pay styling is to my bangs. My hair is pretty thick, so it requires a little wrangling to make my bangs look awesome. Once my hair is done, I head to the closet, but I don't find the uniform Pattie supposedly left for me. I swear to God, if Blair took it to fuck with me, I'm not afraid of punching her right in her new nose.

I close the empty closet door and open the door next to it—another fucking closet—and find the uniforms. Five of them. At least that's one for each day I guess. Who needs this much space for clothes? I'm used to living out of a suitcase... Tour life isn't as glamorous as people think. I'm not sure I've ever had or needed enough clothes to fill one of these closets, let alone two. Pulling the protective, plastic bag from the hanger, I take in the uniform.

The skirt is black and white plaid, which comes with thigh high socks and a starched white shirt. Along with them is a black and white neckerchief thing and a fitted black blazer, both embroidered with the school crest which has accents of a teal green… Someone fucking save me. There's a note taped to the hanger that catches my eye.

Shoe choice is optional.

However, I suggest a pair of Mary Janes or something equally as sophisticated.

My aunt can choke on a dick.

If I have to wear this get up, and the shoe choice is optional, I'm wearing my Chucks. I pull on the excuse of a uniform and groan as I take in my reflection. I knew it was going to be bad, but holy fuck. I spin around and face-palm. My ass is practically on show with how short this stupid skirt is, like I know I have curves, and I've always loved them, but damn. I look like something out of a fucking porn movie.

Please let this be the worst part of my day…

Whispers follow me as I walk from my rental car toward the main doors of Echoes Cove Prep. At this point in my life, rumors and gossip are nothing new. Being the daughter of Stone Royal means this stuff has followed me for almost my entire life. He was the nation's King, and I was their Princess. Whispers were part of the territory.

Except these whispers… They have nothing to do with my old life. These whispers have everything to do with me being back here at Echoes Cove Prep for my senior year. It's not hard to overhear everyone talking about me. Most of it isn't true, so the whispers of whore and slut don't bother me so much. It's the whispers about my dad that sting. I should've known that Echoes Cove would have more gossip than Page Six.

It's obvious from the sneers and lewd glances that these people don't want me here any more than I want to be here. I wonder once again why my dad thought that this would be a good idea, what it was that made him put that stipulation in his Will. There are better schools in the world than ECP, so why send me back to this pit of despair?

The whispers of why I'm back just add to my want to be anywhere but here. The jealousy from having full access to my inheritance seems to be another thing that fuels the rumor mill.

"I heard she fucked her lawyer to get him to change her dad's Will and forge the signature."

"I heard she offed her dad just for the money."

"Well, Becky heard her dad didn't even commit suicide. It was a murder cover up. I bet she did it."

I roll my eyes. The things people say blow my mind, but I know the truth, so I try not to let it get to me. They might not want me here, and honestly? I would have much rather spent the year homeschooling and continuing to travel, so the feeling is more than mutual. Plus, I'm a little worried about how well I'm going to fare in traditional schooling compared to homeschooling as it is.

I know I'm not like a lot of the trust fund babies here, thanks to my dad. While most of them will have limits to what they can access in their trust funds, I don't... And I'll never, ever have to worry about money again, so long as I stick to the stipulations in the Will, and I fully intend on doing that. All that money is one hell of a point of contention with my aunt and uncle. Apparently, despite the mansion on Ballers' Row and the fact that they're both from what Aunt Vivienne likes to call 'old money,' plus the fact that Uncle Nate is a hugely successful investment banker, I'm still an incredible drain on their resources.

Yeah, that was a fun conversation. The one where they told me I'd have to pay my way because they couldn't possibly take me in, out of the goodness of their hearts. It doesn't really bother me, though. Money isn't everything... I'd much rather have one last day with Dad, doing all of our favorite things. Granted, if I said that out loud around here, I'd probably be shot.

I shake my head to clear the thought and focus on the front of the school as I approach. It looks like the type of school you see on TV with the pale stone arch around the large main entry doors. The year the school was founded along with the school crest—a shield with a horse and swords, topped with a crown, surrounded by flora—is engraved at the apex of the arch, just the way I remember it. The red brick exterior is still covered with ivy, and it screams money as much now as it did the last time I walked these halls. It might only be a three-story building, but it's so fucking imposing. It all feels like a lie. This isn't a place where dreams come to thrive. It's where they go to die.

I watch the people around me and wish I was anywhere but here. Everyone around here is so fake, and despite how I grew up—or maybe because of it—fake is everything I despise.

These people... Well, they were my people once upon a time, but everything I've seen in the few weeks I've been back in Echoes Cove tells me that either I'm not the same person I was when I left, or they aren't. My cousin, who was once practically my sister, is nothing short of a vapid bitch from hell, and my once three best girlfriends... Well, from what I've heard from Blair, they're her friends now and every bit like her.

That's before I even think about the boys who were once my rocks... my saviors. If they're anything like Blair has said, then everything about being back here is going to suck. I haven't heard from any of them since I got back into town, and Blair made it clear to me that I was *persona-non-grata* to them. I hate that she might be right, but if they're anything like I've heard, then maybe it's for the best. It seems I'm not the only one who's changed in the last five years.

Thankfully, I've been able to hide out in the pool house since coming back to Echoes Cove. I've been able to avoid the truth of my new reality, but today there's no escaping the facts of it all. Now I'm here, ass deep in it and wishing I was anywhere else.

I try to pull down the skirt of this stupid-ass uniform while I walk, ignoring everyone, and head to the office to pick up my schedule and locker assignment. How this skirt, along with the thigh high socks, can be considered a demure school uniform is completely beyond me. My best guess is that the principal is a perv. That or whoever is pulling his strings likes this ridiculous outfit... and is also a perv. My shirt is almost too tight around the girls, and I'm pretty sure the outline of my bra is on full show, and the blazer is definitely a slim fit too. I look fucking ridiculous. I would kill for my jeans, band tees, and leather jacket back.

I push open the door to the office to find an older, gray-haired woman sitting behind a desk in an excessively lush office. You'd think the wood paneling would be enough, but no. There are gold accents on everything, and a mass of plants that makes me feel like I've stepped into an alternate world entirely. Maybe I'm in the wrong place.

"Hello, dear, can I help you?" She looks me up and down, her bright and sparkly voice at odds with the resting bitch face she looks at me with.

"My name is Octavia Royal. I just started here and was told this is where I should come for my class schedule and locker assignment."

"Oh yes, I should have known. We don't get new students very often at all. Please take a seat, and I'll get your things." I glance over my shoulder as she points, spotting a shiny, black leather sofa. Taking a seat, I try not to wince at the chill of the leather on the back of my thighs. *Stupid fucking skirt.*

She gets up and heads into one of what I'm assuming are smaller offices just as the door to the principal's office opens. My stomach drops. I swear to fuck, I didn't think my day could get any worse, and yet here we are. I knew I'd see one of them at some point, the school isn't big enough for me to avoid them for long, but to see him before my day even starts? It feels like a bad omen.

Maverick Riley walks out of the door, flicking his messy brown hair out of his eyes, swagger on point like he's walking a fucking runway. If it wasn't for the twisted grin on his face, I'd think he was actually in trouble; but when the principal shows his sweaty face, I know that's far from the truth. "It was good doing business with you, teach. Just remember the rules, and this year will go just fine."

That's when he sees me, and his twisted grin turns to

nothing. His dark brown eyes look at me as if he can see all the way through to my very soul. If my icy wake up call this morning hadn't already chilled me to the bone, his look would freeze my black little heart. "You're back."

I roll my eyes because, well done, Sherlock Holmes. "Obviously."

"I didn't think you'd be brave enough to actually do it. Not after the way you ran away," he says, his empty voice giving me goosebumps as he looks me over. I try not to react to the boy who was my best friend once upon a time. Well… one of my best friends. Especially when I have no idea what he's going on about. "Guess I'll be seeing you, princess."

His dismissal stings as he saunters out of the office. His tall, lean form shouldn't be so fluid and graceful, yet somehow he pulls it off with an insane amount of swagger.

I didn't expect things to go back to how they were, but to be treated like we have no history? Yeah, that cuts deep.

The office door closes behind him just as the older woman returns to her desk. I brush off the interaction, instead taking note of the principal retreating back into his office. That only holds my attention for a second because I can't get Maverick off of my mind. Why was he so cold in the short period of time we were in the office together? And what did he mean that I ran away? None of it makes any sense to me. I guess being friends with the guys is off the table, but that's fine. I don't plan on sticking around in Echoes Cove long enough for it to matter too much.

I hope.

My phone buzzes, so I slide it out of my pocket as the office lady shuffles through some papers.

Unknown:

Welcome back to Echoes Cove, Miss Royal. We look forward to seeing you soon.

Yeah, because that isn't weird at all. Nope.

I delete the message with a decisive shake of my head. It's probably just an automated prep school message or some shit. No one really knows that I'm here, especially not anyone who has this number anyway. Though knowing my delightful family, I'm sure Blair probably has it. And considering her feelings toward me, anyone here at Echoes Cove Prep could have it too.

Fuck my life.

"Here you go, dear," the woman finally says, offering me the stack of papers she's been shuffling around on the desk. "Your schedule is as was pre-approved with your guardian. As you know you were a late enrollment, so your guardian picked your classes with the guidance counselor—I know that your old house manager was consulted about your prior education since no one else seemed to have any answers. It's all locked in now, so let's hope it's all okay." She smiles at me softly, but it doesn't bring me joy. I look down at my schedule and roll my eyes. AP English, Business, AP Music, Stats, French, and Gym. This structured schooling thing is going to *hurt*. I can feel it already. But at least Gym is at the end of the day, I guess. "Your locker combination and a map of the school are there too, along with the Code of Conduct, and a few other things. Just have a quick read, sign them, and drop them back here before the end of the day. I've also included your login for ReachMe, it's the school's social media site. Students aren't permitted to use wider social media without permission from a parent or guardian while attending the school, for your safety and the safety of the other students. You will just need to reset your password once you log in. If you don't have any questions, hurry along. You don't want to be late for your first class."

"Thank you." I smile at her, standing with a wince as my skin pulls against the cold leather, and grab the papers before leaving the office. She couldn't be more wrong. I'd love to be late for my first class and every class after that too. Hell, I'd like to just leave and never come back. If it wasn't for my dad's insane demands via his Will, I'd be out of here in a heartbeat, but the thought of giving up my dreams keeps my ass in this school. There's nothing quite like the possibility of my dreams going up in smoke to keep me on track.

I head to my locker. Thankfully, it isn't too far from the office, but unfortunately it is in the main freaking hall as you enter the school. I shove my bag inside before checking my schedule.

"Well, well, well, the princess really is back to grace us with her presence."

I groan into my locker, stomach jumping at the sound of *that* particular voice behind me. I am so not ready to deal with this bullshit right now, but I guess if I get it all out the way now, the rest of my year should be clear. Right?

I turn around to find Maverick standing with Lincoln Saint and Finley Knight. The three guys who were once the closest people in the world to me are now glaring at me like they would prefer it if I'd died along with my dad—and I have no idea why.

"Do you guys have something important to say? I have to get to class," I huff, refusing to show them just how rattled I really am that they sought me out, especially like this.

After Blair's cruel taunts and my run-in with Maverick earlier, I didn't exactly expect a warm welcome from them, but at least when I left here, we were friends. Sure, it's been a minute, but the icy chill coming from them feels like a little much, though it does match the theme of the day.

Despite the chilly reception, I can't help but give them a quick once over. Lincoln still looks just as dark and broody as he did as a kid. All the way from his jet black hair down to his dark gray eyes, he still looks like a permanent storm cloud. His smile never quite reaches his eyes. And Finley... well, he bulked out more than I would've imagined from when I knew him before. He must live at the gym in his spare time. His blond hair falls into his icy blue eyes as he stares at me, and the wave of chilly energy coming off of them makes the hair on the back of my neck stand on end.

They don't say anything. I expect it from Finley; he's always been the quiet one. Lincoln, though, he's always been the leader of their little Three Musketeers boyband. He sneers at me as Blair and her merry band of bitches appear to stand with the guys. I guess this is the royal court of Echoes Cove Prep.

"Little Miss thinks she's better than all of us. I mean, really, look at those shoes. Maybe her having access to her inheritance is a lie. Who would wear those ratty excuses for shoes? Maybe she's just a gold digger here to snatch up a rich husband." Emma—one of my old friends, now seemingly attached at the hip with Blair—taunts, but I turn back to my locker and sort out my books that were already waiting for me. Got to love private school, I guess.

"I think whoever ordered her uniform thought she was skinnier, look how fat her ass is. It's practically hanging from her skirt. What a whore." I don't know which of them said it this time, but I grit my teeth, trying to ignore the comments and the giggling.

I turn back around to face the three boys who were once my whole world, standing among the snarling girls who look like they'd happily smother me in my sleep just for returning.

The guys still don't say anything, and their silence almost stings more than I imagine their words could. Once upon a time, they would have never iced me out like this or let others speak to me this way. Once upon a time is starting to feel like a lifetime ago. So I slam my locker closed and head toward my first class, feeling their stares burn into the back of my head the entire way.

Stares don't bother me. Those I'm used to, so I shut it all out and keep my head held high.

This is just another day in the life of Octavia Royal.

Two

After wandering the halls trying to get my bearings again, I walk into English class, which is mostly full already, to see Blair and one of her vapid besties drooling over two football players. The resulting eye roll is so hard that I worry I won't be able to undo it. I glance around the rest of the room before heading straight for the back corner where there's a seat near the window, next to a girl with the brightest purple hair I've ever seen… And, considering the groupies I've met, that's a feat in itself.

She smiles at me as I slide into the chair, but the teacher walks in the room as I go to say hi, so I shut my mouth and give her an awkward little wave. Her smile only grows in response, and there's just something about her that tells me she and I are going to be friends.

That, or I'm projecting because she's the first person

not to treat me like a pariah since I showed up this morning. But I guess there's still time for that to change.

"Morning, ladies and gents, welcome to the start of your senior year. You don't know me, and I don't know you, so let's fix that. I am Ms. Summers, and I'll be your English teacher for the year. Yes I'm new here, but don't think that I'm a pushover. I don't care what you did over the summer, it's done. Right now, we're going to focus on how I can get you out of this classroom and off to the college of your dreams. If I see your phone, it will be confiscated. I am not afraid of detentions, and bribes will not be accepted. Now that that's clear, let's start with your reading list, shall we?"

Oh my God. She's English. My English teacher is English. Brilliant.

I wonder if she gets hung up on her 'u's?

The girl next to me snorts, and I bite down on my lip to stop from laughing too. I don't know who this teacher is, but she just became my hands down favorite. I'm also glad I'm not the only new person here so I can avoid the whole new girl introduction thing. I make sure my phone is on silent in my pocket, because I really don't want it to be confiscated by my new favorite teacher, and turn to focus on what she's saying.

Ms. Summers passes around a piece of paper detailing the reading list in full, and I grin as I scan it. I've covered half of these with my tutors already. I knew I was ahead, but I didn't realize just how ahead I was. Maybe, just maybe, this structured schooling thing won't be as bad as I've been worrying about.

"I've highlighted the texts we'll be focusing on, but I suggest reading the others because this is AP English, and you're here for a reason. You'll be doing the first assignment in pairs. Pick wisely because you'll be stuck with each other for the rest of the year."

I guess I'll do some re-reads to refresh my mind on them, but some of my favorites are on this list. Plus, *Wuthering Heights* is highlighted, which only makes my smile widen. I've always been an avid reader, so the thought of re-reads just excites me.

Purple Hair glances over at me, pointing at me then back to herself, and I nod. She might be godawful at English for all I know, but she's a decent human, and that's all I give a fuck about.

"Pick your favorite book on the list and discuss with your partner why you believe it's the best one there. Try to convince them that your book should be at the top of the list." She waves at us to begin before sitting behind her desk, and the room becomes a hive of movement as people shift to sit in their pairs.

"I'm Indi," Purple Hair says, turning to face me, and the first thing I notice is that her big green eyes shine like seas of emerald. She literally looks like a living, alternative pixie. The ring in her nose and lip, plus metal studs all the way up her ears shock me. I'm surprised she gets away with them with the dress code. "And you're Octavia Royal."

Normally someone knowing who I am in this sort of situation would make me uncomfortable, but there's something about her that makes me feel at ease. Maybe it's her laid-back demeanor, or maybe it's that she very obviously doesn't look like one of the ECP drones, but I like her already.

"I swear I'm not like a crazy, psychopath stalker or whatever... Though I will say I listened to your dad somewhat obsessively in my tween years, *but* I'm past that little obsession. Sorry about him by the way. Also, I have really bad verbal diarrhea when I'm nervous, so sorry about the babbling. Oh my God, I need to stop." She covers her mouth with her hands, and I just can't. I laugh quietly at her, feeling my eyes crinkle at the edges as I do.

"Dude, you're fine. Take a breath."

"Sorry, yeah okay. Right, let's start again, shall we? I'm Indi, it's nice to meet you." She puts her hand out for me to shake, looking more than a little awkward, so I take it to make that lost puppy look on her face disappear.

"Octavia, though a lot of my friends just call me V."

"I like that." She grins and scoots her desk closer to mine. It's then I notice the pattern beneath her shirt.

31

"Midnight Blue?" I ask, and her grin grows.

"I am more than a little obsessed with them. And the lead singer... I swear I'm not into girls, but Jenna B gives me such a lady boner. I can't even."

"Yeah, she's pretty cool." I laugh, relaxing in her presence. She just radiates warmth and joy, and it puts me at ease despite myself. "And they put on an epic show."

"Oh my God, have you met her? I'm going to hyperventilate. You know Jenna B?" She's practically fangirling, and I have to say it's pretty refreshing to find someone in Echoes Cove who isn't so up their own ass that they care about shit like this.

"I've met her a couple times, yeah," I tell her, downplaying how close I am with her. Some people get weird when they know the people I'm friends with. "They were on one of Dad's tours in their early days. They only did about seven shows, but they were amazing even then."

"I am officially going to die. I dub thee my new bestie." She cackles, and Ms. Summers looks over at us, narrowing her eyes at us in a way I do not like. Especially on my first day here.

"Done. Now... let's talk about *Wuthering Heights*." I bring our conversation back to the class because I don't want to fail before I even start. I grin at her, and she shakes her head, feigning a look of betrayal as she lays a dramatic hand over her heart.

"Oh no, you're one of those. I take it back," she scoffs before shaking the list in my face. "How can you pick Catherine over Jane Eyre?"

"Ah, the great sister debate… This is going to be the start of a beautiful friendship."

I leave Indi behind and head to Business. I'm early, so I snag a seat in the back corner again and watch as the sea of new and old faces filter into the room. There are more than enough whispers and side glances in my direction for me to know that my return isn't a small thing. I knew it wouldn't be, and that's exactly why I didn't want to come back. Despite the fact that the people I grew up with in Echoes Cove have grown while I've been away, nothing much changes in a town like this. It's still just as judgmental and gossipy as it was when I was a kid.

It's not even that shocking that my mom ran off when she did. While I hate her for abandoning me, I'd like to run the fuck away from here right now too, so a small part of me almost understands her actions.

I sigh at the thought of my mom and pull my phone out, only to see a video waiting for me from Mac, the head of security and a general pillar of my dad's touring team. He basically helped raise me on tour. I find the video along with a few messages from the roadie group chat about how much I'm missed and wishing me luck. My heart pangs with sadness. This group of people are my real family, the people who always had my back no matter what. It may not have been a long time since I've been away from my found family, but fuck I miss them. I send them a message back, telling them just how much I miss them and wish I was back with them before a shadow washes over me.

"You're in my seat." I look up to see Lincoln staring down at me as he towers above. Why the fuck does he have to be so freaking tall?

"There's plenty of others." I jut out my chin, the action practically begging him to fight me over it. I don't know where the defensiveness is coming from, but after my run in with him and the others earlier, it isn't hard to see that we aren't going back to the way things were before I left.

"Mr. Saint, please take a seat, any one will do," the teacher says as he breezes into the room, dropping a ton of textbooks on the table.

Lincoln glares at me before dropping into the seat beside me. Maverick and Finley finish out the back row.

Well, this is going to be fun.

I listen to the teacher drone on, introducing himself and the curriculum for the semester, trying to remember why I picked Business as an elective in homeschooling. I know I'll never start my own label without it, and yeah, I plan on pursuing a Business degree eventually, but fuck. Could this guy's voice be any more monotone? The guy's rocking a monobrow too. I bet his name *is* Mono. Mono fucking Peters.

I look around the room, and spot Brittany, Blair's best bitch, leaning back to talk to Maverick. She flicks her blonde hair at him, and her shirt is undone so far that I can see her bra from here. I roll my eyes when he throws a pen between her tits and she starts to giggle.

I turn my focus back to Mr. Peters and try to pay attention to what he's talking about, but something about his voice just makes me tune out. Maybe I got my hopes up too early. Passing this class is essential. Not just to my GPA, but for my college applications too. I bite my lower lip, trying to pay attention again. I knew structured school was going to be an adjustment, but shit. If the teachers here are all like him, I'm fucked.

"What's wrong, princess? Too good to be here with the rest of us?" Lincoln's voice startles me. The question is quiet enough that I'm pretty sure Mr. Peters didn't hear, but the snickering from the row in front of us tells me that they definitely heard.

I try to ignore him, but I can feel his stare burning into the side of my head. Why the fuck is he being such an asshole? "I just prefer different company."

"Oh, I bet you do. I heard you enjoyed slumming it on

the road." His sneer, along with the obvious insinuation, pisses me off more. He doesn't know one fucking thing about me.

"And here I was thinking Lincoln Saint wouldn't ever lower himself to reading tabloids."

I don't deny his statement because there's no point. If I deny it, it only makes it more true in their minds. If I say he's right, I become a dirty slut. You've got to love the politics of Echoes Cove.

He doesn't get a chance to respond as the teacher draws the class to a close. Shit. I didn't take any notes. I couldn't even tell you what he talked about. Fuck my life. I need to ask someone to help me with some notes.

As soon as the bell rings, I grab my bag and try to haul ass from the room but find myself cornered anyway.

"You shouldn't have come back, princess," Maverick snarls. "You're not wanted here."

I roll my eyes at him and try to push past him, but he's a wall of immovable muscle. "Trust me, no one wants me to be here any less than I do. It's just this year, and then I'm gone. How about you stay out of my way, and I'll stay out of yours?"

"Look at baby Royal trying to tell us what to do like she runs this place." Lincoln barks out a laugh, and other laughter rings out. That's when I realize the only person who left the room was the teacher.

Fuck, I hate private school.

"I'm not trying to tell you anything," I insist, standing taller as I try to leave again, only for Finley to block my path. He's always been a guy of few words, but when he says something, he always makes it count. I've known him to make people cry with less than a handful of words.

He still doesn't say anything, though. He may be quiet, but he's loyal as they come. He won't move until Lincoln says so. It's always been like this with them, but now I'm learning what it's like to be on the other side of their team.

"I suggest you get with the program, princess. This is our school now. And you? You're nothing but a minnow. Piss me off and see what that gets you."

I narrow my eyes at Lincoln, hating the gauntlet he just threw down. I am not some weak-ass bitch. My dad might have come to a bitter end, but he raised me to be a boss-ass queen. "You already seem pissed off to me, so what's the worst that could happen?"

The grin on my face only seeks to add fuel to the fire my words have ignited.

Lincoln's eyes turn icy, and he curls his lip. The wicked smile on his face doesn't quite meet his eyes as his gaze roams over me from head to toe. The stare causes an icy drop of dread to run down my spine, but I try to keep my face impassive. "Sad, sad lost little princess. Nobody wants you, nobody loves you, and well… Let's just say that when you're gone, nobody will miss you either. You have no idea of the game you're playing. Don't say I didn't warn you."

"What the fuck is that supposed to mean?"

The absolute quiet that follows me challenging him is enough to charge the air and make my hair stand on end.

"That means, Nobody, that you shouldn't be here. This school doesn't cater to the weak and pathetic. You're not wanted here. You should have stayed gone with your coward daddy." His sneer pricks at my heart, but I refuse to let myself be beaten on day one, and I'm becoming very aware that this really is going to be day one of what, I'm sure, is sure to be a nightmare of a year at ECP.

"But even your coward daddy couldn't stand the sight of you, could he? Did you enjoy finding his cold dead body? His note to you telling you how you weren't enough to make him stay in this world? You'll never be good enough, Octavia Royal. Not for him, not for this school, not for any of it."

Rage pulses through my veins, but I refuse to cry in front of these assholes. I hate how he's airing out shit that I didn't think anyone in the general population knew about. Things like the note from my dad, or the fact that I'm the one who found him. We kept all of that from the press. I stand, trying to compose myself, but all of the eyes crawling over me, looking for cracks in my armor, make me want to vomit. I shove it all back, trying to piece myself back together while he just smiles that dead smile of his back at me.

"You are nothing, Octavia, and while you might like to pretend you're more, you never will be. The longer you resist, the more it's going to hurt. You made yourself free game by coming back here. It won't ever stop, not until you leave."

Maverick steps toward me, leaning forward before pulling a face. "I guess they forgot to take the trash out."

He turns and leaves with the other two close on his heels, but everyone else simply watches as I stand here trying to piece my armor back together.

"Fuck this." I leave the room, determined not to let them get to me, but fearing it might be a losing battle.

The morning passes in a blur, but for the most part, I'm left alone after Business. Mostly because the guys, Blair, and her friends aren't in my Music or Statistics classes. That doesn't mean that more of the same bullshit whispers and taunts haven't followed me, though. I always thought I had a thick skin, but apparently something about being back in Echoes Cove has me feeling a bit more sensitive. It's only been half a day, and I'm already exhausted by it all. The whispers, the structure, the classes. Thankfully my Music and Stats teachers were better than Mr. Peters, and the classes were engaging enough to hold my partial attention. I'm used to chaos breaks between my lessons, so four in a row has my brain all kinds of numb. I'm seriously starting to question if a 4.0 GPA is actually doable. I might need to hire a tutor if I want to meet the terms of the Will because I can't seem to get my brain to play ball.

After I leave Statistics, I head to the cafeteria, which of course is on the other side of the freaking building. At least the walk gives me a chance to decompress a little, as I try to shove down the rising panic about passing my classes along with surviving this cesspit of a school for the rest of the year.

I spot Indi waiting for me at the doors, and my anxiety goes down by about three levels. I might be Stone Royal's daughter, used to paparazzi and crazy fangirls, but I'm still a seventeen-year-old girl on her first day at a new high school. This is a whole different ball game. Knowing that Blair and her bitch squad will be behind those doors makes me want to grab lunch off campus.

"Hey! Rough morning?" she asks as I approach, and my mood lightens with each step. There's something about her that's just all sunshine and rainbows. Even with the whole alt/emo thing she apparently has going on at heart.

"My morning has been filled with Blair and her vapid

bitch squad as well as a delightful run in with Lincoln and his merry band of jerks, so yeah, you could say that." I groan, and she tucks her arm through mine.

"Oh no, not the Saint Squad." She sighs dramatically, and I can't help but laugh. "I don't know where these assholes get their sense of power from, but they know this is just high school, right?" I let her drag me through the doors, my stomach tightening as I get my first look at the cafeteria. The people are no less cliquey now than they were the last time I was here. The popular kids occupy the rectangular tables near the center of the room, with everyone else taking the space around them.

"You're not from around here, are you?" I ask, and she shakes her head.

"Nah, I grew up back East, but my dad is a tech genius and landed a job in the Valley, so now I'm here... With all of the California sunshine and vapid assholes I can handle." She laughs as we walk to the lunch line, and I can't help but roll my eyes when I see what's on the menu for the day. At least there are still burgers and pizza. Fuck the salad bar. I don't do a rabbit food diet. I tried it once, and it was the most miserable and cranky two hours of my life.

"Well, what you've probably learned is that the Saints basically own this town. Maverick and Finley have been his best friends since we were all kids. Even when we were younger, everyone just gravitated toward them. I have no idea why. Back then, I was too young to notice it, but I guess the power is something they were born into." I shrug as we make our way to an empty table by the windows. We pass the jock table and the table filled with Lincoln, Blair, and all of their pseudo-sycophants. "Table in the corner?"

"Sounds perfect, away from all the crazy."

"There's a spot here without crazy?" I pull a face of faked shock, and she laughs as we head toward the table and slide into the empty seats.

"Back to the power system... I've noticed it. It's just really different from the public school I was at before I came here last year. But hey, now you're here and I'm not the new kid anymore, so thanks for that." She tips her can of soda toward me, and I laugh.

"You're welcome, I guess?" I take a bite of the cheese pizza I slapped on my plate and groan at how good it is. I mean, it's not as good as Denny's in New York, but for high school cafeteria pizza, it's the fucking shit. "So you only came here last year?"

"Yeah." She nods before taking a bite from her burger. She chews thoughtfully before she picks up a fry, points it at me, and continues, "And you better believe my alt loving, purple hair rocking personality wasn't exactly par for the course around here. I mean, my hair was blue when I started, but I'm pretty sure the change to purple hasn't made a difference."

"Dude, I love your hair," I tell her with a shrug.

"V, you love Midnight Blue, lived life on a tour bus, and love my hair. I knew I was making the right decision having you as my bestie."

I grin at her because I obviously think she made an awesome decision; and while I might not be here for long, surviving this year with a friend like her will make it much easier. We eat in a comfortable quiet, and I download the social media app for the school onto my phone while Indi scrolls through the reality news on hers, showing me random articles about shit I've never heard about. I nod and smile regardless.

I sign in to the app, change my password, then close it down. Social media always seemed a bit icky to me, but if this is how stuff works here, then I'm willing to give it a go. I slide my phone away as I finish eating and look up at Indi. "Want to go catch some sunshine before lunch is over?"

She stands, nodding, and I follow suit. We dump our trays in the trash cans, and I turn in time to walk straight into Blair, her lunch spilling straight down the front of my uniform. "Watch where you're going, you stupid bitch."

The way she smiles at me tells me this wasn't an accident, not that I ever actually thought it was. Granted, the spaghetti making its way down my shirt only serves to confirm how unaccidental this fucking run-in was. This bitch doesn't eat carbs.

"Here, let me help with that stain." Brittany cackles before throwing her drink over me, the sticky liquid staining my uniform further. The entire cafeteria is silent until Maverick starts laughing, and then the rest of the students join in. Fury and embarrassment burns in my veins, and it takes every ounce of control that I have to not lay this bitch out.

I clench my fists and remember that Mac taught me never to hit someone first. Finish the fight, but never start it. Even with this crazy bitch.

"Blair, that shit is out of order." I look up and see some of the football team heading in our direction. I look over to Lincoln who is scowling over at us, but he just sits there, watching it play out and not bothering to intervene. If he's pissed off, he could've stopped Blair himself, but fuck him because we both know he started all of this.

"Come on, let's go get you a new uniform," Indi says, trying to pull me away from them when Blair leans in.

"I told you this was my school, Octavia. You should leave because this isn't going to get any better for you. If anything, it's only going to get that much worse. Don't say I didn't warn you because this is the only warning you'll get."

"That's enough, Blair," a male voice shouts across the

cafeteria, but Blair pays no fucking attention.

I shrug out of Indi's hold and lean in closer, making sure she can see the fire in my eyes. "Blair, you have no fucking idea what I've lived through. A vapid little bitch like you isn't going to scare me."

She laughs loudly, like I've told her some hysterical fucking joke, before turning and flicking her hair in my face and walking away. Brittany's at her side like a perfect little lap dog.

Fuck this shit. I walk out of the cafeteria with my head held high. I won't give them the satisfaction of my tears. They're just angry tears, but they won't fucking know that, and they wouldn't believe it anyway. I refuse to let them see me cry.

"Are you okay?" the blond football player asks, pulling me to a stop before I get past the doors, and I try my best to smile up at him though really, I'd just like to get cleaned up.

"I'm fine, this uniform sucks anyway." He offers me a megawatt smile, and I think Indi nearly drops dead beside me. I think she's actually holding her breath, her hands shake at her sides before she sucks in a breath and clasps her hands together, looking at him all googly-eyed. It's like she's star struck.

"It does, but you rock it. Even with the additions." He shoves his hands in the pockets of his slim fit pants, and his megawatt smile only brightens as he says, "I'm Raleigh."

"Octavia." I smile back, not wanting to be rude since this is the only guy who stood up for me. I glance around him into the cafeteria. I don't want to be dismissive, but I really want to get the hell out of here.

"I have a spare uniform in my locker, come on." Indi swoops in and saves the day, like a fucking superstar. I wave at Raleigh as she loops her arm through mine, pulling me into the hallway.

"Definitely didn't think you'd be into the jock type," I joke as she leads me in the opposite direction of the cafeteria.

"I'm so not, well usually anyway, but dude, that smile. Exceptions can always be made." She fans herself, making me laugh as she leads me to a bathroom. I strip out of my shirt as she disappears and do the best I can to get the soda out of my hair. I tip my head under the hand dryer, but it's a useless effort, so I focus on drying my bangs and put the rest up into a ponytail.

It doesn't take long for her to get back, handing me a shirt as she leans against the wall. "This isn't the first time this shit has happened, so I tend to keep at least three spares in my locker at all times."

I'm pretty sure my jaw just about hits the floor, but she only shrugs in response. "Like I said, I know what it's like being the new kid."

I'm not sure if I'm more pissed off for her or for me at this point, but I make a vow to myself right then.

I am not letting these assholes win. Not now, not ever.

Three

Indi meets me at the door after I finish my AP French class, and we head to the locker rooms for Gym. We're the last ones to arrive, and I groan internally at all of the bitchiness I can already sense swirling around in here. It's just a fucking gym class, not the Olympics, of course we all look like shit. I tune everyone but Indi out as we get changed, and since we were the last ones in, we're the last ones to head to the gym. I'm so glad this is the last period of the day. It feels like I've been here for twelve hours.

As I push the door open to the gym, I hear, "Is that you, V?"

No fucking way.

I look up and find Easton Saint grinning at me. His startling gray eyes light up as he watches me. I take in a grown up East, raking my eyes over his mouth-watering…

everything. Tall, broad, and ripped as fuck. His once long and floppy dark hair is now short on the sides, and longer on top, and I can tell from looking at it that he's been running his fingers through it all day. He has that mussed, just woke up, I don't give a fuck, look going on.

I head straight for him and practically jump on him. He catches me and spins me around before putting my feet firmly back on the ground. "East, what the fuck are you doing in this hell hole?"

He belts out a laugh before taking a step back. That's when I notice the whispers, the phones pointed in our direction... and what he's wearing. "Picked up a job till Linc is out of here. Just something temporary, and the school board was desperate after Coach White quit suddenly just before the semester started."

"You're my freaking Gym teacher?" I groan, and he nods, the glint in his eye dimming a bit. "So, I guess wrapping myself around you like that is going to really help with these assholes all calling me a whore."

He leans in, glaring over my shoulder before whispering. "Fuck them, V. You know who you are, and you always have." He pulls back, his megawatt grin firmly back in place. "Now line up, it's track day."

The round of groans around me makes me smile real hard. I don't know if he did it for me, or if it was already his plan, but I've always loved running. It's never been a secret among my friends. I follow everyone outside and line up on the track. East winks at me, and I get the feeling we probably weren't meant to be out here, but fuck yes.

"You're enjoying this, aren't you?" Indi moans, and I nod.

"Hell yes, there is nothing quite like running on a clear track."

She rolls her eyes at me, and I laugh softly. "This is the peppiest I've seen you all day, so I'm not going to rain on your parade. Move up front, Running Barbie. Leave my slow 'I don't wanna' ass back here. Might as well get some joy out of the day."

"You're officially my favorite person." I beam at her and move through the crowd to the front, where some of Blair's bitch squad are all simping over East. Damn, these girls need to pick one guy and stick to him. They call me a whore, and yet they're drooling fucking everywhere they go.

"Ready!" East shouts before he blows his whistle, and I shoot off, ignoring the entire fucking world except the track beneath my feet. I run, not paying any attention to one damn thing until the whistle sounds again. It's not until I stop that I realize the cheer team, which includes Blair and the rest of her bitch squad, and the football team are all out here too. Who knew cheer was a replacement for Gym?

By the time I make it back to where East is standing, pretty much everyone else has already headed back to the locker room. "I see you still like to run."

The look on his face is a total contradiction to his cheery, laid-back tone. He sounds light and breezy, but he looks at me like he's haunted. "Running soothes my soul. Usually it's music, but I haven't been able to play since…" I trail off, and I hate the pity I see in his eyes. But I can't play right now, I've tried picking up my guitar a dozen times over, and I just can't do it. Even in Music today I just mumbled my way through. Music has always been the thing I did with my dad.

"I guess that explains a lot. You did good today, though I didn't realize you were back. Honestly, I didn't think you'd ever come back here."

"I didn't have much of a choice. I'm only here for the year," I tell him, trying not to focus on just how much even hinting about my dad hurts. It's like a stab straight through the heart—the sting of a thousand cuts. It's fucking unbearable, and I can barely breathe.

"Yeah, I heard about your dad. I'm sorry, V. That sucks. Where are you staying?"

"With Blair." I sigh, rolling my eyes. "I'm in the pool house at least. Their McMansion is just weird. It's like a fucking museum."

"Yeah, that place has always been creepy," he laughs,

running a hand through his hair. "Okay, you better head to the showers, otherwise you'll be late. We should catch up sometime, though."

"I'd like that." I smile at him. "Drop me a text, and we'll sort something out."

I give him my number before heading to the locker rooms. Indi is the only one hanging around, clearly waiting for me, so I haul ass in the shower. I leave my hair up because I can't make myself care enough to wash it just to go home.

"You want to grab milkshakes before heading home?" Indi asks when I reappear in nothing but my underwear. I've never been particularly shy about my body, especially since growing up on a tour bus meant that privacy wasn't exactly something there was an abundance of.

"Sure, as long as there are burgers. I'm fucking starving."

"After leaving us all in your dust out there, I'm not surprised. Though why Coach Saint let you just keep running rather than doing sprints like the rest of us was unusual." Her observation isn't much of a surprise. My hello with East wasn't exactly discreet, but then, I didn't realize he was our Gym teacher. I have to admit that hearing him called Coach Saint is pretty fucking hilarious.

"East and I go way back, actually. Let me finish getting dressed, and I'll explain everything over food." I grin widely as I shimmy back into this ridiculous uniform. She just nods and swings her car keys around on her finger.

"Sounds good, you need a ride?"

"No, I have my rental, but if you want to follow me home, we can ride there together. I don't have my own car yet. It's just another thing on my never ending to do list."

"Then that sounds like a perfect way to spend our weekend," she says with her infectious smile. She nods on a pause, like she's confirming a car shopping trip on her mental to-do list. After a moment of what I'm guessing is unusual quiet for her, she says, "But yes, that absolutely sounds like a plan. No need to take both cars."

I nod along as I stuff my gym gear into my bag, pulling my blazer on as I turn to face her. "I am so here for that. But first, let's eat!"

I pull my phone from my bag as an afterthought and groan at the ton of messages flashing at me from unknown numbers. Oh awesome, I guess this is going to be a thing now. I flick through a couple of them—the vitriol reflecting back at me isn't anything I haven't already seen on social media—and just delete all of them before looking back up at Indi and smiling. A few hateful remarks are not about to ruin my day.

We head out to the parking lot, and she heads to the pale blue, old-school Jeep Wrangler sitting in the lot. "This is yours?"

"Look, my obsession with Stiles is real, and if you tell me you don't know who that is, I'm going to have to rethink this entire friendship," she deadpans, and I start laughing so hard.

"Girl, he is a beautiful man. I watch everything he's in. Of course I know who Stiles is. Teen Wolf is an obsession of mine too."

She grins at me as she unlocks the doors. "Good, then we won't have any issues here."

We pull up at Penny's in Indi's Wrangler after dropping off my rental, and I'm not even surprised that it's absolutely packed. Penny's has always been the spot to hang since the food is to die for. It might just be burgers and shakes, but when I tell you they're the best burgers and shakes you'll experience in your life, I'm not messing around.

"Hey, Octavia." I look up and see Raleigh sitting with a few guys from the football team at one of the booths. I wave as we pass by him and weave through the masses to a booth in the back, sliding in opposite each other. I pick up a menu and grin. This place hasn't changed at all. I mean, sure, it's been updated inside a little, but it still looks like a sixties diner, all bright pink and white with splashes of orange. It absolutely shouldn't fit in here in Echoes Cove, but it somehow does.

"You know what you want?" Indi asks as a server heads in our direction on skates. Man, I really do love this place. I nod at her, and she drops her menu just as the server comes to a stop by the booth.

"What can I get you girls today?" the blonde woman asks with the warmest smile I think I've ever seen in Echoes Cove.

"I'll have the double bacon cheeseburger with a chocolate shake and extra fries, please," I say, grinning at her while Indi snickers at the look on the poor woman's face. I may be reasonably small, but I like to eat.

"I'll have the same."

The server nods before skating away, and Indi looks at me like an evil genius, wagging her eyebrows at me. "So... you and Coach Saint?"

"And here I was thinking that I'd at least get a bite in before the inquisition commenced."

"Oh, I am definitely not a sit around and wait for something to happen for me kind of girl." She grins. "Now spill the freaking tea."

I roll my eyes and let out a deep breath. "Okay, so I already told you I lived here when I was a kid. Back in the day, Linc, Mav, Finley, and East were a fearsome foursome. They were tight as tight could be, and nobody fucked with them. Back then, when my mom was still around, I lived in the house next door to East and Linc, so we were pretty friendly, I just wasn't one of them. But then one of the bigger kids at school thought it would be fun to push me off the swing set when I was like five, I think? East, who didn't take shit even back then, basically made the kid eat dirt and took me under his wing. The other three accepted me into their circle, and we were inseparable.

"I don't think I'd have gotten through my mom disappearing the next year if it wasn't for those guys. I remember feeling so lost, but between the four of them, I was literally never alone. I remember Linc sneaking over and climbing the tree next to my window. He'd sneak in my bedroom and stay with me overnight just so I didn't have to be alone."

She just leans back in the booth, staring at me with wide eyes. "Are you sure we're talking about the same people? Because I'm not going to lie, that doesn't sound like the guys I've seen jackassing around here at all."

"We were all crazy close until Dad hit it big and took me on tour with him just before my twelfth birthday. It wasn't as easy to stay in touch then, cell phones were a thing, but not like they are now, and my dad wasn't a fan of me having one. He was weird about technology. We lost touch, and by the time I had a cell, we hadn't spoken in so long that it didn't feel right getting back in touch with them. I have no idea what happened while I was gone, but the icy reception I got when I came back isn't exactly what I expected. But I can't hold it against them, not really."

"Hell yes you can. You left with your dad—it's not like you had a choice. They have zero reason to be the giant bags of dicks they were today."

"I mean, they didn't really do anything…" I trail off just as our shakes are brought over. I take a sip, groaning at how good it tastes when my taste buds come alive. So thick and chocolatey. I would happily go into a food coma after having this.

"No, but they didn't stop Blair from being a catty bitch either. You and I both know, even if you have been away, that they could have stopped her if they wanted to." She's not wrong, and now that I think about it, I realize they could also be behind the wave of messages coming through to my phone. I can't prove any of it, so I just shrug.

"I can handle Blair and her bitch squad. They can give me their worst, and it still won't top some of the shit I've been through before."

She scowls over my shoulder as I finish my mini-rant, so I turn in time to see the guys, Blair, and her bitch squad walking in. Awesome.

They don't immediately spot us in the corner as they take up one of the bigger booths on the other side of the diner. As if hearing my thoughts, though, Linc glances in our direction, his frown deepening when he sees me.

I really wish I knew what I did to piss those three off, especially since East was so chill with me.

"Well, at least Coach still seems to be on Team V," Indi says, pulling my attention away from the guys and bringing my focus back to her.

"East was always the most laid-back of them all. Linc was the protector, Finley was the quiet one, Mav was the psycho, and East was the glue that held them all together."

"Not much has changed there then," Indi laughs, and I join in.

"It doesn't seem like it."

Our food arrives, and I grin at the size of the portions. Seriously, salads are for the birds. "Oh man, this is going to be so worth the extra laps I'll have to do in the pool tonight."

"You're going to swim even after all the running? Girl, you're crazy. I work out as much as they force me to, and that's it. I'm not going to feel even a little bit of guilt over it either. I'm going to spend my night in a food coma, and maybe, just maybe, I'll pick up my sketch book at some point. I'm not going to stress if I don't, though."

I grin at her and take a bite of the burger, and I swear I come a little in my panties. "Goddamn, this just became my new favorite thing in the world."

She nods, agreeing as she sinks her teeth into her own. "So come on, it's your turn. Catch me up on the hierarchy around here. Obviously the boys are at the top of the food chain still, but how the fuck did Blair attach herself to them?"

She swallows her mouthful and takes a slurp of her shake before she starts to speak. "I have no idea how she attached herself to them. By the time I got here last year, this is how it was already. I had the unfortunate pleasure of being Blair's target last year, so as much as I hate that it's on you now, thank you." I laugh at her, and she shrugs, chomping down a few fries before continuing, "After the bitch squad, you have the jocks and the cheer team. Though Blair and some of her squad are on the cheer team, so maybe that's how that works. Then it's the rest of us, though being the new kid and outcast definitely put me at the bottom of the pile."

"That's so shit."

"It is what it is, and I'm pretty chill about it. I'm good with being left alone." She shrugs like she doesn't care, but I can see that she does really. No one in high school wants to be the kid with no friends. No matter how okay you are on your own.

"So Linc and the guys, Blair and the bitch squad, then Raleigh and the team. Who are the party people these days?"

She snorts a laugh. "Oh that's easy. Raleigh's best friend, also the wide receiver on the team, Jackson Jones—

there's a back to school thing at his place this weekend. He started here the year before I did and by the sounds of it, he's a freaking NFL guy, which in football speak basically means he's something of a superstar." She blushes a little talking about him, so I nudge her foot with mine.

"You like the superstar?"

"He's a jock, and I'm, well… me. Pretty sure he doesn't even know I exist." She dips one of her fries in her shake, looking down at the table like she's embarrassed by what she admitted to me. I might have only just met this girl, but there is something about her that calls out to my goddamn soul. If she wants an intro to the superstar, I'm going to figure out how to make it happen. Even if I hate the idea of partying with these people.

I glance over at the jock table and catch Raleigh looking over at me, so I smile at him. "Maybe we should get ourselves invited to that party."

"Good luck with that," she snorts, and I grin wider.

"Oh, Indi, I know you've been here a while, but you've only just met me. They might be treating me like the new kid, but I can guarantee that I can get us invites to that party." I sound conceited as fuck, but I don't care because the grin on her face makes it worth it.

"Then hell yes, let's get us an invite to that party."

I turn back around and wave Raleigh over. A puppyish smile crosses his face as he jumps up from his booth and saunters toward us before slipping into the booth next to me. "Hey, how was your first day?"

"It was like being chum in a fucking shark tank outside of meeting my girl Indi here and my run-in with you. Indi tells me there's a party this weekend?" I smile at him as his arm goes over the back of the booth. He doesn't quite have it wrapped around me, but it's pretty damn close. This QB is smooth, I'll give him that. He also seems like a genuinely nice guy, so I'm not opposed to the closeness.

"There is, and my boy Jackson is throwing it. He's only like three houses down from you, so you could just walk down the beach if you guys want to come." He gives me that megawatt smile of his, and I smile back at him before glancing over at Indi.

"We could probably do that," I say, and Indi nods in agreement. "Are you going to be there?"

"Of course, I wouldn't miss it. Especially if you guys are coming. You probably know a lot of people here already, but I'm sure I can introduce you to some of the half-decent humans at Echoes Cove Prep." I can't help but laugh. It seems I was right. He actually is a nice guy.

"You weren't here before I left the Cove, right?"

He shakes his head, the smile of his still in place as he gets comfortable beside me. "Nope, I came here freshman year. I've been dominating the field since. It's been my only focus because man, some of the people here fucking suck."

"Yes, yes they fucking do," Indi snorts. I offer my plate to Raleigh, who takes a handful of fries as I take a bite of my burger. I sit and listen while he and Indi talk up a storm about people I don't know, but I'm glad that she seems so chill with him too. Maybe it won't be so bad making some friends before I ditch this place at the end of the year.

"I better get back to the guys, but I'll catch you both tomorrow."

"See ya." I grin as he drags himself out of our booth and makes his way back to his friends. I wait until he's gone to say, "See, easy as pie."

My skin prickles and I look up, feeling someone's eyes on me. I find Linc glaring at me from his booth. His jaw clenches as he looks from me and over to the table where Raleigh is sitting before saying something to Maverick. He turns his dark-eyed glare in my direction too.

Fuck both of them.

If they don't want to be my friend these days, that's fine. But they don't get to pick who I *am* friends with either. I turn back to Indi who looks happier than I've seen her all day, even with her evil genius smile on.

"You, Octavia Royal, are my new favorite person in the entire world." I cackle at her words and take a sip of my milkshake.

"Right back at you."

We sit, chatting about the other politics of Echoes Cove.

It's the standard bullshit that's probably worth knowing before attempting day two at prep, considering just how bad day one went. Our phones buzz in sync on the table, pulling our attention away from our conversation.

Indi grabs hers, swiping on the notification, and all of the blood drains from her face.

"What's wrong?" I ask, picking up my phone. The notification is from the ReachMe app. I swipe across on it, and the app opens to a picture of me wrapped around East from gym class today with the caption 'School slut screws the Coach.'

It's been up for less than a minute and already has over fifty comments. I scroll through them, and the hatred and degradation is beyond disgusting. These people don't even know me.

Blair laughs across the diner, and I clench my hands around the edge of the table.

"I'm sorry. This is so shit. I've reported the picture already, which means it will be taken down—" Indi starts, but I shake my head, cutting her off.

"The damage is already done." I sigh, shaking my head again. I almost feel bad for East because this isn't going to be good for him either. He could lose his job. My skin crawls as people's eyes rake over me all around the diner. "Can we go?"

Indi shoves the last of the burger in her mouth as she

stands up. "Sure."

I grab my bag, and hightail it across the space. Leers and catcalls follow me as I go, along with laughter and calls of 'whore.'

Just as we reach the door, Lincoln's voice reaches me, almost cutting me deeper than everything else. "Don't be stupid, no one will believe this. East would never stoop so low as to fuck a disease-ridden whore. You all saw how she grew up; she's probably ridden more dicks than we have at the school. East thinks way too much of himself to slum it with her."

"You're right," Blair's shrill voice follows his demeaning vitriol. "We're going to have to burn her sheets rather than just wash them. Nothing else will get out the smell of cheap perfume and desperation."

Maverick's laughter booms around me, like the last nail in today's coffin, and Finley looks at me, his lip curled up in disgust. I thought I could come back and live a quiet life for a year before escaping.

How fucking wrong was I?

Four

I ask Indi to drop me off at my childhood home after everything that happened at Penny's rather than at my aunt and uncle's stupid-ass mansion. I don't want to be near my cousin or anything else relating to the other people in Echoes Cove. I just want the sanctuary that my old home brings. Technically, this is still my house since, you know, I own it now. I just can't live here because of the stupid term in my dad's Will stating I must live with my legal guardians, which is complete and utter bullshit if you ask me.

I use the code to open the gates, making sure to re-lock them behind me, and make the long walk up to the house.

It looks exactly how I remember it. It's like something from a haunted house movie, but I love it. The house itself is a tall dark stone building, with the windows and door arched in a paler stone. Finished with dark gray window frames and a matching door. I'm pretty sure my parents had a 'we want to be scary' vibe going on when they picked this place. If I remember correctly, even the back balconies are black wrought iron and a bit pointy on top. Dad used to joke it was to keep the boys away from my room.

If he only knew.

The door opens before I even reach it. I pause, wondering who the fuck is in my house already. Once it's open fully, Smithy steps out and grins down at me. "Miss Octavia, it's so lovely to see you. Welcome home! I've been wondering if I'd be seeing you."

I run up to him and hug him tight. He's much older than I remember, but I guess being away from here for five years coupled with a child's memory will do that. Smithy was the house manager when I was younger, but he was also like a surrogate parent. He was there for me when my mom left, when my dad drank too much... even just when I fell and needed patching up. He might have been the house manager, but to me, he was so much more.

"I had no idea you were still here, otherwise I'd have come to see you sooner," I tell him as he squashes me against his chest. Just over two weeks I've been in this godforsaken town. Seeing him would've made it feel more like home. I could kick myself for being too chicken to check the house out before now.

"Of course I'm still here. Who else was going to keep this place in working order and ready for your return?" He grins down at me before ushering me inside. I follow him to the kitchen, which looks exactly as I remember it—all black and white marble tops and white cabinets with silver handles. It's maybe a little more updated, appliance wise, and I don't remember the espresso machine, but I'm not sad about it. As I'm taking everything in, he pours me a glass of peach iced tea with extra lemon slices. I love that he remembers my favorite drink. I sit on a stool at the center island, and he sits opposite me.

"If I'd known you were here, I'd have fought harder about living with Vivienne and Nate. I'd much rather be here with you."

"I thought your father put me down as your guardian in his Will. I assumed you chose to be with your family after going through such an ordeal." He smiles sadly at me, and I nearly spray tea out of my nose with the derisive snort I let loose.

"Those people are not my family. I'm going to call the lawyer to see what he says. If I can be back here, I'll be here before the end of the week."

He smiles widely and claps his hands together. "Nothing would make me happier, Miss Octavia." The genuine happiness in his tone hits me a little harder than it might have before, and I fight the urge to rub the place on my chest just over my heart. Damn. I didn't know how much I missed being wanted. "Now then, have you eaten? I can whip you up some mac and cheese. I assume that's still your favorite."

I groan at the memory of his mac and cheese and find myself wishing I hadn't already eaten. "I had a burger at Penny's with a new friend, but now that I know you're here, I'm definitely coming back to eat tomorrow. If that's okay?"

"This is your home, Miss Octavia. You're always welcome here. Feel free to bring your friend with you." His smile reaches his eyes, and it warms my heart. I missed him more than I ever thought possible. I freaking adore him.

"That I can totally do. Am I okay to go have a look around?" I know this is technically my house, but if he's been here the last five years, it feels wrong to just stomp about the place.

"Of course, this is your home. Do as you like. I packed your father's things away. I didn't want you to have to do it, but I've put the boxes in his old study. I left your room alone, but if you're coming back here, we can update it or even move you to the master."

I hadn't actually considered any of this, and it's enough to make my mind reel with the possibility. But I'm glad he's packed away my dad's things. I still haven't been through the stuff that he had on tour with us. I imagine that was all brought back here too. I definitely don't have it in me to go through the boxes. Picking at that wound isn't something I'm strong enough to face yet.

"I'll speak to the lawyer and make sure that it's okay that I do move back here. I don't want to lose access to anything. If he says I'm good to go, I'll sit down and think about where to go from there."

"Sounds perfect," he says as he stands, taking my empty glass and putting it in the sink. "It will be nice to have some life around the place again."

"It'll be good to be home." I smile up at him before heading upstairs. The thought of being able to move back here, away from Blair, makes me happier than I've felt since I found out I had to come back to Echoes Cove. I might actually be able to relax in my own space rather than being on edge twenty-four fucking seven.

I head straight to my room and cringe as I step inside. Yep, this room definitely isn't suitable for me any more. There's a single bed with a white canopy, and the entire room has a pink and white theme... None of this is even close to the person I am now. I smile at the blossoming tree still outside my window, then frown from the memories this room pulls to the forefront about Lincoln and the others.

This definitely isn't my room anymore. And those are

not memories I need haunting me, especially when it's clear the guys have no intention of even being civil toward me.

I pull my phone from my pocket and send an email over to the lawyer who's been in charge of my inheritance and my father's estate, asking him to give me a call as soon as he can. Hope blossoms in my chest, and I do what I can to quash it. Hope can be a dangerous thing.

I head toward the master suite on the other side of the house. My heart aches in an echo of the emptiness on this side of the house. There isn't even any furniture in here. I don't remember Dad having much in here before anyway, but this still seems extra barren. He rarely spent time here because of his insomnia, but my heart still pangs a little from being here in the room that was once his. I'm pretty sure I've cried every tear I have in my body for him, and so I find myself flickering between anger and sadness. I suppose if I give myself a moment to really consider everything, I'm overall just kind of sad.

I know some people might find it weird to move into a room like this considering the circumstances, but it feels right to me. I don't really remember ever seeing my dad in here, so it's not like there are *that* many memories to dredge up in this room. Plus, he left the house to me—he'd definitely want me to make use of it. I pad over the cream carpet to the wall of glass that looks out over the backyard and open the door that leads to the balcony.

If I lean just the right way, I can see the tree that stands by my old bedroom window. I push away thoughts of the guys that threaten to rise and focus on the rest of the view of the yard. The pool sits covered and undisturbed in the middle of the expanse of yard, and the loungers dot the edge. The outdoor kitchen still gleams. Smithy really did keep this place spick and span, and I can't help but smile. I'm glad that someone had some love left to give to this place.

My phone chimes, pulling my attention away from my slow perusal of the property. I glance down, and my stomach clenches at the sight of an email from my lawyer confirming he'll call me in half an hour.

Awesome.

I lock the balcony door back up and head back downstairs, making sure to say goodbye to Smithy before heading down the drive so I can walk back to my aunt's place. It's not too far from here, and while their house might be on the beach, I'd rather be up here looking over the cove than right on the beach anyway. Fingers crossed my lawyer confirms what I want him to, so I can move up here.

Just as I'm locking up the gate, a black Porsche Cayenne stops on the road in front of me. The window rolls down, and I try to hide my shock as Lincoln's face comes into view. "What are you doing here?" he spits, eyes narrowed as he all but sets me on fire with his eyes.

I cross my arms, refusing to let him get to me. "I was just checking in. Problem?"

"You shouldn't be here, Octavia. You should crawl back in the hole you came from."

I roll my eyes and sigh. For the life of me, I truly cannot work out exactly why he's in asshole mode. "It's my house, Lincoln."

"I meant in Echoes Cove. You left this place behind and never looked back. Why the fuck would you come back now? You're not wanted here. And don't think cozying up to my brother is going to make things easier for you. He wouldn't touch you if you paid him." The bite in his tone hurts me more than it should, but I refuse to let it show.

"I didn't exactly plan on coming back here. My dad fucking killed himself—I didn't have a choice. Now if you'll excuse me, I have places to be." I turn quickly on my heel and walk away from him, not giving him a chance to answer. I don't dare to breathe those first few steps, listening with bated breath for him to throw his car in reverse and come back to tear me down some more. What a fucking asshole.

I quickly swipe at the tear that falls down my cheek. I hate that I'm crying because I'm angry... Angry at Lincoln. Angry at my dad. Angry at myself for letting it all get to me. I'd really like to go back three months and try and get my dad the help he needed. But I didn't know, and now I have to live with that.

I slide the door closed on the pool house just as my phone starts to ring. I kick off my boots as I see the lawyer's company name on my caller ID. "Hello?"

"Octavia? It's Derek. You asked me to call, so I thought I'd check in. Is everything okay?"

"Hey, Derek," I say, putting as much of a sunshiney tone into my voice as I can muster. Considering that I cried most of the walk back here, it's not actually much. "I'm fine, I just had an interesting conversation with my estate manager, Smithy—sorry, James Smith—so I wanted to clear something up with you."

"Oh," he mutters, and even without being face-to-face with him, I know he's pulling the collar of his shirt. During the few meetings I had with him, I noticed that he did it when he was uncomfortable. "How can I help?"

"I was just told that my aunt and uncle *aren't really* my legal guardians, so I'm just curious as to why I was told I was required to stay with them until I graduated."

"Oh, well. You see..." he trails off, and I sigh as I drop down onto the sofa. I don't know whether I should be relieved or pissed off. I settle somewhere in the middle of the two.

"Spit it out, Derek."

"They thought it would be best if you came to stay with them even though they weren't named your sole guardians, so they approached me about ensuring you would be with them." I cackle at his words, but of course they did. This explains the exorbitant rent they demanded. They wanted my father's money. "I figured since they were actually related to you and wanted you with them, that it was probably for the best."

"What are the *actual* stipulations of my inheritance, Derek?" I try not to be a total bitch, but I've been in this fucking house for weeks now, absolutely miserable. I was dragged here by child services from my hotel room where I was staying with Mac after my dad died. I was told I needed to stay with my aunt and uncle which has been miserable, so yeah, I'm in full bitch mode.

"The only stipulations your father made for your inheritance remaining in your control were that should you be under the age of eighteen in the event of his death, you would be required to graduate from Echoes Cove Prep with a 4.0 GPA and remain in the care of your guardian or guardians. Failure to do either of these things would result in you not having access to any of the inheritance until your twenty-fifth birthday."

"Thank you, Derek." I smile, and for once, I don't have to force it. I might not *want* to be in Echoes Cove, but at least now I know I don't have to stay with my shitty aunt and uncle and their demon spawn.

"Was there anything else, Octavia?" he practically stammers, giving away just how nervous he is. The first thing I'm going to have Smithy do for me once I sort out the house is find me a new goddamn lawyer. I want a shark, not a fucking minnow. I hang up the phone, but my grin only grows as I stare up at the ceiling.

I have to make a checklist of everything I need to buy for the house before I can move in. I'm pretty sure Smithy will handle everything for me if I shop online and get shit delivered. I bounce off of the sofa, practically skipping up to the main house.

Aunt Vivienne is in the formal dining room with Uncle Nate and Blair, finishing their dinner. Blair was just at Penny's. Her mocking still rings in my ears. I guess she couldn't possibly eat in front of her friends. Vivienne sneers at me as I enter the room, and I practically laugh. The sheer audacity of this woman trying to make me feel like a burden when she demanded I be here is astounding. "Octavia, you're late. You'll need to sort something out for yourself."

Goddamn, her voice is so fucking shrill. Just a few more days, and I'm out of here. "No problem, I already ate.

I was just coming to find you to let you know I spoke to my lawyer. I'll be moving out of the pool house this weekend and moving back into my house. I'll make sure to pay you in full for the time I stayed here, though, don't worry. But you won't be seeing another penny of my father's money beyond that. I'd say I appreciate you letting me stay here, but since you manufactured it that way and then made me feel like a burden, I'll just say fuck all of you."

I spin on my heel, not giving any of them the chance to respond. I walk from the dining room, leaving Nate spluttering, Vivienne uttering strangled curses under her breath, and Blair glaring.

All things considered, this might just be the best night ever.

Today was a bad day. I spent the day with Linc and East because Dad was so angry. I don't know what I did, but he just kept yelling at me to leave too. So I ran away next door and spent the day with my friends. By the time I got home, Dad wasn't mad anymore. He was just sad. All he does since Mom left is write songs with his guitar and drink that brown stuff that makes him smell funny. Smithy said he'd look after him and that I should get to bed, but I just can't fall asleep.

My sadness is too big.

I cry into my pillow, trying to keep my sobs quiet. Dad doesn't like it when I cry because it makes him sad too. He's been so sad since Mom went away, and I don't know how to make it better. I still don't know where she went or why she left us, but I really wish she'd just come back. It's been nearly a whole year since she left, and I still miss her every day.

I go still when I hear a tap against my window. After a moment I turn over to find Linc standing in the tree branches, trying to open my window. I rush from the bed and open it for him. He grins as he climbs in. "What are you doing here?" I whisper. He's going to get in so much trouble if his mom finds out he's not in bed.

"I knew you were sad; and I didn't want you to be alone, so I'm here. Now get back into bed before your dad hears us." He closes the window, and that's when I notice he's in his pajamas. I crawl back beneath my sheets, and he slides in beside me, lying so he's facing me. "You don't need to cry anymore. I'm here now."

I smile at him as a tear runs down my face. He smiles back, a little sad too, and wipes it away.

"But if you need to cry, that's okay too," he says as my tears come faster again. He hugs me tight and whispers, "I've got you. I'll always be here."

I cry into his shirt until I can't cry anymore. "Won't

you get in trouble for being here?" I finally manage to ask.

"Nah, East knows I'm here. He'll cover with Mom." Lincoln seems so grown up sometimes, and I just feel like a cry baby. He's only nine months older than me, but sometimes he's more of a grown-up than East is.

"I'm okay now. You can go home if you want to," I tell him through my sniffles.

"Don't be silly. I'm not going anywhere. Now go to sleep. We have a pop quiz in the morning."

"Linc…" he cuts me off by putting his hand over my mouth. I lick it, and he narrows his eyes at me, making me giggle.

"Go to sleep, V," he whispers before wiping his hand on the sheets and closing his eyes. I smile and close my own, happy that he's here. He always makes me smile, even when I cry.

I believe him when he says he's not going anywhere, so I drift off to sleep feeling happier and safer than I have since Mom disappeared.

Five

Feeling much lighter than I did last night, I practically bounce out of the pool house and over to the main house for breakfast. Nothing will bring down my mood this morning. Not even my dream about Lincoln. I'm marking that down in the 'going back to the old house and shaking up my memories of a time lost to the past' column and leaving it there.

I smile at Pattie as I skip through the kitchen, beyond happy to find I'm the first one here for breakfast. I pile up my plate with all of the breakfast goodness I can manage and dive in. Pattie and her cooking skills are pretty much the only good things that came from being at the McMansion.

I eat happily until my phone buzzes. I pull it out of my pocket, smiling when I see Indi's name popping up in the notifications.

Indi:

Need a ride? I can swing by and grab you.

Me:

That would be amazing. I'm at the house of horrors rather than where you dropped me yesterday though.

Indi:

LOL! That's fine, I know where that is. I'll swing by in 15?

Me:

Sounds good. I'll be ready

Indi:

See you soon!

I take a bite of my toast and slam back the last of my coffee before jumping up from the table and escaping the McMansion without a run-in with my so-called family. Thank God. I change out of my pajamas and into my uniform, and despite hating this ridiculous outfit, it doesn't put a damper on my day.

I pull my hair back into a high ponytail. It's a little messy, with tendrils of hair surrounding my face, but I kinda like it, so I leave it as it is. I finish my look with eyeliner and a swipe of mascara, then slip on a pair of black Louboutin heels. I might usually be a Chucks kind of girl, but today feels like the kind of day where I'm going to need the boost these shoes give me. I grab my bag and dash out the front in time to see Indi pulling up the drive.

"Morningggg!" Indi grins at me like the alt sunshine child that she is as I jump into the Wrangler. She turns down the Midnight Blue blasting through her speakers as I buckle up, and she peels away from the McMansion like zombies are chasing us. I can't help but laugh at her, and she chuckles along next to me. She slows once we reach the main intersection before looking over at me. "Coffee?"

"Hell yes. There could never be enough coffee in my system to deal with going back to this hellhole of a school." She laughs, turning away from the direction of school and swinging into the drive-thru at the closest Starbucks.

"How was visiting your old place last night?" she asks, and I grin so freaking wide.

"Well, it turns out my old place is my new place. Long story short, my family are assholes and wanted access to my dad's money, which is the only reason I was apparently ever with them."

"Wait, don't they have enough of their own?" she interrupts, eyes wide, and I shrug.

"I thought so, but there's no such thing as too much with people like them. Either way, it turns out my house manager, Smithy, was also in my dad's will as a legal guardian, so this bitch is escaping the house of horrors and going home. Also, before I forget, you're invited over for dinner tonight—Smithy insisted. He'll be serving up some mac and cheese goodness."

She goes to answer when the speaker box crackles outside her window. "Good morning! Thank you for choosing Starbucks; what can I get started for you?"

"Peppermint Mocha Frappe with extra cookie crumble, extra whip cream, and mocha drizzle," she says into the box, before turning back to me and laughing when she sees the look on my face. "Don't knock it till you've tried it. What do you want?"

"I'll just take a cold brew with mocha and almond milk," I tell her, reeling off the floofiest drink on my personal coffee menu. It's too goddamn warm for hot coffee right now, and I know if I have her sugary drink, I'll crash before lunch.

Once we get our drinks, she cranks up the latest Midnight Blue release and we sing at the top of our lungs until we pull into the parking lot at school. I smile when I see Raleigh and his friends standing near the steps up to the school, and we head straight for them.

"Octavia, hey!" Raleigh calls out, and I smile at him. I loop my arm through Indi's, practically dragging her along with me.

"Hey, guys," I offer with a smile, and Indi gives them all a small awkward wave. Oh my God, she's the cutest. I love her so much, and it's only been a day.

"I hear you guys are coming to my party this Friday?" one of the guys says, beaming at us with a classic puppy dog smile.

"If you're Jackson, then you'd be right."

He clasps his chest, acting like a swooning heroine from some fifties movie. "The girl doesn't even know who I am, my poor little heart."

I can't help but laugh at him as Indi giggles at my side. The girl fucking *giggles*. She must be downright smitten.

Raleigh drops an arm around my shoulder and puffs out his chest. "She doesn't need to know your name, bro, she already knows mine."

Jackson pulls a face, and Raleigh removes his arm from my shoulder before lunging at him. They start wrestling and laughing, so we say our goodbyes and head inside to our lockers. I drop off most of my books, only keeping what I need for English, and groaning at the thought of repeating the day I had yesterday. The monotonous schedule is one thing I didn't miss about traditional schooling. On the road, my tutor would change up what we did each day, because ya know, variety is the spice of life. The thought of having the same lessons at the same time every single day makes my little black heart shrivel some more. I'm just hoping that today I can focus enough to take notes at least. Hopefully I'll actually even learn something. The only classes that I feel confident about are English and French, because languages have always come easy to me. Music would usually be on that list, but right now, the thought of playing or singing makes me want to die a little.

"You ready for another bright and sunny day at Echoes Cove Prep?" Indi asks, shoving her head in her locker like she's trying to disappear into it.

"Oh yeah, it should be joyous," I quip, wishing I could disappear too. If she has a portal to Narnia in there, she better not be fucking keeping it from me.

"Whore," one guy coughs as he passes, and I flip him the bird as his friends laugh like he's just told the world's funniest joke. It's good to see that the delights of yesterday are going to continue today.

I need way more coffee than I've already had this morning if I'm expected to actually deal with this shit. If I make it through the day without being arrested, it'll be a good day.

English was a breeze. A debate with Ms. Summers about which main character from all of the books on our list fit best into the stereotype of a Byronic hero got my day off to

a stellar start. Obviously I chose Heathcliff because well…
duh. It's freaking Heathcliff.

I didn't even have time to care about Blair and her
bitch squad being catty the entire class. Though, knowing
I'll be moving out of her house at the end of the week is
definitely keeping my mood nice and breezy.

My entire day is going great until I find myself sitting
in Business class, the not-so-proud co-owner of a project
with Lincoln fucking Saint… A project that's going to last
the entire fucking semester and make up nearly half of our
grade.

Fuck my actual life.

The lesson draws to a close, and I escape to Music
without incident. I might need to work with Lincoln on the
project, but I'm just stubborn enough that I'm positive I
can do it without actually speaking to him.

I slide into the back of the music room, just the same as
yesterday. This lesson is a refuge as much as it's a waking
nightmare. None of the assholes haunting my life are in
this class. In fact, the only person I know here is Raleigh.
The problem is that everything about this lesson reminds
me of my dad.

Miss Celine flounces into the room, her scarf waving
behind her as she flourishes her arms to bring the chatter
to an end. "Morning, everyone, I hope you're ready for
the day! I've done some thinking after we finished the

vocal seating assignment yesterday, and I couldn't help but reflect on the skill level of this group in particular. I want to challenge you, so I've decided that a solo will be required from each of you. The solos will be performed at the end of the semester, and I'd like it to be an original piece. You are permitted to work with another on the composition if you don't have the skill to play an instrument yourself, but you will each be required to perform a solo performance."

I fight the simultaneous urges to groan and pull out my hair. There goes my refuge. This class was meant to be easy. I mean, it's not like I got a choice with the class since my schedule was picked by my guardian. I know Smithy didn't mean anything by it, so I can't hold it against him… But *fuck*.

It's not that the project will be hard. I literally spent as much time composing music as I did studying when I was growing up. The problem is that I haven't been able to play, or even really sing, since my dad died.

I got through the last class by the skin of my teeth. I only had to sing one solo line and mumbled through the rest, and I handled that okay. It's just that I totally hid in the bathroom for ten minutes after that, trying to pull myself out of the dark hole that threatened to consume me from the inside out.

Everyone says that senior year is meant to be one of the best years of your life. I dare those fuckers, whoever they are, to live through the past few months of my life and tell me it's the best time ever.

"The music rooms will be open to you before the day begins, during lunch, and for an hour and a half once the school day is over. Use your time wisely. Now, let's warm up!" She turns on the music system, and I can't help but grin at the song that blasts through—"She's So Gone" by Naomi Scott. I'd be totally lying if I said this song didn't feature heavily in my early teen years.

Miss Celine blushes a little before shrugging. "You guys probably know the words, so let's do this."

The words wash over me in a wave, and I remember the time I sang this with Dad's band before one of his shows. It was my first arena performance, and I was hyped for weeks after it. I've never been one for performing publicly, but that performance was what solidified my desire to work in the music business. I just wanted it to be in a different way from my dad.

Music has always been a higher power of sorts for me. There's something about a song that can say more with a few words than I could ever manage in an essay.

I take a deep breath when the song reaches the chorus, singing along quietly. It's not really a quiet kind of song, but I don't have it in me to belt it like it deserves. As sad as I am, the song is still too fun to not get lost in it, so I manage to lose myself just a little. When the music wraps up, Miss Celine splits us into groups. I end up paired with Raleigh, and he saunters over to the back corner where I've been hiding all class long.

"I did not expect the QB to be a singer," I tease as he takes the seat beside me.

He grins at me before twisting his chair so he can face me with ease. "There's a lot more to me than being a QB."

"I have no doubt. You seem like the white knight type," I say with an easy laugh, and he brushes off the backhanded compliment, completely unfazed.

"I might have something of a hero complex, but only when it's needed. I'm all about independent women owning their shit." His grin widens, and I can't help but laugh at him. He really is something else. "As for singing, my grandma was a singer. She used to have me singing blues with her as a kid, and I've loved it ever since. This was a just-for-fun class for me this year. I don't need the art credits or anything."

"An overachiever too, I see."

"I do like to excel at everything I do." He flexes his arms as he talks, wagging his eyebrows in an over exaggerated sort of way, making me laugh once more. "Speaking of, you should come to our first game. We're playing the Asheville Allstars. The guys there can be total douchebags, but I have a feeling we're going to fucking annihilate them this year."

"When's the game?"

"Next week."

"I'll be there! I'm sure Indi will come with me, and I hope like hell she has a better understanding of football than me. Otherwise, we're going to end up cheering for the wrong team. Either way, we'll definitely be there!" He looks horrified at the thought, which only makes it that much more comical.

"Don't worry," he says, nodding sagely as he pats my arm, "I'll make sure to give you an idiot's guide at the party this weekend."

"You usually spend time at parties explaining football to girls?" I ask, an eyebrow raised.

His shit-eating smile is back as he pretends to dust off his shoulders. "Nah, I don't usually have to flex that hard."

"You're such a jock!" I tease, throwing my pen at him.

"I'll show you how much of a jock I'm not. Come on," he says as he stands, offering me his hand. This is the most fun I've had inside these walls, so I place my hand in his and let him lead me from the room. He pulls me inside one of the other music rooms a few doors down, and I crane my neck while I look around. The ceiling is ridiculously high and one of the walls is fully glass, looking out over the field at the side of the school. A lone piano sits in the corner of the room near the windows, and he takes a seat, clearing his throat before placing his fingers on the ivory.

A lump threatens to choke me as he starts to play a haunting melody, and then… it hits me. It's a remix of one of Dad's songs. I go to stop him, but he opens his mouth, and I'm struck fucking stupid.

The boy can sing.

How does he get to look and sound like sin?

He sings the entire song, with so much passion and emotion that I feel a tear trickle down my cheek—I've not listened to any of Dad's songs since his death, and I can't lock my emotions down. I swipe it away quickly, not wanting him to see just how affected I am. "That was amazing."

My voice is scratchy as fuck, and it's instantly obvious that I didn't hide my sadness well because he jumps up and rushes over to wrap me in the biggest hug I've had in months. "I didn't mean to make you cry."

"It's okay, it's all just kind of… raw still," I murmur, enjoying the feeling of being wrapped in his arms. It's rare that I take comfort from people I don't really know, but there's just something about him that tears down all of my carefully constructed walls.

"This looks cozy." My spine goes rigid at the voice, and dread pools in my stomach with his presence. I pull back from Raleigh at the words and turn to find Maverick standing in the open doorway.

"What is it to you, Riley?" Raleigh snaps at him,

keeping his arm hooked over my shoulder.

Maverick's dark hair falls into his brown eyes as he smirks at Raleigh in that ruthless, malicious way he has. It's like every super villain's smile you see on the TV. He somehow seems fucking lethal with just a goddamn smile. "She's off-limits."

"What the fuck does that mean?" Raleigh says, maneuvering himself so he's standing just in front of me. Maverick saunters forward until he's toe-to-toe with Raleigh, crazy-bastard vibes rolling from him.

"You should leave now, quarterback, or I'll end your promising career before it begins." He stays in Raleigh's space, and I watch as Raleigh pales. Maverick pushes him, hard enough to make him shrink just a little, so Maverick turns his focus to me. He steps toward me, and I hate that I falter, that I take a step back. The smile on his face grows until he has me pushed against a wall.

"You won't get away with this," Raleigh hisses.

"Oh really? Who's going to do anything about it? You?" Mav taunts him without taking his eyes from me, and I shrink under his intense gaze.

"Yeah, I am," Raleigh says, but what he thinks he's going to achieve other than pissing Maverick off is beyond me.

Mav grins that ruthless smile down at me, ignoring Raleigh entirely.

"You can't do this," I stammer, looking around for Raleigh, but I can't see him. I hope to God he's gone to get a teacher.

"Can't do what, princess? Talk to you? Get in your space? Declare you off-limits?"

"Any of it!" The words fall from my lips in a rush, and I clench my fists, digging my nails into my palms in a desperate attempt to center myself. I hate how easily he can make me feel so small. He puts one hand on the wall just by my head, and reaches behind him with the other. When he brings it back, he has a knife in his hand.

A fucking knife.

He presses the blade against my throat, and I swear my heart stops. I can't even breathe with the cold, sharp metal pressing into my skin.

"Your pupils dilate so pretty," he murmurs as he pushes the blade harder, and I wince at the bite against my skin.

"You can't do this," I say again, my voice shaking despite my paralyzed state.

"Are you going to stop me? Are you going to fight me? Poor lost little princess. Sad little princess. Everyone would believe it was you if I slit your wrists and walked away, wouldn't they? The apple never falls far from the tree."

I look up into his eyes, and the delight in them as he stares down at me makes my blood run cold. "Please, Maverick."

I hate that I'm begging him, but I don't know just how

far he's willing to push this. I've only been this scared a few times before in my entire life, and each time, I froze.

"That's it, beg me like the pathetic dog that you are." He sneers at me as he drags the knife down from my neck to my chest, cutting the skin as he goes. I can't help but hiss at the sting of the blade as it makes the shallow cut. "You sure make pretty sounds for me, little slut. Make some more."

I cry out as he cuts through my shirt, drawing blood as he goes, until the blade is at my navel. He removes it, and I almost sigh in relief until he places it against my thigh and draws it higher until it's at my panties. He breathes in deeply with his nose against my neck before rolling his tongue over the skin he cut.

"I bet you're wet aren't you, whore? I bet being fucked by my knife wouldn't even be the most fucked up thing you've done. I'd put money on you enjoying it too. I bet I could get you off with just my knife, couldn't I? Look at how hard your nipples are. Pebbling under my touch like a whore begging for more. I bet if I pushed my fingers past your panties you'd be wet, wouldn't you? Fucking pathetic. You're nothing but trash."

"N…n…no."

"You really think you get to tell me no?" He quirks his brow and pushes the cold metal harder against my skin, and I squeak again. I hate how small he makes me feel. I flinch as he brings his face close to mine, almost nose to nose. I turn my face to the side, closing my eyes, praying he got what he came here for because I'm not sure I can take much more.

"Off. Fucking. Limits, Octavia. You've been warned."

He pushes off the wall and walks away without another word. My misery is burned away by my fiery fucking rage. My hands shake, and I feel warm from the flush on my face. How dare he do that shit, say that like he owns me? Shame, embarrassment, and anger flood my veins. He has no fucking right, and no reason either. I haven't done anything to him.

The boy I once knew is definitely no more, in his place is a psychotic savage of a man. I already know there will be no reasoning with him. He's become the honed weapon his father always seemed to want him to be.

I'll give him fucking off-limits.

I clutch my shirt to my chest and send Indi a message with an SOS for yet another shirt. I need to clean up this blood too. Fucking Maverick Riley.

I curse myself for not finding this rage when he was here. Next time, I promise myself I'll be stronger.

Next time… because I already know that this won't be the end of it.

My rage stays with me all fucking day, like a close friend keeping me warm, with that cold, slimy shame lying just beneath it. Raleigh did eventually come back with a teacher but Maverick was long gone, and Indi had already saved the day with a new shirt, thankfully I managed to clean up the majority of the blood with the neckerchief.

I scurried off with Indi after reassuring them both I was okay. She didn't ask questions, just helped me out, and I'm glad. Because reliving what happened isn't something I want to do. The shame of enjoying what happened, having him pressed up against me, that his words sparked something primal in me, is still too raw.

Raleigh didn't seem to put much stock in Maverick's words, but I know that those three assholes hold more power here than people let on. They rule this fucking place with an iron fist.

That much has been drilled into me time and again.

It was more than apparent at lunch that Maverick's decree had been heard when even Jackson refused to meet my eyes. Apparently *off-limits* means being my friend puts you on a hit list, and no one wants to be on the wrong side of Lincoln and his faithful followers.

Though considering what happened with Maverick, I don't blame Jackson and the others. But if Lincoln and his two besties think they can actually control my life, they have another thing coming. I've had just about e-fucking-nough of that lately, thank you very much. I just need to find my rage sooner when they're around. Thankfully this shirt covers all of the marks he left on my skin, and the cuts weren't deep enough to scar.

To top it all off, it seems like we're back to our regularly scheduled programming in Gym class. Rather than taking us out to the track to run laps and practice sprints, East has us working circuits. Thirty minutes of the intense routine isn't even enough to burn away my rage.

At the end of class, he sends us to run suicide drills. I throw myself into them wholeheartedly, running until my heart feels like it's going to burst out of my chest.

The bell rings, and East blows his whistle, calling the drill to an end. Everyone leaves the gym while I stand, bent over, trying to catch my breath. I'm seriously considering continuing to run until I'm too numb to do anything else.

"V, what's going on with you?" East calls once the gym is clear. His footsteps echo in my direction when I don't answer right away, but I keep my mouth firmly closed so I don't flay him with all of the vitriol bubbling up inside of me. "Hey, V."

I stand to face him, and his eyes go wide. I guess my fury is written all over my face. I'm usually pretty good at hiding my emotions, but I'm beyond all that today. This whole fucking town is toxic.

"What's wrong?"

I take a deep breath, trying my damnedest to tamp down some of the boiling rage, because I know I'm going to have to answer him. I just don't want to piss him off.

"Your fucking brother and his crazy-ass friends," I say, my jaw still clenched.

"What did those little dicked, sons of bitches do now?" His question actually makes me laugh for the first time since Maverick's little declaration earlier. Fuck, I needed that.

"I assume you saw the crap on ReachMe?"

He rubs the back of his neck, his discomfort obvious. "Yeah, I did, but don't worry. No one will believe that it's true."

His words sting, echoing Lincoln's yesterday.

"If you say so." I shrug, trying not to let the sting of his words show. I refuse to believe that he shares the same views about me that his brother does. "But between that and the three of them casting me out publicly—I'm untouchable, and being my friend will make you an outcast. Being anything more than that is, well… social suicide. You know as well as I do that that'll extend beyond school."

"Those boys are fucking idiots," he grumbles, rubbing a hand down his face. "Let me see if I can't talk some sense into those assholes."

"No, don't bother. We both know that'll just make it

worse. I've got this. You know me, I never start a fight, but I will sure as hell finish it." He barks out a throaty laugh before pulling me in for a hug, and I just hope I find the strength to see my words through.

"Damn, I missed you, V. You show those assholes what you've got. Maybe they'll pull their heads out of their asses." He squeezes me tight again before releasing me and looking back down at me with a soft smile on his way too pretty face. "How are you settling back into the Cove?"

"It's been pretty shit, honestly. Though, I did find out yesterday that I don't have to stay with Vivienne and Nate, so I'm heading back home this weekend."

His eyes go wide as I tell him my plans, and then he grins. "I guess it'll be just like old times, well, kind of. I'm still at the house with Linc. Since Mom fucked off not long after you guys left and Dad is always gone with work, it's like we have the place to ourselves."

"Your mom left?" I ask, shocked as hell. I had no fucking idea, I know I haven't been here, but that seems like the sort of thing I'd have heard before now.

"Yeah, I figured Linc told you after you left." He scratches the back of his neck and shifts from one foot to the other. He offers an off-kilter smile before shrugging. "I guess not, though. That's all in the past now anyway. But it'll be good to have you back around. Smithy still makes me a birthday cake every year, so now I'll have an excuse to come back around more often."

"You're welcome whenever." I smile, then notice the time. "Shit, I better go get changed. Indi is going to kill me if I keep her here too late."

"Sure, go. I'll talk to you later." He hugs me again quickly before I run to the locker rooms and jump in the shower. When I head back into the main part of the locker room, the place is empty. I open my locker, pull out my phone, and see a message from Indi.

Indi:

Got to grab a book from the library. I'll meet you by the car.

Me:

Sorry! I didn't mean to take so long. I'll be out in a minute.

Indi:

No rush, the parking lot is still practically full so I can't get out yet anyway.

Weird. Most people would usually be gone by now.

I throw my phone back into my bag, slipping out of my gym clothes and pull out my uniform. It takes me all of a second to notice the giant holes cut into my shirt.

Fucking bitchy asshole girls.

I check out my skirt to find it in tatters too.

I fucking hate this school.

Fuck this, I could leave in my gym clothes, but fuck them all.

I throw the shirt and skirt in my bag, slipping on my untouched underwear and blazer. I let my hair down from its ponytail and fluff it up. If these assholes think I'm going to cower just because they fucked with my clothes, they have no idea who they're fucking with. I have bikinis that show more skin than this.

I pick up my bag, slip on my heels, and check out my reflection. At least I picked pretty black lace underwear today. I look like something out of a fucking Victoria's Secret ad. It's so fucking stupid, but you can bet your ass I'm going to rock this shit. I refuse to be beaten twice in one day. These assholes have no idea who I am, and the girls at this school don't scare me.

I hiss as I apply a little foundation over the red line down my skin to hide the mark Maverick made earlier before sliding on some lip gloss. I head out of the locker room in nothing more than my underwear and blazer.

The comments are almost instantaneous. I guess news of what the bitches in my gym class did spread around the school, which explains Indi's message about the parking lot. I hold my head high and strut through the halls, owning my shit like a badass bitch. I find Blair and her bitch squad all giggling by my locker, phones out and taking pictures. They stop laughing when they see the look on my face. I know I'll see those pictures online later, but what's one more at this point?

"I look fucking awesome, right?" I ask with a small wave as I pass them by. If they thought this would break me, they can think again. I've survived worse than their attempted humiliation.

I get to the end of the hall just to come face to face with Lincoln, Maverick, and Finley. Linc's jaw ticks as he takes in my appearance. Maverick's heated gaze on my chest where the cut on my skin is hidden almost makes me want to cower. But not again, not today.

"Not so off limits after all, am I?" I wink at him, and I swear to God Finley smirks as I push between him and Linc.

The catcalls and shouts I get as I pass the football field to where Indi is parked just make me shake my head. I can't help but laugh when I hear Raleigh tell them to shut their mouths before yelling, "You look like fire!"

I finally reach Indi, and she gawks at me as I climb in the car. "Don't even ask."

"Bitch, you just owned that. Whoever did this to you fucked up. There's no way in hell you look as good as you do right now and don't get half the school simping over you by tomorrow morning."

I bark out a laugh as she throws the car in drive and peels out of the parking lot. I knew I loved her for a reason.

Six

I survived.

Kind of.

Well, my first week anyway. It's been pretty fucking hellish. Between Lincoln, Maverick, and Finley terrorizing me daily, plus the general taunts and social media hate from the rest of the student body, I'm worn thin.

A girl can put on a brave face, but on the inside, I'm crumbling a little. Bullying isn't something I've ever dealt with before, not like this anyway. The online stuff I can handle, I'm used to tabloid bullshit, but my dad was there to shield me from most of it. Now I'm alone, and I'm not so sure I can handle it. I've questioned more than once this week if my inheritance is worth staying here. Between that and the struggle I'm already having trouble focusing in some of my classes, I'm not sure I'm going to meet the requirements of the Will anyway.

I'm just glad I made a few good friends who haven't even blinked at the social bullshit that seems to come with being associated with me. Indi is my fucking rock, and Raleigh has all but ignored the *off-limits* warning. We've sat with the jocks everyday at lunch since then, which meant that at least at lunch, I've felt somewhat safe. Some of the players still won't talk to me, but Jackson seems to have gotten over his aversion to eye contact, at least. He mostly spends time talking to Indi rather than me, but that, at least, makes me happy. Jackson chatting up Indi was always my endgame anyway. Becoming friends with Raleigh along the way is just an added bonus.

Throughout the week, I've managed to get lost inside my own head and packed up my meager belongings in the pool house. I also returned my rental in fear of it being fucked with because I wouldn't put it past the animals I go to school with to do something like that. Surprisingly, my aunt and uncle haven't put up much of a fight, though that could have something to do with the money I've already transferred to them for my 'rent'.

The few boxes of my dad's records are stacked in the corner along with the three duffel bags full of my clothes.

My new furniture has been delivered to the house throughout the week, and according to my regular updates from Smithy, everything is coming along nicely. Indi is going to help me drive the few things I have here over to the house in the morning, and then I never have to grace this house of horrors with my presence again.

It's almost enough to make me let out a whoop of joy. I focus on getting ready for Jackson's party instead. I'll save the celebrating for tonight.

I finish the final touches on the waves of my hair and add a batwing of eyeliner to each eye before adding a swipe of mascara. It's simple, but that's all I've ever done anyway. I'm not a cake-it-on kind of girl. I have mad respect for those who can, but contouring my face is basically the same as asking me to contort my body... It's just not going to happen. I'm hopeless.

I'm just glad that the cut Maverick made has mostly healed and what's left can be hidden with makeup. I sure as fuck don't want to spend my night explaining that away.

Indi sashays out of my bathroom, and I can't help but grin. She looks like an emo princess. "Damn girl, you are fire!"

"Why thank you." She blushes, taking a curtsy in her tutu, and I laugh. I'm not sure many people could pull off a black tutu dress with a leather jacket and flip-flops. "I don't want to get sand in my boots, so I figured I'd make this work."

"Dude, you look amazing! You're totally making it work."

"Are you ready to go?" she asks as I shrug on a kimono over my white tank top. I glance at the storage box of my shoes and ultimately decide to go shoeless. It's on the beach anyway, so fuck it.

I look outside at the pitch black sky and grin. I mean, who turns up to a party on time anyway? "Yeah, let's hit it."

I pull my phone out of the pocket of my cutoffs and send a message to Raleigh.

Me:

You still there? We're heading down now.

Raleigh:

You know I got you. I'll meet you at the bottom of the stairs.

I shove my phone back into the safe in my closet before we head down the stairs from the McMansion down to the sand below. I'm not going to need it tonight, but I learned long ago not to be stupid enough to just leave it lying around.

It's impossible not to see or hear the party from here, but it's nice of Raleigh to come get us anyway.

I think he might be one of the nicest guys I've ever met.

Indi's phone goes off, and she squeals a protest when she looks at the screen.

"What happened? Is everything okay?"

"*Adams Ever After* was canceled. Goddammit!" she exclaims, stomping her foot. I want to go on whatever journey this is with her, but I literally have no fucking idea what she's talking about. "Like, I know Ken died, but dammit, I was so freaking invested! I need to know what happens next. Natalie just went back to Banner-Hill. For fuck's sake."

"What on earth are you going on about?" She looks at me like I just kicked her puppy and took away her eyeliner stash all at once.

"You don't know what *Adams Ever After* is?" I wince at her screech as we reach the bottom of the stairs. Luckily, Raleigh is there waiting for us to save me from whatever this mini-tantrum is. I bounce across the sand toward him while Indi stops to take off her shoes.

"I've never heard of it," I yell back to her before turning to Raleigh. "Hey!"

"You and I have a trashy TV marathon coming up, V. This is an atrocity!"

"What is she yelling about?" Raleigh asks, laughing as she stomps across the sand toward us.

"*Adams Ever After*? I don't know." I shrug just as Indi catches up, waving her flip-flops at me.

"You mean the TV show?" he asks, and Indi grins wide at him.

"See, he knows! Natalie just went back into Banner-Hill. I need to know what happens. I know I'm whining, but you don't understand! I've watched this show for years! I know they haven't finished airing all of this season, so I still have a little more, but this is bad, bad news. What am I supposed to do on Thursday evenings now?"

I can't help but laugh at her dramatics. TV has never really been my thing, but if she's this invested... "I've honestly never heard of it, but for you, I'll give it a go."

She does a weird little dance in the sand, and Raleigh shakes his head before leaning down and saying, "You're going to regret that."

He's right, I might, but she's happy. I can live with it.

It doesn't take long for us to reach the outskirts of the beach party, and everyone says hello to Raleigh as we pass. The school might be for rich kids, but they seem to love football as much as any other town with a half-decent football team. I might as well be fucking invisible, though.

Raleigh leads us to where Jackson and a bunch of the jocks are sitting around the fire, beer in hand. Music thumps loudly all around us, but not quite so loudly that I can't hear myself think. It also doesn't quite drown out the squeals of girls being dunked. It's not like other parties I've been to, but then, technically this is my first high-school party.

Indi gravitates toward Jackson, while I chat with Raleigh and some of the other guys on the team. Apparently after my whole strut through the school half naked thing, everyone's just straight up ignoring Maverick's decree because I'm too hot to ignore, at least according to Raleigh.

I'm pretty sure that's the most backhanded compliment I've ever gotten in my life, but fuck it.

I drink a little, not so much that I'm going to feel it tomorrow, but enough that I can feel a buzz and loosen up a little. I can't believe it's only been a week since I started back at Echoes Cove Prep. It feels like a fucking lifetime with the amount of shit I've already dealt with.

So I decide I'm going to have a little fun tonight.

What's the worst that could happen?

Tonight has been way more fun than I expected it to be. Raleigh told me that the only reason Blair is here is because the cheer team is always invited, but they've basically left me alone. In fact, I haven't seen them around for a while. I'm not exactly sad about that either.

I lean into Raleigh, who's had his arm around my shoulder most of the night. He's so warm compared to the cool breeze, so I haven't complained about it, even if it does feel a little possessive. He's so chill, I'm sure that's not his intention. I'm new at this whole 'being around people my age all the time' thing, though, so who knows?

Man, I miss the roadies.

My attention is pulled back to the group when a roar of laughter goes up across the fire. I go on high alert when I notice Indi gasp. Her eyes go wide as she looks over my shoulder.

I look behind me and groan when I see what has her so on edge. Lincoln, Maverick, and Finley. I should've known that I couldn't have one fucking night of peace. After a week of shit, of course they have to show up at a party I know they weren't invited to. Even if it is on the beach.

Fuck my life.

"It seems the party started without us, boys," Maverick snarks as they approach, the firelight glinting on the bar in his eyebrow. Somehow the lighting makes him seem more menacing than normal. How an eighteen-year-old guy can look so menacing in a muscle tank and a pair of ripped jeans is beyond me, but he manages it. It also reveals the ink I hadn't realized he had. All of it is normally hidden by his uniform, but tonight his colorfully painted skin is fully on show.

"I didn't realize you guys were coming," Jackson says, pulling Indi closer to him. "You know you're always welcome."

Raleigh throws a sharp glance over at him, and Jackson just shrugs. I get it. Those three run the school. Just because Raleigh dislikes them on my behalf doesn't mean Jackson can afford to as well. I elbow Raleigh softly, bringing his gaze to me, and smile at him before looking over to Jackson to let him know I'm good.

"Of course we're welcome. This is our beach just like ECP is our school," Maverick says before grabbing a beer and heading toward the gaggle of squawking girls by the water, crashing into my shoulder as he does.

Jackass.

"Surprised you showed your face, Royal," Lincoln says, his tone biting as he grabs two beers from the cooler. He offers one to Finley who refuses it. The refusal doesn't surprise me. His mom always had substance abuse issues, and he definitely seems like the straight edge type.

"Why wouldn't I? My friends are throwing a party—of course I'm here." I raise an eyebrow in challenge but bite back any other response. I couldn't be anymore fucking annoyed with myself for responding to him, but prodding probably isn't going to make my life easier either. I haven't spoken to him since he saw me in my underwear as I left school the other day, and it isn't like he's made any effort to talk to me either. He's just watched as his loyal sycophants have terrorized me all week.

He stares at me, his expression blank, before walking

away to another group as Finley drops onto the sand and gets comfortable.

Of course he fucking does.

I try not to let their appearance fuck with me and turn my attention back to Raleigh and the guys, but it feels like the whole tone of the party has changed. The music is lower, and everyone's mood seems a bit more subdued. It's almost like a parent just crashed the party. My buzz sure as shit took a hike when they appeared. I let out a sigh and untangle myself from Raleigh. "I think I'm going to call it a night. I have a big day tomorrow."

"You sure?" He frowns down at me as I take a step back.

"Yeah, I'm sure."

"Okay, you want me to make sure Indi gets home okay? I've only had one." I look over at her, and she looks so happy I don't want to rain on her parade.

"That would be awesome if you don't mind?"

"Nah, it's good. I'll make sure she's safe."

"Thank you." I smile at him before heading over to Indi. "I'm heading home. Are you still cool to go car shopping with me tomorrow?"

"You know I am." She grins at me, and I can tell from the faraway look in her glassy eyes that she's quite a bit more buzzed than I am, and I bite my lip.

"You okay staying? Do you want me to get you home?"

"I'm good," she giggles. "I haven't drunk that much, and I'm sure Raleigh the Protector will make sure nothing nefarious happens."

"He did say he'd get you home for me," I tell her, and she giggles again.

"See, I'll be fine. I'll pick you up bright and early in the morning!" She moves from Jackson and wraps her arms around me, holding me tight for a second before letting go.

"Have fun." I grin and wink at her before turning and heading back up the beach toward the pool house. I definitely have a lot going on this weekend. Between moving, car shopping, and homework, I'm sure I'll barely have time to breathe. And I'll bet there's probably more that I've forgotten about, but I mean... I need a car, and I need to get out of the McMansion. Stat.

I rub my hands up and down my arms as I trek down the beach. It's definitely cooler than I thought it would be. I lose myself to thoughts of the rolling to-do list in my head, but the sound of sand shifting behind puts me on high alert. My heart rate spikes as I look over my shoulder, but it's so fucking dark out here, there could be someone there and I wouldn't know it.

I pause for a moment, but I don't hear anything else, so I pick up my pace. I practically run up the steps to the house, but freeze when I take in the backyard.

The doors to the pool house are all open, and my

clothes are in pieces and scattered across the yard. Fuck. Some of them are in the pool too.

I decide to leave them and head into the pool house. There's no point trying to collect the clothes outside. They're in shreds. I just hope whoever did this didn't find my band tees. Dad and I collected those from his shows, as well as some others that we went to together. They're more than just t-shirts.

I flick on the lights and stop dead in my tracks.

No.

My dad's records... They're in pieces around the room.

This cannot be happening.

I fall to the ground, my knees crashing against the wood flooring with a bang. I can't breathe.

This is like losing him all over again.

This is all I had left of him. All that really mattered anyway.

All I can see is the destruction around the room. Of my memories.

Of my dad.

I think I might officially be losing the tenuous grip I've been holding over everything since Dad died.

This? This might be the thing that actually breaks me.

I didn't have much that mattered left in this life, just the contents of these boxes. And now everything's gone. Destroyed. In a matter of hours.

I don't even have to think twice about who did this. I knew there was a reason the bitch squad disappeared from the party. I just hadn't considered that even Blair would be this hateful. What did I ever do to her?

"Lookie what we found here, boys… You know, you really shouldn't spend so much time alone, whore." I spin around at the voice and see four guys I don't know. I recognize their faces from school, but I couldn't name them even with a gun to my head.

"What do you want?" My voice sounds as broken as I feel. I climb to my feet, tired of all of this already. All I want to do is tidy up and then drown myself into oblivion, preferably with tequila. Because this week has been fucking awful.

They press closer into my space, and the hair on the back of my neck goes up. It didn't occur to me to be afraid of anyone that wasn't Lincoln, Maverick, and Finley, but the smiles these four give me tells me that was stupid. "We just want to have some fun. You're already putting out for Coach. Why not us too?"

"I didn't put out for anyone," I argue, folding my arms over my chest to hide the shake of my hands. I don't even have my phone to signal for help, it's locked in my goddamn safe.

The leader of the pack steps even closer to me, so close I can feel his breath on my skin. "That's not what we heard.

What's wrong? Are we too good for you?"

"I said scare, not play." I look up over the guy's shoulder and see Lincoln, Maverick, and Finley, all leaning against the glass wall that makes up the front of my pool house.

Of course this was them.

"You heard him," one of the other four guys says, and they rush me. I kick and shout, trying to get them off of me, but they hold me while tearing at my clothes. Pawing at me in the process. I call out until my throat is raw, but it's no use. No one is going to help me but me.

They have me down to my underwear, and I thrash harder. They are not getting me naked. Not a fucking chance. I throw out a fist, catching one of the guys in the face, but I don't have time to take any happiness from my victory when he clasps me around the throat. "Stupid bitch."

"That's enough!" Lincoln's voice booms around the room. "Leave."

At his decree, the four of them pull away from me, grumbling under their breath as they leave the pool house. They each look like they'd like to complain, but they don't actually speak up. Who would dare complain to the King?

I clutch my arms around my body, trying to cover myself up as humiliation burns through me. "What the fuck do you want?"

My voice is harsh, but it doesn't affect them. Not at all.

They close in on me, and I stumble backward until my back is pressed against the wall. I might not have had the sense to be afraid before, but I know for sure that these three have zero hesitation in regards to hurting me. Maverick already proved that. And money talks in this town, so even if I went to the police, nothing would be done. Nothing is ever done with people like this.

"You came back." Lincoln shrugs, like that should explain everything. Tears well in my eyes, but I blink them back. I refuse to let them see me cry.

With a slight nod from Lincoln, the other two step forward. Finley grasps my wrists, and despite my attempts to break his grip, he lifts them and pins them above my head on the wall. I'm usually all for consensual restraint, but this is different, despite the shudder of excitement that runs through me. I struggle against him, but Maverick pulls that knife of his again. "Please, don't."

"You don't make the rules here, Octavia. We do. The moment you set foot back in our town, we owned you. You want control? Leave," Lincoln says as he smirks at me. "But don't worry. You'll enjoy this."

He drops to his knees at my feet, and I lock my ankles together. "What the hell are you doing?"

He glances up at me before his gaze moves to Maverick. The sinister grin on his face as he steps toward me makes me fight Finley's hold even harder. He is not putting that knife near me again.

"Stop. Wait. Fine," I say because really, what other choice do I have? I uncross my ankles, and Mav steps back, watching me like a bird of prey. I am most definitely the mouse in this situation.

Lincoln reaches forward, his fingers brushing softly against my skin as he pulls my panties down my legs. Goosebumps erupt all over my skin at his touch, and I hate that my body reacts to him like it does. He smiles up at me knowingly, so I can't help but taunt him. "This is the only way you'll ever be able to touch me. Pathetic."

The light dances in his thunderstorm eyes as he chuckles softly. "By the time I'm done with you, Octavia, you'll be begging for me to touch you again."

"You think this is a game?" I pull against Finley's grip again, but it's futile.

"Princess, the sooner you figure out that life is a game, the sooner you'll understand." Lincoln throws that bit of fucked up philosophy my way right before his tongue does a leisurely swipe of my pussy that has my entire body shaking with need.

"I hate you!" My words are harsh, but my delivery of them is weak as hell. My traitorous body has abandoned me, leaving me alone with my thoughts.

"That's okay," I hear Finley whisper in my ear, his erection rubbing against my hip as he keeps a steel hold on my wrists above my head. "We hate you too."

I turn to face him, and the fire in his eyes is enough to shock me to silence. It takes a second for me to remember that I want to answer his retort, but Lincoln swiftly grabs my thighs and throws them over his shoulders—giving him open access to my pussy to do with it as he wishes—stealing my attention away from Finley's hurtful words.

The first full contact of Linc's mouth on my body sends shivers down every inch of my skin in slow fucking motion. How is this even possible? Why am I reacting this way?

Rustling sheets to my left catch my attention, and when I turn to see what's happening, I see Maverick leaning back on one arm as he sits back on my bed, his other hand gripping his eye-wateringly big cock like he lives here. Like this is his room, his bed.

Like I'm his to admire.

Narrowing my eyes at the sight before me, I try to growl at him, but it all comes out in a moan like I'm the star of an orgy video. None of them miss the sound, the smirks on each of their faces telling they heard it loud and clear.

"Nice. I might just come in my pants if you do that again," Finley whispers, lips tickling the shell of my ear.

"Fuck you!" I hiss, and Lincoln pulls back from me to look into my eyes. You'd think him being on his knees would give me some form of power, but it's glaringly obvious to all involved that I am not the one with power here.

"Maybe one day, but first, I want to see how fast I can make you come," Lincoln taunts, which only pisses me off more.

"You're delusional if you think you can force me to come," I spit at Lincoln just as his mouth latches back onto my pussy. Finley's cock rubs up against my naked skin as he grips my chin, turning my head toward Maverick who's jacking himself off, eyes fixed on where Linc's mouth is fucking my pussy like he owns it.

"There's nothing more powerful than owning a cunt's orgasms. And trust me, Octavia, while you stay in Echoes Cove, we own you."

I can smell my arousal, hear the wet sounds coming from Linc's mouth, and the slapping of Maverick's cock as he increases the rhythm of his strokes. I squeeze my eyes closed to try to shut out everything else. I am trying really fucking hard not to enjoy any of this.

What kind of fucked up person am I that I have to force myself not to enjoy being taken by three guys I hate?

I'm going to Hell. Yeah, scratch that.

I'm already in Hell.

Finley's grip on my chin tightens before his hand moves down to hold my throat, and he squeezes. "Open your eyes, whore. Watch him."

All of my good intentions go flying out the window as Lincoln pushes two fingers inside my pussy and curls them just right, hitting some sort of magic button deep inside me that no-one before him has managed to find.

"So tight for a dirty little whore." Lincoln grins up at me before letting out a dry laugh.

"Fuck you," I pant, wishing I didn't sound as turned on as I do, and I grit my teeth at his degradation yet again. If only he knew the truth of it.

He thrusts his fingers inside of me again and I see fucking stars. A shudder runs down my spine, and the sound that comes out of my mouth isn't normal. It's animal-like. Something uncontrollable and unwanted.

Maverick grins from where he's splayed out on my bed. "There it is. Keep going, Linc, I think she's enjoying herself."

Fucking Finley and his dirty whispers.

Pressing my head back against the wall, I make the mistake of looking down. What I see undoes me completely.

Lincoln is eating my pussy like it's his last supper, two fingers pumping in and out of me as his lips latch onto my clit and squeeze hard enough to make me groan in pleasure. I'm almost resolved to just letting it happen, but then I look at Maverick, and the smug expression on his face gives me the strength to keep fighting them. Until

Lincoln hits that spot again, and every thought but their touches and stares leaves me.

"Stop! Oh God, right there! No, yes! Yes!"

I don't know what the fuck is spewing from my mouth, but the sight of Maverick's forearm tensing with every stroke, veins popping with the effort, the sound of Linc's mouth and fingers fucking my pussy like he owns it, and the feel of Finn's body rubbing up against my naked skin as he squeezes my throat, not letting me take a full breath… It's making my brain melt.

Fuck it, I can't control my body's needs, so I just let it happen.

As I make that decision, I relax my body and feel my juices trickling down my inner thighs, eliciting a moan from Linc. It's the first time I've realized his enjoyment, and I get a small feeling of empowerment from that. Because they may be using my body against me, but my body is making them lose control just as well.

With a small grin on my face, I bask in the knowledge that I might be having the same effect on them that they're having on me, and it feels like a small victory.

I open my eyes once more, focusing on Maverick's face and notice he's about to come. His dick is a deep, angry red, ready to explode and that, too, gives me a sense of power.

It's only when I feel another breach of my body that I

lose all self-control.

Gathering my juices on his finger, Lincoln pushes one then two fingers inside my ass, and that brief moment of pain is like fuel to an already blazing fire.

The sound that escapes my body is probably loud enough for the entire town to hear, but in that moment, I don't give a shit.

In that moment, all I want is bliss.

So, I let it happen. I even rub my pussy in Linc's face, making sure he'll be tasting me for hours to come, smelling me on his breath long after he's gone.

I writhe and groan, watching as the first spurts of Maverick's cum splashes on his chest. I watch him as my body, my pussy, makes him lose his own control. His cum coats his entire hand before he smears it on my bed, smirking at me as he does. Oh, how the tables have turned.

Linc doubles down on fucking me with his mouth like it's his only mission in life. He's all lips, tongue, and teeth. His fingers move in sync, fucking my pussy and my ass, and I'm a goner. Beside me, Finn whispers filthy words that only add to my orgasm as it hits me like a Mac truck.

"You're our dirty little whore."

"That's right, that tight little cunt of yours is begging for us."

"I can't wait to bury my dick inside your pretty little pussy."

"Next time, you'll be sucking my cock."

My senses can't take it anymore, and my entire body erupts with an orgasm so powerful I think I actually pass out for half a second.

When it all ends and I come back to the reality of my situation, I hate myself almost as much as I hate them. My brief feeling of empowerment is stolen by the shame coursing through my veins. Looking down at Lincoln as he takes one last leisurely swipe of his tongue across my soaked pussy lips, I glare at him.

They won, and I hate them for it.

He must read my thoughts because his next words are like a bucket of ice spilled over my naked body.

"I told you, Octavia. We control everything. Even things as primal as this. The only way to be free is to leave." Lincoln glares at me as Finley finally releases my wrists and Mav tucks his dick back in his pants.

"Leave," I somehow manage to say around the painful lump in my throat. I swallow and clear my throat, but my voice still comes out scratchy as all of my emotions hit me at once. "Get out."

They just stand there watching me, and I hate how I gave in to them. No matter how much I enjoyed it. I slide down the wall until I'm sitting on the floor, knees pulled against my chest, protecting myself from them the only way I can.

"Get out. All of you. Just get the fuck out." They don't move, and my anger burns hot and ugly in my gut. I slam my fists on the hardwood floor as I yell, "Leave!"

Lincoln steps toward me, a glare on his face, but Finley puts a hand on his shoulder, stopping him. They all turn and leave without a backward glance.

I swipe furiously at the tears that stream down my face and shut down the hurricane of emotions that are swirling around inside of me.

Tonight was too much. I lost too much.

The second I know they're gone, I break.

And I'm not sure I can be put back together the same.

Seven

I wake up, feeling bleary-eyed and stiff, and sit up from where I lie curled on the rug. I blink through grainy eyes and take in the destruction from the night before. The stiffness in my body is a stark reminder of last night, of just how much I've lost in the past month.

Once I showered, trying to scrub away the feel of them on me, denying how much I enjoyed their touch, I managed to get everything in one pile and even salvaged a few records. My band tees were completely unscathed, though I have no idea how. I found the duffel under my bed, so either someone knocked them under there by accident, or I shoved them under there and forgot I put them under here. Everything else is gone.

I literally have nothing but the clothes on my back.

They destroyed everything else.

I cannot wait to get the fuck out of here. I'm tempted to set fire to the fucking pool house with everything in it on my way out, so I don't have to see what they did to me anymore.

I stretch out my stiff limbs and climb to my feet before packing the few things that I salvaged in my duffel with my band tees. It doesn't take long, and as soon as I'm finished, my phone buzzes away in my pocket.

Indi:

Morning! I'm on my way. I'm bringing coffee, because shit.

Me:

I'll wait for you out front

Indi:

Sure thing. I'm going to get you a floofy coffee, prepare yourself.

I can't help but smile at her and her floofy coffee. At least something can still make me smile. Maybe I'm not beyond help after all. Something inside of me definitely broke all the way last night, though, and there's no coming back. I am so done with these Echoes Cove assholes. But I decide to keep what happened with the guys to myself.

Indi doesn't need to know my shame. Telling her that I didn't hate it, even admitting it to myself… I just can't.

I'm keeping my head down and getting the fuck out of here the second I can. It's not hard to see why both of my parents left this hellhole the second they got the chance. My phone buzzes just as I reach the gate at the side of the house.

Indi:

Here!

Me:

2 secs

I don't even bother going through the house. If I see Blair, I might smash her face in, and while she deserves the beating, my aunt and uncle would definitely press charges. No question. That's just not something I want to deal with on top of everything else right now.

I jump into her Wrangler, throwing my one lonely duffel bag in the back. She looks at me, and I can tell the questions are on the tip of her tongue, so I shake my head and ask, "Coffee?"

"I got you the Java Chip Frappuccino. Not too floofy, considering you usually like a Mocha, but it is life."

I laugh at her, shaking my head before buckling

myself in. She peels out of the drive, whipping through the neighborhood. We drive in silence for a few minutes, but I can tell her curiosity is eating her up from the inside. She taps her fingers against the steering wheel and glances at me every few seconds. I sigh with a roll of my eyes but incline my head in her direction. I'll have to tell her eventually, about some of it anyway.

Her silent questions are damn near suffocating. I take one long, deep breath before answering, "Blair and her bitch squad destroyed most of my shit, so that bag is all I have left." The car swerves as she jerks her head in my direction, jaw slack.

She focuses back on the road quickly and straightens out, but her knuckles are white on the steering wheel. "Those fucking cunts," she all but growls, and I can feel my eyebrow inching upward on its own accord. "Sorry, bitch just isn't cutting it. Who the fuck even are they? Entitled little twats."

"What the fuck is a twat?" I laugh.

"Girl, you and I need to watch Green Street. Charlie Hunnam, with a British accent, calling people a twat is a whole experience," she gushes, and I can't help but laugh at her. "A twat is basically a British insult that covers most things, and just sounds good. But at least now you're smiling."

I finish telling her about my evening and then realize

I'm being a terrible friend. I shove down all of my misery and vow to be at least a little happy—I'm still getting out of my aunt and uncle's house after all. I refuse to bring her down just because my shit is all kinds of fucked up at the moment. "Wait, screw my shitstorm of a night! How did your night go with Jackson?"

She grins, and I swear I can spot a sparkle in her eyes. Damn. Must've been good. "It was fun, nothing really happened, but it was fun to hang out. Him and Raleigh made sure I got home safe, and he was a perfect gentleman the entire time."

"Uh-huh, if you say so." I grin, and she sticks her tongue out at me before pulling into the Jaguar dealership. "So, we start here?"

I take a look at the cars on the lot and shake my head. "No way, this place just screams evil villain. I want something a little more me." I pull up one of the car ads I found online and show it to her. "I'm thinking something more like this."

She grins at me and nods, putting the car back in drive. "I know exactly where to go."

She pulls out of the lot and jumps on the highway. We sing and dance around like idiots to "You Me at Six", and I feel a little more like myself. This girl is literally the embodiment of sunshine and joy. I swear to God if anyone tries to take that from her, I'll flay them alive.

She pulls off the highway, and it's not long before she pulls to a stop in front of a showroom full of vintage cars.

Now this is what I'm talking about.

I look across the lot, and within seconds, I see the car I'm leaving with. It's fucking beautiful. A black 1967 Chevrolet Impala gleams in the sunlight, and I want it. No, I need it.

It doesn't take long for me to convince the salesman that I want what I want, and he's not going to sell me on anything else. Less than thirty minutes later, after a swipe of my pretty little plastic and a call to Smithy to confirm the sale, I leave with the keys to my newest joy. Got to love the way that money makes everything go faster in Echoes Cove.

"I'm gonna call her Izzy the Impala." I grin at Indi who laughs at me. "You want to follow me back to my house, and then I can show you the place properly since you ditched me earlier in the week?" I pout at her, and she rolls her eyes.

"Oh please, I ditched you to have dinner because my aunt came into town as a surprise. We both know I'd rather have been eating mac and cheese with you."

"Oh I know, it's just fun to poke."

"Yeah, yeah, Royal." She rolls her eyes and spins her keys on her finger. "Now get your pretty little butt in your car so I can follow you home in your beautiful new

Impala."

I grin at her and practically skip over to my new car. Once I'm in, I take in the fact I just bought my first car. I refuse to dwell on the fact that Dad and I talked about this day way too many times for this not to hurt a little, but I already hurt so much that I just can't think about it properly.

I start the car up, practically quivering over the pure American muscle growl that it makes. I peel out of the lot, heading back toward Echoes Cove. The car drives like a dream, and I almost wish the journey was longer.

By the time we pull up to the gates of the house, I'm grinning from ear to ear, having played more than a little to see what the little beauty is capable of. I lean out of the window and hit the buzzer, smiling into the camera lens. It buzzes again, and the gate starts to open. I head up the drive, with Indi following behind me in the Wrangler. Our cars so do not fit into the whole uptown rich bitch vibe of Echoes Cove, but I kind of love that.

I jump out, before grabbing my duffel from the backseat of the Wrangler, and head to the door with Indi on my heels.

"Miss Octavia, welcome home." Smithy greets me with a huge smile as he opens the door. "You must be Miss Indi. Welcome."

"Oh, I like him. Where can I get one?" Indi snickers,

and Smithy laughs in that deep, throaty way he does.

"You are welcome here at any time, Miss Indi." He waves us in the house, and I swear, a weight I hadn't realized I'd been carrying lifts from my shoulders. Even with the bullshit of everything that's happened in the last twenty-four hours, I'm finally home, and I almost feel content. "I've had the bedroom put together as per your directions, and all of the deliveries are arranged in the room for you too. I'll start putting together something for lunch. Will you both be eating?"

"Thank you so much, Smithy." I hug him tight, and he squeezes me just as tightly back. "We'll both be here for lunch and maybe dinner too. And thank you for handling everything, really. I appreciate it."

"That's what family is for, Miss Octavia. Now then, head upstairs! Do you need me to get the rest of your things?"

I twist my lips instantly, still a little pissed off about everything, and he frowns in response. "This is everything I have left. Blair and her friends destroyed everything else."

"That girl... I swear..."

"It's fine," I say, waving him off. If I go down this path again today, I'm never going to pull myself out of the pit of despair that's always lurking just beneath the surface and threatening to pull me under. "You said you packed most of Dad's stuff up in the basement, right? And all the other stuff that was sent back from the tour bus is there too? I'm sure I'll find some more momentos in that stuff, so no worries."

"Yes, of course, if you say so." He twists his lips like he disapproves but shakes his head before smiling at me again. "Now you girls head on upstairs. If anything isn't to your liking, just let me know, and I'll get it all sorted out for you."

"Thank you, Smithy," I say before turning to Indi. "Ready?"

"As a church goer on a Sunday." We head up the stairs, and I show her my childhood room, which gives her more than a few laughs. The pink really needs to be sorted out. Maybe I'll have Smithy arrange for the room to be painted and turned into a spare room or a music room. Anything but this pink nightmare.

We leave the pink disaster behind and head to the master suite. I can't help but grin as I take in what Smithy did to the room. He didn't just do what I asked—he decked the room out to the extreme. There are guitars hanging on one wall with a keyboard sitting just beneath them, regardless of the fact that we have a baby grand downstairs. The carpet is a cream colored blanket of thick, plush luxury, and the walls are dark gray. All of the furniture is a shabby white, and it's just… perfect. I smile as my eyes catch the accents of teal peppered throughout the room.

"Dude, can Smithy be my interior designer? This room looks amazing."

"Right? He nailed it." I walk in further and notice a ton of bags from what looks like clothes stores lined up beside the bed. Then I notice the envelope sitting on the pillow with my name on. "What the…"

I pick it up and take the note out.

To replace what was damaged at my behest.

Linc

"You have got to be fucking kidding me," I practically spit, seething with the anger burning deep in my gut.

"What?" Indi asks, and I pass her the note. She reads it, and her eyes go wide as I clench and unclench my fists. What the actual fuck? "Oh boy, did he actually just buy you a new wardrobe?"

I reach for one of the bags, recognizing the lingerie brand and my anger ratchets up another thousand degrees or so. "He bought me fucking everything, including underwear."

"Is he crazy? Why would he do this?"

"Because Lincoln Saint is a control freak, and he always has been. Apparently that's one thing around here that hasn't changed." If he thinks I'm accepting this bullshit, he has another thing coming. This isn't an act of kindness. This is just another reminder of his words last night. Money means nothing to him. This is just another show of control."

"I mean, some of this is nice, though," she jokes, spinning a lacy black thong around in the air, and I can't help but laugh. "Maybe after seeing how hot you looked earlier in the week, he was inspired."

"He can shove his inspiration up his ass." I start snatching up the bags, and Indi joins in, grinning even though she's out of the loop of my plan.

"What are we doing?"

"We're going next door."

"Next door?"

"To the Saints' house." I grin, and her eyes go wide.

"Wait, they still live next door too? This is so delicious. Girl, I can't even." She's practically giddy as she follows me out of the house and down the drive. I buzz on the Saints' gate and wait, trying not to sigh as I bounce from foot to foot. My hands clench around the handles of the bags as fury pierces through me. I still can't quite believe Lincoln had the nerve to do this, and yet, I don't know why I'm really that shocked.

"V? Is that you?" East's voice comes through the system, and I smile. Better him than his brother. I can't help but wonder if he knows what Lincoln and the others did to me over the weekend? I can't help but wonder if East would have joined them. Would he have pinned me and whispered dirty words to me like Finley did? Or watched me like Mav? Or would he have touched me like his brother did? Shame floods me at the thought, and I push it back the best I can.

"Yeah, it's me. Can I come in? I'll only be a minute."

"Er, yeah sure," he says, and buzzes me in, sounding more than a little confused. Indi follows me up their drive, and I ignore the onslaught of memories that threaten when the house comes into view. We find East standing in the open front door, eyes wide when he takes in the sight of us with all of the bags. "V, what is that?"

"This is all for Lincoln. You can tell him to shove his so-called gift up his ass."

East drags a hand down his face as I drop the bags at his feet and groans. "What the fuck did he do now?"

I give him a quick run down of some of the shit I've been going through, leaving out the more… graphic parts… and the look on his face tells me he has had no idea about anything that's been going on beyond what I told him that first day in Gym.

His rage over everything is obvious. His hands shake as he clenches his jaw, looking more like Lincoln than normal, though they could be twins on a bad day. "My little brother needs to get a fucking clue. I'm sorry, V."

"You don't have anything to be sorry for," I tell him before giving him a quick hug.

He frowns at me and says, "I'm still sorry, V. If there's anything I can do to help, you know I will. I can't believe they trashed your dad's stuff. I'm going to have words with that little fuck head."

"There's no use, we both know that it won't stop anything. It might just make him worse. I just wish I knew what I did." He frowns at my words as I wrap my arms around myself. He steps forward and hugs me tight, and for a moment I let myself relax into his arms. Taking comfort that he, at least, is still my friend. "I'll see you soon?"

"You know it," he says before Indi and I head back home.

"Actually, fuck going home, do you want to go shopping? I do need a new wardrobe after all." I smile at her, and she squeals happily.

"Hell yes!" We head inside and grab my keys before heading back out. Shopping has never been something I massively enjoy, but then I've never had a girlfriend like Indi to shop with.

I chew on my lip as I climb in the car, trying not to get lost in my own head as Indi gets in. I thought coming home would solve all my issues, but I have a feeling being next door to the Saint boys again is going to bring a whole host of new issues.

At least life won't be dull, I guess.

Eight

"You think he was pissed?"

I glance over at Indi sitting in my passenger seat, chewing on her lip. She's been fidgety ever since I picked her up for school this morning. Gone is the badass that helped me dump clothes on Lincoln's doorstep, and in her place is the sunshine child who doesn't want to hurt anyone.

"I mean, probably, but he was pissed at me anyway. This won't have made much of a difference. Plus, I don't give a shit if he's pissed. After everything they've done to me this last week, they deserve to be pissed off." I smile at her, trying to reassure her, but she wrings her hands in her lap. I haven't even told her everything that's happened, and right now I'm glad for that. I'm not sure her sunshine persona could handle the avalanche of bullshit I've been buried under. "Don't worry, even if he is, I won't let anything happen to you. You did your time with the bitch squad already. I won't let being my friend drag you down harder."

Her eyes go wide, and she shakes her head. "Oh please, that isn't what I meant at all. I just mean like, the bitch squad are the ones who have been messing with you so far. What if the boys step up their assholeness? I'm not worried for me, just for you. You've only been back at ECP a week, and look at what you've already dealt with."

My heart swells at her words. Total sunshine child. She is literally the embodiment of joy in a dark little alternative shell. For the first time in a long time, it's nice knowing that I have someone who is one hundred percent on my side and has my best interests at heart. "Don't worry about me. I grew up here, playing these games is practically a part of my blood. Blair and her little minions already took the last few things that were precious to me. There isn't anything more they can do to truly hurt me."

My mind flashes over everything they've already done. I'm not really sure that it can get worse than it has.

"I don't know, you have some pretty banging hair, and I've seen the Saint Squad do some pretty shitty things."

I shrug as I pull into a space in the student lot. "It's just hair, it'll grow back. But trust me, they won't go after my hair. I swear, Blair's hair is her greatest treasure, so she wouldn't want me to retaliate that way. She might seem like a dumb bitch, but she's calculating as hell."

"Okay," she starts but cuts off with a squeak as Raleigh jumps in front of the hood.

He lets out a whistle before walking around and opening my door for me as I grab my bag from behind Indi's seat. I look up and see Jackson at her door, and she's blushing like crazy. I wink at her, which just makes the red on her cheeks deepen closer to maroon as he opens her door.

"Good weekend?" I ask Raleigh as I lock the car.

"Yeah, not so bad, just chilled and slayed Jackson on Apex and all that. It was a pretty chill weekend. You?" We circle toward the back of the car, reaching the other two as he asks, and Indi's eyes widen comically, looking like a deer in headlights. I give her a small shake of my head.

"It was fine," I tell him, the lies like ash in my mouth. No need to dump my baggage everywhere since it won't help me anyway. "We went car shopping, obviously, and I moved back into my old house. It was a pretty chill one too."

"That is one sweet-ass ride," Jackson says with a whistle as he slings an arm over Indi's shoulder. "I mean, compared to the others in the lot, she stands out. She's got that old school beauty."

"Yes, yes she does." I beam, glancing back at my car before climbing the steps to the school. "I need to hit the library quickly before I head to class, so I'll see you guys later."

"Oh, I'll come with you, I need to ask Mrs. Smith to source a book for me," Indi exclaims, ducking out of Jackson's hold. He protests weakly, and her blush goes damn near as purple as her hair as we walk away with a wave.

"Well, that looked cozy," I tease, bumping her shoulder with mine.

She grips her books against her chest and glances at me from the side of her eyes. "I have no idea what that was."

"That was the start of *something*." I grin and then hum the High School Musical song at her until she pushes me away laughing.

"You are such a dork."

"I know, but I totally rock the dork thing." I grin as we reach our lockers. My smile drops when I notice the new 'art' engraved into my locker door.

Slut.

How original.

"People are such assholes," Indi hisses, her anger worse than mine.

I shrug and open my locker. "Fuck them and their opinions. Words can't hurt me if I don't let them." I smile over my shoulder at her, but she doesn't look like she agrees. "Let me just throw my stuff in my locker, then we can hit the library on the way to English."

"Sounds good to me, I'll do the same." She huffs, and I hope she'll just ignore the latest attempt at tearing me down. I need her to treat it the same way I am. As nothing but pathetic. She ditches her stuff while I unload mine and is back before I'm even done.

"Octavia, we should talk." I groan at the sound of Lincoln's voice.

"Will you run to the library for me, get your thing, and then check out *Jane Eyre* for me? There's something about the feel of a real book when you're reading the classics, you know?"

"Are you sure?" Indi asks quietly, her gaze bouncing over my shoulder to Lincoln. I don't need to actually see his face to know how annoyed he is that I haven't actually addressed him. I can already picture his face, which is exactly why I'm still facing her instead of him.

"I'm sure. I won't be long." I smile at her, trying to reassure her, and she nods before scurrying away. I love that she's willing to go against Lincoln, Maverick, and Finley on my behalf, but I also totally understand her fear of them after surviving a year at this school alone.

I take a deep breath and shut my locker before turning to face the guy in question, with a saccharine smile on my face. "Lincoln, what can I do for you?"

"You can take back the things I bought for you. I told

you, you have no control until you leave. Don't make me force the matter again." He leans against the locker, like he's as casual as casual gets, but the tightness of his shoulders and the tic in his jaw tells me just how tense he is, really. I can feel the eyes of people in the halls on us, but I'm determined not to make a scene. I've had enough of that already.

Then it hits me what he means, and I feel a blush creep up my chest. I know he notices because his jaw relaxes, and he has that smug-ass smile of his back for a moment. He's too close right now, but I don't want to take a step back. I don't want him to know that he's getting to me as much as he is, so I take a deep breath and tough it out.

"I don't want the things you bought, Lincoln, so no, I will not take them back. I already went shopping for myself. Return them, burn them, donate them—I don't care… That's a lie, I'd totally rather you donated them, but still. I won't take them. What was taken from me was irreplaceable—control or not."

"Why do you always have to be so obstinate?" he growls through clenched teeth.

"Pot, meet kettle," I say, flicking my hair over my shoulder, pulling on the rage from everything that's happened so far as I face him down. I'm sure this moment of stupid bravery is going to be short lived and something he'll make me regret later. But for now, I'm going to cling to it like it's my last lifeline. "Now if that's everything, I have to get to class."

He doesn't say a word, just narrows his eyes and glares at me. I know I've poked the bear. And I know I might possibly regret it later, but dammit, I don't want to be the weak damsel he and his friends keep turning me into.

Compared to last week, this morning has been a breeze. My classes have been easy enough, and even Music didn't send me into a spiraling melt down. I'm calling it a good morning.

Even Blair didn't bother to acknowledge my existence, and I for one, am thankful for it. Because if she tries me today, I'm likely to lose my shit. I've been just about keeping myself together, like a reasonable human being, but if she mentions Friday night, I will not be held responsible for my actions.

I walk into the cafeteria, arm in arm with Indi, and I wave over at Raleigh when he calls my name. We grab a tray each and slide into the line, but then the room goes so quiet you could hear a pin drop. I'm immediately on alert in the seconds before I feel heat at my back. Indi turns to face me and startles. I don't have to question who's behind me.

I paint a smile on my face as I turn to find Maverick standing way too close behind me. "Can I help you?"

He smirks back at me before leaning into my personal space and whispering, "I can think of a lot of ways you can help me, V."

I jolt back, hating that I'm giving him the power yet again, but I don't want him that close, or even in my space at all. Shoving him backward would only start something I'm not willing to finish here in the cafeteria.

"Pretty sure you can help yourself with that," I sneer before turning my back on him and facing Indi again. I grab my tray from the counter and encourage Indi to move forward. She still doesn't know what happened, and I'm not ready for Maverick to out me. I've helped him plenty already.

When nothing happens to satisfy the needs of the drama-seeking student body, the noise in the cafeteria starts back up, and we make our way to the table we claimed as ours last week, waving at the football guys as we pass them.

"That was weird," Indi says as she slides into the chair opposite me.

"Maverick has always enjoyed games," I tell her, trying to breeze past it and dig into the chicken and broccoli Alfredo I picked for my lunch, groaning at how good it tastes. I swear the food in this place is the only redeeming feature of the entire school. I mean, the teachers are okay for the most part, minus the whole 'being afraid of the students' thing. I can *almost* understand that, though. They're just here to get a paycheck, and these kids could ruin their lives in a heartbeat; but shit, it's frustrating.

"He definitely seems like the crazy one of the three," she says, cracking open her soda and taking a sip. She has no fucking idea.

"Who's crazy?"

I groan as Maverick slides into the seat beside me, and Indi about chokes on her drink, spluttering over the maniac of a boy sitting next to me.

"Why are you here?" I ask, glaring at him.

"It's lunchtime, where else would I be?" His eyes dance with delight, and I want to nut punch him, just to wipe the stupid smile from his face.

"Why are you sitting here, Maverick?" The words come out through a tightly clenched jaw. I hate how much they affect me without even really trying.

He clasps at his chest, a look of mocking disbelief on his face. "Why, Octavia, are you saying I'm not welcome here? And here was me thinking we could be friends."

"Maverick Riley, you made it all too clear that we are not friends. So fuck off and sit with your actual friends." I try to put a brave face on, letting my anger lead me, and point over to where Lincoln and Finley are watching us. Their matching frowns almost make me want to laugh, but

147

I clamp it down in favor of maintaining the stern look I'm giving Maverick.

"I don't remember doing any such thing." He's so fucking nonchalant as he reaches over and takes one of Indi's fries. I slap his hand so he drops the fry while Indi just watches us. Her panic is clear. She has no clue what to do right now, so I smile at her.

"Leave her fucking food alone, you heathen." I swear his grin grows, and I just want to roll my eyes at him.

He turns his gaze on her, and I swear she blanches. "She doesn't mind, do you, Indigo?"

"Don't be such a dick, Maverick." I sigh, leaning back in my chair. "Of course she minds. If she wanted you to have her lunch, she'd have offered it, and she didn't."

"Fine, fine. I see I'm not wanted." He brushes his hands together as he stands, but leans down to whisper in my ear again. "But don't think that I'm done, V. I told you you were off-limits, and you bucked against it. You'll see what happens when you defy me if you keep this up."

An icy drop of dread runs down my spine, making my entire body shiver, but I keep the bored look on my face as he pulls back. There's no way in hell I'm letting him think he's actually managing to intimidate me. Not again. I don't know what his little show today has been about, but I'm going to work it out. How can they possibly think that what they've already done isn't enough?

Those three are frustrating as fuck, and I am already so over it.

He saunters back toward his usual table, and Indi's color comes back to her face more and more with each step away from us he takes.

"Sorry," I sigh at her, but she shakes her head.

"No, I'm sorry. I need to grow a backbone when it comes to those three. I can face off against Blair and the bitch squad without really thinking twice, but there is just something dark about those three that makes my blood turn to ice."

I shrug before picking at my lunch again. "I get it. Something's definitely changed with them since I left, I just wish I knew what their game was."

"With the rumors I've heard around this place, it could range from just some bored fun to something fucking deadly. Please be careful." My eyebrows raise at her comment. What the actual fuck does she mean *deadly*? Apparently I've been away from here for way too long, but if they've set their sights on me, I'm not about to back down.

Deadly or not.

We make it through the rest of lunch without any drama,

and I leave Indi to head to her class as I meander toward my locker. I have French next, and considering the amount of time I've spent in France, it's not really a class I'm worried about passing. I speak six different languages, all fluently, thanks to my badass tour tutors.

"Octavia!" I groan at the sound of my name on Lincoln's lips again. What is it with him and Maverick trying to steal the small moments of peace I find?

"Yes, Lincoln?" I turn to face him, crossing my arms. It might be a small barrier between us, but I'll take any barriers I can get until I work out what the fuck he's playing at. I don't think he'd attack me in the hall, but I wouldn't put anything past him at this point.

"I want you to reconsider the gifts." He frowns at me, and it's more than apparent that he's not used to people telling him no. Despite their father not being around much, the Saints basically own this town, so I'm sure no one has ever really told him no in his life.

I sigh and pinch the bridge of my nose. "I don't want the clothes, Lincoln."

"Why not?"

"Because they weren't a gift. I'm not a willing participant in this game you're playing. You can try to intimidate me all you like, but I'm not budging on this. You already took enough from me."

His frown deepens, and his shoulders tense. "You

always could see me like no other."

His muttering makes absolutely no sense to me, so I just raise an eyebrow and wait for him to get on with whatever it is he has to say.

He takes a step forward, so close I can feel the heat of his skin as his warm, earthy scent assaults me. I refuse to step back and give him the space I did Maverick in the cafeteria. I can feel that he's a different kind of dangerous, and I just need to work out exactly how. "A lot has changed since you left. You'd have been better off not coming back here."

"Oh awesome, we're back to this again. You're a broken record, Lincoln. I already told you, I didn't have a choice."

His entire demeanor changes, turning icy cold. He narrows his eyes, and his calculating stare makes me hold my breath. Something just changed, and I have no idea what or why.

He grips my arms, so tightly I think I might bruise, before leaning down until we're eye to eye. "Don't get me started on things you don't have a choice in, Octavia. You should've stayed away. But you're here now, and that means you need to get the fuck in line before you get hurt."

"The only thing hurting me right now, Lincoln, is you." I try to pull away, but his grip is ironclad.

"You can't imagine the things that could hurt you here.

Everything so far… that's just a small taste. Your dad might have taken the easy way out, but at least he got out. He left you here to fend for yourself in his stead like a fucking coward." His biting tone has nothing on the pain piercing my heart.

"You don't get to talk about my dad like you knew him," I hiss, pushing him away from me. "You have no idea what he went through or why he did what he did." Tears threaten to fall at the thought, but I won't let them fall here. Not in front of him. Not like this.

"You have no idea what I know," he growls before standing up straight and smoothing down his blazer. I have no idea what the fuck he's talking about, but I don't have a chance to ask him before he turns on his heel and stalks away from me.

My emotions roar inside of me like a storm I can't outrun.

Anger.

Confusion.

Devastation.

The emotions build to a roaring pitch inside of me as I watch him walk away. I'm startled by the bell followed by the principal's voice through the intercom. "An assembly has been called in place of your next class. Please make your way to the auditorium. Attendance is mandatory."

The halls fill with noise and bodies in an instant as kids

spill out of their classrooms. It's damn near suffocating, and I struggle to breathe as they force their way past me in the halls to get to the auditorium. This is all way too fucking much.

"Fuck this," I mutter, and walk in the opposite direction of the auditorium. I need a refuge right now, and there is only one place I can think of to go.

I sit down on the piano bench, my fingers touching the cool ivory. It feels like it's been forever since I played. The quiet of the room soothes me. I know that no one else is on this side of the school, at least no one that truly matters, not when everyone else is in the auditorium. My chest aches with thoughts of the last time I played, messing around with my dad on his stage before his show, just playing because we loved it. It was our thing. Before every show, he'd clear everyone out except for Mac, and we'd just play the songs we loved the most. Him on his guitar, me on the keys.

I start to play, the soft chords fill the room as silent tears fall down my face. I know the reason I haven't played in forever is the exact reason I'm playing right now. It makes me feel. Too much. Everything. I just need to let this raging storm of me out. Just a bit of it though, otherwise I'm going to break so catastrophically that I might not come back from it.

I fall into the music, playing out every swirling emotion that's been rotting inside of me since he died.

Every single thing I've dealt with since I came back to Echoes Cove pours out of me, and I start to sing my old favorite song for any kind of heartbreak. I put every piece of myself into the music, like cutting myself open and letting myself bleed over everything, while ignoring the tears that track down my face, instead focusing on feeling every fucking thing I've been avoiding. I never usually let myself cry, despite being pushed to it by others so far this year, but just this once, I let go of the walls I've kept around myself since everything happened with my dad.

The song draws to a close, the soft tinkling of the ivory echoing in the room, eventually giving way to absolute silence beyond my own breaths.

"Octavia…" I spin on the bench and find Finley standing in the doorway, his voice barely more than a whisper. Just like the dark knight that he is, watching me in the shadows. The emotion on his face isn't anything I've seen before. At least not from him, but I don't care. Not anymore. Not after everything that's happened recently. I stand, clutching my arms against myself. I have no idea how long he's been there, and even though I'm fully clothed, I've never felt more exposed in my entire life.

I rush past him, tears still streaming down my face. I do not have the emotional capacity to deal with Finley Knight right now. I hear his heavy footsteps behind me, and he reaches me before I make it to the end of the hall. He grabs me from behind, pulling me back until my body is flush to his chest, and just holds me against him. I cave and lean into him, pretending the comfort is coming from anyone but him. He turns me around once he realizes I'm not going to struggle, and wraps me in his arms as I war with myself over taking comfort from someone who is one of the main reasons I need it.

He holds me until my tears slow, pulling back to wipe them from my face after a couple of minutes. He cups my face gently. "Octavia..."

His voice is like a bucket of cold water.

This isn't right.

I untangle from his arms, despite his protests, and turn and walk away from him.

Finley Knight is not the guy who comforts you. He's the guy that makes you cry. Something I'm all too fucking aware of. He's still the guy who iced me out the second I got back here, and I'm not stupid enough to think this means something now. He might have caught me at my weakest, but I'd be an idiot to think this changes anything.

We're still not friends, and we're definitely not what we used to be.

I doubt we ever will be again.

Nine

FINLEY

Octavia fucking Royal makes my world spin off axis.
Always has.

Always will.

Ever since she came back, my entire life has been upside down and ass backward. Something about that girl pulls all of my attention, and everything else just goes to shit.

Which is exactly why I hoped she'd never come back.

It was safer with her gone. For us, and for her.

OCTAVIA

"Where did you disappear to earlier?" I look up from my locker to see Indi leaning against the one next to mine.

"I went to the music rooms, which was a huge mistake. I should've just gone to the stupid assembly. Did I miss much?" I ask as I pull my books from the locker into my bag and slam it shut. Apparently, I'm still not over my run-in with Finley earlier.

"Just Principal Evans droning on about his expectations for the year and some new rules being introduced after the summer of war between us and ECH." I lift my eyebrows in question, and she continues. "Echoes Cove High... a guy called Ryker Donovan and his boys practically run the place, and to say the rivalry between this school and theirs is epic is an understatement. One guy ended up in critical condition after a fight over the summer apparently."

"Well shit, I think I remember Ryker... He's a twin right?" I ask, as we start heading down the hall to escape this living nightmare of a school.

"Yeah, that's him. Ellis is his twin. They have an older brother, Diego, and a younger sister, Scout," she says, nodding as she opens the door. She freezes on the threshold before peeking over her shoulder at me. "Uhm... Octavia..."

She grimaces as she turns back to me all the way. I look over her shoulder, and rage floods my system. Most of the school is out front with their phones out, pointed in our direction. Waiting. My eyes flick from my brand new car, which now has bright yellow paint poured all over it, to the smirk on Blair's face. My eyes slide to Lincoln, Finley, and Maverick, who are watching me, straight-faced.

I take a deep breath and paint a smile on my face. These assholes would love a video of the nation's princess losing her fucking shit to go viral online. I'm not about to give that to them.

"Do you want me to give you a ride home? The garage dropped my car off at lunch," she asks, but I shake my head.

"No, I'm good. Come on, let's go face my adoring audience." My sarcasm is thick, but she looks as devastated about the state of my car as I feel. Fucking assholes, the lot of them.

I'm not sure what they think any of this is going to achieve, but I'm not going anywhere. My only stipulation in the Will was a 4.0 GPA from this school and staying with my guardian, so even if they burn my shit to the ground, I'm here to stay.

Indi steps fully out of the door, and I follow her out, pulling my aviators from my bag and sliding them onto my face. I finger wave at those with their cameras out, smiling like I couldn't give a fuck about the state of my car. Lincoln and company watch me as I head to my car before they climb into Lincoln's 4x4 and head out of the lot.

Fuck them all.

Fuck every single asshole here that thinks making my life hard is funny.

I get in the car and hook up my phone before blasting "Fuck You" by Don Vedda. I hit the wipers, smearing the paint just enough that I can actually fucking see and peel out of the lot. I clutch the steering wheel so tight my knuckles go white. Yellow paint spills down the rear window as I drive, fueling my rage. Angry tears fall down my face, which just pisses me off more.

I end up stuck in a row of traffic, and the stares from people when they see the car just prickles me further. The car can be fixed, but it's the sheer fucking audacity of it all. What gives these pricks the right to fuck with me just because I came back to this hellhole?

If they're not careful, they're going to push me too far, and they're not going to like it when I fight back. I don't fight like these prissy rich bitches. I'm all about getting my hands dirty. Be it blood or actual dirt, I'm not afraid of throwing hands. The one thing about growing up with roadies and a security team... My life was different from all of the people here. Their petty bullshit is just that.

It takes way too long to get home, and just as I'm pulling up to the house, I spot Lincoln leaving his house. Finley and Maverick are with him, and both of them look surprised to see me pulling into my drive. I guess the details of my move hadn't made it to them yet.

Interesting.

I hit the clicker on my keys, and the gates swing open. It doesn't take a minute to reach the front of the house, but the yellow paint is dripping all over the drive. I fucking hate people. It's official.

I need to run. It's the only way I'm going to destress. Usually I'd use music, but after this fucking day, there isn't a chance I'm touching an instrument again any time soon.

I grab my bag and head inside, finding Smithy in the kitchen. "Good day, Miss Octavia?"

"Not exactly," I sigh, and jump up onto one of the stools at the island.

"This calls for a milkshake," he says, frowning. I'm not

sure how he always knows the perfect thing to aid my calm, but in less than three minutes, the thickest, chocolatiest milkshake is in front of me, and he smiles sadly. "Drink up, then tell me all about it."

I take a sip of the shake. It's like a mouthful of happy and ecstasy, and the flavors burst over my tongue. I tell him about my car, though I leave out some of the other, more delightful, parts of my day. I'd have hidden the car thing from him if I thought it was possible—he's already done more than enough for me, he shouldn't have to deal with shit like this too. But there's no way he would have missed the damage to the car. He's not blind.

"I have a man who can fix your car, let me handle that. It might take about a week, but I'm sure we can sort you out a lease in the meantime." He pats my shoulder gently before getting up and pulling his phone from his pocket. "I'll call him now. You head upstairs and take a nice long, relaxing bubble bath."

"I'm thinking about going for a run, but that sounds perfect. I'll do that later. Thanks, Smithy, you're the best."

"It's no trouble at all, Miss Octavia, and I think a call to Mr. Evans to remind him exactly who funded that new football field is in order. Your father was very generous to that school, and it's appalling that Mr. Evans forgets who was good to him when he needed it."

"You don't need to do that. It'll just make things

worse," I tell him with a sigh before taking another sip of the heavenly milkshake.

He frowns at me and shakes his head. "Let me go and make a call about your car, the rest we can discuss later." He leaves the room before I can respond, leaving me alone with my thoughts, which is possibly the worst place I could be.

Fuck this shit, I'm going to run.

My run through town takes the edge off of the burning anger, but it's still a fiery pit inside of me. Mac thought I should see a therapist after Dad's death, but I've never really been the kind to sit and talk to a stranger about how I'm feeling. Usually I'd write it out and put it into a song. Dad always said every experience in life is just another plot line, but considering the fact that every time I try to play I end up crying, that isn't an option right now.

So I run, and I keep running, until I can't anymore… Then I go a little further. Except this godforsaken town just won't let me have any peace. If it's not someone from school staring and pointing, it's the paparazzi who think I can't see them, trying to get a picture of me being anything other than the picture of perfection they've always made me out to be.

You'd think the death of my dad would excuse me from the paparazzi chaos I've experienced since I went on tour with him, but apparently not. I managed to get some privacy when I first came here, but I guess more than one video or photo of the shit from school told the vultures where I ended up.

Wonderful.

By the time I reach the shoreline, my chest burns, but my anger hasn't subsided in the slightest. If anything, it's grown. So I push myself onto the sand and keep running. The summer sun beats down on me, and sweat trickles down my back as I run. The burn in my legs intensifies, but I push through.

I run until the beach is desolate and I'm beyond all of the houses that back up onto the beach. Until I can pretend I'm the only person in existence and the rest of the world isn't trying to beat me for a reason I haven't worked out yet.

I come to a stop, lifting my hands to the back of my head, and suck in lungfuls of air before downing water like it's going out of fashion.

Echoes Cove, in a lot of ways, is the same as I remember, but something definitely changed while I was gone, and I have no fucking idea what it is. I don't remember the people here being so… secretive. So sadistic and twisted.

My mind wanders back to the four boys who were once

my saviors. I wonder what happened to them to make them so twisted. I get that the parents in Echoes Cove aren't the most attentive... The greed here makes me sick, but the sadistic streak in Maverick is worse than I ever remember it being, and Lincoln was always dark and broody, but the anger that seems to fuel him is insane. I can't quite get a read on Finley, but something definitely isn't right there either. The only one who seems reasonably unscathed is East... And none of it makes any sense.

Not that I expect it to, but Indi's comment about deadly secrets has been swirling around in the back of my mind since she said it. Part of me wants to just put it down to the rivalry she mentioned... But another part of me tells me not to be so dismissive.

Echoes Cove has always been a web of lies and deceit.

"I can't stay here with all of this, Stone, we need to get out. Now. Before they come for Octavia." My mom screams at my daddy, and I rock back and forth in the pantry with my hands over my ears. All my parents seem to do now is argue and shout. I wish I could make it stop.

"There is no way out of this, Emily. What part of that don't you get? The best thing we can do for V is to just do what we need to do." My dad's voice gets quieter. He sounds so sad.

A glass smashes, and my mom shrieks again. "Why do you have to be such a fucking doormat? I didn't sign up for this, Stone. I'm taking our daughter, and I'm getting as far away from this cesspit as possible."

"If you run, they will chase you. It's what they do."

"We can't just let them dictate our lives like this. I'll suffocate if I stay."

"You think they'll let you live if you leave… if it's not on their terms? What about that is safe for her, Cami?"

I don't understand any of what they're talking about, so I stay quiet. No one knows I'm here, and I don't want them to yell at me too. Mom yells all the time now. Ever since they went to that party I wasn't allowed to go to. I wish I'd never made such a fuss. Maybe then they wouldn't fight anymore.

"Have either of you seen Miss Octavia?" Smithy's voice interrupts them, and I scurry into the back corner. If they find me here, I'm going to be in trouble. I push harder on my ears and close my eyes, counting my numbers like Daddy asked.

I wish they wouldn't fight about me all the time. Maybe if I was better they wouldn't fight. Maybe if I could just learn my numbers, the yelling will stop.

I drop to my knees as the memory hits me, the ache in my chest growing. I don't have that many memories of my mom from before she left me… or so I thought.

What even was that?

I take a deep breath and close my eyes, racking my

brain for more of the memory. What on earth would my parents have been trying to run from?

I shake my head, trying to clear the memories. Before who comes for me? Surely my dad wouldn't have sent me back here if it wasn't safe? All he ever tried to do was keep me safe.

That's why he took me on tour, he wanted me with him after Mom left. It was our big adventure, a way to keep us together. I was safer with him on tour than here in the Cove on my own.

None of this makes sense, and I only have a fragment of the puzzle. It's probably nothing, just my stressed out brain trying to manifest my trauma or some bullshit.

My phone buzzes in my arm strap, so I slide it out. Any distraction is better than this.

Indi:

You doing okay? Did you get the car sorted out?

Me:

I'm fine, just out for a run. Smithy is getting the car taken care of, but it's going to take at least a week. FML.

Indi:

Want a ride in the morning? I don't mind playing taxi for a week if you need me.

Me:

You are a lifesaver, floofy coffees are entirely on me the whole week.

Indi:

See this is why we're going to be BFFL. You understand me on a baser level.

I can't help but laugh at her. Coffee is definitely one way to this girl's heart. That, reality TV shows, and good music. I can get down for most of that. The train of thought gives me an idea.

Me:

Exactly... speaking of BFFL, when is your birthday? A good bestie requires this information.

Indi:

Uhm... it's actually in a few weeks. I don't usually do much, birthdays aren't a big deal in my family.

Me:

Are you shitting me? You turn 18... this requires celebration!

Indi:

If that comes in the form of eating so much I pass out, that's a celebration I can get down with. Beyond that, just nope.

Me:

Deal!

This totally gives me an idea for her birthday, and I smile wider than I have in a week. I am going to rock this bestie thing.

Indi:

eye roll emoji If you say so. You sure you're okay? Running doesn't sound fun.

Me:

Running is awesome. I promise I'm good, just burning off some anger rather than going to jail. This seemed like a better option. Orange isn't my color.

Indi:

cowboy emoji You slay me. Okay, if you're good, I'm going to get started on my Econ assignment. Enjoy your run. *shudders*

Me:

*Have fun with that. *middle finger emoji**

I laugh a little and slide my phone back into the strap before finishing my water. Maybe the Cove is the cesspit my mom thought it was, but with people like Indi bringing the sunshine, I'm pretty sure I can survive the chaos.

I'm Octavia fucking Royal... How bad can one year be?

I get home from my run, exhausted but feeling lighter than I was when I left. The thought of the bubble bath Smithy suggested puts an extra bounce in my step as I finish running up the driveway.

I flick through the mail on the entry hall table as I kick off my sneakers. Bills, junk mail... and a black envelope with my name embossed on it.

Different.

I flick it over to open it and notice it's sealed with red wax and stamped with a symbol I've never seen before. I peel it back and pull the card from inside.

Octavia Royal
You are cordially invited to the Echoes Cove Orphan
Society fundraiser ball.

Date: December 5th
Location: The Nesthood Hall

Dress Code: Black Tie

Please RSVP by August 20th with note of any additional
guests.

Yours
TKS

Apparently charity gala invites got bougie. Who would've thought? And the Nesthood Hall? Not on your life. I've avoided that place my entire life. The building creeps me the fuck out, so I don't think so.

I drop it back onto the pile with zero intention of going. Balls have never been my thing, and Dad stopped taking me to red carpet shit after the first one we did. It was horrendous. I don't have a pretentious bone in my body, and my whole 'speak your mind' attitude didn't exactly go down well. I know my place, and charity balls are not one of them.

"Did you enjoy your run, Miss Octavia?" Smithy appears, startling me, but the smile on his face brings me joy.

"It was amazing, thank you."

"What would you like for dinner this evening?" I think it over, craving tacos way more than I should... But it's been a hot minute since I actually ate a vegetable, so I know I need to make some good decisions, shitty as they are.

"Chicken and veggies?" I say, biting my lip, and he pulls a face at me.

"I know you're not that uncreative, Miss Octavia," he scoffs, and I stifle the laugh that threatens. "I have a perfect idea. Give me an hour."

"Sure thing, Smithy. As long as you join me. Eating alone isn't so much fun."

He softens a little and smiles at me. "It would be my pleasure."

"Awesome, I'm going to grab a shower, then I'll be down." I jog up the stairs, the bubble bath can wait for the minute. My stomach growls at the realization that food is far higher up the priority list right now.

It doesn't take long to shower and wash my hair, though blowing out my waist length hair takes longer than I'd like. I'd cut it, but well... My hair is the only thing I'm really fussy about when it comes to my looks. It's weird, but it is what it is. I'm allowed to be vain about one thing.

I throw on a pair of leggings and a hoodie, pulling my hair up into a messy bun before making my way back down to the kitchen. I find Smithy humming along to the music he has funneling through the speakers in here, almost dancing as he's standing at the chopping board. If I wasn't hungry before, the smells coming from this room would have me ravenous.

"Anything I can help with?" I ask as I enter the room, and he shakes his head as the gate buzzer sounds.

"Expecting anyone?" he asks, frowning.

I shake my head. "Not that I know of. I'll go see who it is, don't let me interrupt you. Whatever you're cooking smells delicious."

Smithy offers a noncommittal grunt in return, so I turn on my heel and go to the monitor in the small room just by the front door. I peer into the monitor, but I don't see anyone at the gates. I push the button to the microphone while frowning. "Hello?"

No one responds, and the monitor flickers to another one of the cameras we have set up, and I catch sight of something leaning against the gate.

Flowers?

That's weird as fuck.

"Who is it?" Smithy calls out as I leave the security room.

"Looks like a flower delivery, but they left them at the gate. I'm just going to go get them." I slip my sneakers back on, giving zero fucks that I look like a hot mess, grab my keys, and jog down to the gate. I use the clicker to open the gates, standing back and waiting to see if anyone jumps out. Apparently the assholes at school have me a little on edge. I've seen too many movies where the mean girls cover the girl in honey and feathers, or worse… If they fuck with me like that, I'll do far worse to them than has already been done to me. I've not really retaliated at this point but that doesn't mean I won't.

When I'm confident there's no one there, I rush forward and grab the flowers, hitting the clicker for the gates as soon as I'm clear.

It doesn't take me long to get back to the house, and I drop my keys back into the bowl next to the mail and take the flowers to the kitchen.

"Oh tulips, how lovely," Smithy says as I lay the flowers down on the counter. "I'll grab a vase as soon as I slide this into the oven."

I look at the veggie lasagna he's layering and practically drool. "Smithy, you are a culinary wonder."

He ignores my compliment in favor of studying the flowers for a moment. "Who are the flowers from? Yellow tulips aren't a usual gifting flower." He moves across the kitchen and grabs a vase from fuck knows where and fills it with water.

I pull the card from the flowers, but there is no inscription on the envelope. It's sealed with red wax, a horse inside of a rose. Weird. I break the seal and find a black card inside, embossed with the same image on the seal. "No idea who they're from. There's nothing on the card."

I show him the card, and I swear I see fear flicker behind his eyes, but it's gone as soon as it appears, so I question if I even saw it at all. "Well, a mysterious suitor. How quaint."

He takes the flowers and arranges them in the vase, placing them on the windowsill. Smithy admires them for a short moment before turning back to me and asking, "Now, are we eating in here or with a movie, Miss Octavia?"

"Serial killer TV?" I ask hopefully, knowing he won't really tell me no.

He shakes his head, smiling softly. "Why not? Maybe we'll learn a thing or two."

I grin at him and clap my hands. "That's the spirit, Smithy. Every girl should know how to hide a body."

My phone buzzes on the counter, and I see a notification from the ReachMe app. Dread pools in my stomach. The last time I used the app was when the picture of East and I was on there. I haven't opened it since. I don't need to see the vitriol being hurled at me from every angle reflected on the school's shitty app.

Smithy turns his focus back to cooking, so I leave the room quietly and curl up on one of the sofas in the main room. Curiosity bites at me. Maybe the notification isn't about me.

My phone buzzes again, though, and I glance at it to see a message from Indi.

Indi:

I'm sorry, they're such assholes. Just ignore it. I've reported this too, so it should be gone soon.

Butterflies kick up in my stomach at her message. My curiosity gets the better of me, and I open the stupid closed network app. My notifications are insane. Apparently pictures and videos of me on here are rife. I'm tagged in so much shit, each caption more hateful than the next.

I clear the history of notifications, going to the most recent tag. *"Royal really is just this pathetic. Who cries to the guy who hates her? Just how fucked up is she? Maybe she's as fucked up as her dad. It takes a special kind of fucked up to off yourself the way he did."* I click on the attachment, and the sounds of my crying fill my ears.

No.

Someone recorded my breakdown on Finley. Someone took that moment of weakness and decided to use it against me. What the fuck is wrong with the people around here?

Tears prick my eyes, falling down my cheeks, and I wipe them away angrily.

How much longer can I do this? I don't know if I'm strong enough to survive another month here, let alone a whole fucking year. I've tried to be strong, but there's only so much a girl can fake. I thought I was doing so well hiding my shit. I thought if I put on a brave face, they'd get bored and back off but I'm getting the feeling that isn't going to happen.

Echoes Cove Prep isn't just where dreams go to die... it's become my waking nightmare.

Eleven

After a sunshiney start to my day with Indi, literally bouncing our way into school with Midnight Blue blaring through the speakers, my day actually hasn't been that bad.

The repercussions of the video haven't been exactly fun, and people around the school have been anything but nice about it. Not that I expected them to be, the entire Cove is full of shrivel-hearted assholes. The fake love notes in my locker 'from Finley' have been the highlight for me. Declarations of love for a slut who throws herself at the guy who hates her.

It's been awesome.

I should've ignored it, pushed it down with all of the other shit that's been bothering me, but I couldn't help torturing myself by watching it a few times over. Every time I watch it, I can't help but focus on Finley. He seemed so sincere in the moment, and he even looks it in the video, but I know better than most how good those guys are at wearing a mask.

All things considered, today could have been significantly worse, that much I'm sure of. As much as I'd like to become a wallflower while the boys keep up the tirade of terror, encouraging everyone else to be giant assholes along with them... Well, I know that isn't going to happen.

Everyone used to assume—and I guess they still do—that I wanted attention, being the daughter of 'The King.' I was blasted across the tabloids, and people think that life is all fun and games when you're in the spotlight like that... Until you get your period without notice and have to hide from the world because you had a moment of actually being *human*.

I've always preferred to fade into the background, which is why I want to open my own record label and just write music. I'd get to do what I love with music without having to be the face that everyone wants to see. I'm very aware of the chaos that comes with fame. Having had more than a little taste of it, I'm beyond over it.

So after a relatively quiet morning when I slide into what I've dubbed our table in the cafeteria, and Maverick drops into the seat opposite of me, I am overwhelmingly not prepared.

"Sitting alone, princess?" He reaches over to grab for the garlic bread on my plate, and I slap his hand, making him grin. "Maybe if you were a little nicer to people, you'd have more friends."

"Maybe if you weren't such a psychopath, you wouldn't think that," I bite back, making his grin widen. "You're in Indi's seat."

At that exact moment, Indi sidles up to the table, eyes wide as Maverick leans over so that he is very much in my space. "We have unfinished business, V. You'll be seeing me around."

I roll my eyes. Of course I'm going to see him around. Echoes Cove isn't big enough for me to avoid him, or I'd have already made that my number one mission.

"You don't get to call me V," I tell him as he stands, and an evil glint appears in his eyes, a malicious smile on his face.

He circles to my side of the table, standing behind me and caging me in as he leans over me to whisper into my ear, "You don't get to tell me what to do. You have no power here, princess. You'd do well to remember that."

I look up to find a wide-eyed Indi, who stands watching us, fidgeting like she doesn't know what to say or do. I smile up at her to let her know it's fine, despite his proximity.

He pulls back and saunters away from me, all eyes on

him as the whispers start again.

Indi slides into the chair he vacated and drops her tray onto the table. "Do I even want to ask?"

"Probably not." I take a bite of my pasta, hoping the joy of carbs can take me back to the happy place I was *almost* in ten minutes ago. I make myself smile up at her because I'm not going to ruin her day too. "How's your day been?"

"I can't complain. I saw Blair trip and faceplant into her locker, so that was fun." She grins wide, and I can't help but laugh. "I just wish I'd been able to record it so we could bask in the bliss of it together."

"I'd have paid good money to see that."

"To see what?" Raleigh asks as he drops into the seat beside me.

"Blair faceplant into her locker," Indi tells him, practically bouncing in her seat as she takes a bite from her burger. He bursts out laughing, which only makes my smile widen.

"Yup, I'd have paid good money to see that too." Jackson and some of the other guys on the team join our table, and lunch break passes in the blink of an eye.

When the bell rings, I can't stop my frown. I am so not ready to go back to class, French might not be one of the classes I'm having issues with, but I'm starting to panic at how behind I'm getting in Business and Statistics.

Focusing on those lessons is beyond hard. Paying attention for four lessons in a row isn't a strong suit of mine. I really do miss my chaos breaks.

"I'll see you after school?" Indi asks, and I nod.

"Sure thing. You still good to give me a ride?"

"You know it!" She blows me a kiss before scurrying out of the lunchroom and off to class. If I had my car, I might just head out to the beach by my damn self and skip the rest of the day. You know, if that 4.0 GPA wasn't hanging over my head. I let out a deep breath and grab my bag.

"I'll walk you to French," Raleigh says as he waves off his boys. I can't help but smile. I don't think I've ever met someone as sweet, yet as cocky, as him.

"You totally don't have to."

He scoffs and drops his arm around my shoulders. "It's on my way, and I wanted to talk to you about Friday."

"About the game?" I ask as we head out of the cafeteria. I can't help but catch Finley's eye as we're walking, and his stare is like a brand on my back as I leave with Raleigh. A part of me wants to shrug off Raleigh's arm because I don't want those three going after him too, but I don't want to cower from them any more than I already have. I hate feeling so weak, especially where they're concerned.

"Kind of. I was wondering if you wanted to hang out after. Just the two of us…" he trails off as we hit my locker, and I swap my books over.

"You mean like a date?" Color me fucking shocked. I mean, I know he's been a little tactile, but I figured that was just his way.

"Yeah, I mean like a date." He hits me with that megawatt smile of his, and I find myself nodding, despite my reservations about going on a date with him. This probably isn't a good idea, I don't think him and I will ever work, but one date can't hurt, right? Maybe I'll be wrong, and it won't be so bad.

I can't help but think this is likely going to piss off the guys even more, but fuck it. That's their problem, not mine.

"Awesome." His excitement is contagious, and I find myself smiling up at him before letting him walk me to class.

He kisses my head when he leaves me at the door to French before running off toward his own class when the warning bell sounds. Maybe this isn't a bad thing... Except I've never actually been on a date. The guys I dated before now were all roadies or people I met out on tour, and we hung out on tour, so actual dates weren't really a thing.

Nerves hit me as I take my seat at the back of the room. This totally isn't what I had on the cards for this year. It's just one date, what harm could it do?

My phone buzzes in my pocket, so I sneak a peek at it while the teacher isn't looking.

Indi:

I am so sorry, but my mom called an SOS. She had a fender bender and needs me to pick her up from the garage. I had to leave early.

Me:

Dude, no sweat. I hope your mom is okay, I can get myself home.

Indi:

Thank you, I hate letting you down.

Me:

You're not, I have legs and if all else fails, there's Uber.

Indi:

Sorry! I'll make it up to you.

I can't help but laugh at her. Not giving me a ride isn't the end of the world, but her sunshine heart really is just that big. While the thought of walking home doesn't exactly fill me with joy, things could be much worse.

Then I realize she's not going to be around for Gym.

Fuck my life.

I groan as the bell rings, knowing I'm going to have to face the bitch squad alone. Here's hoping that my weirdly quiet day continues. The only hiccup in my whole day was lunch when Maverick joined me uninvited, and I'm hoping that this new turn of events continues.

I pack my shit away and head to the locker room, grabbing my gym uniform on the way.

It's only once I get to the locker room, and the stares intensify, that I really even notice them. I head to my locker, keeping my head held high. Being the nation's princess for the majority of my existence taught me a few things, and keeping your head up despite the bullshit is one of them.

I change in silence, double checking the lock on my locker once I'm done before heading out to the gym. I'm practically the first one out of the door, despite being one of the last in.

What the fuck's happened now?

I head to where East is already talking to a few people and start stretching out. Circuits are killer, but doing this shit is going to get me in better shape than I've ever been in before. Mac would be proud.

Thinking of him, I realize I should probably find a

self-defense class around here somewhere to keep up on the training I was doing with him before. He'd be so disappointed if he found out I'm slacking, and that is more of a dagger to the gut than I need. He was basically my second dad on tour, disappointing him totally isn't something I want to do.

I really need to text him back later too.

East blows his whistle, calling my attention back to him, and I stop my stretching. His sadistic grin inspires a little bit of fear to spear through my gut. Circuits are already a bitch without that smile.

"Ladies, since you all enjoyed them so much, we're going to start today with suicide drills and learn not to fuck with other people's shit. Am I clear?" He glances over to me. Goddamn, why does he have to be so pretty when he's going all white knight on me? Those gray eyes of his practically fucking sparkle. I smile down at my shoes as everyone groans.

Serves those assholes right for what they did to my clothes and my car.

I'm not surprised he knows, though I am surprised he's doing anything about it. Not one other faculty member has even mentioned what happened to me. Though considering Maverick seems to have the principal wrapped around his little finger, I'm not that surprised. That and the sheer amount of money floating around this school is enough to keep any teacher under their thumb.

East blows his whistle again and starts the drills. Personally, I have zero issue with them. I mean they fuck my shit up, but I like running, so it's not exactly a hardship. The other circuit shit is worse for me.

He keeps running us until half the class looks like they're going to pass out. I can't even laugh because I'm so freaking out of breath, but it's such a good feeling seeing the others so fucked up that I'm not sad about it. Not even a little.

East blows that fucking whistle of his again, his sadistic grin still in place. "Get your asses up off the floor, we're not done yet. Start your circuits; and if I see anyone slacking, I'll keep you extra long!"

I laugh under my breath and head toward one of the empty circuit points, smiling at East as I do. My foot suddenly catches on someone else's ankle, and I trip and fall, barely managing to catch myself without smashing my face on the hard, wood floor. I may have saved my face, but my knees are fucked.

I turn to see one of the bitch squad, whose name I literally haven't cared to learn, snickering as she skips away from me like she didn't just trip me. "You stupid bitch!"

I push myself to my feet and go to charge her, finally seeing red because today was a good day, goddammit.

An arm wraps around my waist, and I'm literally lifted off of my feet. "Calm down, V. She's not worth it." East plants me back on the floor, pointing in the other direction. "Serena, detention tonight."

"Sounds fun, sir," she flirts, fluttering her lashes, and I almost want to be sick when East smiles back at her.

"I didn't say it was with me, did I? Detention tonight is with Mr. Avery. Have fun with that."

I burst out laughing because Mr. Avery has some serious hygiene issues and is more than a little bit of a creep. Obviously he wouldn't do anything to her, but just the thought of detention with him is enough to make her almost cry. She stomps her foot as East turns his back on her before blowing his whistle again. "Circuits!"

This time when he yells the word, I don't even care. I'll do all the circuits in the world if it means she has to suffer.

I practically bounce through the halls after class. Gym wasn't exactly fun, but seeing someone in this school finally getting punished for being a giant bag of ass has me all kinds of gleeful.

Even the fact that I have to walk home doesn't get me down. The sun is shining, the sky is clear, and today might just have been the best day I've had since being forced back to this horror show town.

I make my way through the parking lot, slipping my aviators on, when a white Mustang pulls up beside me, the roof retracting. "Need a ride, V?"

I smile at East, who looks way less like a teacher right now with his backward cap and his sunglasses. He's rocking that whole hot as fuck college frat boy vibe with his music blaring from the car. "I'm not going to say no if you're heading straight home?"

I can practically feel eyes on me as I walk around his car, dropping my bags on the back seat before climbing in. Maybe I should feel a little more wary of him, considering how his brother has treated me since I got here, but I'm not about to hold him accountable for Lincoln. That would just be a shitty thing to do.

"Yeah, I'm heading straight home. Buckle up." I do as he says while he grins wide at me, and as soon as I'm secure, he peels from the lot so fast that my head shoots back against the headrest. A laugh rips from me at the exhilaration that comes from the speed. He drives like he's a street racer, but he seems so confident and at ease that I don't panic at all.

I enjoy the thrill as he drives through the town, the disapproving glances bounce off him like water off a duck's back, and it is so refreshing. I'm almost disappointed when we pull up to the gates in front of my house. "Thanks for the ride."

"A gentleman doesn't drop a lady at the gates," he says, wagging his eyebrows. "Drop the code in. I need to see Smithy about some cake anyway."

"You and your cake," I say, shaking my head as I have to almost crawl over his lap so I can key the code to the gate. I can feel his breath on my neck as I reach out to the box, realizing I should have just given him the stupid code. The tension ramps up by about three thousand degrees when I realize just how close my hand is to his dick as I lean on his thigh.

I shift back, accidentally brushing my hand against it and gasp, looking up at him with wide eyes as my heart races. Part of me wants to lean in and kiss him, but the other part, the part who doesn't want to be rejected by him, freezes. His eyes are hooded as he stares down at me, and I can't breathe. His face is so close to mine, and he leans in further just as the gate groans open.

The noise seems to pull him back to reality, and he jerks back. The moment is shattered, and I hurry back to my seat. Heat creeps up my chest as I blush. East might have featured heavily in my fantasies for as long as I can remember, but I've never considered that he'd feel like that too. And well… I wasn't imagining the fact that he nearly kissed me just then.

Was I?

When we reach the house, Smithy is already at the door waiting for us.

"Good afternoon, Miss Octavia. Master Saint, it is wonderful to see you again." I beam at him as I jump out of the car. East struts around to my side, grabbing my bags before I get a chance to.

"Smithy, my man! How are you doing?" East hugs Smithy, who looks almost relieved to see my old friend.

"Fine, thank you, Master Saint. Are you joining us for dinner this evening?" Smithy looks so hopeful that when East glances back at me, I just shrug. Who am I to say no? East has been nothing but my white knight since I got back. I have zero issues with him. If he wants to stay for dinner, it doesn't bother me at all. We head inside, and East finally gives my bags back to me.

"Sounds good to me, Smithy! Now… let's talk about cake." I laugh as Smithy leads East to the kitchen as I head to the laundry to dump my gym stuff. I wait for the light to flicker on, trying not to shudder at the thought of entering the small dark room.

You'd think life on a tour bus would've forced me to get over my issues with small dark spaces, but even the small bunk couldn't cure me. After being trapped in my closet for almost a whole day when I was younger, the fear manifested, and I've never really gotten over it. Dad felt so bad when he finally found me. He was at work when there was a smaller earthquake and my dresser fell in front of the doors after I hid.

It was the first time I experienced an earthquake, and they still make me almost shit my pants. Though not quite as much as small dark spaces. I shudder just thinking about it. No thank you.

I empty my gym clothes into the hamper and then head upstairs to change. It doesn't take me too long. I don't ever really obsess about how I look, so leggings and a hoodie with messy hair is absolutely my go-to. By the time I get back downstairs, Smithy already has a milkshake for me on the counter, and East is halfway through the one in his hand. "Making yourself at home, I see."

He grins over at me before taking another sip of his milkshake. "If Smithy makes you these every day, I might never leave."

I climb onto a stool at the counter, and somehow he still towers over me. What the fuck are they feeding people here, super grow Wheaties? "I mean, you're only next door. It's not like you're exactly far away, is it?"

"This is very true. Smithy, one of these days I'll convince you to jump the fence and come live with us." Smithy scoffs at his words and shakes his head.

"Very unlikely, Master Saint. Then who would look out for Miss Octavia?" He smiles warmly at me as I take a sip of my milkshake. "But, as long as you treat her well, you will always find a milkshake here for you. Now then, if you two want to go get comfortable, I'll start dinner."

"What are we eating?" I ask as I jump from my seat.

"My main man Smithy is making homemade pizza," East says with a grin as Smithy shoos us from the kitchen, and I blow the old man a kiss. My love for pizza knows no bounds. I could literally eat it every day and not get tired of it.

I head into the lounge with East and drop onto one one of the sofas. "Movie?"

He sits on the sofa with me and makes himself comfortable. "Sounds good to me. Anything in mind?"

"There's that new one out about fighting a war in the future…" I offer with a small shrug. Why does this feel awkward all of a sudden?

"Action movie. Girl after my own heart. Glad to see that much hasn't changed." His smile is sad, and I get the feeling that I'm missing something. I have no fucking clue what, though, so I put the movie on and settle in.

The uncomfortable feeling leaves once we get into the movie. I'd almost forgotten how alike East and I can be. While Linc was always my savior in the shadows, the dark protector, East was the sunshine on a cloudy day. It's funny to me that East is the older of the two when Linc has always acted like the eldest.

Smithy joins us once he brings the pizzas in, and it

warms my heart to have him back in my life so much. I missed him when I was gone, even if I did have Mac and Dad. There's no one quite like Smithy.

Time passes in a blur as we eat and watch the movie, and once it's over, Smithy makes his excuses to disappear. Not that I blame him, he has his own life to be getting on with, rather than spending all of his time with me. I hope he does anyway. The thought that he's putting his life on pause for me doesn't exactly fill me with joy.

"I should probably head back before the world implodes," East says once Smithy has left. He stands and his t-shirt rides up, giving me a glimpse of his abs and that freaking 'V' making me want to groan. Goddamn. "Do you need a ride in the morning?"

"No, I should be good. Indi will be back to playing chauffeur tomorrow. She just had to go rescue her mom tonight, but thank you." I stand and stretch out as I yawn. Apparently, I'm more tired than I thought.

I walk him out, and as he stoops to slide his shoes back on, he picks up the black envelope on the mail table. "What's this?"

"Just some stupid charity gala invite. I'm surprised you guys didn't get one too." I shrug and lean on the wall as he drops it back on the table and turns his attention back to his shoes.

"You going?" he asks, eyebrows raised as he slips the

shoes on and leans down to tie them.

"What do you think?" My sarcasm is on fire, and he just starts laughing.

"Fair point. Octavia Royal and charity galas don't go hand in hand. I'll see you tomorrow?"

I roll my eyes at him as I usher him out of the door. "You'll see me in Gym, unless you plan on quitting anytime soon. You having that job still seems so weird to me."

A look of guilt flashes across his face, and he runs his hand through his hair. Weird. "Nope, no quitting till Linc can escape."

He jogs down the steps and jumps back into his car, driving off with a wave before I shut the door. This has been the strangest fucking day, but I'm too tired to try and dissect it. I call out a good night to Smithy before heading upstairs.

The door to the balcony is open, which is unusual, but I guess Smithy has been in here cleaning. I shut the room up and climb into bed, shutting off the light. The moon shines in from the windows, still lighting the room enough that the darkness doesn't make my heart race. Thinking about being trapped always puts me on edge in the dark.

I close my eyes and try to unwind, and just as I start to drift sleep I hear soft music coming from outside. It's one of my dad's songs. Just like that, my good mood disappears, and I drift to sleep with tears slipping down my face.

Twelve

I went out for a run first thing this morning, trying to burn off the funk last night left me in. Things have been too quiet, and that's making me almost as jumpy as when I was being attacked almost daily.

Quiet usually means the calm before the storm, but after everything the guys and Blair have pulled so far, I can't imagine it getting much worse. Even with Lincoln's sideways warnings.

I get back to the house to find the gate open, and my stomach drops.

The gate should *not* be open.

I run up the drive, spotting the open front door. Fear trickles down my spine, and I curse myself for thinking things couldn't get worse.

Moving as silently as I can, I enter the house, my heart

beating so fast I'm scared it'll be heard.

The place is trashed. The artwork is slashed and the knick-knacks and decor smashed, but I can't think about any of that because Smithy was here.

If they hurt him, I swear to God...

I creep through the rooms, trying not to make a sound while hoping like fuck whoever broke in isn't still here. The squeak of my shoes on the floors seems so loud that I pull to a stop, holding my breath so I can hear if anyone else is in here.

I try to keep a hold on the panic threatening to take over my entire body, but I need to find Smithy before I do anything else. That one thought is the only thing holding me together.

I stumble over one of the smashed statues, falling and cutting my palms as I do. I curse under my breath for being so loud.

Fuck it. If anyone else is here, they already know I am at this point.

"Smithy!" My shout echoes in the giant space, but when there's no response, my heart thunders in my chest. I hurry through the rooms and head for the kitchen, hoping Smithy is in the panic room under the island.

I find Smithy in the kitchen, face down on the floor, blood spilling from a wound on his head. "Shit!"

I rush toward him, trying to wake him. I shout at him

as I shake him, but it's no use, so I do what any reasonable person would do. I call the police, while trying not to sob and freak out that he won't wake up.

When I hang up, I take a deep breath, trying to calm myself and roll Smithy onto his side, moving his arms and legs into the recovery position, making sure his airways are clear and that he's still actually breathing.

Who the fuck would do this? And why would they hurt Smithy? He hasn't done anything to anyone.

I look up and see a piece of paper stuck to the refrigerator.

No one you love is safe while you stay here. Don't say you weren't warned.

Those fucking assholes. This can't have been them, right? They wouldn't have hurt Smithy. Would they? I see red, snatching the paper from the fridge and crumpling it in my hand. If the police see this, I'll never hear the end of it. All I want is an ambulance for Smithy.

He has to be okay.

He can't be seriously hurt because of me.

When the buzzer at the gate sounds, I make sure it's open wide as one cruiser and an ambulance come up the drive. The paramedics come in first, and I direct them to the kitchen. The officer pulls me to the side and asks a ton of questions I don't have the answers to.

"Is he going to be okay?" I ask as the paramedics wheel

Smithy's unmoving body out of the house.

"He has a contusion to the head and has lost quite a lot of blood. They'll be able to assess him better at the hospital. Will you be following?"

I nod, and the paramedic rushes out to join his partner. The officer asks me a question, but I don't hear it as the sirens start up.

I can't believe they hurt him.

Guilt churns in my stomach, more powerful than any rage I can feel. This is my fault. I should've listened to them. I could have stopped this.

"Miss Royal?" The officer calls my name, and I shake my head, pulling myself from my thoughts.

"Sorry, Officer, this is a lot."

"Sure, I can imagine. Do you know if anything was taken?"

I shake my head again, clasping my arms around my waist, holding myself tight. "I'm sorry, I have no idea. I went straight into the kitchen and found Smithy... sorry, James."

Just saying the words makes me feel cold. How is this my life?

"That's understandable, are you okay to walk through with me quickly before you leave for the hospital?"

I find myself nodding before I start walking him through the house. The main floor is completely destroyed.

Anything that wasn't bolted down has been thrown or smashed. The contents of the kitchen are spilled over the counters and floors. We head down the stairs to the basement, and I choke back a sob when I see the music room.

The place that was my dad's sanctuary, it's… almost unsalvageable. The smell of urine makes me gag, and I leave, unable to look at it anymore.

Finally, we head upstairs, and I find much of the same. More destruction. My clothes aren't shredded this time, but they are strewn across the room. The only things left alone are my dad's guitars hanging on my wall.

I nearly fall to my knees as relief floods me in waves.

"Everything seems to be accounted for, but I can go through more thoroughly later once I've been to the hospital. Is that okay?" I say to the officer, my voice thick with emotion. This has been one hell of a day, and it's not even eight in the morning yet.

My week has been a clusterfuck, but I refuse not to let today be a good day. Smithy was released from the hospital last night. He had a slight concussion, but other than that, the cut was his only wound. Though if you ask him, his pride was wounded more. The doctors wanted him to stay overnight, but the man is stubborn as a mule. So I ended up bringing him home.

While we were waiting for the doctors to finish their tests, I called in a cleaning company to sort out what could be salvaged from the house and throw away anything that couldn't. It's just stuff. It can be replaced, and besides, I didn't want Smithy going home to that madness.

When I asked him who attacked him, he said there were five thugs but that he didn't recognize them because they were wearing masks and gloves. Which I guess makes sense, but it doesn't explain why my wall of guitars was left untouched or why nothing was actually taken.

It hurts my head just to try and make sense of it all. I can't help but hope it wasn't Lincoln and the others. Surely they wouldn't hurt Smithy. But who else would leave that note?

I pushed him a little harder on the drive home, but he didn't have anything else to say. I get it, he was tired, and he'd answered all the police's questions as well as mine, but he doesn't seem... angry enough about it? Maybe that's just my response to everything these days.

Then this morning, he demanded that I go to school despite everything that happened, so I made him promise to take it easy. It took some doing, but I threatened to have Pattie come and check on him if he didn't behave. I'm not entirely sure why those two hate each other so much, but it worked, so I'm going to take the win.

Lincoln, Maverick, and Finley are suspiciously absent from school, which has the gossip mill all aflutter. Luckily, it means I've actually been able to relax—the thought of confronting them about what happened to Smithy fills me with anger and fear at the same time. I hate that the fear is there, especially when I've never been the kind of girl to cower, but something about those three and what they're capable of… It puts me on edge. Catty pettiness from Blair and her girls I can cope with, but the boys… They know me so much better than anyone else here.

They know the real ways to hurt me if they want to.

And for some reason, they seem to want to.

So a day without them here is a good day, and I haven't let it go to waste. Even circuits in Gym isn't getting me down. Though that could be because Indi, the sunshine child extraordinaire, has done nothing but bitch and whine as we've worked the course together, and it gives me such life.

"If I do another squat, my thighs are going to explode," she complains, and I can't help but grin as I finish my round of burpees before sitting cross-legged on the floor.

"Want to swap? I will happily do your squat set if you want my burpees."

"Not on your fucking life, my friend," she practically hisses, and it makes me laugh out loud. She looks like she's ready to collapse by the time East blows his whistle, calling an end to the lesson before the bell actually goes off.

"Thank fucking Christ for that. I hate Gym. Exercise is not for everybody. This body of mine was made for coffee, chips, and pizza. Not exercise." She leans against the wall while I climb to my feet.

"I so feel that."

"You have much going on tonight?"

I groan in answer. "I have to finish dealing with the house shit. I'm trying to work out what we need to replace to take some of the pressure from Smithy. At the same time, I have *so much* homework to catch up on. How can we only be like two weeks in, and I'm this behind already?"

"Same! It's like the teachers want to torture us or something. Want to have a study date? I could use a few hours where Mom isn't trying to talk to me every two minutes so I can work. Plus, I can help with the house stuff. Or try at least."

"Sounds good, I'll let Smithy know you're coming over. Just remember the house is a disaster. I mean, the cleaners came in, and I'm sure Smithy didn't rest today, but still." I shrug a little, and once I reach my locker, I drop the man in question a quick message to let him know my plans. I get a smile emoji back, which, considering he didn't text before I showed him how to last night, is a definite win.

I go to drop my phone back in my bag before I head to the showers. It buzzes before I put it away, and it's like a surround sound of pings goes off. My stomach drops. Everyone getting the same notification from ReachMe is never a good thing.

Indi's eyes go wide as she looks at her phone before looking back up at me. Her discomfort is instantly obvious as she bites down on her lower lip.

"What?" I ask, and she shakes her head, so I pick up my phone and open the app. The post just has a link in it. So I click on it, and immediately really wish I fucking hadn't.

My screen fills with something from a porn movie… Except that's my face… And my voice—did they record me in the pool house?

I close my eyes as the breathy sounds fill the locker room.

This can not be happening.

I know I've sure as shit never fucked the guy in this video, and I sure as hell never videoed myself having sex… That would require me having had sex, which I haven't. Fuck my actual life. Whoever made this is a fucking pro.

Even though I know that it isn't me in the video, shame and humiliation floods my system, and I want to fucking cry. My hands shake as I shut down my phone, shoving it into my pocket. I can usually keep my head held high, but despair filters through me. I haven't even been here three fucking weeks. How is this my life?

"What a whore."

"Nice tits, Octavia. Why don't you show us since you don't seem to mind baring all to the world."

"Of course she made a sex tape. She's nothing but trash."

Their words hit their mark, and I struggle to breathe around the pressure that's sitting squarely in the center of my chest. Why is this happening to me? There's a buzzing in my ears, and my blood runs cold as my skin goes prickly. I need to get out of here. "Let's shower at my house?"

Indi nods, bundling her shit into her bag almost as quickly as I am. I'm not usually one to run from bullshit, but this... This is too much. "Let's go." She wraps her arm around me, squeezing me quickly once, while everyone around us laughs and watches the stupid clip on repeat. I try to keep my head high as we rush from the school.

"Want to ride on me, Octavia?" someone leers, and Indi flips them the bird as she tries to get me out of here as quickly as she can. The taunts and jibes follow us all the way through the school, each one like another dagger to the heart.

These people don't know me. If they did, they'd know I'd never do anything like that; but that doesn't matter to them. It doesn't make their words hurt or fill me with shame any less.

We leave the building and head toward Indi's car. The shouts and catcalls follow us the entire way. I nearly manage to keep my tears at bay, until I catch Finley's eye as he stands by his car. He wasn't at school today, so why is he even here?

The smug look on his face tells me everything I need to know.

He did this.

I bite down on my lower lip to stop myself from crying harder. Why would he do this? Indi has her car unlocked before we even reach it. I climb in, blinking back my tears. She starts the car up and peels away from the school. We're out of the parking lot before the first one falls.

What did I ever do to deserve any of this?

Indi says nothing the entire drive back to my house, and I whisper the code to her so she can go straight to the house. Once she pulls to a stop out front, her hands clench around the steering wheel. She takes a few deep breaths before turning to face me. "Do you know who made that bullshit video?"

"You don't think it's real?" I ask, shock coloring my voice. I might not be answering her question, but the fact that she didn't even ask me if it was me has me shook.

She shakes her head and squeezes my hand. "I may not

have known you long, V, but I'm pretty sure you're not the type of girl who fucks on camera, even with the wild rockstar shit that happens. So no, I don't think it's you in the video."

"I think… No, I know… It was Finley," I say quietly, picking at the skin beside my thumbnail. I swallow what little of my pride I have left and finally tell her what happened with the three of them. Telling her every little thing that I've been withholding. It's like a weight has been lifted from my shoulders, but she looks horrified.

"What a fucking dick stain! The fucking lot of them. I am so sorry, V. About all of this, I wish there was something I could do… say… to make it better for you."

"You're here, and you're my friend, in spite of everything. That's what I need."

"Then I've got you." She clasps my hand and squeezes before she climbs from the car. I follow suit, finding a worried looking Smithy waiting for us.

He twists his hands in front of him, and I can't tell if he's worried about me or about what it is he's waiting to tell me. I take a deep breath and try to prepare myself for whatever it is. He ushers us inside, and I know it's bad when he pulls out the teapot, one of the few things that apparently survived the break in.

I slide onto one of the stools, and Indi does the same as we wait for him to pour us both a cup. I pull my phone out of my bag and turn it back on before placing it down on the counter as Smithy turns and looks at me, frowning. "I heard what happened, Miss Octavia. The lawyers are already working on getting it pulled down... but I'm afraid that it's already online—more than just your school network. And that stupid gossip rag TV show, Celebrity Time, are threatening to pick it up for their news cycle. Obviously they can't run the video, but they *can* run the story."

"Of course they are," I sigh, putting my head in my hands. "I wonder who leaked it? I mean, being on the school network is bad enough, but to go wide..."

"I've been speaking with a friend in the police to get this shut down. She believes she already has the source of who leaked it wide, and they're working on finding out how it was posted to the school network too. Someone will be punished for this. I've also arranged for personal security too, just until we get this under control."

"I don't want that. I'll hide out in here if I need to, but I don't want someone following my every move ever again." He nods, taking my wishes into consideration, even though I can tell from his frown that he disagrees with me.

Indi sits, practically shaking with rage, on the stool next to me. "This is such horseshit. Can they even play or print it? You're still a minor!"

"The tabloids don't care about that. They won't play

it… but the 'nation's princess' in a sex tape scandal, even if it's fake one, is hot news," I explain, and she curses enough to make a sailor blush.

"My sentiments exactly, Miss Indi."

My phone starts blowing up and I groan, covering my face with my hands. "What a fucking mess." I look back up at Smithy, seeing the concern in his eyes and let out a sigh. "You know that isn't me right?"

"Of course, Miss Octavia. I would never believe such things." My heart warms at his words. His unwavering faith in me is fucking everything. Though my guilt over him dealing with this when he should be resting makes me feel sick.

I nod and look over at Indi, loving that she never thought it was me either. "I'm going to fucking murder someone. How fucking dare they!" My sunshine girl is gone, but I'm so grateful to have somebody this fucking angry on my behalf.

I shrug, hating how resigned I am to the fact that this is my life now. "This is going to be absolute fucking chaos."

Thirteen

I wake up bleary-eyed, dreading the day. I shut my phone off almost as soon as I turned it back on last night. I couldn't bring myself to look at it, so Indi and I hid in my room, binging reruns of Gossip Girl, trying to convince myself that it could be worse.

My lawyers called to advise that lawsuits had been drawn up against the publications who said they were going to run the story, which should stop it from ending up on the actual news, but that doesn't mean it hasn't already gone viral.

I cover my face with a pillow and scream into it. I want nothing more than to roll over and go back to sleep, to ignore the world for a week, a month, hell, even a year. But I'm not letting these assholes fuck with my GPA, and missing any school means getting even further behind than

I already am. Needless to say, I did not get my study date last night.

Fuck this shit. They don't get to win. Not now, not ever. I'm not the type to tuck tail and run.

They can go fuck themselves up the ass with no lube.

I'll face the day the way my dad always rode out a storm. By looking and feeling fucking fierce. I mean, he didn't tend to do it sober, but that's not exactly an option for me—I don't have that choice. If I did... well, fuck being sober.

I kick off my blankets and stomp into the shower. Today, I'm going to look like a bomb-ass bitch because I need the armor. It's the only way I'm going to either stay out of jail or not break down to a puddle of nothingness.

I turn my phone on, flicking quickly over to airplane mode before linking it up to the sound system, and blast "Queen" by Loren Gray. There's nothing like music to help reset your mindset. I put it on repeat because this song is absolutely fucking life right now. It's like they wrote it just for me.

I take my time scrubbing, shaving, and preening every inch of my fucking body till I almost shine. I let the music wash over me, sinking into my pores to help build up the mental walls I need for today. This is the one part of being my father's daughter that I hate. The paparazzi, the media storms, the inability to have much privacy at all. If I was anyone else, this wouldn't be a potential national news story.

There have already been some paps here, but this… This will reveal to everyone where I am, which only makes Echoes Cove have the potential to become even more of a nightmare for me than it's been already. I wish my dad had thought through the stipulations of his Will. Why would he make me come back here?

When we left here, we never looked back. Or, at least, I didn't think so. I guess since Dad kept Smithy on, he had more intention of coming back here than I ever realized.

I lose myself in the monotony of getting myself ready for the day. Once I've picked out the most badass underwear I have, I sit down to do my hair and makeup. I pay special attention as I blow my hair out, letting it cascade down my back in dark, shiny waves. I finish the look with thick winged liner and a lipstick called *Bitchcraft*. It's a deep purple and makes my eyes pop in contrast.

It's not lost on me that I have to practice my smile in the mirror to make sure it's somewhat convincing today. But if this is what I have to do to show them that they won't break me, then this is what I'll do. I just wish I knew why.

What did I do to inspire such venom from the people who I was once closest to in the world?

I shake off the thought. Focusing on that shit isn't

going to help me today.

Today, I need to keep my head high and rise above.

Fuck being a princess, today I'm going to be a goddamn queen.

I finish dressing by slipping my feet into a pair of black Louboutins to complete the look. I check out my reflection in the full-length mirror in the closet and feel almost prepared to face the day. After grabbing my bag, I head downstairs to find Smithy in the kitchen making pancakes.

My stomach revolts at the thought of even trying to eat anything. I take a deep breath as my mouth fills with acid. There is no way I'm going to vomit right now. No fucking way. "Smithy, I adore you, but I can't eat."

He startles a little as I put my bag on the stool and head to the coffee machine. The sweet nectar of the gods is going to be absolutely necessary today. I can feel it already. "Oh, Miss Octavia, you really should eat."

"And you should really call me V. Or at the very least, Octavia," I tease.

He scoffs at me, waving the spatula in my direction, looking highly offended. I'd worry if he wasn't smiling with his eyes. "That, Miss Octavia, is never going to happen. Now, please sit and try to eat something. There were some developments overnight. I've already called Miss Indi. She won't be able to get you this morning thanks to the vultures camped at the gates."

My stomach drops at his words, and I drop onto the closest stool with a heavy sigh. Why is this my life? "Well, I guess school really is out of the question today then."

He frowns at me and shakes his head, piquing my interest at what he could possibly have up his sleeve this early in the day. "I've already been on the phone with the school this morning. They've put more security measures in place. It's not the first time they've needed to keep the media away. They are also aware that if we find out someone at the school created and leaked that video, we will be pressing charges, and including the school in the lawsuit if any of their equipment was used."

"Thank you, Smithy." Relief floods my system at not having to face school with people trying to take my picture all day. I mean, they will definitely try, but if there's extra security in place, it's unlikely any will be too successful.

He moves behind me to the refrigerator and pours a glass of juice before placing it in front of me. He pats my shoulder before saying, "Drink your juice, Miss Octavia. Only having coffee won't be a good start to the day."

I pick the juice up and take a sip as he raises an eyebrow, watching me to make sure I actually drink it before he moves back to the stove. He plates up a few pancakes for me, topping them with blueberries and whipped cream, before sliding it in front of me. "Now then, I've also arranged for you to ride into school with Master Saint. You can use the gate between the yards so that you don't have to go out the front. Then they won't know for some time that you've left."

Relief floods my body at the thought of not having to go out the front of this house. The thought of facing it all before I even really start my day is enough to make me want to crawl back into bed. Bad bitch persona or not. "You're the best, Smithy."

"Just doing what I can, Miss Octavia." I jump up and hug him tight. It takes him a second to react, but then he holds me just as tight.

I feel safer now than I have in a while. I guess I have more pseudo-dads than I realized. "Thank you, Smithy."

He nods before motioning to the plate on the counter before me. "Anything for you, Miss Octavia. Now eat up, you don't want to keep Master Saint waiting."

I take a few bites of the pancakes, since my stomach is basically the home of nothing but butterflies right now. Enough to make him happy, but not so much that I feel sick. I love that Smithy arranged for East to take me in. Maybe going for a spin in his car will be a good start to the day.

I hop down and grab my bag, planting a kiss on Smithy's cheek. "See you later!"

"Have a good day, Miss Octavia."

I feel a little lighter as I cross the yard to the hidden

gate between our property and the Saints'. It wasn't there originally, but once I became such good friends with East and Lincoln when we were younger, Dad installed the gate for us.

I cross over onto the Saint property, and a shudder runs down my spine. It almost feels like I'm in enemy territory, but I just need to find East and haul ass out of here. I walk around the property, and it feels like I've gone back in time. Nothing over here has changed. This far back in the yard, it's like I'm in a secret garden, protected from the rest of the world.

Walking around to the front of the house, I'm assaulted by memories of my childhood, which are not welcome considering everything that's happened since I got back here.

I reach the front of the house and freeze, an icy drop of dread runs down my spine when I see the black Porsche sitting in the drive. Smithy wouldn't have done this to me, right?

Then Lincoln walks out of the house and glares at me.
Fuck my life.
"Nope."

I pop my 'p' and turn the fuck around. I'll just take extra credit for my GPA.

"Octavia, stop being a brat and get in the fucking car." The growl in his voice causes goosebumps to erupt over every inch of my skin.

I spin back and glare at him, my anger like a writhing beast beneath my skin, just to find him leaning against his car. "You don't get to call me a brat when this is your fucking fault."

When he rolls his eyes, I swear my blood ignites. My rage grows to natural disaster levels.

Fuck this. He doesn't get to win, and his total lack of denial is staggering. I strut back to the car, stopping before him and mirroring his pose. I fold my arms over my chest, stand tall, and jut out my chin. He raises an eyebrow before he stands up properly. I almost feel small standing before him. He's easily a head taller than me, but I don't give up any ground.

He moves and opens the door for me, I keep the smile from my face at the small win. "Get in the fucking car, Octavia. I won't say it again."

I climb into the car without another word and sink into the soft leather seats. I'm not usually one for foreign cars, but this one is a wet fucking dream. Not that I'm going to tell him that. He slams the door closed and stalks around the car before climbing in himself as I buckle in. He doesn't say a word as he starts the engine. The throaty sound does things to me that it definitely shouldn't.

And it definitely isn't linked to being in such a small space with all of his growly big dick energy.

Nope.

He puts the car in gear and heads toward the gate. I hold my breath, hoping that the crazy people stalking me and trying to get through my gates don't notice me.

"They can't see you, the windows are tinted enough that they won't have a clue." I look over at him, wondering why he cares enough to reassure me. Not that I take his words as gospel. It's not until we're past the savage masses of paparazzi that I relax even a little. Not that I can relax fully, I'm still in a moving vehicle with someone who very obviously doesn't want me around. The only reason I know I'm safe is because Lincoln has always had too much ego to off himself.

We ride the rest of the way to school in total silence. The worst part about it is that it's not even uncomfortable. Other than the fact that I can't stop glancing over at him. Why does the asshole have to be so pretty to look at? And since when are forearms a thing that are so goddamn hot? I can't help but steal glances at him. He's changed a lot since we were kids, and I haven't exactly had a chance to watch him without care before this point. His thunderstorm colored eyes are focused on the road, and his dark hair is just a smidge longer than I imagine someone as controlled as him likes since it's long enough to fall into his eyes. His blazer looks fit to burst around his broad frame, which is almost enough to make me bite my lip, but I refrain as his strong jaw stiffens.

I think I might have been caught checking him out. Oops.

His hands clench around the steering wheel when he looks over. He definitely catches me looking, so I stare back at him with a raised eyebrow, almost begging him to say something. He stays silent.

I can't help the smirk that plays on my lips as we continue the ride in silence. Finally, he's the one on the back foot and uncomfortable. This might not last long, so I'm going to enjoy it while it does. I slide my phone from my pocket and pull up the thread with Indi.

Me:

You will never guess who my ride is this morning.

Indi:

Smithy said it was Coach???

Me:

I thought that too… turns out it was the **other** Saint.

Indi:

Fuck your life.

Me:

My sentiments exactly.

Indi:

How is it?

Me:

Other than choking on my own resentment and his big dick energy? It's totally fine. Most quiet I've had in days.

Indi:

cowboy emoji Well, there are worse ways to start the day? Maybe? You're not dead at least...

Me:

Definitely... the madness at my gates was beyond insane.

Indi:

I'm sorry. Did Smithy get the legal shit sorted out?

Me:

Yeah, I'll explain everything when we're at school.

Indi:

I'm already here, floofy coffee in hand. I'll meet you in the library.

Me:

Indigo Montoya you are a freaking goddess.

Indi:

I know, see you soon **heart emoji**

It doesn't take long for us to pull into the student parking lot, and he drives straight up to the front of the lot nearest the doors. Of course his spot is just left empty. He pulls in between a white Lamborghini that Finley climbs out of and a Ducati Panigale V4. That's when I notice Maverick sitting on the steps of the school, helmet on the ground between his legs.

Why am I not even surprised he's the one with that deathtrap of a bike?

I look at Lincoln, and he pauses before unlocking the doors. "Was it you? That attacked Smithy? That leaked that tape of me?"

He watches me, not saying a word but quirking his eyebrow in a way that makes me feel ridiculous for asking. As if he'd stoop so low as to bother. But he and I both know he's been on a mission to get me to leave, so it's not that ridiculous if you ask me. Except now I feel kind of stupid for even mentioning it.

I move to open the door, but Finley is there already opening it for me. I guess Lincoln warned them that he was bringing me in today. I slide from the car once the door is fully open before turning back to Lincoln. I hate thanking him for anything, especially when I know this mess is his fault, but manners don't cost a goddamn thing, and I'm not that bitch.

"Thank you." He glances over at me and just nods, effectively dismissing me as he climbs from the car. The other two just watch me, as silent as Lincoln has been all morning. I huff and head toward the school to meet Indi in the library.

I've had enough big dick energy today already. I can't deal with the three of them right now. More so because I know that the current chaos in my life is entirely their doing. As much as I'd like to confront them about it, I know I won't get anything from it. They won't be sorry, they won't apologize, and they can't take it back.

Pandora's box is officially open.

Just as I reach the doors, I hear Blair's screeching voice yelling my name across the lot.

Fuck my whole life today.

I contemplate pretending I don't hear her as my hand finds the handle and twists. But she screeches again, and this time she's closer, so it's louder.

Delightful.

I take a deep breath and prepare myself for more emotional warfare. I turn and find Blair at the bottom of the steps, practically foaming at the mouth. "What do you want, Blair?"

Her eyes go wide at the blatant lack of fucks in my

tone. Her hands clench at her sides, and I can't help but wonder what's gotten her so worked up. It's not like it was her fake sex tape everyone was watching yesterday. "Why the fuck did you ride in with him?"

You have got to be fucking kidding me. "That's seriously why you were screeching my name like a banshee? Because I got a ride to school with Lincoln?"

She climbs the steps so that she's face-to-face with me. I'm glad I put my heels on today otherwise she'd be looking down at me. Fuck that.

"Answer the fucking question." She practically spits the words at me. "I warned you before the year started, he's mine."

I burst out laughing because I just can't help myself, and she slaps me across the face, shocking the shit out of me. "Don't fucking laugh at me."

She practically vibrates with anger, and her eyes are wild. Apparently laughing at the self-appointed queen of ECP isn't something that happens around here. A crowd gathers around us, but the last thing I need is another video of me circulating. I take a deep breath and try to calm myself down so I don't retaliate, because breaking her new nose isn't going to help me right now. "I needed a ride to school because my house is a circus right now."

"That better be all it is. Next time, call the pathetic, depressive dirty emo puppy you've adopted to save you."

My sight bleeds red at her words, and I shove down all of my good intentions and punch her square in the face. The crunch of her nose, followed by her scream and the gush of blood, makes me feel better for about two seconds until the reality of the situation seeps in.

Never start the fucking fight, Octavia.

I turn on my heel and walk into the school while she wails on the front steps. Her bitch squad fawns over her and leads her away from the school. Her nose probably isn't broken, right?

I close my eyes and take a deep breath—I *can* survive this day. And maybe if I do actually survive the day, I can survive the year.

I open my eyes and head to my locker. My stomach bottoms out when I catch sight of them… Dozens of stills from that fucking video are taped all over the walls and lockers.

You have got to be fucking kidding me. Could this day get any worse?

I start tearing them down before anyone else heads inside, but I'm sure if they're here, they're everywhere. I throw a ton of them in the trash before realizing that it's a waste of my time. The video is already out there. The pictures are just another taunt.

Fuck it, I'm not wasting any more time on this bullshit.

I drop my stuff off at my locker before going to find

Indi. *Please fucking Christ let this day get better.* I don't think one fucking good day is too much to ask for.

I strut into the library to find Indi waiting at the table for me with the biggest Frappuccino possible topped with *so much* whipped cream that all of my bad mood disappears. Well, at least for the moment.

She hands it to me, her grin matching mine. "There is nothing that whipped cream can't fix."

I take a sip of the sugary goodness, wondering how I ever came around to this drink, and sigh. I think she might be right.

I look up from the drink after a quiet moment, and my eyes catch on a trashcan stuffed to the brim, realizing after a moment that it's full of pictures from the sex tape. Indi blushes a little and shrugs when she notices me looking at it. "I took down as many as I could on the way here and then all of the ones that were taped up in here too. I know I couldn't get them all, but I figured the more I got the less there were for you and everyone else to see."

I hug her tight, and she squeaks a little. I fucking love this girl. She has my back without me even needing to say a word. "It's official, you are my ride or die, bitch."

She grins at me enthusiastically and nods when I let her go. "You had me at ride or die."

225

English with Ms. Summers is always a dream, but there's a rock in my stomach as I walk to Business. I need this class so badly, but I literally can never focus. Mr. Peters' voice is so dreary and monotone. And after having already focused for a whole lesson, it feels like my brain just won't engage during this time period.

It sucks.

I sit in my seat next to Lincoln, groaning when he glares at me. What a joy.

"Ladies and gents, as per the email last week, your first proposals are due at the end of the lesson," Mr. Peters says as he drops down into the chair at his desk.

I look at Lincoln, who looks smug as fuck. I didn't get any damn email, and I'd put money on him being the reason why. "Why didn't you say anything?"

"I didn't realize I was your keeper." He rolls his eyes, and just once, I wish I was brave enough to fuck him up a little. I've fought bigger guys than him, but there's something almost feral underneath that calm surface of his that gives me pause everytime I think about lashing out.

"Of course you're not." I sigh, exasperated. Why does he take everything I say the wrong way? "But we're supposed to work on this together."

Mr. Peters draws my attention back to him as he drones on about plentiful returns and profit margins, and it takes everything I have not to zone out and panic about the project I'm meant to be doing with Lincoln. After most of the class has passed, Mr. Peters tells us to finish up our first proposals before handing them in.

The first part of our project is to write a proposal for a business venture with full-scale profit projections. Apparently, Lincoln has taken it upon himself to decide what the business venture is. I look over at him and he's got a smug smile on his face as he watches my panic ensue. "Are you going to show me what you've worked on at least?"

"Why would I do that?" he asks, smug smile firmly in place.

I let out a deep sigh and rub at my temples. "Just this once, don't be an ass, Lincoln. Please?"

Here I am, begging again. I'm starting to despise Lincoln Saint and his web of bullshit.

"Fine," he says, dropping the file onto my desk before leaning in close. "But only because I like the way my name falls off your lips when you beg."

The bell rings before I have a chance to even read the first page. Fuck. Fuck. Fuck.

He takes the file from my hand, nodding once before stalking to the front of the room, dropping the proposal he wrote up on Mr. Peters desk. "I did this myself. Octavia felt she was above the task, so I completed it on both our behalf."

Mr. Peters looks over to me with an eyebrow raised. "Miss Royal, if you'll please stay behind."

I groan and drop my head onto the table, waiting for the rest of the class to filter out, the snickers following as they go. When the last person has left and closed the door, I grab my bag and head to his desk. "Mr. Peters, I wasn't aware that our proposals were due today, and Lincoln hasn't exactly been open to being my partner—today was the first time I knew he'd even been working on it. If you give me an extension, I can make notes on his proposal and expand on the presentation."

He leans back on his chair, and the look of indignation on his face tells me just how much he believes me. I could fucking kill Lincoln. Does he have any idea how much I need to pass this class?

"Miss Royal, it's obvious from your work and lack of attention that you are not dedicated to this class." He stands, moving closer to me before perching on the edge of the desk. "At this point, with what you've done so far, you are looking at a failing grade on this project."

The blood drains from my face, and I feel a little woozy. I can't fail this class.

I just can't.

"Please, Mr. Peters, if there is anything I can do, I'll do it. I need to pass this class." I hate that I'm begging. I hate what Lincoln has reduced me to yet again.

The lewd smile that crosses his pasty face makes me feel sick. He stands up and brushes back my hair behind my ear, and I shudder. "I'm sure we can think of some way for you to earn extra credit."

"Mr. Peters, that isn't exactly what I was intending." I take a step toward the door, and he follows again, reaching for his zipper.

"I hear things, you know. No one would have to know, not that they'd believe you if you said anything. I'm a respected teacher and well... I saw that video. A few times."

My stomach rolls as he pulls his dick from his pants, and I look anywhere but at him.

"No, Mr. Peters. I won't do it."

"A little whore like you must be very good at sucking dick. Imagine how easy that A would be. I'm sure you're a girl of many talents." He walks closer toward me until my back slams against the door. This can't be happening to me right now. "Be a good girl and get on your knees."

"No!" I shout, pushing him away from me. "You're a fucking pervert. I'm not going to do anything for you."

His face turns red as he tucks his dick away. "You'll regret that. And you'll fail this class no matter what you do. No one would think twice about a girl like you failing this class."

Angry tears prick at my eyes, and I blink them back.

"Fuck you, Mr. Peters."

"I did offer," he says, with the creepiest smile I've ever seen. I tear the door open and storm from the class, feeling dirtier than I ever have. But he's right, who is going to believe me after everything that's happened since I came back here?

Why is this year not over yet?

My morning has not gone the way I hoped it would, but the sugar rush definitely carried me through it. The bell for lunch rings just as my sugar crash hits, and I groan. At least I can eat and recaffeinate. Caffeine is absolutely necessary to ensure no more fists are thrown.

I haven't seen or heard anything of Blair since this morning, but most of her bitch squad have been MIA too. I'm taking it as a blessing, because the whispers and looks have already been so insane today, that, despite my armor and the sugar, I feel like I'm bleeding out.

I pack my things up into my bag and head for the cafeteria, not paying attention to anyone around me. I guarantee I've taken nothing in during any of my lessons today, so I'm definitely going to have to beg someone for their notes at some point.

I meet Indi by the doors for lunch, and the grimace on

her face tells me that she has bad news. "Blair is back… and she is pissed."

"Of course she is," I groan. I mean, she definitely deserved at least a bitch slap, but I definitely saw red earlier. You can fling shit at me, and I'll let it go, but you do *not* insult or fuck with my friends. All reason disappears when you cross that line.

"Apparently her nose isn't broken, though." She shrugs and links her arm with mine. I love her show of loyalty, even if it is a subconscious thing. "So ya know, she has no real reason to be pissed."

"I'm almost disappointed that it's not broken," I joke, and she snickers.

"The day isn't over yet."

We walk into the cafeteria laughing, and it goes so quiet you could hear a fucking pin drop. *Just awesome.*

Indi stills at my side, and I love how fierce she looks right now. There's a nasty sneer on her face like she'd happily throw hands if anyone says one goddamn thing.

I jut out my chin and glance around the room. I don't see Blair here yet, but I catch the eyes of at least half of the room as I go. My eyes dare them to be brave enough to say something to my face rather than whispering about me behind my back. No one says a fucking thing or even moves until I lock eyes with Lincoln. He raises an eyebrow at me, but I refuse to look away first. Finley leans over and says something to him, drawing his attention from me, and I smirk.

Once he looks away from me, conversation starts again, and Indi leads us toward the line to actually get some food. I grab a cheeseburger, fries, and a soda despite the fact that eating feels like that last thing I want to actually be doing.

As we head to our usual table, coughs of 'slut' and 'whore' follow me across the room. "Fuck you all, like you're the virgin fucking Mary," Indi snaps at someone who I don't remember having ever seen before.

"Not worth it," I tell her, pulling her to our table and letting the words slide off of me like water from a duck's back.

She slams her tray down, and her hands shake as she sits, her face red with anger. "People are such fucking dicks. Not one of them would call you out on shit to your face. Cowards, all of them."

"They are." I shrug. "But they're not worth your rage for exactly that reason."

She shakes her head and jams a fry in her mouth. Apparently, her hangry is showing. "I don't know how you do it. I'd have already broken under the pressure of everything you've been through the last few weeks."

"Nah," I say, shaking my head as I unwrap my burger. "You're stronger than you think. You survived last year here on your own."

"Let's agree to disagree."

We sit and eat in a comfortable silence until Raleigh and some of his friends join us. No one says a thing about the video, Blair, or my outburst this morning. They just talk about the upcoming game this week, and it's just so fucking normal. I love it.

"Are you okay?" Raleigh asks when everyone else is distracted with another conversation about the Asheville Allstars.

I think about his question for a quiet, contemplative moment. Am I okay? I feel okay considering everything that's happened, so I nod and smile. "I could be worse."

He frowns a little, the lines on his forehead deepening as he does. "How come you didn't call me for a ride today if you needed one?"

I swear it takes everything in me not to roll my eyes. I don't get why me coming in with Lincoln is so out there. I mean, yes, he hates me. That much is obvious, but still. I bite back my frustration at being called out, especially since it's really not any of his business. Yeah, he's been a good friend, and he asked me out on a date, but that doesn't give him the right to question me.

Despite all of the mild resentment swimming in my head, I answer him, trying to sound as rational and as calm as I can. "Smithy, my guardian, arranged it. I thought I was coming in with Indi, but with the amount of press at the house, it wasn't possible. Lincoln is my neighbor, and it was easy for me to get to his house undetected, so I could actually get to school."

He frowns again, but nods. "Okay."

That's all he says. Like I needed his permission. I grit my teeth together and take a deep breath. I'm on edge today, so I'm not going to snap at him. This could be me fully taking it the wrong way. He's been nothing but nice until now, so this has to just be me.

Just as I find my zen, Blair enters the room and glares at me. Her nose isn't strapped up, so it obviously wasn't broken. Though even from here, I can see the extra concealer on her face, so I guess there's some bruising.

Shame.

She stalks toward me, pissy as hell, but Finley steps in front of her and diverts her attention to Lincoln. I don't know why that pisses me off more, but when she smiles smugly at me, I clench my fists under the table.

The bell rings, and Indi glances over at me. "Want to skip?"

I love her so fucking much.

I shake my head and grab my bag and tray. "Not a fucking chance. Then they'll think they've won, and they need to learn that I'm not going anywhere."

"Damn, you are slaying this badass bitch vibe today," she says, smiling wide. We say our goodbyes to the table and hurry out of the cafeteria to my locker.

They're going to learn that I'm not just another one of their lowly subjects. This bitch doesn't take it lying down.

Fourteen

I'm woken by my phone pinging like crazy on the nightstand. Groaning as I roll over, I look at the messages.

Indi:

I need you.

Indi:

I was carjacked.

Indi:

I don't know what to do.

Indi:

Help.

I blink down at the screen in horror.

What the actual fuck? I dial her immediately, my heart racing at all of the possibilities of what could have happened to her. My panic flips to anger as I wait for the line to connect. I swear to God, if she's hurt…

She answers on the first ring and her sobs echo across the line. "Where are you?"

"V… I…" she stammers like she can't get her words out around her panic. "I'm just past the railroad tracks on the other side of town. I'm hiding down an alley right now. But, V, they took my car, they hit me…" her words taper off as her sobs pick up again.

"I'll be there in a few, okay. Just stay on the line."

I rack my brain, trying to think of how the hell I can get to her when my car is still in the shop. I run down the stairs and head for the security room where Smithy keeps the keys for my dad's cars that are locked in the garage. I haven't touched anything in the garage since I got back to Echoes Cove. My dad's things were his, but right now, I need one of his cars. I grab the closest keys to me and run to the garage. When I push the button, the lights on the black SUV flash.

I don't hesitate, I just climb in and start the engine. The tires screech as I pull down the drive, smashing the gate clicker so it opens. "I'm on my way. I'm in the black Range Rover."

"Okay." I push the button on the dash so my phone connects to the bluetooth, keeping the connection to her open, her sniffles filling the car.

"Did you call the police?" I ask, but I'm pretty sure I already know the answer.

"No," she hiccups. "I panicked. I ran. I just texted you. I don't know what to do. They hurt me, and I'm so fucking scared they're going to come back." Her sobs start up again, and I grip the steering wheel tighter as I fly through the city toward the less savory part of Echoes Cove. I can't help but wonder why she was over there in the first place. That's a question for later.

I scan the roads as quickly as I can. Once I cross the tracks, I slow the car. "I'm nearly there, can you come out to the street side so I can see you?"

"Okay." Her voice is so small, and I hate that someone did this to her. She's possibly the nicest person that I've ever met. She didn't deserve this.

I see her appear on the right. I jerk the wheel in her direction, screeching to a stop before jumping from the car. A bruise is already forming on her cheekbone, and she's bleeding from a cut above her eyebrow.

"Oh, Indi," I sigh and wrap her in my arms. Her knees give way and I take her weight, lowering us to the ground, holding her while she sobs. Her entire body shakes as she buries her face into my neck, clinging to me for dear life like I can save her, and my anger blazes again that someone would do this to her.

We're in the middle of some residential buildings, and it doesn't look like there are even any businesses here where she could've gone for help. This entire place looks sketchy as hell. "We should get you to the hospital to get checked out and then call the police."

She shudders in my arms before pulling away and wiping at her tears, wincing as she touches her cheek. "My mom is going to be so mad."

"Your mom will be happy you're okay, I promise."

I usher her into the car before taking her to the hospital, calling her mom on the way. It doesn't take long to reach the hospital, and thankfully we don't wait long before someone comes to tend to her since it's so early in the day, but I'm instructed to stay in the waiting room. Her mom breezes through the waiting room and heads straight for me, looking fucking terrified. "She's okay, she's just in with the nurses."

"Thank you, Octavia." she says, taking a deep breath before she heads into the room. I can't imagine how she feels; that's her daughter in there. Though her helplessness and rage are written all over her face. And after everything I've been through the last few months, I get it.

I move to actually sit in the waiting room and stare up at the tiled ceiling, searching for some answers. I drop a message to Smithy to let him know I'm going to miss school today, and he confirms he'll let the school know. It isn't like Thursdays are a typical skip day, and while I might be worried about my grades and getting behind, I'm more worried about my friend.

My phone buzzes again, and my heart stops when I see the message.

Unknown:

We told you nobody you loved was safe. When will you listen?

This is my fault.

Holy shit.

I can't breathe.

I put my head between my knees as I try to stave off the panic attack that threatens. My heart thumps in my chest and my hands shake; my temperature rises as everything around me becomes overwhelming. The noises in here sound like I'm underwater as I struggle to focus on my breathing.

This can't be my fault. It has to be a coincidence. They wouldn't do that.

Right?

Friday morning at school is like nothing I've ever experienced. The hype for tonight's game is *out of this world.* School spirit's at an all time high, and it's like everything else that happened this week is long forgotten. It feels like I'm not here, as if everyone's forgotten to make my life a living hell, and I'm so fucking here for it.

Indi's excitement is palpable. The cut on her head was small enough to not need stitches, and makeup covers the bruising on her cheek. I showed her the message I got when the nurses finally let me in her room, but she refused to put any of the blame on me. She said the guys that stole her car were older, so that it was likely someone heard about what happened and was trying to use it against me.

I hate to hope that it's true, but she's been adamant about it, and despite everything, she's still my sunshine friend. When she appeared at my gates this morning in her Wrangler, I was beyond shocked. Apparently it was found not an hour after we reported it stolen, without a single scratch on it.

That alone makes me think she's wrong about it being a coincidence. She won't hear any of it, so I keep my thoughts about it to myself.

As I walk through the halls with Indi, I can't help but be amazed once more about the complete change in the whole mood and demeanor of the entire fucking student body. "This is weird, right? It's just a high school football game."

Indi looks at me with wide eyes full of fear, which is sobering but makes me want to laugh at the same time. "Please, sweet baby Jesus, do not let anyone hear you saying those words. Football is basically a religion here. Why do you think that Raleigh and the guys are basically untouchable? Even Lincoln and his merry band of assholes don't tend to fuck with the team. *Religion*."

"It's still weird," I say with a shrug as we reach my locker. I open it and put my bag inside, grabbing my phone and sliding it into my pocket before locking it up.

"Oh, it's absolutely fucking nuts, but is that even a surprise about this place at this point? Everything about Echoes Cove is fucking weird. The sheer amount of money that gets funneled into the team is staggering. If there isn't some shady shit going on with that, I'd be amazed." She pops her bubblegum when she finishes speaking, and I consider her words. She's not wrong. Echoes Cove is a web of lies and secrets. There's no way there's this many rich people in such a small place without there being something shady going down.

I'm just glad I've managed to keep out of that shit.

She shoves her stuff in her locker and we head to the cafeteria in time for a mass exodus. The cheers and chanting leave me at a loss as the loudspeaker sounds with the principal's voice. "Today's pep rally will start in thirty minutes. Please start making your way to the gym."

Indi groans beside me, rolling her eyes. "I totally forgot they wipe the whole fucking afternoon for this bullshit."

My stomach growls at her words. "Okay, well, if I have to deal with this much school spirit and not kill people, I need food."

"Same, girl. Same," she says as she heads into the near empty cafeteria. I follow her, stoked to see that the one advantage of the insane pep rally is that there's no one in line for food. Some of the tables still hold kids, the ones who are obviously choosing to study instead of going to the pep rally.

Maybe they have the right idea.

I grab a couple slices of pepperoni pizza and a bag of chips before heading to a table with Indi, who carries her own pizza and a brownie. "Maybe we should skip and study? We never had our study date."

She pauses, her slice of pizza halfway to her mouth before shaking her head. "If I wasn't a football fiend, I would usually say yes... Except for the fact that Jackson asked if I'd be there, and I already told him yes."

"Ooh, how's that whole thing going?" I ask, wagging my eyebrows, and she blushes.

"It's going." She takes a bite of her pizza and groans. I won't push her for details if she isn't comfortable giving them. I get it. "I also heard that you have a date after the game tonight."

"I totally would've said something, but well…"

She interrupts me by putting up her hand and shaking her head. "You've had shit going on, and I'm not worked up about it. I was a little shocked since he doesn't seem like your type."

I can't help but laugh at that. "I have a type?"

She shrugs as the bell rings again, letting us know the pep rally is about to begin. I grab my pizza and chips, ditching my tray. There's no way I'm leaving my food behind. Indi follows suit and we start heading to the gym. "I mean, I've never seen you date anyone, but a typical high maintenance, golden boy quarterback doesn't really seem to scream *Octavia Royal's type.* But I mean, what do I know?"

"I've never dated a sports type, but Raleigh's nice. Plus, it's only one date, even if I'm not all that confident about it. Who knows what will happen? I have bigger worries before my date tonight," I quip and she looks at me, eyebrows raised in question. "What the fuck happens at a pep rally? It can't be like what I've seen on TV, right?"

She bursts out laughing at me, her shoulders fully shaking, and she pauses walking as she pulls herself together. "Oh man, I'm not even going to explain. This is too good."

I mean that doesn't exactly fill me with joy, but I follow

the swarm of people to the gym with her. We take a seat toward the back of the bleachers, and I already know that I'm going to hate whatever this is. The hype in the room is enough to choke a girl, and while I might like that sort of thing, this is totally not the place for it.

The principal walks up to the podium in front of the bleachers and lifts his arms. A roar of shouts and applause echoes around the room as the entire fucking school loses their shit.

This is fucking insane.

He lowers his arms, and the room goes quiet. "Are we ready for tonight, Raiders?"

The response is almost fucking deafening as people stomp their feet and shout. Indi leans over, grinning at the look of horror on my face. "Oh girl, this is only the beginning. Just wait for the dancing, the glitter, and the streamer rockets."

My eyes widen at the very thought of it. I barely have time to question it as the dance team struts onto the hardwood floor in shiny shorts and bandeaus made of sequins. Fucking sequins.

Music blares through the PA, and everyone goes crazy again. I glance around and even the three boys who have made my life hell seem to be enjoying themselves. I think I'm more shocked to see them actually smiling. I hate that despite everything else that's happened, I still seek them out in a crowd. Not that they're hard to miss. There's a ring of empty seats around them, as if everyone else is afraid to get too close. The girls who would usually, are all on the dance or cheer teams who are going crazy on the floor below us.

This level of hype should be reserved for concerts, not high school football games.

"Do you think anyone would notice if I escaped to the Music rooms?" I ask Indi, having to lean into her to be heard over the chaos. I have to give props to the dance team because they're fucking slaying their routine to AWOLNATION's "Sail", but still... This amount of pep is kind of gross.

Indi points as the football team breaks through a banner and runs into the room, joining the dance team as the crowd screams and cheers. "Pretty sure your boy would notice."

Fuck my life.

Someone please fucking save me.

Tonight's game has been bad.

I don't know much about football, but the triple threat of players from the Allstars—according to Indi—is fucking lethal. I literally only know the names Xavier, Hunter, and Tobias because she's cussed them out so hard all night. I'm assuming they're the other team since I don't recognize the names, but who knows at this point?

All of the student body's pep and cheer from earlier in the day is officially dead. The score is 35-14 to the Allstars, and apparently there's no coming back from that with the amount of time left on the clock. I have zero idea what's happening on the field, except for the fact that these guys spend more time taking breaks than they do running plays.

The mood's grim as the game ends, which doesn't exactly leave me hopeful for tonight. I accepted the date without really thinking it through, and I've regretted it ever since. Indi was right, I'm not the one to date a sports type... I'm also not looking to date. Having Raleigh as a friend is one thing, but anything else... I'm just hesitant. Dating was not on my radar this year, and I don't want the tentative friendship we've built to be ruined by him thinking this could be more.

Blair and her bitch squad look so salty about the loss that I almost want to throw them a bottle of tequila.

Almost.

The team heads for the fieldhouse after the clock runs out, and the stands start to empty. Indi drops into her seat and folds her arms across her chest, looking equally as pissed off as the cheer team. "Well, that was a fucking shit show. I know the Allstars are good, but fucking hell. Our defense was fucking useless tonight." I sit down beside her, feeling bad for her and our friends, but I don't really get the whole 'football is a religion' thing. "Those Allstars fucking annihilated us."

"I'm sorry?" I say, unsure if there's anything else I *can* say.

She shakes her head, shrugging. "It's just a bad start to the season. If we have too many losses, the chances of a championship slip away."

"Dude, you're totally a football nerd, aren't you?" I tease her, and she blushes a little. I never would have pegged her for a secret football lover but here we are.

She nods and tucks a strand of her freshly colored purple hair behind her ear. "I totally am. It's all Dad's fault. He's a fucking football freakazoid. He didn't have a son to share his love for the NFL with, so he shared it with me, and now I'm somehow hooked."

I smile, thinking of all the things my dad shared with me. There really isn't anything quite like the bond between daddy and daughter. "Hey, no shame. I get it. My dad shared music with me."

"Am I ever going to hear you play, by the way?" she asks, and I shrug. The thought of playing in front of people still makes me want to be sick.

We wait in comfortable silence until the stands are empty and head toward the back of the fieldhouse. With a loss like this, apparently the coach will be bitching them out for a while, so I prepare myself for Raleigh to cancel on me. I wish that made me more upset, but it doesn't, which isn't a great omen. I'm almost sad about not being sad.

"What are your plans for the rest of the night?" I ask her while we wait, and she blushes.

She fidgets a bit as she looks down at her feet. "I'm heading to a party over at ECH with Jackson."

I grin at her and nudge her with my shoulder. "Look at you go. Are you excited?"

"A little," she nods. "I'm more nervous than anything, though. He's a football god, and I'm… well, me." Her self-deprecation is not okay with me. Not even a little.

I grab her by the shoulders and force her to look at me. "Indi, you are a fucking amazing human, and he's the lucky one here. Football gods come and go, but you are literally the nicest human I've ever met in my life. Your sunshine sparkle mixed with your sassy as fuck snark gives me life. If Jackson can't appreciate that, then fuck him. You are a goddamn goddess."

She blushes in response to my words and starts to laugh softly. "Dude, you are so freaking fierce. I know you hate that you had to come back here, but I'm so glad you did."

I hug her tight. I know she's deflecting, but I totally understand. Compliments are hard to handle when they're not something you're used to. I let her go as the doors behind us open and the team filters out. The unwavering pep from earlier is noticeably absent. I guess the party at ECH is going to end up being a commiseration rather than a celebration. "Be careful tonight. If any shit goes down, call me, and I'll be there in a heartbeat."

"Awh, look! You do warm and fuzzy too," she teases, and I roll my eyes. "But yeah, I'll be careful. I know the rivalry is real, but things are usually pretty okay at parties. Everyone just wants to get fucked up." She looks over my shoulder, and her smile widens. I glance over my shoulder and see Jackson heading toward us.

"Have fun," I whisper in the moment right before Jackson reaches us and slings his arm over her shoulders.

"You ready?" he asks her, and she nods. "Awesome. We'll see you later, V."

I salute him as he leads her toward the parking lot before turning back to the locker room door. Most of the team has already left, but there's no way in hell I'm heading in there. Especially with the bellowing voice from the football coach filtering under the door. Not on your life.

I sit on the grassy mound behind the fieldhouse and play a game on my phone while I wait, ignoring the world around me.

"Sorry that I took so long." I look up and find Raleigh standing above me.

I smile and climb to my feet, dusting off my ass as I do.

I'm only in denim cutoffs and a tank with a shirt over my shoulders. I wish I felt more excited, but maybe that will come later. "You're good. Are you ready?"

He nods and takes my hand. It feels a little weird, but I go with it and follow him to his car. "Where are we heading?"

"That's a surprise," he says with a wink as he opens the truck door for me. I slide into his pickup, and he closes the door before slipping around and climbing in the driver's side.

I'm not really a fan of surprises, but I'm not about to tell him that and ruin whatever he has planned. Though if anyone actually jumps out at me and yells surprise, I won't be held responsible for my actions.

He drives us through town and pulls up outside a Mexican place that I haven't seen before. "Indi said you were a sucker for tacos, so I figured my family restaurant was the perfect place to eat."

My eyes go wide, and I get a flutter of panic as my heart starts to race. His family restaurant means his family is in there, and that feels like way too much for a first date. Even if the food is some of my favorite. "Oh, uhm, yeah, I love Mexican food. I didn't know your family had a restaurant."

He puts his hand on the handle of the door before winking at me. "There's a lot you don't know about me."

The night ends, and I'm more than a little underwhelmed. I mean the food was fucking amazing. I've never had Mexican food that good, and I'm definitely not mentioning that to Smithy, but I'm never going to be able to eat there again.

His mom and older sister were there, and they fawned over us like he was literally their little golden prince and I his prize. That was turn off number one. I wasn't even that pampered out on tour with my dad. It was kind of sickening.

Then there was how he totally changed once we were out. He was so controlling, and like, not in a good way. At first, I thought he was being a gentleman. Opening doors, pulling out my chair... until he commented on my clothes and how he thought I should've dressed better for him. Then he ordered for me without even handing me a menu, talked down to me about the amount of food on my plate, even about ordering a soda. All massive red flags to me. Some girls like the controlling thing, but I am not one of them. Not like that.

Don't get me wrong, he's the nicest guy usually, but as anything more than friends... It's never going to work with us. Of that much, I'm already pretty sure. He pulls up to the front gates, and turns off the engine.

This doesn't feel weird for me or anything. No, not at all. Fuck my life. I grasp the door handle quickly, wanting to escape before this gets any more awkward. I'm preparing myself to say goodnight before I close the door, but he gets out of the car too.

He stalks round to my side, golden boy grin on his face, with his hands shoved in his pockets. "Tonight was fun."

"It was, your family's restaurant was great, and the food—"

His grin widens, and he nods, interrupting me. "Yeah, my mom knows how to cook."

I twiddle with my thumbs, wishing I was better at this. He's been nothing but nice since the day I met him, which is why I don't want to lead him on. I don't want to crush his feelings either, though after tonight, I'm not entirely sure that'll be an issue.

The sound of metal cogs whirring fills the silence as the gate to the Saint household opens, and I spot Finley's pearly white Lamborghini rolling through it. He and Maverick look over in our direction as the car rolls forward, windows down, and Raleigh moves closer to me.

He wraps his arms around my waist and pulls me against him. My hands press on his chest; but before I can say another word, his lips are on mine. Shock has me paralyzed for a moment before I pull away. He looks over his shoulder, grinning at Finley and Maverick, who glare in our direction. Maverick says something to Finley that I can't hear despite how close they are, and Finley shakes his head once, his knuckles turning white on the steering wheel before the car speeds away from us.

Did he actually just try to claim me in front of them? With the world's most underwhelming, no fireworks kiss at that? That's not exactly how I pictured my first kiss with him going, though I hadn't pictured kissing him at all. That should probably have been my first warning sign. I pull myself out of his grasp, and he frowns as I quickly dash through the gate and close it.

"We should do this again," he calls out, and I try not to grimace.

How the fuck am I going to do this right? "Yeah, maybe. I'm tired, so I'm going to head to bed."

"Yeah okay." He grins at me like he can't tell how grossed out I am by him right now.

I turn to head up the driveway, calling out a 'night' when I realize he's still standing there, watching me.

"Night," he shouts back, and I hear the slam of his door before the engine starts and he drives off into the night.

I run a hand down my face and pull my phone from my pocket, clicking on the message thread with Indi.

Me:

I'm home, alive and well... Just wanted to check in with you. Hope you're having a good night with J.

Indi:

I will require all of the details, but yes, having an awesome night.

I smile at her message, glad that one of us is having a successful night, and repocket my phone before entering the house. I need a shower to wash the night off of me.

If this is how actual dating works, I'm not sure I'm a fan.

I groan as I roll over in bed and stare up at the ceiling. Last night was... Well, it wasn't great.

I tossed and turned most of the night trying to decide what to do, but I'm convinced that Raleigh's going to go strictly into the friend zone. The more I think about that kiss, the more disappointed I am.

There were no fireworks, it was underwhelming, and the whole claiming thing skeeved me out.

It was a weird fucking night. I was extra glad that the press wasn't camped out at the house again. I guess

Smithy's legal threats finally hit home with people. At least that's one less thing to worry about now.

My phone buzzes on the bedside table, so I grab it and groan when I see Raleigh's name on my screen.

Raleigh:

Morning beautiful. Last night was great, we should do it again. You have anything planned for the weekend?

Apparently the eager beaver thought last night went much better than I did. Now I have to work out how to walk us back to being friends because this isn't going to work for me. I should have trusted my instincts and cancelled the date.

Me:

Hey, I've got some shit to do this weekend, but I'll see you at school on Monday?

My phone buzzes again almost as soon as the message is sent.

Raleigh:

Well that sucks, but it's cool. Yeah, I'll see you Monday. Have a good weekend.

The sulkiness that comes through with his message is unreal, and I groan again as I run a hand down my face. This was a mistake, a huge one. I hope he takes the 'let's be just friends' talk okay.

I take a deep breath and decide to start the day off with a run. It's been too long, and I swear my blood feels itchy under my skin with the need to pound pavement and escape the world. I pull up my thread to Indi and smile at the picture of her and Jackson down at the beach that she sent me last night.

They're so stinking cute together.

Me:

You look like you had a good night.

Indi:

You could say that **laugh emoji**

Me:

I feel like I need details. Want to come on my run with me?

Indi:

You and your run can fuck right off.

I burst out laughing at her response. Coming back to

Echoes Cove has fucking sucked, but I can't be too mad about it since it gave me her.

Me:

pouty face but running is good for the soul.

Indi:

Running is the devil's work. Burgers... now they're the work of the gods. We can grab lunch if you want to?

Me:

Grease sounds perfect

Indi:

I'll swing by and grab you, just let me know when you're back from your run.

Me:

Will do

I jump up and get dressed, pulling my hair into a high ponytail and sliding on my arm strap. I absolutely need this run today, even if only to process how I'm going to talk to Raleigh. I bounce downstairs and find Smithy waiting for me in the kitchen. "Miss Octavia, good morning."

"Morning, Smithy. You have a good night?" I ask as I

head to the fridge and pour myself a glass of juice. I grab a bottle of water for my run when I put the juice back.

He smiles at me as he motions for me to sit down. "It was fine, thank you. The repairs to the house were finally completed yesterday, so it was nice to not have to think about that anymore. I'm glad all of that nonsense is done with. Now then, I was wondering if you have anything planned for Labor Day weekend?"

"Nothing at all yet, why's that?" I ask as he slides a plate of Eggs Benedict in front of me.

"My sister informed me that she's hosting something of a family get together back east, so I'm thinking about going, but if you're going to be home…" he trails off, and I shake my head.

"Go. Absolutely go!" I tell him, excited for him. I didn't even know he had a sister! "I'll find a way to keep myself busy and alive. You deserve a weekend off."

"Well, I don't know about that," he utters as he sits opposite me with a plate of french toast. *Gross.* Syrup on eggy bread is just a no from me.

"You have to go. I'll be so sad if you miss out on seeing your family because of me." I have to practically beg him to go before he agrees to it. Silly man. I have no blood relatives left—I'm not counting my runaway mother—and I'd do a lot to have some time with my dad again.

Suddenly the itch to run is replaced with an urge to

play, and I haven't felt like this since Dad died. I can't help but smile. I've missed music so fucking much.

I finish my breakfast with a smile on my face as we discuss his plans to go away, and I confirm he managed to secure my birthday present for Indi. Happy that everything's in order, I put my dishes in the sink. "I'm having lunch with Indi today, so you don't need to worry about me. I'm going to go and chill in the music room for the rest of the day."

He motions to my outfit and frowns at me. "I thought you were running."

"I don't feel like I need to run right now. There's a song burning under my skin. I might not have played much since I got back, but there's no way to ignore a song like that. Plus now that the repairs are done, I want to play. I might reschedule with Indi too…" He nods at me, and I grin before I practically skip upstairs and then head to the music room in the basement that sits in a soundproofed space, along with a small recording studio.

This is my happy place.

I changed a few things with the repairs to make it more my own space now. The chairs are comfier and the colors a little warmer. I'm glad they managed to erase all evidence of what happened here. If I didn't have this space, I'm not sure how I'd stay sane.

I drop a quick message to Indi to reschedule until

tomorrow, because God only knows how long I'll be in here, and her relief is real at not having to get out of bed. I laugh softly at her insanity before locking myself in the music room.

I sit at the baby grand piano and close my eyes, feeling the music inside of me before placing my fingers on the keys. I can hear it before I even press a single note.

This is what I needed. So I start to play, and nothing can take this from me.

And if anyone tries… well… there will be blood.

Fifteen

A knock at the door has me pausing the movie in the theatre room and hopping over to the door. I open it to find Smithy smiling at me on the other side.

"Miss Octavia, I have a surprise for you!" He's so excited that I can't even bring myself to remind him how much I dislike surprises. He turns and heads down the hall, so I turn off the projector, pull down the sleeves of my hoodie, and follow him. This might be interrupting my Sunday chill, but it's Smithy, so I don't mind. The man is a freaking saint.

He heads outside, and I follow, beyond curious at this point. He's like a kid in a candy store. I step outside to see what has him so excited.

"They just delivered it." His grin matches mine as I take in the sight before me. My beautiful Impala, in better condition than she was in when I bought her. Not one spec of that hideous yellow paint is on her.

I clap my hands together as joy swells in my chest, and I practically squeal as Smithy holds out the keys for me. I grab the keys and hug him tight. "Thank you, Smithy!"

He pats me on the back, finally getting used to my random hugging. "Anything for you, Miss Octavia."

I pull away and slide my phone from my pocket, snapping a picture and sending it over to Indi.

Indi:

Holy shit, she looks good as new!

Me:

Right, want to go out?

I'm suddenly over my Sunday chill, imagine that.

Indi:

Sure thing! Give me 10 so I don't look half dead. **Skull emoji**

Me:

I look half dead, but I don't care. I'll be there soon, send me your address **heart emoji**

Indi:

middle finger emoji #attachment

I can't help but laugh at her as I slide into the car, joy pulsing through my veins. I bring up the pin drop she sent me, feeling a little bad that I've never been to her house before. "Thank you, Smithy! I'll be back soon."

He waves as I start the car, and I head down the drive and out of the gates. I use the clicker to make sure they're shut behind me before driving toward Indi's. It thankfully doesn't take me long to find her house. I pull up out front, and she's already sitting on the steps waiting for me. She jumps up when I pull to a stop and skips down the path toward me.

I unlock the door, and she climbs in, grinning at me like a crazy person. "You look happy."

"I spent yesterday with Jackson again, *and* you have your beautiful baby back. What's not to be happy about? Oh, and I forgot to ask yesterday 'cause I was so wrapped up in myself, but how did Friday go?" I groan and bang my forehead on the steering wheel, which makes her laugh. "That bad?"

"Don't even get me started," I say before restarting the car and heading out to the Pacific Coast Highway to coast around in my pretty, not so little, car. I tell her everything about Friday night as we drive around, and she pulls as many faces as I wanted to on the night in question. By the time we end up back in Echoes Cove, she's as confused about his behavior as I was.

"It doesn't make any sense. Maybe it was because they lost the game?" She shrugs, trying to offer an explanation.

It doesn't really make a difference to my decision though, and I tell her as much.

"Makes sense, if it's not right, then it's not right. I'm sure it'll be fine. He's pretty chill," she says as I pull the car to a stop in the lot by the pier.

"Here's hoping. You want to fuck around on the pier? It's been ages since I rode the rides and did all the fun shit." I unbuckle and turn to her, finding her eagerly nodding.

"Hell fucking yes I do. I love that shit."

We climb from the car, and I strip off my hoodie, leaving in the car. The sun's beaming down, so I grab my cardholder and phone, stashing them in my pockets before I slide my aviators on. It's such a beautiful day and spending it on the pier sounds like the best idea.

"To the games," Indi yells, pointing toward the pier before linking her arm with mine, and I can't help but laugh at her.

"To the games!"

Indi left the pier after a call from her mom, who picked her up, so I sit at the edge of the pier looking out over the water. It's so beautiful, so vast, and so fucking terrifying. I've always had a love-hate relationship with the water.

When we were younger, one of the girls in our class was swept out to sea and was never found. Ever since, I've had an issue with the ocean. It took years for me to even dip my toes in again. Swimming pools are fine, but natural bodies of water? No thanks.

All that being said, I do still love the sound of waves crashing in the surf. It's possibly the most soothing noise of nature there is.

I find myself humming along to the songs being played by the booth closest to me as I watch the sun begin to set. I hadn't even realized the time.

I stand when I hear my dad's voice, and my heart stops. I close my eyes, and for a second, it's like he's back here with me. I smile for just a moment before that hope slips away. I clutch the railing of the pier as his laugh sounds on the speakers, and a lump forms in my throat.

This is why I don't listen to the radio.

I can't move as the interview plays; and when they start playing one of his more popular songs, I break. Tears stream down my face as my heart shatters in my chest. Without even thinking about it, my feet move, and I'm running down the pier. I keep running onto the sand and down the beach, trying to escape the pain.

It feels like I can't breathe. Like the pain of hearing his voice is going to be the thing that finally sends me over the edge. Hearing him sing hurts so bad, but hearing him talking and laughing like that hurts even worse. For a second, just one, it was like he was here again. Like my life wasn't a fucking mess. It was as if my mind forgot he was gone and felt peace before having all of my safety barriers torn away once more.

I run until there's no one else in sight and fall to my knees in the sand, letting out a scream filled with so much pain that it makes me cry harder.

My dad was my safe haven. He was the person that didn't leave. He was always there.

Always.

And now he's gone, and it's like I can't breathe properly anymore. My whole world crumbled once he died, and I feel so lost.

I've tried to find myself ever since I lost him... Since he left me... And I've done so well at pretending like I didn't lose myself at the same time.

I shift in the sand and clutch my knees to my chest as I sob, hoping that the tears dry themselves out. I've tried to be strong, but I'm so crushed without him here. The pain of not having him with me is so devastating, especially after the second of mindlessness on the pier where I almost convinced myself that he was here with me again. The legacy that he left behind for me, his music, was meant to be his gift to me, but it haunts me instead, and I'm raw.

Placing my forehead on my knees, I cry until I feel hollow. Even then, I can't stop. It feels like losing him all over again.

I hear footsteps coming toward me, and look up to find Finley staring over at me before heading in my direction. I let out a deep breath and wipe away the still falling tears. "I can't deal with you today, Finley. Please."

My voice cracks on the last word, and he hesitates as if he's fighting an internal battle of his own. He shakes his head and finishes stomping over to me, dropping down beside me in the sand. He doesn't say a word. Instead sits, staring out over the water with me while I try to stop the flow of tears.

Another wave of grief crashes over me, and my shoulders shake as I struggle to control the sobs. I hate being this weak, especially with him here. This is the second time he's seen me lose it.

"Fuck it," he growls, standing and lifting me out of the sand. He sits with me in his lap and holds me. I don't want to be here, but I'd be lying if I said being in his arms didn't make me feel less alone. So I allow myself the weakness of leaning into him once more, vowing that this will be the last time.

But for now, I let myself crumble as I mourn losing my dad all over again.

By the time I lift my head, darkness has blanketed us, and the moon in the sky is the only source of light. My heart feels empty and broken, but I push myself out of Finley's arms and stand.

"Octavia," he starts, and I glare down at him.

"Did you make that video?" I don't have to say anything else or even wait for his response. His guilt's written all over his face.

He stands, brushing himself off, the wet patch on his white t-shirt obvious despite the dark night. "Let me explain."

"There isn't anything to explain," I hiss. "You don't get to keep comforting me when you have no issues with making me cry. I am not a toy you can pick up and put down."

"Please—" he starts, and I cut him off with a wave of my hand.

"No. Thank you, for this, but no. This doesn't make up for anything else, Finley. We were friends once, and I have no idea what I did to incur your wrath so badly that you'd do something as horrific as you did." His face falls, and he looks as defeated as I feel.

"I…" he starts but trails off, shaking his head. He puts his hands in his pockets, that stoic, passive glare back in

LILY WILDHART

place. "You're right. We were friends once, and we're not anymore. This was a mistake."

He walks away from me without another word, leaving me speechless.

How the fuck did he cut me and make me bleed with only his words when I thought I was already broken beyond repair?

Mondays fucking suck. After last night at the beach, I decided to skip my run today. I had to talk myself into it, but I decided to swim laps instead. Swimming a mile isn't too hard. I used to be able to do it in forty minutes, but it's been a minute since I swam.

I'm about halfway through my mile when I spot a shadow at the end of the pool. I finish my lap and come up for air to see who it is. I take a deep breath and lift my hands to wipe the water from my eyes, but I find myself plunged back under the water. A hand grips my hair, keeping me beneath the surface. Panic sets in.

I claw at the hand, but I can't focus. My entire body is freaking the fuck out.

I never thought to worry this morning about drowning in my own pool.

I never considered how deep it is.

270

As I try to push up for air, I see a flash of my dad's face and a dark thought hits me.

Would it be so bad if I didn't fight?

But then I see a flash of my Smithy's face, and I think of Indi. I see all the people who would be disappointed in me if I just gave up, and I start fighting again.

My lungs burn as I struggle not to draw in a breath.

My limbs start to feel heavy as I continue to fight, but the lack of oxygen slows me down.

The thought of that girl being lost at sea hits me; and I vow that if I survive this, I'm never getting in the water ever a-fucking-gain.

As quickly as it appeared, the hand leaves my hair. I sink a little before pushing up from the bottom, gasping as I clutch the side of the pool. I wipe the water from my eyes, but I don't see anyone around.

How is that even possible?

I stay where I am until my eyes focus again and my hands stop shaking before pulling myself from the pool.

I look around the lawn, but there aren't even footprints in the dirt thanks to the dry summer.

I grab my towel and wrap it around me, trying to get a hold of myself before I go inside. My entire body starts to shake as the adrenaline quickly wears off, and I sink to the ground as my knees give out. I suck in a breath as my emotions get the better of me and hold it, trying to stop the noise in my head. I cling to the towel, hoping the pressure helps stave off the panic, as I curl up as small as I can.

Hot tears slip down my face, and I don't bother trying to wipe them away. Why does this shit keep happening to me?

I let myself break, before trying to piece myself back together. Once I can breathe normally again, and my heartbeat doesn't sound like thunder, I splash myself with cold water to try and hide my red, puffy cheeks. It takes a minute before I'm sure my legs will hold me, but I climb to my feet before hurrying into the house. My only thought is finding out who did this. I don't think we have security cameras out back, but I'm sure as hell going to check them if we do.

Whoever it was obviously wanted to scare me—I just wish I knew why.

That's when I see the note taped to my back door. It says *'Leave. It will only get worse from here.'*

I leave the note exactly where it is and head off to find Smithy. I don't know who the fuck did this, but I'm done.

I find Smithy and tell him what happened. He has his phone in his hand, dialing the police in less than five seconds. "No, I don't want the police involved. We both know they're just as corrupt as the rest of this town."

He knows as well as I do that this town is run by those who have money… Except my dad left and pissed off a ton of people before he did, so I don't get the same privileges that others do. I've only heard whispers of the shit storm my dad left behind, but I've heard enough to know that in this situation, the police won't be of use to me. He hangs up and drops his phone on the counter. I shake where I stand, wrapped in a towel, in the middle of the kitchen. "We can't just let this go, Miss Octavia."

"And we won't. I still have to get ready for school, but can you check the security feed? And if we don't have footage, we need to increase the security on the property." He nods at my words, and I can see his guilt, clear as day in the set of his jaw. "This is not your fault."

"I'm supposed to be looking after you." He frowns. "I'm letting you down. I'm letting your father down."

My heart sinks at his words. "You're not letting anyone down. None of this is your fault, and I won't hear another word about it. Can we increase the security some more?"

He nods, looking a little less defeated than he did a minute ago. "Yes, I'll get it sorted as fast as we can."

I feel a little better, taking care of the situation, or at least preventing the chances of it happening again. It could have been anyone. It doesn't seem like a Lincoln move, but I wouldn't put it past Blair or one of her little cronies. "Perfect, thank you. I'm going to go and wash up, get ready for school, and try to forget this morning ever happened."

I climb the stairs to my room and shudder at the

thought of going back under the water, but I need to wash the chlorine off of me.

You've got this, Octavia, there's no one else but Smithy in the house. You are safe.

It takes a minute after my pep talk to actually get my ass in the shower, and I rush through my usual routine; but once I'm out, I feel a lot better.

Though if this is an example of how this day is going to go, I'm not even going to bother to hope for a good day.

I make it through the morning without issue, and Indi's been almost glued to my side since I told her about what happened this morning.

Whoever did it didn't hide their reasoning behind it. The note was crystal fucking clear, but I'm not going anywhere. I do want to know why someone wants me gone so badly, though.

None of it makes any sense.

I'm here for my diploma, and I'll happily leave once I have it.

Indi meets me after Music, like she has after every lesson so far today. She's like a snapping turtle, losing it at anyone who so much as looks sideways at me. I love this badass sunshine version of her almost as much as the dancing in the rainbows side.

"Do you mind if I talk to Raleigh for a minute? I'll meet you in the cafeteria." I feel bad because I should've said something when she got me from Statistics, but I spent my entire period pep talking myself to have this conversation with Raleigh. I hadn't intended on doing it till after school, but he was overly touchy in class, and I can't go through the rest of the day without saying something.

She eyes me, making sure I'm okay before nodding. "Sure thing. I'll grab you a tray so you don't end up with the dredges of what's left."

"You're the best."

She squeezes my arm before heading down the hall while I wait for Raleigh to finish talking to Miss Celine. It doesn't take long, and the slimy smile he gives me when he sees me waiting for him, sends shivers down my spine confirming that I'm making the right decision.

"You waited." He beams at me and slings his arm over my shoulder.

I pause, extracting myself from his embrace, and he frowns. "We should talk." I wince a little hearing the words fall from my lips because well, cliché much.

"That doesn't sound great." He folds his arms across his chest and leans against the wall. And it occurs to me just how alone we are... how empty the halls are.

I know it's just my paranoia from this morning rearing

its head, so I shake it off. I'm not having this conversation with people around. I won't do that to him or to myself. "It's not... I really like you, Raleigh. You're an awesome guy—"

"But you just want to be friends." He laughs haughtily after cutting me off. "Of course you do."

He scrubs a hand down his face, and I shift from one foot to the other. This could go either way, and I really hope it doesn't go badly. I don't need another enemy at this school, and he has been a good friend to me. We're just not a good match otherwise.

"Yeah, pretty much. I wasn't really feeling it," I tell him, trying to be as honest as I can.

He shrugs, stuffing his hands in his pockets. "I get it. I don't like it, but I get it."

I smile up at him sadly. "I totally don't want to say it because it's awful, but I'm really hoping we can still be friends."

He belts out a laugh, and I wince again. This morning really has left me on edge. "You're right, that was awful. But yes, we can still be friends. What's one date between friends? It isn't like we fucked or I declared my love for you."

My eyes go wide at his words, making him laugh harder.

"Chill, I don't love you." I let out a breath of relief at

the clarification. "Now let's head to lunch, I'm starving."

I make it through the rest of the day without issue. In fact, everything was looking up until I started the drive home.

Stupid me didn't think to check my car after school.

That was my first mistake.

So when I need to stop the car at a traffic light, and my brakes fail, I smash into the car already sitting there. Thankfully there *was* a car there, otherwise I'd have hit the kids crossing the road. But fuck my life.

So now I'm sitting in the back of an ambulance getting checked over while the police look over the road.

What an awesome way to finish this day.

My neck's so fucking stiff, and a bruise is already blooming on my chest from the seatbelt. The pain relievers the paramedic gave me aren't helping much, but I don't want to take anything stronger. A police officer approaches the ambulance, and I spot Lincoln's Porsche pull to a stop behind the cop car.

"Miss, are you okay to answer some questions?" I nod and stand, only a little dizzy from where I hit my head in the crash. I'm pretty sure I look worse than I feel. I'm glad no one was hurt too badly, but I am beyond pissed that my car is fucked up yet again.

"Can you please tell me what happened here, in your own words?"

I sigh at the question. I know it looked like I just plowed straight into the back of that woman, but they're not going to believe me until they check out the car. I explain everything that happened about my brakes not working.

His look of skepticism isn't lost on me. "Who would want to mess with your brakes?"

I look over at Lincoln, and he smirks at me as he leans against his car, arms crossed over his chest. Jackass. I don't know why he's here, but we both know that if he backed me up right now, this cop would believe me without hesitation.

Of course, we're not friends anymore, so I don't expect his help. But it's likely he knows who did this if he didn't do it himself. Though this seems too blue collar for Linc. He knows his way around an engine—he's always had a fascination with how things work—but I doubt that even if it was his idea that he did the damage himself.

"I don't know, Officer. All I know is that they didn't work. I never said that someone messed with them." The officer's cheeks go red as he splutters an apology. "Is there anything else?"

"No, miss. We've called a tow truck for your car pending investigation for your insurance company, but once everything's cleared up, someone will contact you."

I nod at him, wishing I hadn't because pain rips through

my skull. Well, that's a fun little side effect, awesome. "Thank you, Officer."

He heads back toward his car, and the paramedics pack up, leaving me with my smashed up car to wait for the tow truck. The woman I hit scowls at me, and I smile apologetically. I don't know how many more times I can say sorry to her. Thankfully, her car isn't too damaged, so she climbs in and drives away, leaving me with my undrivable Impala.

Lincoln saunters over to me, smirk firmly in place. "I do not have the time or patience for your bullshit today."

"And here I am, a nice bystander, waiting to offer you a ride home." I scoff at his words. There is no way he's here just to be nice.

I roll my eyes at him, beyond exasperated and so done with this day. "Yeah, right, I totally believe you." My smile conveys every ounce of snark I have building up inside of me. "Besides, I already called Indi, she's on her way."

"She isn't. I was at the library too when she got your call. I told her I'd come and get you since I was heading home anyway."

I let out a growl of frustration. "Of course you fucking did. If you're being so helpful, why not help me with the cop?"

He laughs at me and crosses his arms, watching me like a hunter watches his prey. "Why would I help you with that?"

I roll my eyes again, but it makes my head pound. I wince, grasping my head. God, he's such an asshole. We're interrupted as the tow truck arrives, asking me to sign a dozen different forms before he hooks up my poor car and takes it away.

"Do you want a ride home or not?" He's so fucking shitty about it. I almost want to say no, but the world starts spinning. I groan internally because I don't think I'll manage it if I try to walk home.

"Yes, please." I grind out the words through a clenched jaw, and he grabs my bag from the ground.

"After you," he says, waving to his shiny black SUV. I start walking, and my stomach flips. I really hope I don't vomit. Though the thought of fucking with his impeccably spotless car does give me a sadistic sort of satisfaction.

He opens the door for me and closes it once I'm buckled in, striding round to his side before climbing in. His gaze runs over me—almost as if checking for injury, but I know better than to think that—as my stomach rolls, and I practically feel the blood run from my face. "If you vomit in my car, I'll make you clean it."

I flip him the finger and open the window, taking deep breaths.

At least that wouldn't be the worst part of my day.

Sixteen

"**H**APPY BIRTHDAY!!!!" I practically jump on Indi when I meet her at school. The last couple of weeks since my car crash have been pretty shit, but she's the sunshine in my life, and it's her birthday. I've been planning her gift for what feels like forever.

I grin at her when I release her from my hug, and she looks all sassy and beautiful. Her long hair is now a cascade of rainbow colors, and I fucking adore it. "Here. This is for you!"

Not bouncing up and down in excitement about her gift is fucking hard as she opens the envelope.

She gawks down at the tickets in her hands, blinking. I think I might've broken her.

It only takes a second or so before she comes back to life, and her squeal is so high-pitched, I think dogs on the other side of town can hear her. "Oh my God! You absolute fucking rockstar! Are these real?"

She waves the All Access Passes I got her for the Midnight Blue gig in San Diego in my face; and when I nod, she squeals again before jumping on me and hugging me so hard I almost fall over. I'm glad the bruising on my chest is gone, otherwise I'd be fucked right now.

"You're coming with me right?" she asks.

"Yup!" I say with a nod, popping my p. "I have a hotel sorted out for us already, and it's only a few hours drive away, so *road trip!* We just need to make it through to lunch because Smithy and your mom have already let the school know we won't be around this afternoon." I might need a 4.0 GPA but bringing her this joy is so worth missing class. Plus, I already spoke to East directly, and he's not going to penalize us for missing one class. I'm caught up on everything else, having gotten straight As on all of my assignments so far. Except for the project I have with Lincoln. That class I'm worried about, especially considering Mr. Peters being a grade A pervert, but I'm hoping I can work on Lincoln to actually work with me since I'm pretty sure he doesn't want a bad grade either. I can afford to skip a little, because Business is going to hang in the balance either way.

"I'm so fucking excited. Oh my God. I'm going to meet Jenna B. What if I fangirl too hard and make a total ass out of myself? Oh shit, that's definitely going to happen. This is going to be so good and so terrible, and I don't even care. I'm too excited." The babble continues to fall from her lips, and I can't help but laugh a little. It brings me so much joy seeing how happy she is.

"You'll be fine, she's excited to hang out too. I spoke to one of my friends earlier, since he's on her team now. Jenna basically hired my dad's entire road team and I love her for that, so we have All Access Passes for the entire thing."

She stills and blinks at me for a second before whispering, "You spoke with Jenna B?"

I nod, and she covers her mouth with her hands. "Holy. Fucking. Shit."

"Are you okay?" I ask, a little worried about her. I don't care about everyone watching us, they can fuck right off. This is Indi's day, and if she wants to be crazy and loud, then so be it.

She nods, looking back down at the tickets with wide eyes. "My bestie just got me the best present ever and told me she talks to my ultimate girl crush on the regular. I'm just having a moment."

She grins up at me, and I burst out laughing. "I love you."

"I love you too," she says, linking her arm with mine, practically skipping as we head toward the main entrance of the school. "So where are we staying?"

I run through the details with her as we hit our lockers before heading to English.

The day passes quickly, with Raleigh finally back to being his usual laid-back, cheerful self during Music. He's been understandably distant the last few weeks, but it's nice having him back to how he was before the world's most unfortunate date.

By the time the bell rings to signal lunch, I'm beyond excited to get out on the road with Indi for the gig tonight. Her squeal reaches me before she does as I head down the hall toward her. I grab my shit from my locker, and then we head straight out to the parking lot. "Head home, pack yourself a bag, and I'll be there in less than an hour to get you."

"Holy shit, I'm too excited, my heart is racing." She grins and hugs me. "Okay, I'll see you soon."

I head over to my newly repaired Impala, checking to make sure every inch is safe before I jump in and drive home. I already packed my overnight bag, but I still need to get ready for tonight. I say a quick hello to Smithy as I climb the stairs to my room to shower and get my shit together.

Opening the door to my room, I freeze. The balcony door is open again and there's a note lying on my bed. Fuck, that's so creepy.

I pick the thick cream paper up, taking a deep breath before opening it.

I told you to leave. You didn't listen. You're going to regret that.

Fuck this, I'm not letting whoever this is ruin my weekend. I should probably be a little more concerned after the car crash and everything else that's happened, especially when the note is on my bed; but today is Indi's birthday, and I refuse to be rattled. I drop the note back onto the bed and head for my bathroom. I'll let Smithy know about it before I leave and ask him to look into it, since we're still waiting on his security guy.

I take extra care getting ready and pep talk myself into not breaking down on Indi's birthday. Going back to the stadium I was at last with my dad has me all kinds of fucked up. Tonight isn't about me, though, so I'm shoving all of my bullshit in a box to deal with another day.

Once I'm ready, I grab my bag and head down to find Smithy. He's waiting for me in the kitchen. "Oh good, Miss Octavia, I'm glad I caught you. I got a call while you were upstairs. My sister is in the hospital. Since I know you're away tonight, I was wondering if you would mind terribly if I flew home to be with my family?"

"Smithy, of course not! Go, family comes first, always!" Fuck the note, we can deal with that when his sister isn't in the fucking hospital.

"Thank you, Miss Octavia. I've made a call to a friend at the security company, he's going to come and check on the house a few times while we're gone to ensure nothing untoward happens in our absence. He'll also be upgrading the system to a new state of the art system, so I'll ask him to leave instructions for you."

"You don't need to thank me, Smithy, she's your family. Can I have your friend's details? Just so I can let him know when I'm home. That way I won't get freaked out by people I don't know being in the house when I'm back."

"Yes of course. I'll send the contact over to you. I need to organize a flight, and then I'll sort it out."

"Take the jet," I tell him, and his eyes go wide.

"I couldn't."

"You could. It's just sitting there doing nothing, and it's way better than flying commercially. It's not like I need it." I shrug because I'm not wrong. Why pay for a drop hat staff if you don't use it?

"If you're sure," he says, looking uneasy, so I smile and nod.

"Beyond sure. I don't need it, and you do. It'll get you there faster too. Then you can come back whenever you're ready without having to worry about flights."

"Thank you, Miss Octavia. Enjoy your trip away. I'll keep you up-to-date with the details of when I'm coming home as soon as I know exactly what's going on."

"There's no rush, honestly. If you need to stay there, do it. I can ask the security guy to be here if I need to." I'd rather not, but considering the note, it might be a good idea. Smithy almost looks uncomfortable at the thought but nods anyway.

He thanks me once more, so I hug him and tell him goodbye before heading out to the car to go grab Indi. Excitement bubbles in my chest at the thought of how much fun this weekend is going to be.

I slide my aviators into place and start the car.

San Diego, here we come.

"Please don't pass out," Indi murmurs to herself as we walk toward the doors of the stadium, and I can't help but laugh softly under my breath. I take her hand and squeeze it, just to find that she's shaking like crazy.

I nudge her shoulder with mine to grab her attention from where she's staring at her feet. She looks all kinds of amazing in her knee-high rainbow Converse, little shorts, and band tee coupled with her rainbow hair. "You okay?"

"I'm good," she says quietly. "Trying not to freak out. You'd think I'd be more chill than this. But I've never been to a concert before, and you did all of this for me. I'm a little overwhelmed."

I pull her to a stop before moving us out of the crowd of people heading toward the stadium. "If this is too much, we can wait out here before going in. Or we don't have to go in at all."

She takes a deep breath and looks up to the sky. "There's no way in hell we're not going in. I tend to avoid big crowds because they make me anxious as fuck. I thought I'd be okay, but apparently my brain is working against me. I just need a minute, and I'll be fine. Sorry."

"Dude, you have *nothing* to apologize for. You do whatever you need to. I'm chill." We move to sit on a bench, and I give her the space she needs to get herself together. My phone buzzes in my pocket, so I slip it out and take a quick look.

Panda:

Are you here yet?

I can't help but grin. I've missed his face so goddamn much. I've been away from tour life for too long.

Me:

Yup! Just outside, shouldn't be too long. I'll find you as soon as we're in.

Panda:

I'll hang around near the back doors, so just head this way, don't worry about going through the front.

Me:

You rock, P! See you soon

I drop a message to the security guy too, so he has my number should anything happen, before tucking my phone away and focusing on Indi. Her eyes are closed and she's breathing deeply, as if she's meditating, but her smile grows. That's all I really give a fuck about anyway. An anxiety attack definitely wasn't part of the plan today, but I've been there, so I totally get it.

She opens her eyes and bounces to her feet, practically vibrating positivity. "Let's do this!"

I grin at her, glad to see her back to her usual self, and get to my feet. "Hell yes! Panda messaged me, and he's waiting for us round the back. We can head to the crew entrance, so we don't need to deal with the crowds and lines out front."

"You freaking rock. Sorry for freaking out just then. Also, who the fuck is Panda?"

"You have nothing to be sorry about, and you don't need to explain. If I said I'd never had a panic attack, I'd be flat out lying. And Panda is... well, Panda. He's one of my dad's old roadies. He isn't much older than us, and he's a fucking legend." I shrug and link my arm with hers. "Now let's go enjoy the rest of your birthday, shall we?"

"Lead the way, oh wise one!" she jokes, and I laugh. It doesn't take long to get to the back, and I drop Panda a message when we're close.

"V baby!" I look up and see the metal door opening, and I squeal. I run toward him and leap into his giant fucking arms. The guy's a fucking tree, catching me easily before spinning me around. "I missed you!"

"I missed you too, P!" I squeeze him before he puts me down. Indi reaches us, and I smile at her sheepishly as she checks my friend out. "Sorry, P, this is my girl Indi. Indi, this is Panda."

"That's one hell of a name." She gives him a wicked grin, and he groans.

"You wear eyeliner one time and end up with a name like Panda. I swear to fuck, it's going to follow me for a lifetime. My name is Evan, it's nice to meet you! You must be the birthday girl. Welcome to the Psycho Girl tour." He shakes her hand, and her excitement goes up a few notches as she bounces on the balls of her feet. If I wasn't convinced she's head over heels for Jackson, I'd swear she was crushing. P has that charm about him that puts you instantly at ease. He also looks like a golden fucking Adonis, so I get it. I'd be lying if I said I hadn't rocked a major crush on him before now.

"I mean, was it questionable eyeliner?" she asks, and he grins. I laugh, thinking about that night.

"He forgot he had it on, rubbed his eyes, and well… It was really hot in Atlanta. It smudged a lot, so he became Panda." He grabs me by the waist and lifts me, tickling me while Indi laughs.

"What the fuck's going on out here?" a shout comes from inside the stadium halls. Indi's eyes go wide with fear, but I smile wider as P puts me down.

"Mac!" I basically attack him as he walks into view, and his anger disappears as soon as he sees me.

"V, is that really you?" He blinks down at me for a second before hugging me back, and P moves to stand by Indi, making her feel included. I love him for that. This is her birthday, and I'm sucking all the fun up.

"Hey, Mac," I say quietly, squeezing him before I let go. "Indi, this is Mac. Mac, this is Indi, my bestie from back home."

"It's good to meet you, Indi. I didn't realize you were coming tonight." He almost looks sad to see me, but I know that's because of the last time we were here together. I feel the pain in my very fucking soul, but I refuse to let all of my baggage ruin this day for Indi.

"P helped me keep it a secret so I could surprise you guys. It's Indi's birthday, and she's a huge Midnight Blue fan," I explain, and he nods.

He moves over to Indi and talks to her quietly for a minute before hugging her. "Thank you for looking after my girl."

I swear I get all misty, and I look up to the sky to stop the tears that threaten to spill over. Tonight is not about me, and I'm not ruining this eyeliner.

"Now, that's enough of this mushy shit. Let's go find Jenna and the girls, shall we?" Mac coughs and bangs his fist against his chest, going hyper macho. I can't help but giggle a little.

"Let's do it," I say, grabbing Indi's shaking hand. "Tonight is going to be fucking awesome."

"You're in for a treat tonight too. They're unveiling the new single live tonight," P tells us as we enter the stadium and the chaos that is the backstage area before a show. Indi huddles closer to me. I'd almost forgotten how nuts it can get backstage, but at P's words, her excitement overtakes her. She practically bounces next to me, eyes wide.

"Best. Birthday. Ever!"

We head to the green room to meet the girls before the gig, and Indi is so nervous. She keeps shaking out her hands before clenching her fists, over and over again. It's like she's literally fizzing.

I adore her so freaking much.

It's the only reason I'm clinging to the happy she's putting out. Because inside, I feel like I'm dying a little. Walking these halls is crushing. The last time I walked them, I found my dad. He just looked like he was asleep, and then I saw the pill bottles, the bottles of whiskey, and the tinge of blue on his lips. I'll never forget that moment. Sometimes I see it when I close my eyes, and I hate that it's my last memory of him.

I still don't believe he was trying to kill himself. They ruled it as a suicide, but I think it was accidental.

Mac squeezes my shoulder as we close in on the green room, and I guess he's remembering the same thing I am.

At least we're not heading to the dressing room. I'm pretty sure that that would break me fully, and that's the last thing I want tonight.

"You ready?" I ask Indi, forcing as much excitement and happiness into my voice as I can. Hopefully she can't see the strain in my smile through her nerves.

"I am *so* ready."

She's like a kid at Christmas, and it's adorable.

"Please don't let me word vomit on them?" she asks, clutching my arm, and I giggle a little.

"I swear I will stop you if that should happen."

She nods and hugs me, just outside the green room

door. "This is why I love you the most."

Panda grins at me, his hand on the door handle before opening it a little and popping his head through the space.

"Get out of the way, Panda! Where's my girl?" Jenna's low, husky voice reaches me seconds before her beautiful face appears around the door frame. "There she is!"

She rushes me and hugs me, jumping with excitement. It's been a minute since I saw her last, but she's one of the few people who was there for me throughout all of the stuff with Dad. Indi's eyes go wide as she leans against the wall, and I pull out of the hug. "It's so good to see your face."

"Yours too, bitch, don't hide from us for so long next time. Selena's been like a nagging mom, totally on my ass about getting you out to see us." I can't help but laugh at her dramatics as she flicks her long pink hair over her shoulder. Truthfully, though, Selena, who's the drummer of Midnight Blue, is totally the mom of the group.

"I'll try not to get dragged, kicking and screaming, to a hellhole the next time I can't be on tour." I stick my tongue out at her, and she rolls her eyes like I'm the drama queen here. "J, I want to introduce to you my girl, Indi. She's literally been my saving grace since I went back to the Cove. She's something of a fan."

"Hi," Indi squeaks, waving awkwardly at her, and I half want to die on her behalf as red spills across her cheeks.

Jenna's a pro and takes it in her stride, though.

"Thank you for watching out for our girl. Come on, I'll introduce you to the others." She slings an arm over Indi's shoulders like they've been friends forever and drags her inside the green room.

I move to follow them, but Mac stops me with a hand on the shoulder. I turn to face him, and he looks me over like the over protective papa bear he is. He watches me closely while I stand for inspection, cocking an eyebrow at him. "Are you going to be okay being here tonight?"

I nod at him, acting like there isn't an open wound in my chest and I'm not bleeding out all over the floor. "Yes. Tonight isn't about me. I'll be fine."

He gets my hint and nods wordlessly. I'm glad. I don't want him to prod because it won't take much to bring down the carefully constructed walls I put into place to deal with being here tonight. He lets me go into the green room, and Indi is grinning like a cat who got the cream as P snaps pictures of her with the girls. I lean against the doorframe, letting her have her moment with them before they spot me.

She looks so fucking happy, and I'm not going to take that from her. Then Jenna grabs her acoustic and starts playing a ballad version of one of their most popular songs. Indi drops onto the sofa with P, absolutely rapt. It's kind of adorable.

Selena heads over to me and pulls me into her arms wordlessly. To look at her, you'd never think she was the mom of the group. She's absolutely covered head to toe in ink, her eyeliner's thick as fuck, and her blunt black bangs frames her face in a way that almost makes her look like an intimidating badass. But she's one of the softest, cuddliest humans I've ever met in my life.

She lets me go, asking me with a look if I'm good, so I nod and sway with her as Jenna sings. Indi doesn't take her eyes from Jenna as she plays. The song comes to close as a girl I don't recognize enters the room, clipboard in hand. "Time to go, ladies!"

"Let's do this!" Emmy, the bassist shouts, and a whoop goes up around the room. "You going to come hang with us later?"

I look at Indi, who looks fully starstruck, so I answer Emmy myself. "You bet your ass we are."

"Yes, bitch!" Jenna high fives me as she passes me. "Enjoy the show, Indi!"

They leave us with P, and Mac follows them, ever on guard. "You ready to go watch?"

"I don't think my legs are working," Indi says, the awe in her voice evident.

"Want to watch from backstage?" P asks, and I love him a little more in that moment. Watching without the crush of the crowd is absolutely my favorite way to gig, but I look to Indi because this is up to her.

She nods, and she finally jumps to her feet. "Lead the way, maestro!"

Seventeen

"Morning, sunshine!" Indi bounces onto my bed, and I groan, rolling over. The sun spills into the room through the open windows, and I pull the duvet over my head. We stayed out way later last night than I've stayed out in forever, and I definitely forgot how much roadies drink. I never used to partake; but when Jenna and the girls invited us out with them, and the crew came too, I decided to let loose. Indi was there with me, shot for shot, so I have no idea how she's exuding her usual dose of sunshine like she is, but I am so not ready for it right now.

"Oh come on, grump. The sun is shining, the views are beautiful, and yesterday was possibly the best day of my life!" She literally bounces on the bed, singing her words. It's a little bit annoying, but it still draws a smile out of me. I peek out from the sheets to find her grinning down at me.

"I have coffee coming."

"Thank fuck," I groan as I squint through the blazing sunlight. My head pounds, and I almost want to just crawl under the covers again. "I'm glad you had so much fun."

"Are you kidding me? After my little meltdown over meeting the girls, I thought I was toast. But everyone was so nice, and watching the show from backstage was fucking epic! Then going out after and being treated like a freaking goddess... What about that isn't something I'd love? Best. Night. Ever!" Her joy is infectious, and my hangover ebbs a little.

I climb out of the sheets and sit up in bed, basking in her joy as she scrambles over me and jumps under the covers beside me. She rests her head on my shoulder, and I lean my head against hers, resting with narrowed eyes until a knock on the door jolts us into action. I climb from the bed in my tank and boy shorts, sorting out the tray of room service she ordered for us. I groan as I lift the plate lids and piles of bacon and eggs stare up at me. She walks into the main room of the suite and grins while I drool over the food and coffee. "You are a goddess."

"I know." She grins before coming to sit with me at the small dining table. We spread the plates out and pick at the food in a comfortable silence as music plays softly in the background. It doesn't take us long to inhale the food and coffee, and once we're done, I feel like I could sleep for an eternity again, but I don't want to waste the time we have on our trip.

"What do you want to do today before we head home?" I ask, and she almost looks shocked.

"We're not going straight home?" she asks, and I shake my head, finishing the dregs of my coffee.

"No, I figured we could chill here for most of the day and head home later, but if you want to go straight home, we can. It's your birthday, and the world is your oyster."

She claps her hands together and does a little dance in her chair, and I can't help but grin at the sheer amount of joy bottled inside of one very small human. "Zoo! I want to go to the zoo so bad, and then maybe we can go snorkeling at La Jolla? Can we do both? Do we have time?"

"We can do whatever you want." I grin, basking in the glow of joy she's emitting. "So if you wanna do both, we can totally do both."

"Yes!" She jumps to her feet and continues her wiggling happy dance. "I'm going to get ready. I am too excited."

She bounces all the way to the bathroom, and I laugh, pouring myself another cup of coffee. Pulling up the San Diego zoo website on my phone, I buy us two all inclusive passes before looking for a snorkeling company in La Jolla. My dad always made a big deal out of birthdays, and it's the one tradition I'm determined to continue.

By the time she's done in the shower, I have everything

booked that she asked for, and then jump in the bathroom to get ready myself. I wash off the grime from last night. As much fun as gigs are, they're totally gross. I hate myself a little for not showering before I passed out last night.

It takes a little longer than I'd like to get myself ready for the day, the sluggishness from last night slowing me down. By the time I'm washed and dressed, Indi has our bags packed and the room straightened up.

She's like the goddamn Energizer bunny.

I wouldn't have her any other way, though. "Ready to go?" My question is a little redundant, but her eyes flash with mirth as she nods and grabs her bag.

"I am so ready. Let's do this, San Diego!"

Our day in San Diego was fucking amazing. I don't remember the last time I went to the zoo or went snorkeling. Or even just had a fun, almost regular day. It's been so fucking refreshing and clarifying. It woke my soul up a little.

The drive home has me exhausted after the last forty-eight hours, so as I pull up out the front of Indi's house, relief floods me. Reds, purples, and pinks paint the sky as dusk hits, and my bed is calling my name. I texted the security guy before we left and confirmed the new cameras and sensors were in place, but he said he'd be gone by the time I got home, and also confirmed that whoever got in before was a tech wizard, because the tapes were cut, but there was no trace of the hack into the system at all. Not scary at all. Nope.

He also sent me some lengthy instructions on how to set the new system but I'll check that out later.

"Thank you so much for the best birthday ever," Indi says, wrapping an arm around my neck and hugging me tight.

"It was my pleasure. Thank you for being the best friend ever."

"You're going to make me cry if you keep being this nice to me," she says as she pulls back, her eyes already a little watery.

I smile and shake my head at her, the little softie. "Then prepare to cry, my friend, because I'm not going to stop. You're a beautiful human, and if I can do things to bring the joy to you that you give me, then I'm going to."

She laughs as a tear runs down her face. She wipes it away with a shaky sigh before saying, "See, look what you did. I'm going to go now, before I start ugly crying."

"Go on," I laugh. "I'll see you tomorrow?"

She shakes her head, looking a little sad. "Tomorrow is family day for my birthday, I have aunts and uncles and all sorts coming in for a big dinner. I'd invite you, but my family is weird as fuck. Plus, one of my cousins is weirdly obsessed with you."

I bark out a laugh. There are absolutely zero interesting things about me to be obsessed with. "You're fine. I should probably get some decent sleep and down time. I'll see you on Monday then."

"You will," she says before climbing out of the car and grabbing her bag from the back. "I love you, and thank you again for the best birthday ever. Drive safe and let me know when you're home."

"I absolutely will. Have a good sleep. I'll speak to you soon."

She closes the door, and I wait until she's in the house before I pull away and head home. I swear my eyes hurt— I'm that freaking tired, but it was so worth it. The drive home doesn't take long, but as I get closer, the thumping sound of loud bass shakes the car and I groan.

Of course Lincoln's having a party. The one night I want to sleep, there's going to be so much noise that sleep is going to be a long time coming. I can't complain too much. It isn't even that late, but damn. All I want to do is crawl into bed.

I put in the new code for the gate that the security guy sent over and head up the drive. I should put the car in the garage, but I really can't be fucked. One night out front won't hurt. I groan at myself and decide to move it into the garage, especially with the party next door. Knowing my luck, some asshole will discover the gate and egg my car or some shit, and this car has been through enough in its short time with me.

Once the car's secure, I trudge into the house, shutting off the alarm. It's so eerie when it's this empty and dark. It's way too big for one person really. I have no idea how Smithy survived years in this place alone, but it's home, so I doubt I'm going to change it any time soon.

I drop my bag in the entry hall. The bass from next door isn't so bad in here, but I swear I can feel the low thump inside of my chest, almost in time with my heartbeat. I head to the kitchen and put on the coffee pot, and the smell is freaking divine as it brews. I figure if I'm not getting any sleep for a while with the noise anyway, why not?

I finally go through the new security details, happy that this new system has a room by room system, meaning I can have the ground floor protected but still keep the door in my room open to let in some fresh air. I don't like to sleep with the air conditioning on if I can help it.

A crash out front draws my attention, and I groan. If their party overspills here, I'm going to be pissed. The Saint house is plenty big enough—there's no reason for people to sneak over here.

Fuck my life.

I slip my Chucks back on, glad I left my hoodie on, and

check the monitors before I head out front. I can't really see anything on the monitors, though, and sigh. Of course I can't. That would make my life too simple. The new alarm system might be awesome, but maybe I need to call him back and upgrade the cameras.

I find a group of drunk assholes literally starting an orgy around the side of the house. "How the fuck did y'all get over here?"

My shout seems to startle them, like they hadn't even considered there would be someone home. The girl giggles as she does the buttons on her shirt up and one of the guys groans. "We didn't think there would be anyone here. The lights were all off."

"Well there is, but you didn't answer my question." I fold my arms over my chest. I'm aware I don't look even remotely intimidating, but fuck it.

"There's a break in the fence, through the trees. It isn't easy to find, and we came across it by accident," one of the other guys says as he zips up his jeans.

Of course there fucking is. Fuck my life.

"Show me?" I ask, and the guy nods. They lead me over to the hidden entry, and I curse under my breath. It isn't big—they had to have squeezed through—but it's big enough. I mean, it wouldn't be the end of the world usually; but with Lincoln having a party, it's a problem. They head through the gap, and I follow them through, coming face-to-face with the man in question.

"What are you doing?" he sneers as I come through the trees with the disheveled group. They scurry away at the sound of his voice, leaving me alone with him. Cowards.

"Coming to find you. I found them up against the house, starting a private party of their own. They showed me a weak spot between the properties," I explain, and I can tell he doesn't believe me from the sneer on his face. "I'll get it sorted out, but if you can keep your drunken rabble of friends away from here, that'd be awesome."

"Where were you? The house was dark. It's never dark," he asks, completely ignoring my request. I don't know why I'm shocked, but I can't tell if I'm more shocked that he ignored me or that he noticed I was gone.

"Not that it's any of your business, but I was away with Indi for her birthday."

"The girl with rainbow hair?" he asks, and I nod. "Where's Smithy?"

I sigh, exasperated. "With his family, there was an emergency. Can you keep people away from here, or do I need to call someone out tonight to sort it out?"

"I'll keep people off your property." He scans the front of his house. The party is in full swing and spills out here. There are people everywhere, so good luck to him with that.

"Thanks," I say before turning my back on him and

heading home through the gap in the fence. He doesn't say anything else, and I don't expect him to.

I pull out my phone and set a reminder to call someone about the fence tomorrow, then remember to text Indi as I head back into the kitchen. I make sure all the doors are locked and the alarm is set on my way.

Me:

I'm home, party next door. All the fun

Indi:

Assholes. Earplugs?

Me:

Nah, I'm going to fuck around in the music room for a bit, just exhaust myself so I don't care about the noise.

Indi:

Sounds like a plan. I'm going to pass out. Good luck with the noise!

I pour a mug of coffee and pad downstairs to the music room. The quiet is such joy after an intense few days. I sit down at the piano, flicking through the sheet music I started writing when I was down here last.

I twinkle my fingers on the ivory, falling back into

the place of utter peace at the feel of it at my fingertips. Emotion swells in my chest as everything I shoved down last night wells up. Being back there, with the people who loved my dad almost as much as I did, hurt me. But they're the only people who seem to miss him like I do. Nobody else knew him like we did, not really. They didn't see the highs and lows that came with tour life, with the success and the fame, or with the crazy fans and people who only seemed to want things from him.

I won't lie and say it was easy, but his love for music made it all worth it to him. I can't say that I agree with those decisions, but they weren't mine to make for him. Even if I think the toll of it all is part of why he isn't with me anymore.

I let my emotions flow out through my fingertips and onto the ivory as tears stream down my face. I find myself playing the song I wrote with him at the beginning of summer, and I sing through my tears. My voice breaks as I sing, but I keep going. Music's the best therapy I'm going to get. I play and cry until my shoulders shake and until my tears blur my vision so much that I can't see anymore. I close the lid on the piano and fall apart in the one place that I can feel my dad in this entire house.

I curl up in a ball in the corner, my heart in a million pieces in my chest, until the tears won't come any more. I miss him more than I can express, but music makes me feel so close to him. Being at that stadium last night with everyone made everything so raw.

Once I've gotten a hold of myself, I trudge up the stairs to my room, too broken to care about the noise anymore. I crawl into bed still in my hoodie and leggings. I close my eyes and let sleep take me to a place of peace that I can't seem to find when I'm awake.

Something startles me awake. The room is still dark and silent, but it feels wrong somehow. An icy drop of dread runs down my spine and my hair stands on end as I spot something moving in the darkness of my room. My heart races, and I can hear the blood rushing through my veins, like white noise in my ears as I become hyperaware of my surroundings.

Someone is in here with me. I don't know how I know, but I just do.

I move to try to grab my phone from the bedside table, but a hand clasps around my ankle and pulls. I scream, and another hand clamps over my mouth.

Everything Mac ever taught me about self-defense goes right out the window as I try to fight off my attacker. More hands cover me, and I suddenly realize there isn't one person here.

There are at least three.

Fear floods my system with icy dread, and my blood feels like it's on fire as I try to kick and wriggle out of their hold as I'm ripped from my bed.

They don't say a word as they manhandle me. I lash out with my hands when one of them captures my wrists in one hand, and it would be silent if not for my grunts of protest.

I try to bite the one who has their hand on my mouth. I just barely manage it, and the attacker lets go, hissing. The top half of my body starts to fall, and I think I might have a chance, so I flail. They drop me, and the breath leaves my body as I crash to the floor.

I can't move for a second. It's like my soul is ripped from my body for a minute, and then everything whooshes back to me. I scramble onto my hands and knees as I try to crawl away. I can't see shit—it's too dark—but there's a pressure on my back, and I'm forced to the floor, face down. One of them is on top of me, grappling with me until they have my hands bound in theirs behind my back. I scream out again, and someone pushes my face harder into the carpeted floor to smother the sound.

I suck in a breath, but my mouth's covered again as I'm lifted.

I hear the door open before they start walking with me, but we don't go far before I'm thrown. I smash against a wall. A door slams closed, and what little light there was completely disappears. I move to stand and get stuck.

That's when I realize where I am.

The half closet in the hall.

No, no, no.

This can't be happening. I can't even stand up in here, it's so small.

I bang on the door, screaming at the top of my lungs when I can't get it open.

Please, God, no.

"Please! Please let me out," I beg, my voice breaking as fear grips me round the throat. "Please."

I feel a pressure against the door, and I know someone's out there, leaning against it.

"You don't have to do this. Please. You can take whatever you want, but please don't keep me in here."

I push against the door with everything I have and scream until my throat is hoarse.

I can't be trapped in here.

Not again.

Panic swells in my throat, and it feels like I can't breathe.

I need to get out.

So I bang, kick, and push against the door until my hands bleed. I scream until no more sound comes from my ravaged throat. Tears stream hotly down my face.

I hear movement outside the door as someone walks away from the cupboard. I push against the door in hope, but I'm crushed, realizing that the door is locked. I'm trapped.

I fall to the floor, spent, curling in a ball and rocking.

I can get through this.

Someone will come for me.

Someone will find me in here.

Right?

Eighteen

EAST

I've messaged Octavia five times since she was due home, and she hasn't responded to one of them. Usually I wouldn't worry, but Smithy isn't at the house, and he asked me to check in on her. That's hard to do when she won't answer the goddamn phone. I've paced around my room for the last half hour trying to convince myself not to go over there.

She could still be sleeping. She had a big weekend. But it's nearly lunchtime, and she's usually an early riser.

I could be worrying about nothing. Considering the threats that hang over us all—especially her, though she doesn't know it yet—I'm feeling overly paranoid.

I know Lincoln has a plan to get her to leave, but it doesn't seem to be working. I don't want her to leave, which is why I've kept myself removed from it all. Do I want her to be safe? Yes. But I'm the only one who seems to think I can keep her safe by keeping her close.

My brother doesn't agree with me, but from what I've seen, he doesn't seem to be able to stay away from her either.

When she first left, the four of us moped around for about a year. We might have been young, but every single one of us was in love with her. Sure, we might not have realized it back then, but seeing her again was like a punch in the gut. I thought I'd gotten over the puppy love, but I obviously haven't.

I can't say the same for the others—they're all so coveted these days—but I wouldn't be surprised if they felt it too. There's something about Octavia Royal that is completely undeniable.

I look down at my phone again and growl. "Fuck this."

Grabbing my hoodie, I head out through the back of the house and through the hidden gate that joins the two properties. Stone Royal installed it when we were kids.

All of the lights are still off, which isn't unusual, and I can't shake the feeling that something's wrong.

I grab the spare key that Smithy left me for emergencies and let myself in.

The alarm isn't on.

My heart rate spikes. There's no way she wouldn't have set it, right? She wouldn't have been in this giant house alone without the alarm on.

"Octavia!" I yell out, not giving a fuck if she's asleep. My blood feels like it's on fire, and I'm frantic to figure out what the fuck is going on. I move through the house, yelling her name, before I hear a whimper coming from upstairs.

I swear to fucking Christ, if they got to her, I'll burn down their world and bathe in their blood.

"Help me, please," she yells, sounding so fucking broken as I run up the stairs and crash into her room. She's not here, but there was clearly a struggle.

There's a faint tapping down the hall, so I follow it, trying not to panic. It gets closer before disappearing again.

"Octavia!" I shout, hoping she calls out again.

"East…" her voice is scratchy as fuck, but I realize she's in the cupboard at the top of the stairs. What the fuck happened here? She would never crawl in there on her own. She hates small spaces. I try to open the door, but it's locked.

Fuck this shit.

"V, sweetheart," I say as softly as I can while rage pulses through me. I know she needs a sense of calm right now, so that's what I'm going to be for her. "I need you to cover your face so you don't get hurt when I get this door open, okay? Move as far away from the door as you can for me."

She whimpers a soft, "Okay," and anger floods me again.

I take a deep breath before punching a hole in the door to the left of the handle and ripping my way through it.

My heart breaks when I see her.

She's curled up on the floor, her fingernails bleeding, looking completely broken. I lean down and slide my hands under her, lifting her and cradling her against my chest. "I got you, V."

I murmur and coo comforts to her as I walk her down the hall to the bathroom. She needs to be cleaned up, but the way she grips my shirt makes me want to commit fucking murder.

I sit her on the counter in the bathroom and start the taps on the clawfoot tub, all while keeping contact with her. Once the taps are running, and I've poured in some bubble bath, I focus all of my attention on her. The way her hair's ruffled and her tear-stained cheeks. Then there's the fact that she won't look up. Instead, she stares at the floor like she's still afraid. The dried blood from where she tried to escape, or maybe even fight back, coats her skin. I clench my hands at my sides because getting angry won't help her. I tuck a finger beneath her chin and lift her head so that she's looking at me. My heart breaks for her, and I declare war in my mind on whoever did this to her. "What happened, V?"

My voice is gentle, trying to coax her to talk; but when she tries, there's barely a noise. It's as if she screamed herself silent, and I hate that I didn't hear her screams and get to her sooner. I'm furious that I wasn't here to protect her so she didn't have to scream at all.

"It's okay. You can tell me later. Let's get you in the bath, yeah?" Her eyes go wide, and she shakes her head frantically. Her fingers dig into my forearms, like if she lets me go, I'll leave her alone again. "I'm not going anywhere, okay? I've got you. We just need to clean you up a bit."

I try to get her out of her clothes, but she's shaking so badly, it's almost impossible. She won't let me go, so I quit trying to make her.

Fuck it.

I shut off the taps and kick off my shoes before lifting her into my arms. She's still shaking, even when I hold her, and it pisses me off. I take a deep breath, shoving my rage down to deal with once I know she's okay. After that, I'll gladly lose my shit.

I step into the tub fully clothed with her against my chest and sit with her. I try to clean the blood from her arms, hands, and legs as much as I can, but it's difficult since she's still mostly dressed. "V, can you take off the hoodie so I can make sure there's no more injuries?"

She nods, but it's barely a movement as she curls up on my chest. I strip the hoodie from her and drop the sopping wet bundle on the floor. I don't give a fuck about the mess, that's a problem for later. I scour her with my eyes, but it doesn't look like she has any other physical injuries. No, whoever did this knew it would hurt her in a much deeper way than that.

Then it hits me.

Those fucking little assholes.

I clench my jaw and take a deep breath. I'll deal with them as soon as I have her settled. I help her wash, stripping her down as we go, then wash and rinse her hair. "We need to get out now, okay?"

She nods, and I lift her from the bath, grabbing a towel and wrapping it around her. Doing this fully clothed wasn't the greatest idea, but there's no way I was stripping down and climbing into a bath with her naked when she's like this. Once I pat her hair dry and drop her robe around her shoulders, I climb out of my clothes and quickly wrap a towel around my waist. "I'll be back in two seconds, okay?"

She looks up at me with those big brown eyes of hers and just blinks.

I run to the spare room, which I know probably still has some of Stone's old shit in it, and grab a pair of sweats. I throw them on and rush back to her, finding her sitting where I left her, staring down at her cut up hands.

I contemplate whether I should ask her to walk but

think better of it and pick her back up in my arms and carry her to her room. "Let's get you dressed and back into bed."

She blinks at me as I sit her on the stool by her dresser before I rush into her closet, grabbing a pair of leggings and a tank for her. I don't bother with underwear. She needs to sleep, and sleeping in a bra doesn't sound like a good time.

I finish getting her dry and help her into the clothes, but she's still shaking like a leaf.

Blood will be spilled today.

"Let's get you into bed, okay?" Her eyes go wide, and she shakes her head, clinging to me like I'm her only lifeline. Right now, I just might be.

It suddenly hits me that she was probably asleep when they dragged her from the room. Fucking hell.

"I have another idea, okay?" She calms a little and sags against me. "Can you walk?"

She blinks up at me again, still fully mute, and I swear to God I see fucking red.

"It's okay. I've got you."

I gather her into my arms and walk through the house, not bothering to lock it up. I'll deal with that later. Right now, my sole priority is her. I walk barefoot and half dressed across her yard with her lying against my chest. Crossing onto my property, I see Maverick leaving the house. My eyes narrow at him as shock registers on his face.

I'll deal with that twisted little asshole later. I keep her held against my chest as I pad into the house, up the stairs, and to my room. "You can sleep here today, okay? You're safe in here."

She nods, and I tuck her into my bed, drawing the curtains closed to shroud the room in darkness. I leave a sliver of sunlight so she doesn't freak out after being locked in that fucking closet all night.

"Cold." The one word is all her scratchy voice manages, so I root through one of the drawers in my dresser and find her my old college hoodie. If the situation were different, seeing her in my hoodie would do things to me, but right now, I just want to look after her.

I pull it over her head, helping her slip her arms into it, and tuck her back in once she's basically drowning in the sweater.

"Thank you," she sighs as she closes her eyes. "Don't leave."

There's no way on this fucking earth I'm going to deny her a damn thing, so I climb on top of the sheets on the other side of the bed, giving her space. But then she rolls over and tucks herself into my chest and closes her eyes again. It doesn't take long for her breathing to slow, and I'm sure she's so exhausted she has no option but to sleep. I don't know how long she'll actually manage to rest after what happened last night, so I settle in for the long haul, stroking her hair.

I'll deal with those little fuckers later.

I leave Octavia sleeping in my room. Her sleep has been anything but restful, and my rage has done nothing but simmer and grow all day in response. By the time I manage to slip away, darkness is falling. I find Linc in the game room. I grab the nearest thing I can find and launch it at the TV. I'd rather it be his head, but I'd also prefer to make him bleed with my own fists than the random trophy I launched.

"What the actual fuck?" he roars, jumping to his feet and turning, finding me standing behind him. I don't even care that the TV is busted up and he looks spitting mad. His anger has nothing on my pulsing rage.

"What the fuck? What the fuck? You have got to be shitting me, Linc. I know you're not asking me what the fuck I just did because *what the actual fuck did you do?*" I'm practically foaming at the mouth, shaking where I stand. I stay where I'm standing because I know if I move toward him, I'll beat his idiotic face in.

The cold persona that he uses on everyone else washes over him, and he transforms from my little brother into Lincoln Saint, the boy genius who isn't afraid of getting his hands dirty. The kid that makes fully grown men piss themselves. "I have no idea what you're talking about."

I pick up the closest thing to hand, a glass vase, and launch that at him too. He ducks quickly enough that it doesn't hit him, but it still smashes to shards on the wall behind him. "Don't feed me your bullshit company line, Linc. I know you had a plan to get her to leave. I know you did this. You've gone too fucking far. She's broken!"

Emotion flickers in his eyes, and I can see the doubt creep in. Despite my rage, there's still a part of me that knows he's trying to save her in his own way, but this is too fucking much. "You said you didn't want to be a part of this. You don't get to storm in now and tell me what I've done is wrong. Anyway I haven't done anything to her for weeks. At least if she's broken, she'll leave. Better broken and alive…"

He trails off and pinches the bridge of his nose. His words deflate me and my rage entirely. The alternative doesn't bear thinking about, and I'm still not convinced I believe him about not being the one who fucked with her last night. Who else could know the significance of locking her in a closet? But I don't want him to lie to me, and I know just how ruthless Linc is when it comes to her and her safety. I won't ask him outright because we don't lie to each other, and I don't want him to have to, but I am done with all of this.

"We can't put her through this. If she doesn't leave,

you need to find another way. *We* need to find another way. I want her safe, happy, and out of their clutches."

He laughs haughtily, watching me with those hawk-like eyes of his. "You still love her, don't you?"

"Are you trying to tell me you don't?" I ask, quirking an eyebrow. He shakes his head and drops down into the leather chair beside him.

He sighs and leans his head back, looking up at the ceiling. "Even if I did, nothing could ever come of it. She isn't safe here. Plus, the other two... When it comes to Octavia Royal, everything is always way too complicated."

No truer words have ever been spoken.

Nineteen

OCTAVIA

Spending the last day and night in East's bed isn't exactly how I pictured my weekend ending. He walked me back to the house this morning so I could get ready for school, and only left after my insistence that I'd be okay. I'd set the alarm and locked the door as he'd watched from the back patio.

I'm not going to lie, walking back into my house alone might be one of the hardest things I've done these last few months. However, I refuse to let whoever it was that did that to me win. I've already survived too much to let this be the thing that breaks me.

Well, fully break me. I'm definitely partially broken.

Who would have thought that it would only take four weeks to break me?

Except, I'm also my father's daughter, and there's too

much fight left in me to tuck tail and run. I have very little doubt it was someone from school. I'm also fairly certain it was the three people who knew exactly how much locking me in a small space would fuck me up, but I have no proof.

Even if I did, what could I do?

Absolutely fuck all, that's what.

So I'm going to go to school and pretend like nothing happened. Letting them see how fucked up I am about it all gives them more power than I'm willing to relinquish.

So I pad up the stairs, still wrapped up in East's hoodie. I've been wearing it since he found me yesterday morning, but it smells like him, and right now, he's my safe harbor in these shark infested waters.

As I reach my bedroom door, I freeze, my hands shaking at my sides. I close my eyes and clench my fists. I hate feeling so fucking weak. I hate that they found a way to make me crumble, but what I mostly hate is how much rage I feel toward my dad for putting me in this position in the first place.

If he hadn't left me, I wouldn't be here. I wouldn't be going through this. I'd still be safely out on tour, living my life the way I always have. I wouldn't be subject to the webs of lies and torture that is Echoes Cove.

If I don't get my dad's inheritance, it goes back into my trust. If that happens, my guardians might get access to it. I'm not convinced that isn't why people want me to leave. Considering how close Blair and Lincoln seem to be, it wouldn't surprise me if she asked him for help. She must have a magical pussy to get him to bend to her will like that, though.

I hate how fucked up the thought makes me feel. Him fucking her. Him being on her side. That she really has replaced me when it comes to those three. I can't help but wonder if he crawls into her bed and holds her the way he used to hold me.

I shake the thoughts off and cross the threshold to my room, taking deep breaths as I undress before changing into my uniform. I take extra care doing my hair and makeup, making sure no one can tell I've slept like shit the last two nights. I don't want to look affected by the nightmare that plays on a loop when I close my eyes.

A shudder runs down my spine as I think about it again, and tears prick my eyes. I blink them back. I fucking *refuse* to cry over it anymore. They don't deserve any more of my tears.

I find my phone on the nightstand where I left it and grab the charger before heading down to the kitchen. East called Smithy for me yesterday to let him know why I was MIA but told him to stay with his family as long as he needed. His sister is in a bad way, and I don't want to be the reason he isn't there for her.

I plug my phone into the charger once I'm in the kitchen

and start the coffee pot. Looking through the refrigerator, my stomach flips at the sight of all the food, so I grab the cream cheese, then put a bagel in the toaster. I get lost in my own head while I'm waiting, staring out into the yard. When my bagel pops up, I let out a little scream.

Fuck my actual life.

Get a grip, Octavia.

I shake myself off and sort out my bagel and coffee before putting the TV on so there's at least some background noise. I don't need the creaking of the house to freak me out entirely. My phone starts to buzz like crazy as it comes back to life, and I groan.

Twenty text messages and ten missed calls from Indi.

Shit.

Just as I go to open the thread of the messages, my phone rings with a video call. I answer, not bothering to put on a smile. Indi's the one person I won't hide my pain from. She's a true friend, I don't need or want to hide from her.

"Thank fuck you're alive! Where the actual fuck have you been?" she screeches over the line, her eyes crazed.

I run a hand through my hair and sigh raggedly. She stills, her expression changing from angry to concerned at the sound. "Sorry, some shit went down after I texted you Saturday night, and I didn't have my phone until this morning."

"Are you okay? What happened?" Her concern is almost enough to make me cry again. I've never been much of a crier before this fucking year. "Fuck it, I'm coming over. I'll drive us to school, and then you can explain."

"You don't have to—"

"Shut up." She cuts me off, and I can't help but laugh dryly. "I'm already grabbing my shit and heading to the car. I'll be there soon."

The line disconnects, and I stare at the phone. I guess that's that.

My little sunshine friend seems to be finding her confidence, and I couldn't feel prouder.

Now, if only I could find where I put mine.

School's been surreal today. No one spoke to me with disdain. No one spoke about me, or at least not that I heard, and no one tried to fuck with me. Well, except for Blair and her merry little band of bitches, but having them leave me alone would be a goddamn miracle at this point. I don't know what happened between Saturday night and today, but it's like I've become a wallflower, and I'm so here for it.

The football team still sat with us at lunch. Though Indi sat beside me rather than opposite me like normal with me sitting at the end of the table. That way none of them could get too close to me, and I love her for it. To say Indi went nuclear when I explained what happened and why it fucked me up so much is the understatement of the century. I've never heard her cuss quite like that. She was like a stabby little viper spitting venom.

It was crazy and kind of awesome.

She's barely left my side all day. And I genuinely thought she was going to rip into one of my teachers when he tried to hurry her away from my desk. She isn't even in the class with me. Apparently, my little ball of sunshine is also a vicious little ball of fire.

So we're relaxing poolside at my house, sipping on the iced tea I found in the fridge, and sunning ourselves. It isn't normally something I do, but I think after everything that's happened, some decompression time is good.

"Octavia." I sit up, sighing at the sound of Lincoln's unexpected voice. I pull my aviators down so they cover my eyes and I can actually see. Indi looks just about ready to fight him if he starts fucking with us. I can't blame her. She fully agreed with me that they're the most likely culprits for what happened Saturday night.

The only thing that has my guard coming down is that when I look over toward him, I find him flanked by Finley, Maverick, and East.

I know that East won't hurt me. He never has, and

there isn't one thing about him that makes me think he ever would.

"What do you want?" Indi snaps, and I can't help but smirk. Lincoln's face mirrors mine, which only makes me more suspicious. He never reacts well to people calling him out, or at least, he never used to.

"Calm down, little miss warrior. We come in peace," Maverick jabs at her, and she flips him the bird before settling back down on her lounger.

"If you say so, asshole." She lifts her book to cover her face, nodding at me. I know if shit goes sideways, she'll absolutely throw hands for me. Not that I'm sure either of us could fight them physically if we need to. I've trained in some self-defense, but there's four of them, and none of them are small. Plus the last few attacks I've suffered, I've frozen. So I'm pretty sure I'd be royally screwed if they were here to attack us.

"Can we talk?" Lincoln asks, ever the mouthpiece for the band of them. Thick as thieves. I eye them, and while East looks a little uneasy, the rest of them are pretty much unreadable.

Shocker.

I'm not going to give them even an inch. Every instinct tells me that those three are the three who locked me in that fucking closet, so I won't relax around them or forgive them, unless I'm somehow proved wrong. "I guess that depends on what you want to talk about."

Finley steps forward, hands stuffed in the front pockets of his jeans, and I hate him a little for looking so good. He literally looks like some kind of dark and brooding god. It isn't fair that all four of them are so droolworthy when three of them are such giant assholes. "We want to apologize and call a truce of sorts."

I cock an eyebrow, folding my arms over my chest. "A truce? I don't remember declaring war."

"You declared war by coming back here," Lincoln huffs, and Finley turns to face him, glaring.

"You are not helping. Shut up," he growls, and East clips his brother around the back of the head.

It's amusing to see the dynamics changing so much. Finley has never stepped out on Lincoln before. He's always been their unofficial leader. There's obviously a 50/50 split here with this truce, but if this means they're going to leave me alone, I'll take it. All I ever wanted was to keep my head down and get through this year. I want to graduate as per my dad's wishes, and then do what I need to at college to start my record label.

That's all I've ever wanted.

"What brought on the change of heart?" I'm beyond curious. I have a feeling this all came from East. He did such a great job of looking after me over the weekend; and if he, like me, thinks these assholes were behind it, I wouldn't put it past him to call them out on their shit.

Finley looks back toward me, while Lincoln scowls, and Maverick fidgets. I'm not surprised Maverick leaves the talking to the others. He's always been the kind to fix things with his fists and leave diplomacy to everyone else. Even when we were kids, things were the same.

It's Lincoln who steps forward to answer my question, and his *cold prince* demeanor he wears so well is back. "We have more important things to worry about. If you want to be back here, so be it; but don't come running to us when your world's crumbling."

"She doesn't need to run to you assholes," Indi chirps up, and I can't help but laugh.

"What she said. But whatever," I say with a shrug, lying back on the lounger. "I'll accept the truce. I didn't start this mess anyway. Make sure to call off your bloodhound. If you think Blair is going to take your new declaration lying down, you've got another thing coming."

"We can handle Blair," Lincoln grinds out.

His jaw is clenched, and his shoulders are stiff, showing me just how pissed off my words have him. I'm glad. I don't want to let them see that I'm a mess inside. That I'm afraid to go back into my house after this weekend. If he's angry, he won't see it. They don't need to see or know any of that. "Then we have a deal."

Indi didn't go home until after we ate dinner. When she left, I locked all the doors and set the alarms; and I've hid out in the theatre room ever since. This house is too goddamn big to be in alone. Especially when I jump at every little noise. Indi did offer to stay the night, but honestly, I hate putting that on her.

I don't want to be afraid.

So it's time to sit up and get on with it.

I take a deep breath before I leave the room, making sure all the lights are off.

Do I run through the dark house to the next lit room? You bet your fucking ass I do. I repeat my ridiculous routine until I'm in the kitchen and all that's left to do is reset the alarm and go upstairs.

I take another deep breath, trying to calm my racing heart. My hands shake as I set the alarm for overnight and prepare myself to race to my room. I left the light on up there earlier. I know it's bad for the environment, but dammit, so is my car. It makes me feel safer knowing the light's on, and right now, I need that feeling.

I flip the switch for the light in the kitchen and haul ass through the entrance hall and up the stairs. I'm practically panting by the time I reach my room and slam the door behind me. Leaning against my door, I suck in air until my heartbeat slows.

This is ridiculous. But fuck it. No one's here to watch it.

At least, I hope.

I check the room, the closet, the ensuite, and even under the fucking bed to make sure I'm alone before making sure the balcony door's locked; and then I lock my bedroom door, completing my barrier from the rest of the house. The only thing getting me out of here is a fucking fire.

Please, fucking Jesus, do not jinx me.

Once I'm positive the room's secure, I finally get ready for bed. I can't help but wonder what exactly brought on the white flag that was waved earlier today, but I'm not going to question it. Well, not too hard anyway.

I slide between the sheets and turn off the light before trying to lie down and close my eyes, but every time I do, I see the inside of the cupboard.

I put a podcast on, murder and makeup probably isn't the best thing to fall asleep to, but it's what I have, so it's what's happening; and I can't help but wish someone else was here with me. But at least now, maybe with their truce, I'll finally have a good week.

A girl can dream.

Twenty

I slept like absolute fucking shit. Nightmares plagued me all night, so to say there are bags beneath my eyes might be the understatement of the century. If I managed even an hour of sleep, I'd be amazed.

I pull up at school with Indi in the Wrangler almost holding my breath. Despite the white flag that was waved yesterday, there's a part of me that doesn't trust it, even though East was there. It's not like he was in on the bullshit that came before, so why would they listen to him now?

The whole Finley stepping out on Lincoln to agree with East thing has me off kilter too.

None of it quite makes sense to me, but if the truce means the rest of this year is going to be easier, I'll grab onto it with both hands.

Now, if I can just get past my own trauma to actually

sleep properly again, life will be great.

"I still can't believe you passed on sugary goodness for espresso." Indi shakes her head at me as she pulls into a parking spot. "There's nothing good about pure espresso."

I can't help but bark out a laugh. Despite my extreme tiredness, she's managed to keep me smiling and laughing ever since she picked me up this morning. "Tell that to any Italian and see how far you get. Espresso and pasta are basically a religion. At least to the Italians I've met."

I remember when I went to Rome on my dad's world tour. I snapped the spaghetti to make it fit in the pan, and the horror on the face of the Italian tour manager was enough to make me cry with laughter. Apparently that shit's practically illegal there.

I sip on my espresso, exaggerating my gasp of joy as the bitter beautifulness hits my taste buds, and she scrunches up her face in disgust. "Just no," she hisses, taking a sip of the whipped cream topped iced coffee she clutches in her hands. "Now this shit is good."

She starts to laugh, and I join in, feeling grateful again that she came into my life when she did. The laughter is the most catharsis I've felt over the past twelve or so hours.

I try to fight the yawn that overwhelms me and makes my eyes water, but I lose.

"Will you be okay today?" Indi's concern is heartwarming. She frowns at me again, the same way she did when she arrived at my place and saw my disheveled state. "I can stay till Smithy gets back. Or you can come and stay with me?"

I shake my head, smiling softly before yawning again. "I appreciate it, but no. I'm not going to get over this if I let everyone coddle me. I'll be okay. Nightmares can't hurt me. I just need to push through it."

I pull out my phone, shooting a message to Smithy to check in with him like I promised I would.

"Surviving ECP on so little sleep might not be safe," she snorts, before climbing out of the car. I follow suit, shaking my head because she isn't entirely wrong.

We head into the school, arms linked and smiling. When we reach my locker, I start swapping out my books that I need for the morning. "So, I keep meaning to ask, but forget with all of my bullshit. What's going on with you and Jackson?"

She's uncharacteristically silent. Once I have what I need, I close my locker and look at her. A blush spills across her cheeks, and she wrings out her hands. "We're okay. I thought it might get a little weird after you brushed off Raleigh, but it didn't. He's a lot sweeter than I expected him to be, but we're taking things slow."

"I'm happy for you." I smile down at her, genuinely overjoyed that it's working out for her. She brings so much joy to me, I'm glad I helped her take the leap she needed in that regard.

We head to her locker, while she fills me in on her family stuff. I'm the terrible friend who hadn't asked because I'd been drowning in my own drama, but I can listen. "You didn't miss much. Though when Ella found out we were friends, she went a little crazy. I managed to ice her out, but it was weird as fuck. I'm glad my cousins live on the other side of the country. They all have way too much hype for me. I was exhausted by the time they left. They sapped my well of joy and positivity dry with all of their mania."

"I'm sorry I wasn't around to help," I say sadly.

"I mean, you were literally indisposed, you're fine. I wouldn't put them on you anyway. Families are weird."

It's almost like her words summoned my crazy-ass family. Because once she's finished speaking, Blair stalks past us, bitch squad firmly attached to her ass. She flicks her hair over her shoulder as she passes me, and I can't help but roll my eyes when she glares at me. I guess the muzzle Lincoln put on her isn't one she was happy with.

I shudder at the thought of the two of them together. I refuse to think my feelings are anything beyond disgust. There's a small pang in my heart, but that's just a young girl's crush dying. Once upon a time, Lincoln, Finley, Maverick, and East each owned a piece of my heart. As an almost grown-ass woman, I'm aware that I can't have all of them. Hell, I can't have any of them. But that young girl's crush still exists inside of me somewhere whenever I get a glimpse past all of their bullshit and hate.

Maybe even in spite of it all.

But a young girl's wishes are nothing but that. Reality isn't even close to aligned with those wishes, and I don't know that I'm all that sad about it. Especially considering everything they've done since I got back here.

Especially with what I'm positive they did to me over the weekend.

Except for East—he might be the only one of them who hasn't completely changed. The others, though... Let's just say there are some things a girl can't get over. And there's no reason that I can think of for them to have done that to me.

So I tuck that small girl's crushes deep in the back of my compartmentalized heart and take a deep breath.

Indi's eyes go wide as she looks at me. "Did you remember to do your assignment?"

Well, fuck.

After spending last night cramming with Indi and catching up on every assignment and piece of homework that I've left floating, and forgotten about, it occurred to me while we were working that Lincoln and I are still pretty behind on our Business project. Despite the threats of a fail from the creep that is Mr. Peters, I haven't gotten an F yet. That wasn't something I was going to deal with last night, though. So as I head to my Business class, I steel myself against seeing Mr. Peters and talking to Lincoln to catch up on everything.

I didn't sleep much again last night, the nightmares that haunt me when I slip away into sleep are fucking awful, and I woke up hoarse from screaming again this morning. To say I'm tired is an understatement, and the thought of dealing with Lincoln today doesn't exactly fill me with joy.

Lincoln wasn't an ass to me yesterday, but he wasn't exactly warm and fuzzy either. I'm not sure Lincoln Saint *has* a warm and fuzzy side. It's as if he let East take all of the laid-back and chill vibes as they grew up, and he took on the responsibility that comes with being a Saint in Echoes Cove, growing icier as he did it. I can't say for certain about any of it since I wasn't here, but it's sad to see how much he's changed since I left.

I slide into my seat as the final bell rings and Mr. Peters strolls into the room. A shudder crawls down my spine even just seeing him, the same way it has every time since his disgusting proposal. It would seem the fates are on my side today, though, because he sits down and looks around the room, seeming about as awake as I feel. After a moment, he says, "Buddy up with your partners and discuss your project. I expect your second proposal after Labor Day weekend."

I look over and see Lincoln scowling at me. Awesome.

"What are you looking at?" he snaps, and I roll my eyes at him.

The guy is as mercurial as a thunderstorm. It's freaking exhausting. "Well, you are my partner." I sigh. "I was trying to work out how the fuck we're going to catch up."

"We don't have anything to catch up on," he snarls before reaching into his bag and dropping a folder onto my desk. "All you need to do is read up and write your half of the proposal."

"Not this again." I huff. As if what happened last time he pulled this wasn't bad enough. I can't help but frown at him before flicking through the file. An icy rage fills my veins. "I don't expect you to do all of the work, Lincoln. I'm fully capable of doing my part. After last time, I started my own goddamn proposal. Let me read yours, and I'll work out how to merge them."

"I will not risk my GPA, or my chance to escape this place, on some little rock princess who has no idea how the real world works."

I lean back in my chair, blinking at him. I have no idea where this animosity is coming from, but he looks as tired as I feel. I take a deep breath and decide to take the high road. Snapping at him won't get us anywhere. He also doesn't need to know how much I need my GPA to be on track either. "So much for our truce," I mutter. "I'll take a look at what you've done, and I'll give you my feedback before the weekend so we can finish our proposal before it's due in."

He responds with a grunt before pulling an identical file from his bag and opening it. "There isn't anything that needs feedback. The work is solid."

"I'm sure it is." I sigh, exasperated. Why does he take everything I say the wrong way? I decide the truce is on a very thin layer of ice, so rather than pushing, I turn to the work he's already done and start reading. I slide him over the work I've done too, since I'm not risking another chance at a fail or another proposition from our slimebag teacher. There's no way in hell I'm getting on my knees for him.

The first part of our project was to write a proposal for a business venture, with basic scaling and projections. The second part is to rework it based on feedback with full-scale profit projections. I worked blind, considering I didn't have feedback on the first part; and as I read through Lincoln's work, I kind of hate how solid the project is that he's put together.

There are definitely tweaks to be made and other profit streams that could be explored but considering he went at this alone, he's done a fucking lot of work in a short space of time. I am loath to admit that to him though. Especially when he already has a smug asshole way about him. If he was the Lincoln I used to know, I'd have zero issues letting him know how good of a job he did.

But that isn't the situation we're in, so I use the time to sit and scribble notes on the pages while the other groups in the class discuss their projects. The silence wouldn't bother me if I couldn't feel his eyes on me. I look up, watching him practically twitch as I make notes on his well thought out pages. But I refuse to let him do all of the work alone. He might think I'm a useless princess now, but he should know better than that. I haven't done anything to give him that impression of me. I take a deep breath and smile softly at him. "It's a solid plan, but I think there are a few tweaks we could make to widen revenue streams and increase the profit margins."

He looks a little shocked as he leans back in his seat, nodding stiffly before turning to his version of the file. I do a mental fist pump at shocking him into not snarling at me and take the win. Maybe at some point, he'll realize he actually has no clue about the girl I grew up to be and clue in to the fact that I'm far more competent than he wants to give me credit for.

I go through and add notes, waiting until the bell rings before handing him the file. "Have a look, see what you think. If you agree with what I've done, we can merge our two plans, since they aren't worlds away, then write up the final proposal *together.*"

He takes the file from my hand, nodding once before stalking from the room. I can't quite tell if this was a total win, but I head to my next class feeling way lighter than I did before I came to this one.

"Do you have plans for next weekend?"

I glance over my shoulder at Indi who's sitting on the counter of the island in my kitchen. Rooting through the fridge trying to find something to eat is a disappointing endeavor, so I sigh and shut it before turning my attention back to her. I sit down at the island as I consider her question.

I squash down the ripple of sadness that runs through me. Dad and I always used to just get away from everything on Labor Day weekend. We'd escape the insanity that his lifestyle brought and find a remote cabin somewhere. I'm not really one for nature, but staying in a log cabin with beautiful water views and making S'mores at night over an open fire was always a really nice escape. It won't happen this year, and I'm trying not to focus on just how much that thought hurts. "For the long weekend? No, I was just going to curl up in the theatre room in my pajamas and pretend the world doesn't exist. Why?"

She shrugs before jumping down and sliding into the chair next to mine. "I was thinking maybe we could get away for the weekend. You could definitely use some time away from here. I was thinking of a spa weekend. Ultimate relaxation and all the sleep rolled into one weekend."

I smile wide. That actually sounds kind of perfect. It might not be what I've always done, but it might give me a chance to escape the ever-haunting memories of this house. Both of my dad and what happened recently. I might actually get some sleep. "Yes, let's do it. That sounds amazing."

Grinning wide, she pulls her phone out of her pocket, and after tapping at her screen, she shows me the site of a mountain spa. "I was thinking we could go to this place."

I almost can't contain my excitement as I take in the images from the website. It looks so fucking zen, I can't even handle it. It looks perfect. "Yes, let's book it. Right now. I need this way too much."

I grab my purse from my bag while she puts all of the details of our stay in. "You don't need to pay, I can cover my half." She shoves her hands at me as I go to hand her my card, but I shake my head and refuse to take it.

"Hush, what's the point in having money if I can't spend it on the people I love?" I shrug and hand her my card anyway. Money hasn't ever been an issue, and I know I'm lucky that I can say that. I mean it, though, I know she has plenty of her own money; but I couldn't spend what my dad made in three lifetimes, so if I can do this, I'm going to.

She books it in my name and grins at me, showing me the confirmation. "Thank you, I mean you totally paid for my birthday weekend away, so I feel like I'm taking advantage—"

"Hush!" I cut her off, laughing. "No one is taking advantage."

Her phone buzzes, pulling her attention away from the topic at hand, and I see Jackson's name on the screen before she takes it back from me. She smiles down at her phone, and my heart soars for her. I love how happy she is, but I swear to God; if he hurts her, I will literally pop his nut sack. Pop it.

"Do you mind if I jet?" she asks, biting at her lip.

I shake my head. I don't want to be alone, but I could totally try to head to bed early. I might not get much sleep, but I figure the earlier I start trying, the more I might get in overall. "You're good. And don't worry about getting me in the morning either. I can drive in."

"Are you sure?" she asks, conflict written all over her face.

I grab her bag and push it at her, laughing. "Of course

I'm sure, go on, get. Go enjoy that boy of yours. I'll see you tomorrow."

She grins, taking her bag from my hands and slides her books from the counter into it. "Thank you. You absolutely will. I'll grab coffee and meet you in the parking lot."

"Sounds perfect," I say as I walk her to the front door. I disable the alarm and open the door to let her out. "Have fun."

She practically skips to her car, waving once she's buckled in. I open the gate from the remote system as she reaches it and wait for the lock to engage before resetting the alarm. Some might call the level of security I have here overkill, but all things considered, I don't think even Fort Knox would be overkill at this point. I've been attacked in my home twice, and Smithy was attacked once. That's three times too many, and I'm not willing to take chances anymore.

After making sure all of the doors and windows are shut, I manage not to run up the stairs tonight, and I mark that down as progress. At this point, I'll literally claim any win I can. I head straight to my bathroom as I put my hair up in a messy bun and jump in the shower to wash the day off. It's been unseasonably warm today, and I feel kind of gross.

I pad my way into my room in my towel, grabbing a pair of boy shorts and a tank from my dresser along the way. It's way too warm for full pajamas, and I open the balcony to let some of the cool night air into the room. The smell of the flowers from the trellis filters in, and I smile. Wild roses are some of my absolute favorites.

It doesn't take me long to brush out my hair, then shut my balcony door before climbing into bed. I feel so fucking tired after the last few days that it doesn't take long for sleep to pull me under.

I wake up screaming less than forty minutes later and bury my face into my pillow. All I want is one night of sleep—just one—so I set up my podcasts again and try to calm myself enough to sleep. When I see that it's two in the morning on the screen of my phone, I groan.

As sleep finally starts to pull me under once more, I hear noises outside and freeze. I want to move, to run away, but I'm paralyzed by fear. My fight or flight response is, apparently, just die. Awesome.

The balcony door creaks, and I manage to get control of myself. I flip over, sitting up to face the door, and see Lincoln stalking toward me in nothing more than a pair of sweatpants. "What the fuck are you doing here?"

He glares at me and climbs right into my fucking bed.

"What are you doing?" I screech, my fear and anger mashing together.

I grab the sheets, fully ready to kick his ass out when he lies down, grumbling, "I can hear you screaming from my room. Now lie down and sleep, I'm not going anywhere."

I scoff. *The audacity of this guy.* But as he pulls me onto the bed, I can't deny how much safer I feel with him here. Which is ridiculous considering I'm pretty sure he's the cause of my nightmares, but I never claimed I made sense.

I turn my back to him and close my eyes, feeling him move closer to me as he tucks me against his chest, his arm draped over me. Sleep is already dragging me under, so I don't bother complaining. I'm not sure it'd make a difference anyway. As I start to slip away, I hear him murmur, "You don't need to cry anymore. I'm here now."

When I wake up, Lincoln's long gone, and for a minute, I think I dreamed of him being here. Until I roll over and catch his scent on the pillow.

So fucking weird.

Him being here was not what I expected when I heard someone climbing the trellis.

Lincoln Saint doesn't seem like the type to sneak in my window anymore. I didn't think he cared enough to even notice my screams.

But apparently, I am Jon Snow because I appear to know nothing.

I play it all over again in my head, trying desperately to work out why he would come over here. I eventually decide that I'm not going to figure out the enigma that is Lincoln Saint without coffee, if I can even work him out at all.

I try to push it from my mind and get ready for the day. I shoot Smithy a message to check in on him and his sister. They're a few hours behind me, so hopefully I don't wake him. Once I roll out of bed, I head to the shower, trying to clear my mind a little. I slept like the fucking dead after Lincoln came over, and I still feel dazed.

The shower helps a bit, but after I'm dressed, I still stumble down to the coffee pot like it holds all of the answers to life. As I'm waiting for it to brew, my phone buzzes, and I smile when I see Smithy's name.

Smithy:
*Good Morning, Miss Octavia **smiley face emoji***
My sister has taken a turn for the better and things are looking up. I can be home in a few weeks, I hope. Just need to get her back home and settled with a nursing team.

Me:
I'm so glad! You don't have to rush, things are all quiet here now. Take care of your sister, I'm absolutely fine.

Smithy:

If you say so. I did, however, arrange for a grocery delivery. It will be put away before you're back from school. I asked Mrs. Potts, who looks after the Saint household, to sort it out for you. Master Saint will ensure the alarm system is sorted out.

Me:

Smithy, you rock.

I open the refrigerator and wince. I probably should have thought to go shopping myself considering how bare it is in there.

Smithy:

I know. I've asked her to prepare you some meals so you don't live off of take out too.

The guy's a total fucking sweetheart. I miss him so much, and it's hard to remember how I survived without him. I send him a quick thanks before realizing I need to forage food before school. I grab my bag from the counter, making sure I have my purse and keys, and head out to the garage. This morning calls for a breakfast burrito, *STAT*.

I jump in the car and head toward the only place in town that does them. It doesn't take long for me to weave through the early morning traffic and hit up Raleigh's family restaurant, smiling at his sister as I enter. The food smells beyond amazing once I have the take-out bag in hand, so I take it out to my car and basically inhale it before heading to school. I pull into the space beside Indi to find her waving at me like a kid on a sugar high. I guess she had a good night.

Climbing from the car, I hear her door slam, and then there's a chocolatey, whipped cream delight of a coffee floating in front of my face. I grin, taking it from her as she sips on hers and bounces on the spot. "Morning, angel face!"

I laugh at how peppy she is this morning. "Morning, cupcake?"

"You seem cheerier than you have been," she comments as she links arms with me, and I decide to keep the Lincoln thing to myself for now. I don't understand it, and I don't trust it. The last thing I want is her to think it was something I instigated. She's starting to see the truth of who he is and likes it about as much as I do, which is to say, not at all. I'm not going to poke the mama bear.

"I slept better. And I had a breakfast burrito. What's not to be peppy about?"

She beams at me as we enter the school. "You mean other than these unhallowed halls? Absolutely nothing."

The week has been strangely quiet, and since Indi's heading off campus for lunch with her mom, I decided to spend my break in the Music rooms. The longer I spend being back here in Echoes Cove, the more I want to be around music.

After my dad died, I was a little worried I'd never play again, and while I've played piano, I haven't picked up a guitar yet.

Today, that's going to change.

I pick up the acoustic that sits on a stand in the corner of the room and drop onto one of the stools with it in my hands. The smooth of the wood and the rough of the strings transports me to a different time entirely. I go all the way back to the time my dad first gave me a guitar. I revisit learning different chords from him. To the first time he asked me to play a track with him for one of the songs on his album… The first time in a studio. So many memories flash behind my eyes, and I smile despite the tear that rolls down my cheek.

I pick at the strings. The sounds of the first song I wrote with him echo around the room, and I close my eyes, going back to a time before I felt broken. A time when I wasn't so sad. A time before…

I let the music take me away to another place, the sting

of the metal strings a comfort I'd forgotten. The acoustics in this room remind me of some of the places we've played before. It's like I'm back there, with him, and with my eyes closed, I can pretend that's exactly where I am.

I lose myself to the feelings, the music, and the memories. It isn't until the bell rings that I open my eyes and see that Finley is standing there, silently watching me, and I startle.

How wrapped up was I to not notice his presence that almost chokes me now? He stalks up to me, and the stool I'm sitting on puts me almost eye to eye with him. He clasps my cheek in his hand, shocking the hell out of me as he rests his forehead on mine.

I close my eyes at the feeling of him this close, and my heart races. I have no idea what this is or why I'm so calm about it, but there's something so serene about the look in his eyes that makes me sit here with him.

It only lasts a few seconds before he pulls back, stepping away and looking torn.

"I'm sorry," is all he says before he stalks away, leaving me so far beyond confused my world spins.

There are too many things he could be sorry for at this point, but that sorry felt different.

Like goodbye.

Twenty One

"Girls' trip, baby!" Indi practically sings as she slides in her socks across the hardwood of the entry hall. Thank God Smithy isn't here to see her nearly slam into the artwork on the walls. He'd have a conniption. It's officially Labor Day weekend. I'm a little sad he still isn't back yet, but I understand that he's looking after his family.

This past week has been one of the strangest in my life. There hasn't been any bullying, no comments have been made behind my back, and somehow the deep fake sex tape has been wiped from existence. And Lincoln has spent every night in my bed, sneaking in through the window each night and disappearing before I wake.

Some nights I went to sleep without him there, and the only way I knew he was there was his scent on my pillow the next day.

Stranger yet, the three of them haven't said a word to me all week long. It's as if they're pretending I don't exist. It's not much different from when I arrived, just minus the bullshit from the rest of the student body.

Indi dances around in the doorway like an absolute loon, but she brings me so much joy. I laugh at her antics and excitement. "Three whole days of no school, no Echoes Cove, and nothing but utter relaxation. What's not to be excited about?"

"Absolutely nothing!" She slips her feet into her Chucks before spinning to face me. "Let's go!"

I grab my weekend bag, keys, and phone before double checking that the doors are all locked up. Once I'm sure everything's good to go, I grab my handbag, enable the alarm, and haul ass out of the house before locking the front door too.

We jump into her Wrangler, set up our road trip playlist, and prepare ourselves for the couple hour drive inland to the resort.

As we drive out of Echoes Cove, I can't help but feel like we're being followed. There's a prickling on the back of my neck as if I'm being watched, but when I check the mirrors, I can't see anyone there. It's creepy as fuck, but I shrug it off and put it down to paranoia. Despite my nightmares quieting with Lincoln's presence, I'm still not over the whole being jumped in the middle of the night thing.

Which isn't really that surprising considering the trauma from the experience, but this weekend is about getting away from all of that, relaxing, and being at one with myself. I'm totally sure I can do that.

Not.

I finally relax as Echoes Cove disappears in the rearview and sing along to the playlist with Indi, getting into the road trip spirit.

The time passes quickly, and before I know it, the navigation system announces we've arrived at our destination. We turn off onto the entry road, the giant wooden arch welcoming us to Mountain View Spa Resort, and I swear I'm already feeling more relaxed than I have in months. Indi drives us through the green expanses, and it feels like the world falls away as the mountains come into view before us. Tucked away to the left, behind a giant fountain, is the resort.

"Holy shit, this looks better than it did in the pictures!" Indi exclaims, bouncing in her seat as we pull into the valet bay. My door's opened in an instant, and the valet smiles at me warmly.

"Welcome to Mountain View, Miss Royal. Please let us get your bags. If you'd like to head inside with your friend and get checked in, we'll take your luggage straight up to your suite." He offers me a hand and helps me down from the car, and Indi shrugs at me as she reaches me.

"I figured if I put it in your name, we'd get better service, but this is something else."

I shake my head, not caring that she used my name. There are definite perks to being my father's daughter. "Fine by me, let's head inside."

She links her arm with mine, and we head inside. I lift my aviators as we cross the threshold into the building, and the house manager greets us. "Miss Royal, it's good to have you with us. We've already checked you in. If you follow me, I'll show you to your suite. We upgraded you for your stay. There is a private spa space in your suite that you can use as well as the facilities here."

"Thank you," I say, as Indi nudges me like an excited kid. Her joy is officially overspilling. We follow the manager up to the suite on the top floor of the resort.

She opens all of the rooms and shows us the spa menu that's available. She's finishing the tour as our bags are delivered to the room. Indi looks like she's almost a little freaked out by the service, so I try to take charge of the situation, tipping the bell boys before they disappear. Their grins are wide as they thank me before scurrying away.

A knock sounds at the door, and the house manager moves to open it. "Delivery for Miss Royal."

What the fuck?

She takes the delivery and closes the door before turning back to face me with a bouquet of yellow tulips. "For you."

She hands them to me, and I tamp down the freak out that's threatening. What the actual fuck?

I paste a smile on my face as I pull the same envelope sealed with red wax from this bunch as there has been on the others. It felt fine at first, but for whoever's sending them knowing where I am is a little creepy. I check the envelope and again, just a plain black card, embossed with the same image as the wax seal. I quickly put them in a vase and push the thought to the back of my mind. This weekend is about relaxing with my bestie, not focusing on creepozoids.

I turn my focus back to the house manager, who's smiling warmly at me as she asks, "Is there anything else I can help you with?"

"No, this is all wonderful. Thank you."

"Perfect, well, if you need anything, dial '0' on your in-room line. You'll come directly through to me."

"That's great, thank you." I usher her out of the room after tipping her too. I close the door behind her then lean back on it, taking a breath.

I look over at Indi, who still looks pretty overwhelmed from her spot on the sofa, staring at me. "Dude, is this what your life was like before? People tripping all over themselves to be around you?"

"Pretty much," I say with a shrug before moving into the suite and dropping down next to her. "Not everywhere, and not always, but yeah. It can be a little much."

"It's totally out of this world. I'm sorry if putting it in your name was out of line."

"Dude, you're fine," I say, swatting her with a cushion and making her chuckle. "What do you want to do first?"

She picks up the menu, handing me the second one, and grins. "Let's try everything!" Her excitement is contagious, and I'm not about to stomp on it.

I grin at her, happy as hell that she pushed me to get away this weekend. "Sounds perfect."

After two days of total relaxation and treatments, I think I might be tapped out. There are only so many ways a girl can be poked and prodded before she needs some space.

Indi bounces into the bedroom, her excitement at full capacity as ever, before dropping down onto the bed beside me. She shoves her phone under my nose, and I pull away so I can actually focus on the screen. "I found this low-key music bar in the next town over. Restaurant by day, bar by night. Do you want to check it out?"

"Sure, why not?"

"And it's called Midnight Blues! What are the chances?"

"That's kind of brilliant. We can head there in a bit?" I ask with a smile, seeing the open mic night announcement on the website seconds after the agreement leaves my mouth.

Devious little shit. "I'm not singing, though."

"But, V," she draws out the letter, practically singing it. "You're so good! You should share your gift with the world, rather than just me and your shower head!"

I burst out laughing as she wags her eyebrows at me. "My 'gift,'" I say, making air quotes with my fingers, "is a curse. I saw what it did to my dad. I'd rather stay behind the scenes, thank you."

She sighs and flings herself backward dramatically, lying down as she stares up at me. "But it's just a small place, I'm sure there'll be hardly anyone there."

I raise an eyebrow at her and she huffs. "Fine, fine. No singing, but it looks like they do banging chicken wings, and I'm so down for that right now."

"What the fuck is a banging chicken wing?" I ask, completely bewildered.

She sits up and huffs, crossing her arms across her chest. "I really need to get you to watch more British TV. Their language is so much more imaginative. They have such a way with words. Banging means really good. So, banging chicken wings."

"And you couldn't have just said good wings?" I laugh, and she shakes her head violently.

"It just doesn't have that same feeling. The same… pizzazz."

Her pouting makes me laugh harder until she's laughing along with me. "Okay, so no singing but great wings. Sounds good."

It doesn't take us long to get ready and request the car back from the valet. Before long, we're in the Wrangler and heading to the next town.

We pull into the lot of Midnight Blues to find that it's already crazy busy, and I immediately wonder whether we should've booked a table. We can at least see how bad the wait's going to be, I guess. My internal worries are reflected on Indi's face as we climb from the car.

We walk in, and even though it's pretty busy, the hostess greets us straight away. Her eyes go wide when she sees me, and I instantly regret the decision to come here. She visibly gulps before smiling again. "Good evening, just the two of you?"

"Please," Indi says, moving to stand slightly in front of me. It's a bit over protective, but my heart swells anyway.

The girl nods and grabs two menus before motioning for us to follow. "Follow me, please." She weaves us through the tables to the back corner, and offers us a small smile before saying, "I thought you might like some privacy."

This girl is awesome. "Thank you, I appreciate it."

"Of course," she nods, and Indi and I slide into the booth. "I'll give you a few minutes to go through the menu, and then I'll check back in with you."

She disappears without another word, and Indi picks up the menu. "Isn't it strange for the hostess to be our server?"

I shrug as I pick up the other menu and glance over it. "People have always been weird when I go to new places. It's frustrating, but you just kind of get used to it after a while. Plus, she was reasonably chill. Someone else might not be so laid-back."

She clamps her lips together and looks almost guilty. It isn't her fault people are weird. "I didn't ever really think about this side of your life. Not properly anyway. It doesn't seem like much fun."

We chill out and enjoy our food once it arrives. The ambience in this place is so chill, that time slips away without us noticing. When the open mic starts, Indi looks over at me with those big puppy-like eyes of hers. "You sure you don't want to get up there?"

My heart pangs with the memory of doing small nights like this with Dad when we went to places like Nashville. It was always so much fun. I guess it could be again, but I doubt it would be the same. "Not entirely."

"Yes!" She jumps to her feet and scrambles toward the stage before I can say another word. I drop my head into my hands, wondering what the fuck I just agreed to. I'm equal parts anxious as fuck and excited about the prospect of being on a stage again. Even if just for a few minutes.

Indi skips back to the table, sliding into the booth beaming with joy. "They had a spot for you."

She practically sings the words and a flutter of excitement builds in my chest. We watch four acts, and then they call my name and gasps sound around the place.

This might have been a bad idea, but fuck it. I'm here now.

I reach the stage and take the guitar from the sound guy up here. I lift the strap over my shoulder and perch on the stool in front of the mic. As soon as I sit down, I know exactly what I'm going to sing. The song Dad and I wrote together. I lean forward to the mic, the heat of the lights blasting down at me as I try not to squint out at the crowd. "Evening, everybody, it's great to be out here with you all. My name's Octavia Royal, and this is 'Raindrop.'"

I wake up Sunday morning to Indi shaking me. "What's wrong?"

"Uhm, so… I know you shut your phone off when we

got here so you could escape everything, but you should maybe turn it on." She wrings out her hands as she speaks to me, shifting from foot to foot, nervous as fuck.

"What happened?" I ask, scrambling to grab my phone from the nightstand.

She shuffles around so she's sitting cross-legged, looking like she might cry. "I'm so sorry, I didn't think this would happen, but apparently someone recorded you singing last night. And uh… It's kind of gone viral."

I let out a deep breath. The way she was going on, I thought someone had died. "Is that all?"

"You're not mad?"

I laugh softly as she deflates in front of me. "Why would I be mad?"

"Well I basically made you get up on stage."

I put my hand on hers and squeeze. "Indi, you didn't make the video or post it. Plus, this isn't the first tape I've had go viral, even just this month. I'd much rather this one than the deep fake. Honestly, it's fine."

I push the button on my phone, powering it up as she flops backward on the bed. It's barely seconds before it's buzzing out of control in my hand.

I push through most of the junk, deleting all the crazy shit, when I find a text from Raleigh. I haven't really spoken to him properly since we decided to just be friends.

Raleigh:

You were amazing, V.

Raleigh:

I miss you

Raleigh:

I really wish things could have worked out between us.

Raleigh:

Why are you ignoring me?

Raleigh:

Oh I see, you go viral and suddenly you're too good to talk to me. I see how it is.

Raleigh:

Well fuck you too

I let out a deep breath and flop back to lie beside Indi. "Why are boys so gross?"

"What happened?"

I pass her my phone because showing is easier than telling. She sits up, red in the face. "What a fucker. He's been a little weird about you since the whole thing happened, but I figured it was simply a bruised ego. He has no right to talk to you like this."

I shrug my shoulders, resigned to the fact that boys are not worth the hassle. "Privileged football players aren't used to hearing the word no, I guess. Not all of them of course, some of them are beautiful humans, like Jackson. But there's something about quarterbacks. And this is precisely why I don't usually date sports types. The egos are way too fragile."

"I'm sorry, V. What a dick."

I sit up and smile. "Fuck it. It is what it is. Now what are we doing with our last day here before we go back to normalcy?"

"Massages?" she suggests, and I can't help but grin.

I wonder if there's a Dylan O'Brien look alike around here.

Twenty Two

When I got home yesterday, I was glad to see that there weren't any media stalkers at my gates. That's the upside to the video having been taken not in my hometown, I guess. I might have to take Smithy up on the personal security thing if it gets bad again, though.

Lincoln didn't appear last night either, and I hate that I'm conflicted about whether or not I'm happy about that fact.

So much for wanting a normal year.

I head to school, swinging by the drive through to grab coffee for Indi and I, all while losing myself in today's song of the day, "I Am Defiant" by The Seige. The beat of the song has me all kinds of hyped up, which is definitely new for a Tuesday morning. The beat makes my heart race as my blood pounds through my veins. I'm a strong believer that the right song in the morning can set up your entire day properly.

I pull into the parking lot, swinging into the space next to Indi with the music blaring. As I bop along to the end of the song, Indi jumps along to the bass outside of my car.

Fuck, I love her.

I lean over and grab the coffees from the passenger seat before shouldering my bag and sliding out of the car.

"Thank you," she practically sings as I hand her the drink.

"You whore!"

I turn around at the screech and let out a sigh as Blair storms toward me, her hands clenched at her sides as her hair blows around her face in the breeze. She looks pissed.

I glance up at Indi, who looks ready to bitch slap Blair already. She's been too quiet lately. I sigh. I knew it couldn't last. "I wonder what I've done now."

Blair closes in on us, her blonde hair a wild mess as her rage makes her shake. What the actual fuck?

I hand Indi my drink before stepping around the front of the car to meet my cousin, placing my bag on the hood. She reaches me and pulls away before slapping me across the face so fucking hard I swear my brain rattles.

"What the fuck is wrong with you?" My voice is quiet and calm despite the rage pulsing in my veins. I'm not the screeching type, but if she thinks I'm going to take this lying down, she has another thing coming.

Her eyes are wild as she comes at me again, trying to claw at my face. "You just had to come back and ruin everything, didn't you? You couldn't be happy with what you had. You had to take what was mine too." Her words come out in pants as she tries to attack me. I try to hold her off, but her fingernails rake down my cheek, and I hiss as she breaks the skin. You'd think with the amount of self-defense classes I've taken, I'd be better at fending off bullshit attacks like this. I really am rusty. I reach up and touch my cheek. The warm, wet of the blood on my fingertips makes me see red.

Fuck this shit. I push her backward and punch her in her already delicate nose. She should've learned last time.

Her wail is enough to pierce my eardrum as she falls flat on her ass, clutching her nose. Her eyes narrow at me, and she actually fucking smiles. She's a fucking psycho. "You'll pay for this, you little bitch."

Blair gets up and stalks away, leaving me wondering what the fuck just happened. I reach up, hissing as I touch my stinging cheek. My fingers touch the blood that trickles down my face, and my rage pulses inside of me again. I turn back to Indi, who is sucking down her coffee like she's watching a movie, and I can't help but laugh. "Enjoy the show?"

"Like you wouldn't believe," she grins. "Watching her

fall flat on her ass with a potentially broken nose, again, brings me way more joy than it should."

"Any idea what any of that was about?" I ask as I grab my bag, and she hands me my mostly melted iced coffee.

She shakes her head and pulls a wet wipe from her bag, handing it to me. "For your face. And no, I have no fucking idea. She's a legit psychopath, though, so it could be anything."

I take a sip of my drink and take the wet wipe compact she offers me so I can clean up my face. I swear cuts like this sting way more than a deep wound. I'm generally fine with pain, my threshold is pretty high, but fuck, that stings. "Well, that was a fun start to the day. I wonder what other joys this day will hold."

"At least life is never boring?" Indi offers as she tucks the compact into her bag.

I shrug and let out a sigh. "A little bit of boring might be a nice change of pace, though."

I finally turn back to head into school and notice the large crowd of people watching us. Of course there were people here. That's probably why she did it. And I reacted. What a *dick*. I should know better by now.

Do not react to the crazy people.

I keep my head held high, ignoring the whispers that follow me into the building about being an unhinged whore. Because despite no one being in my face about it, and the fact that all traces of the sex tape are gone from the internet, I know some of these assholes still have it. They still talk about it and call me a slut or a skank. But these people don't mean anything to me, and that's what I have to keep reminding myself of.

The world has written lies about me and my family almost my entire life. This is just another one to add to the list. The people who know me know the truth.

At least, I hold onto the hope that they do.

I take a breath and steel myself against this day. It can't get any worse than this, right?

Yesterday morning was such a shit show that Indi and I chose to have lunch off campus at Joe's. There was no way I was heading into the cafeteria for more bullshit. First Blair, then the whispers, and then in Music, Raleigh acted like he didn't even send those messages while we were at the spa, trying to be my friend again.

I can't even deal with this place this week. Lucky for me, I have the world's greatest bestie.

So today, as we head into the school I cross my fingers and hope for a better day. We pass Lincoln, Maverick, and Finley standing on the steps like a group of dark gods surveying their subjects. My gaze is pulled to them as we climb the stairs. I can't help but take in the way they command respect from those around them, even in silence. Each of them drips with the type of confidence you can only be born with. Everything about them screams power, attitude, and raw fucking sex appeal. I almost hate how undeniably hot they all are, my mind drifting to exactly what they could each be capable of. I try to shake the images from my brain.

Nope, I'm not going there.

As we get closer, I realize the only thing they're actually watching is me, like I'm their possession and their enemy all at once. Even Lincoln, who's acting like he hasn't spent every night until last curled around me in my bed.

"Octavia," Lincoln starts, and I swear to fuck I nearly trip up the goddamn stairs. Why am I such a mess around these guys? "You have a minute?"

I look at Indi, who shrugs and crosses her arms. I swear this entire place has me just trying to catch up. I don't get why everything has to be so complicated. "Uhm, sure."

Lincoln pulls me to the bottom of the stairs and back toward my car so we have a little privacy. I'm positive that the other two know exactly what he's talking to me about, and I'm definitely going to tell Indi, so it seems a bit much, but fuck it.

He scowls at a group of kids walking toward us. They squeak and walk around the cars rather than passing us directly. "You don't have to be so cruel, you know." I sigh, and he turns his glare on me before rolling his eyes.

He rubs his fingers against his temples before looking back at me. "You've been gone too long. You have no idea how this place works."

Now who's being dramatic? I know this place is shady as shit, but he could leave as easily as I did if he wanted to. "What did you want to talk to me about?"

His eyes flash, and I watch conflict play out on his face. I have no idea what that's about or why he's giving me a peek behind the mask he wears like a second skin, but I see when he changes his mind about whatever it is he was thinking about before he starts to speak. "The video from the weekend. I know a guy, so if you want it taken down, I can handle it."

My eyes go wide at his offer. This definitely isn't what I was expecting him to say. "Why are you being nice to me?"

I can't help but be suspicious, truce or not.

He glares at me again. I swear his face is going to get stuck that way if he isn't careful.

"We called a truce, remember? Plus, if East mopes around much more, I'll have to make him move out. He's still being pissy with me, and it's fucking with my chill."

And now it all makes sense. He's thick as thieves with Finley and Maverick, but he and East have always been weirdly close. Their bond's the kind that nothing could ever break.

"Well, thank you, but unless shit turns dark, it's not the end of the world. I don't have the media banging down my door this time, so this is the kind of viral I can handle."

He nods at my comment, like he expected as much. I'm pretty sure I wouldn't accept his help, truce or not. After everything that's happened since I came back, I don't see me ever going to him for anything. Whether he's helped with my nightmares or not. I'm still not convinced he wasn't the one responsible for causing them. "Okay, if you need help, you know where to find me."

"Was that it?" I ask, at a loss as to why he'd pull me aside for that. His eyes rake over me, and the conflict from before is back. I'm beyond curious what's going on inside his head. There was a time not too long ago when he couldn't hide anything from me.

Things were so much simpler back then.

Unfortunately, I don't have a crystal ball or a time machine. Either would be useful these days, but I don't live in a fantasy universe. I mean, I wouldn't pass up the opportunity for a mind reading superpower either. That might make my life simpler too.

His jaw sets, and I know he's made up his mind. "Yeah, that was everything. Have a good day." He walks away from me, leaving me slack-jawed staring after him.

Nothing about Lincoln Saint makes sense to me anymore.

I walk toward Indi, and we head inside. "What was that about?"

"Absolutely nothing." I run her over the whole encounter, and she looks as baffled as I feel.

She shakes her head as we walk down the hall. "The people here make absolutely no sense to me."

We head to my locker so I can sort out my books, and the main door slams closed. I look up and see Raleigh stalking toward us.

"Incoming," Indi murmurs, moving so she's standing just in front of me. I really do love her, and it's been so much fun watching her come into her own.

"Morning," she practically sings at him, making herself an obstacle before he can get to me. He straight up ignores her and stares daggers at me instead.

He folds his arms across his chest, practically vibrating with rage. I do not understand this guy at all. I thought I was good at reading people, but apparently I misjudged him a lot. "Why were you talking to Saint? I thought you hated him."

Indi rolls her eyes before chirping up. "Hi, Indi, how are you doing? Yeah, I'm great, thanks, did you have a good weekend?"

He glances over at her before pinning me with his stare again. I have exactly zero desire to justify myself to him, so I don't bother. "Whatever this is about, Raleigh, it's a you problem." The bell rings, saving me from this entire situation. "I need to get to class. When you have your shit together, come find me."

He clenches his fists, but I spin to shut my locker then head down the hall with Indi toward English.

Could this day possibly get any weirder?

My afternoon breezes by pretty easily. Lincoln was almost nice in Business, and it shocked the shit out of me. Not to mention, Blair was noticeably absent after our run-in earlier today. It would've been nice if her bitch squad wasn't in hyper mode about what happened while we were in Gym, but East shut them down so beautifully I almost wept.

There's nothing better than seeing bitches put in their place by the guy they simp over so much.

"V, you got a minute?" East asks as we're heading to the lockers after Gym finishes, and I can't help but laugh at how alike he and Lincoln are. I say a quick goodbye to Indi before turning and heading back to East.

I haven't really seen him much outside of class since the whole *him saving me and making the others call a truce* thing. I should probably thank him for what he did, but the time I spent in his bed after being locked away made things feel weird and tense between us. I'm at a bit of a loss about what to even say to him now that we're alone. "What's up?"

He looks more than a little conflicted when he looks down at me. "How are you doing? With everything?"

I tuck my hair behind my ear where it's escaped my ponytail, wishing this didn't feel so freaking awkward. "I'm okay. The nightmares have almost stopped now. So I'm actually mostly good."

He clenches his jaw and uncurls his fists. "Nightmares?"

My eyes go wide because I figured if Lincoln heard my screams, he would've too. "Yeah, I thought you knew. Lincoln said he could hear my screams when he…" I shake my head, trying not to trip over my words or let it slip that Lincoln snuck in my room and stayed more than a few times when I definitely shouldn't have let him.

"When Lincoln what?"

"Nothing, it isn't important. I'm sorry I haven't been around much since that weekend. I still haven't thanked you properly." I wring out my hands, trying to think of a way to make it up to him. "You want to hang out soon? Maybe have a pizza and Xbox night or something?"

He beams at me in a way that makes my heart race. "Yeah, that sounds like fun. Let me know when."

"I'm free tomorrow if you want to chill?" I swear I feel like a girl who's never hung out with a guy before. East literally bathed and dressed me when I was catatonic, and now I'm a blushing mess over a night of pizza and Xbox? God, I'm so lame.

He grins and runs a hand through his light brown tresses, and butterflies erupt in my stomach. "Sounds good. I'll text you later?"

"Okay." I nod before turning and heading toward the locker room. I can't help but glance at him as I walk away and catch him checking me out. He has the decency to blush, and I laugh, shaking my head as I leave the room.

Most people have already left by the time I hit the locker rooms, and Indi's sitting on the bench flicking through her phone when I reach her. "You don't have to wait. I'm going to shower and then head home. Tonight is totally a study night for me."

She smiles up at me and slides her phone into her pocket. "Okay, sweet cheeks. I'm going to go catch Jackson. But don't book Friday night up. I have plans for us." She winks at me as she stands, and I laugh a little.

"How mysterious."

"Jackson told me about a fight night that's happening. Sweaty hotties, all kinds of adrenaline… It's just yummy." Her grin is so devious, I love it.

A thought hits me and puts a damper on it. "Is Jackson going?" I don't tag on Raleigh's name, but it's more than implied.

"Nope," she says, popping her p. "He was complaining that he couldn't go because of the game."

My grin is firmly in place as I grab my crap from my locker. "Perfect! I'm there."

"Fabulous. I'll see you in the morning." She waves before floating out of the locker room, and I realize I actually have plans like a normal teenager, like, twice this week.

Who would've thought?

I hurry through my shower, not washing my hair, and change into my uniform before heading out. East is leaving the gym as I reach the hall, and he grins at me. "You're running late."

"I wonder why." I stick my tongue out at him, and he bumps his shoulder against mine. We walk through the halls, keeping a reasonable distance. Despite the fact that he's only four years older than me, and we've been friends our entire lives, he's still my teacher, and people are weird as shit about stuff like that. Especially the petty jealous bitches around here who simp over him and wouldn't think twice about trying to fuck me over.

I can't help but wonder what it would be like to date East. It's not only that he's beautiful and has a body that would make the gods weep. The protective side of him both drives me nuts and makes me gooey all at the same time. He's just so fucking nice, which doesn't sound like the compliment I mean it to be, but that doesn't make it any less true either.

He opens the main door for me, and I walk through, smiling at him. But then he looks over my shoulder and his smile drops. He looks fucking terrified.

What the hell?

I look around and find Lincoln, Maverick, and Finley facing off with a guy who makes Maverick look like an upstanding citizen. His black hair musses in the wind, and his ebony eyes are fixated on the boys until he looks up and sees me. His angry look shifts to a maniacal grin.

East moves to stand in front of me, blocking me from the view of whoever is standing with the others. "What do you want, Ryker?"

It takes a second, but it hits me who he is. Ryker Donovan. The Kingpin of ECH. Holy shit, he looks different from how I remember him. He grew up a *lot.* He's easily as tall as Lincoln, with the same fighters build as Maverick, but every inch of skin I can see below his chin is covered in tattoos.

"I came to pay a visit to your brother and to remind him of a few things. Though, I see why he's been so distracted now." His gravelly voice turns my blood cold.

Is he talking about me?

I refuse to cower behind East, so I step beside him and cross my arms.

Belatedly, I notice the gun in Ryker's hand.

How the fuck is this happening?

Ryker raises the pistol, and Maverick saunters toward him like he gives absolutely zero fucks that the guy has a gun pointed at him. My heart leaps to my throat, and the world slows to almost a stop as Mav leans forward and puts his forehead against the end of the gun, grinning like the crazy son of a bitch that he is. "Don't raise a gun at me unless you're willing to pull the trigger, Donovan."

I swear I can't fucking breathe. What the fuck is he doing?

Ryker lowers the gun and tucks it in the back of his jeans, and I feel like I can finally breathe again before Ryker looks over at Finley and Lincoln. East is a fucking statue at my side, and I have no idea what we've stumbled into. Whatever it is, I want no fucking part of it.

Ryker crosses his arms over his chest, and Maverick laughs. Ryker gives him the bird and looks over at East and I before looking back to Lincoln and Finley. "Tell the Knights to back off. I'm not bowing down."

Without waiting for anyone to say anything, he climbs into the idling car behind him and peels out of the lot.

The Knights? Finley's family?

I'm so confused.

Lincoln looks over at me before glancing at East. He looks more afraid than I've ever seen him.

What the fuck are they mixed up in?

Twenty Three

MAVERICK

Well, that couldn't have gone worse. I mean, people could've been shot, so I guess it actually could've; but of course Octavia showed up. And of course Ryker had to see her. I swear, every time we think we have shit figured out, she does something that blows it all to pieces.

It doesn't matter how hard I try to keep a distance from her, it's like I end up gravitating toward her. Like she's the sun at the center of my universe, and it pisses me off like nothing I've ever experienced.

"What the fuck was that?" I look up at the sky, sucking in a breath, ready to do anything I can to distract her from what Donovan just said. Her knowing what he meant could ruin everything. We've worked too hard to have this blow up in our faces now.

I turn to face her while Linc and Finn do what they do

best and plot. East looks at a loss for words, leaving this fully in my lap. I smile the most sadistic smile I can muster and stalk toward her as East moves to talk to the others. We might have called a truce, but that doesn't mean I'm not still convinced that leaving's the best thing for her.

Once I'm in her personal space, crowding her so she can't see the others, I lean down until my nose almost touches her. "What's wrong, princess? A little bit of real life too much for you?"

She rears back, and I can see how much my words hurt as the fire in her eyes dims a little. As much as I hate hurting her, if it'll keep her safe, then I'll do it until I'm so broken there's no coming back. I'm no stranger to pain.

Her eyes go wide, and my dick twitches at how innocent she looks right now. Her soulful brown eyes are like windows to who she really is. Even when she tries to hide, I can see her.

I've always seen her.

"You're such an asshole, Maverick," she hisses, and she clenches her fists.

Fuck, I'd love to see her unleash the fiery rage I know lives deep inside her. The thought of her repressed rage makes me hotter than how innocent she looks. This girl has always been my weak spot—the one person with the power to truly ruin me. Not that I'll ever let her know that.

So I smirk at her again and get in her space, tucking

a lock of her dark hair behind her ear. "Oh, princess, you have no idea." I walk her backward until her back connects with the wall. I lift one arm and place my hand on the brick over her head, boxing her in. "But if you ask real nice, I could show you."

She scoffs at my words, realizing belatedly that I've pinned her in. She slams her hands against my chest pushing me off, and hot damn, that fire is out for all to see today. Her chest heaves as she sucks in a breath, and I can practically see her trying to pull in her rage. I wish she'd let it all out instead.

"What's up, princess, things not so fun outside of your ivory tower?" The taunts roll from my razor sharp tongue so easily. Mostly because I pretend I'm not speaking to her. It's easier that way. I've been in love with Octavia Royal my entire life, but I agreed with Linc when we were all inducted. Keeping her safe is the most important thing, and if that means I have to deny myself from having her, then that's what it takes.

"Fuck you." Her breathy words give away how affected by me she is, and it makes the hunter inside of me excited. I do love to taunt and chase my prey.

"Oh, sweetheart, you're practically begging for it, aren't you? I saw how much you wanted it when Finn had you pinned against the wall in the pool house. I saw everything, including how much you enjoyed it when

Lincoln was between your thighs."

Her eyes flash with a mix of lust and anger, my favorite mix.

"I saw how much you enjoyed me watching you too," I murmur, and she rolls her eyes, pushing me even further away from her. I'm kind of impressed. I'm not exactly an easy guy to move. On one hand, I like knowing that she could probably fight off anyone who was trying to fuck with her, and I know she can throw a punch. Her cousin's broken nose is proof enough of that. On the other hand, all her fight does is make me want to push her harder, to see how much it would take to snap the controlled restraint she has.

My eyes flare at the thought of it. She pushes past me, slamming me with her shoulder as she does, and heads toward her car. My eyes stalk after her as I watch her leave. "That's it, V, run away. You've always been good at that."

She flips me the bird as she climbs into her car. Only once she's in with the door closed, do I head over to my boys to find out what's been going on while I handled the girl we've all been so fucked up over.

When I reach the group, East glares at me. "You look like you enjoyed that way too much."

"Just taking one for the team." I shrug, and his eyes narrow at me, telling me that I'm pissing him off even more. "What did I miss?"

Unsurprisingly, Linc's the one who answers me. "I'm catching East up on the conversation we were having with Ryker before he showed up with Octavia."

"We really need to deal with him and his little gun toting buddies. He can't just show up here with a fucking weapon like that," I growl, and Finn nods his agreement. "This little rivalry is becoming too much of an issue, and we have bigger things to worry about."

I bounce on the balls of my feet. All this anxious energy makes me wish Ryker had pushed me a little harder. Given me a reason to end this stupid rivalry with my fists.

"The rivalry was started by the football teams even if it escalated way beyond that. I'll deal with it," East pipes up, glancing over to V. Of course he's trying to play it down since she's here, in case she hears, but she's not stupid. She'll see through it. I wish it was just a football rivalry still. The minute the Knights set their sights on Ryker, Ellis, and their brother's business, it became more. He huffs before turning to his brother. "We still need to find out who broke into V's house and locked her up like that. Since you three insist it wasn't you."

I grind my teeth at the reminder. I saw her when he carried her to his house the morning he found her. My shock at seeing her in his arms was all too real. Doing that to her is one of my biggest regrets, and I hate myself for it but we thought it would make her leave, and well... Let's just say my fights in the cage have been extra bloody ever since.

The noise of her engine starting makes everyone pause. I don't take my eyes off her until she's out of the lot and I'm sure she's not coming back.

"We need to reassess. What started as a simple year and a reasonably clear chessboard has turned into a fucking riotous mess." Lincoln sighs, pinching the bridge of his nose. "I need to think. The Knights have us bent over a fucking barrel, and I don't like it. If we're not making Octavia leave, we need to think of another way to keep her safe, all while dealing with Ryker and his little band of wannabe bangers. Not to mention we have to figure out whoever the hell it is that seems to be hunting Octavia."

A growl passes my lips at the thought. The only person that should be hunting her is me. "I think I can get some answers at The Nest this weekend."

"I'll come with you. Divide and conquer," Finn adds, and I nod. I'm never against having a wingman with me in that place. I might have gotten into the underground fights as a way to hone my skills before I'm old enough to fight officially, but it's turned into a treasure trove of secrets from the scum that live in the snake pit that is Echoes Cove. Plus, Finn's quiet demeanor scares the shit out of people. Quiet but deadly is his entire persona.

Except for when it comes to V.

Though sometimes, especially when it comes to her.

"We're not going to figure everything out tonight. Let's get out of here before we try to work anything else out. I'm meeting with David about the security at Octavia's since Smithy's still out of town," East says quietly. "I'm going to see if there's any clear footage that captures the faces of whoever broke in. So speak up now if it was you fuckers."

Finn spears him with a look that would have him bleeding out if looks could kill. "It wasn't us."

His ice cold tone is enough to send a shiver down even my spine. I mean, I can see why East would think it was us, and usually we wouldn't lie to him, especially when it comes to her. After our usual go-to guys got way too carried away the last few times we used them, there was no way Linc was outsourcing that particular taunt. But I think the other two regret it as much as I do. What he doesn't know is that there's no way our faces are on any of those tapes. Finley's a tech fucking genius; he already made sure of it.

"Fine," East says with a nod. "You three need to work out your shit with the board. If this keeps getting out of hand, we're going to have to do what they want, no matter how much we hate it."

Lincoln practically vibrates with rage. I don't blame him. East was happy to step back and let Lincoln shoulder all the responsibility that came with the bullshit legacy our families handed down to us. Now he's trying to tell us what to do, all because V's back. It rankles even me.

"Any more leads on who keeps sending her those fucking packages?" Finn asks, looking at Linc who shakes his head.

"That's another fucking unanswered question. I know it's not the board since it isn't their style. Way too creepy. I think I've managed to intercept all of the packages so far. Today's gift was an envelope of pictures. Whoever it is has been stalking our girl hard."

"How do we not know who it is yet? And how are there this many people after her? It's like she's a magnet for psychopaths," East grinds out, his fists clenching, and I can't help but laugh. I'm the only psychopath she needs in her life. I'll eliminate the others through any means necessary.

"I'm on it," Linc snaps, and East nods as he turns to leave. "We'll continue this at my place," Lincoln growls through his teeths before he stalks to his Porsche looking like he's angry enough to kill someone. If only that's the first time this year he's done that.

I look at Finn and clap a hand on his shoulder. "Come on, we better head out. You know he'll pitch a fit if we keep him waiting when he's in this mood." Linc speeds out of the parking lot, almost as if proving my point.

"You want burgers?" he asks, shrugging out of his

blazer before unlocking his Lamborghini. I grab my helmet and leather jacket from the passenger seat and grin at him.

"You know I do."

"I'll swing by and grab some on the way and then meet you there."

I move over to my Ducati and swing my leg over so the powerful machine is between my legs. I shrug into my jacket and grasp my helmet in my hand as I start the bike. "Sounds good to me."

He shakes his head at me as I rev the engine. The purr of his car has nothing on the roar of my bike, but he loves that car like nothing else. I suppose if I'd sacrificed what he had for it, I'd love it like that too. I'm pretty sure the only thing he loves more than his car is Octavia. She hung the moon for him from the first moment she arrived in our class all those years ago.

We all have our own shit to handle, but we agreed when we were inducted that we'd keep her out of it for as long as we could, whatever it took.

I slide my helmet over my head and walk the bike back as it rumbles between my legs.

Octavia might hate us right now, but we'll do whatever it takes to protect her. Even if that means spilling more blood than anyone's ever seen.

This fucking week has been enough to push a saint to kill. So my sinning, pitch black soul's shit out of luck. It's why I grin so hard as blood drips from my knuckles and splatters across my chest.

The tall, scrawny guy in the cage with me is one of the assholes we think has been sending the creepy as shit gifts to V. Whether she knows about them or not, I'm going to get answers out of this dick. I'd really rather she never find out about any of this.

The guy staggers toward me, barely able to stay on his feet. I catch a flash of brown hair behind him, and it distracts me enough for him to land a punch on my jaw.

Focus, Mav.

I shake my head to clear it. There's no way V knows about this place. I swear I see her fucking everywhere.

I shake off the hit and bounce around this dickhead, jabbing him so much he groans as he falls to his knees.

I bark out a laugh at how easy this fight was. I really need to make sure my other opponents for the night are more of a challenge, otherwise the rampant rage burning in my veins won't find the outlet it so desperately needs.

I finish him with an Achilles style punch to the temple, and his eyes roll back in his head as he slumps. He's face down on the ground as the bell sounds and cheers go up around the warehouse.

The ref comes in and lifts my arm, officially declaring

me the winner before making sure my opponent isn't actually dead. I pause for a second until he confirms it, looking out into the crowd. I catch sight of the flash of brown hair again and narrow my eyes until I can see that it's actually her moving through the crowd.

I run a bloody hand down my face and groan.

What the fuck is she doing here?

I jump down from the cage and search through the crowd for her. Once I find her, my eyes narrow in her direction. We've done everything to try and keep her safe, and she strolls into this vipers' nest like nothing fucking matters.

Adrenaline rushes through my veins, and I'm high on the win of my fight as I stalk toward her. I know she sees me because her eyes go wide as she sucks in a breath. The way her chest heaves does things to me it definitely shouldn't, but I'm over denying myself of Octavia Royal. She spins on her heel and walks away, trying to escape me, which makes me grin.

Oh how I love to hunt my prey.

It doesn't take me long to reach her as the crowd parts like the Red Sea before me. These people know not to fuck with me.

I grab her arm and spin her around forcibly. She rips herself out of my grasp, eyes narrowed.

Fuck, I love her fire.

The high of the chase, of catching her, and her retaliating struggle… All she's doing is making my dick harder than it's ever been. She came here for me, to watch me fight. I know it. Her being here tells me all I need to know.

There are a lot less people down this hall of the pit, so I let myself be the animal I know I am. I want her. She wants me. I can see it in the flush of her skin. In the way her eyes go wide as she looks up at me. I grab her chin, my large hand spanning across her cheek and neck, and shove her against the wall. Her gasp rocks me, making me impossibly harder as her eyes dilate.

She wants this as much as I do. I watch as she ghosts her tongue along her bottom lip, and it's like a red flag to a bull.

I push my body against hers, and her eyes flash when she feels how hard I am. "You shouldn't run from me, V."

That fire returns to her as she pushes on my chest, but she isn't going to move me. Not when I'm finally where I've wanted to be since she came back. "Fuck you."

My grin widens as she struggles in my grasp. Fuck, I love the fight in her. Stoking that fire in her is going to be so fucking sweet, I can almost taste it. Taste her.

I crush my lips against hers, stroking my tongue against her lip like I just watched her do, unable to resist any longer. I tighten my hold on her throat. She resists me a little more, pushing against me; and I almost stop, but

I've waited long enough to claim her.

The second I feel her soft, plump lips part, I know what I've always known. She's mine to claim.

Mine.

Twenty Four

OCTAVIA

Maverick fucking Riley has me trapped against a wall, devouring me. As much as I hate it, I can't help but love it too.

If I said I hadn't thought about what being with him would be like, I'd be lying. Fighting against him is a token resistance. Fighting's in my nature. If I wanted him off me, I wouldn't crave him as much as I do.

His lips are brutal, taking and claiming, and my mouth falls open slightly on its own accord. I'm almost putty in his hands.

Almost.

I slam my palms against his chest and push, breaking his kiss so I can breathe. I'm beyond dizzy right now. It doesn't matter how much I might want him. I'll never forgive him for what he's done to me. I can't.

"Get off me, you fucking asshole!" I try to put as much fire and spit into my insult, but even I can't escape the breathy edge to my words. His sheer presence, boxing me in like this, makes me wet. His lips turn up into a devilish grin. I have zero doubts that he knows exactly how wet I am. He all but confirms it with the way he looks down at my half exposed tits in my low-cut tank. He licks his swollen lips.

That, however, is no reason to give in.

Never.

"The lady doth protest too much—" He tightens his hold on my throat, his fingers digging into the flesh to the point I'm afraid I might actually pass out. He trails his nose up my cheek, and my body betrays me as a shiver runs down my spine.

Fuck, the move turns me on, but I can't let him know. His entire upper body bends just enough for his nose to blaze a trail of fire across the skin of my neck, inhaling like a fucking animal before its attack. "—her pussy doth beg to be fucked, way too fucking much."

"Shakespeare was a poet, not a pig like you." I can barely hear my words with his fingers locked so tightly around my neck. I clench my hands at my sides.

"What can I say, V, I like it dirty."

Then his mouth crashes back on mine, his tongue breaching the space between my lips without waiting for any kind of verbal consent. My mind screams at me to run, but my body's primed for the attack. Wanting this. Waiting for it, like I've waited for him my whole life.

For a second, I let the fantasy take over. I enjoy the reprieve of this intimate moment. For a brief second, I forget that this guy's the reason for the literal hell I've lived through since coming home. I forget that he hates me, and that I *want* to hate him. Truce or not.

Our tongues battle for control, stroking against each other like silk, even though we both know he holds the control in the palm of his hand. A hand that's hellishly close to choking the life out of me. I can't explain it, but I fucking love it.

Rubbing my thighs together and trying like hell to ignore the fire between my legs, I wonder if something is seriously wrong with me. Why is this turning me on? Why the fuck do I love this so much?

Maverick groans into my mouth. His body is a punishing weight, caging me in so that no one can see us—see me—and that movement reminds me of where we are. That people can see us. And then like a film reel going backward in time, all the shit he's put me through flashes through my mind. Reminding me of all the reasons this is an incredibly stupid and bad idea.

My hands that pushed him away earlier, press against his sweaty, deliciously inked skin now. My nails curl around his pecs, digging into his flesh and hopefully drawing blood. He deserves the kiss of pain, even if I'm almost sure he gets off on it.

Good sense slams into me, and I'm able to push him away enough to break the kiss once more.

"Get off me!"

"Oh, baby, I thought you'd never ask."

What?

In an instant, his free hand is at my ass, two fingers slipping inside my super short cutoffs, pushing past the thong and making me gasp into his waiting mouth as he returns to his kiss.

An unexpected moan slips from my lips as Maverick thrusts his fingers inside of me. I can feel him smile against me when he feels how fucking wet I am. In an instant, I'm a slave to what my body desires. I can't help but groan at how good it feels. He fucks my pussy with his fingers like he owns it, all the while thousands of people are milling around us like nothing out of the usual is going on.

I slam my eyes shut, refusing to let everything else filter in as I stand here at his mercy.

I freak out a little at the fact that anyone could see us. Anyone could catch us, and after everything I've already experienced these last few months, having this caught on video is the last thing I want. The thought gives me pause as I try to push him away again, but my movements are weak, and I feel his grin against my skin as he kisses me harder. He's treating this like a simple game of push and pull to him.

The span of his large hand is across the lower end of my ass, while two of his fingers are pumping inside me. It makes it really fucking hard to concentrate on anything other than the pending orgasm that I do not want him to witness. I don't want any of these people to witness what's going on here. Yet something about the thrill of getting caught almost makes me hotter, and I feel goosebumps burst over my skin.

Almost is the key word here.

I don't want him to know he has an effect on me, which is ridiculous since he can feel my reaction to him as it coats his fingers.

Maverick pulls back slightly from our kiss, his teeth pressing together with my bottom lip trapped between them as he slams his fingers so deep I nearly buckle under the ecstasy of it all. To anyone passing by, we're a couple making out against a wall, kissing like teenagers often do. They probably wouldn't even notice us with the amount of debauchery that's normal in this place, but it's still enough of a thought to give me pause.

Meanwhile, he's getting me off without even asking me what I want. Like he already knows and doesn't need my input. As his teeth free my lip, I take the opportunity to bite down on his lip. Hard. Hard enough to taste the tanginess of blood as I cut him open in the process. I hate that this motherfucker seems to know my body better than I do.

I thought he'd be pissed and storm off, but as I open my eyes, I see his lighting up. His tongue leisurely swipes at his lip, collecting the blood, and then he licks mine like he's coating them with lipstick.

At that exact moment, it occurs to me that he's an actual fucking psychopath. He adds another finger to my pussy, stretching me to a point I've never experienced, and it makes my knees weak.

Fuck, he knows what he's doing.

He presses even closer against me and rubs his hard cock against the seam of my shorts, hitting my clit like he knows exactly where it is.

My breath catches, and I can feel my eyes widen at the knowledge that I'm about to explode in a public space with thousands of adrenaline-pumped assholes roaming around. The gleam in Maverick's eyes tells me that our location's a huge fucking turn-on for him. I'm pretty sure no one can see what he's doing, but the risk is there, and he's loving every second of it.

It's when he pulls me away from the wall and turns me around like a rag doll that I understand how much control he really has over me. With one hand in my hair, pulling it toward him so he can tower over me and force me to watch his face, now my body faces the wall he uses his other hand to push my shorts down far enough that he can slide his impossibly hard cock between my thighs.

"What the fuck are you doing?" I wish I was screaming at him, but my voice comes out breathy and horny.

"Whatever I fucking want and right now, I want to feel your dripping wet cunt all over my dick."

Without giving me the time to register his next move, he buries his cock deep inside me, filling me to the point of madness. It doesn't hurt like I thought it might, and any sting of pain is lost in the amount of ecstasy I'm drowning in.

I can feel his entire body huddled around me as he bends and thrusts inside me like an animal, like a beast taken over by his baser instincts.

Feral.

Brutal.

Savage.

All of the fucking above, and I'm the prey that's about to come all over his cock. Apparently, I've lost my fucking mind because being treated like a fuck toy is my jam.

I hate him.

I hate this.

But I also can't stop loving it.

I want it. I want more. I want it harder.

To my horror, I say those last words out loud, and the sound that comes from Maverick's throat reminds me of a lion grunting while it fucks its lioness into submission.

Because that's what this is. Maverick's punishing me by fucking the fight out of me, and I'm the crazy bitch loving every second of it.

"You're so fucking wet, don't try to deny that you love this fucked up shit." I don't deny it, not because I don't want to lie, but because speaking is impossible. All I can do is feel.

Feel his velvety dick slam through the walls of my pussy.

Feel the head of his cock ram into my cervix.

Feel his balls slapping against me every time he thrusts impossibly deeper and then deeper still.

"Get the fuck out of here, or I'll slit your throat from ear to ear, motherfucker."

My body freezes at the growl of Maverick's words.

Is he talking to me?

My silent question is answered when I hear a faint, "Sorry, man, my bad."

Fuck. Someone saw me.

I want to care, but when Maverick goes back to pistoning his hips, all other thoughts evaporate.

"Christ, you're even wetter than before. You like that, don't you, you little fucking slut? You like it when total strangers watch you get fucked from behind? Maybe I should fuck your ass. You want that?"

My traitorous body shivers at his words.

My ass?

Hell no.

Yet…

"Oh yeah, you fucking whore. You want me to take your ass, don't you? I bet it's a virgin ass, isn't it?"

To my horror, Maverick slides out of my pussy and glides his wet dick between my ass cheeks making a show of his head circling my asshole.

Oh God.

No. No, no, no.

But curiosity begs me to open up for him, giving him what he would take anyway.

"Yeah, that's what I thought. Good whores like it in the ass."

But he doesn't go through with it. He slams into my pussy and fucks me like he owns me, one hand still pulling my hair, my face angled straight at his face where I can see a sheen of sweat making an appearance on his forehead.

Simultaneously, his free hand reaches around for my clit as his mouth slants over mine and his tongue demands entrance. I fight him on it. Our mouths battle like a war is on the line. A sudden scream escapes me, but no one hears because Maverick's mouth swallows every one of my sounds. He's devouring me, eating up all of my pleasure as he fucks my mouth as thoroughly as his dick fucks my pussy.

I'm shaking in his grasp as the orgasm takes over my entire body, and my legs are unable to hold my weight as the waves crash through me again and again. The power shuts down every one of my synapses. All the while, Maverick owns me, gorging on me like I'm the last drop of water in an endless sea of sand. I feel him freeze behind me, his breaths feeding me as his dick swells inside me. He suddenly pulls out and comes all over my ass, spreading my cheeks to make sure he coats me all over my asshole. It's hot—a psychopath's wet dream.

It's only once the pleasure's gone that I remember he's the enemy and I hate him. He took my moans, but he doesn't get to take my fucking pride with him.

"I told you to get off me, you fucker!"

"My bad, I thought you asked me to get you off."

"You're an asshole." I spit the words at him for effect, hoping I'm as feral as I feel.

After dipping three fingers in my still soaked pussy like he's collecting honey from a beehive, he puts them in his mouth and sucks on them like a damn lollipop. "Your wish is my command. Next time, I'll just fuck your ass."

I pull my shorts back up over my ass, the remnants of my orgasm ghosting my skin as he trails his fingers over my hips. I look up and he has the fucking audacity to give me a good little boy grin like he's the preacher's son.

Fuck that.

"You can dream, I guess. This isn't happening again." He takes advantage of my open lips and pushes his wet fingers into my gaping mouth.

I can taste myself and him all mixed together, and it does something to me. My tongue slips against his callous tips without thought, and I lose myself to him again. It stirs up things inside of me that shouldn't be there. I shouldn't be feeling any of this. I don't want it.

This has to stay as something he will never know I feel. *Ever.*

"Screw you!" I cry out once I free myself of him and his spell, pushing everything rising up inside of me down, before ducking out from under his huge, sweaty arm. The cords of his triceps pull tight as he strains against the wall.

He grabs my arm, looking as menacing as he did in the cage earlier, and my body tenses. "Go home, V. And fucking stay there. Nobody wants you here."

"He did what?" Indi screeches as we climb into my car. To say I hauled ass out of that warehouse after escaping Maverick's clutches is an understatement. The guy is giving me severe whiplash.

"He, uhm… well… we fucked." I shrug, glazing over the whole I just lost my virginity thing, because I don't put much stock in the whole virginity thing.

I start the engine as she squeaks beside me, fully losing her shit. "How exactly did this happen?"

I pull the car out of the space and head out of the rundown, old industrial area of Echoes Cove, trying to find the words to explain this properly. "He, uhm, grabbed me, and well, shoved me against a wall."

Indi slams her hand against the dash and curses. "He forced himself on you? Fuck me, I'll kill him. Who gives a fuck about jail. I'll saw his dick off."

"He didn't force himself… exactly. There were mixed wires, and while my brain was in two minds about it all, my body was definitely on board. I could have stopped it if I'd wanted to. Maverick Riley is a lot of things, but he isn't a rapist."

She grumbles incoherently under her breath as I cross the train tracks and the buildings begin gradually turning back into the picture of wealth that Echoes Cove likes to portray itself as. "Was it good at least?"

I bark out a laugh. Of course that's her next question once she knows I'm okay. "It was possibly the best orgasm I've ever had."

She whistles before grinning over at me with a shit-eating grin. "Hot damn. Why are the psychos always the best in bed?"

"I don't know, but uh… How would you know?" I poke at her, and she blushes, shaking her head, so I leave it for now. I'm sure she'll share when she's ready. "Anyway, it won't be happening again, no matter how good it was. This was a blip. A lapse in judgement. It absolutely can't happen again."

She scoffs and crosses her arms, moving in her seat so she's facing out the windshield. "We'll see. 'Cause, girl, they might act like they hate you, but I've seen how all three… no wait, how all four of them look at you when they think no one's watching. Now that's a party I'd insert myself into. No offense."

"None taken. But that plan's not in the cards. I'm here to graduate—to get the grades I need to finalize the terms of my dad's Will—and get into college. There's a whole world out there, and I have plans. The four of them don't factor into them, no matter how pretty they are. They made that choice when I arrived." I clutch the steering wheel, hating how the words taste like lies on my tongue, despite the fact that I absolutely intend on them being true.

"Girl," she drags out the word, and I can't help but laugh. "If you say so."

We spend the rest of the short drive to her place in a comfortable silence, with just the sounds of Brynn Cartelli's

"Last Night's Mascara" playing through the sound system. I pull to a stop in front of her house, the brakes squeaking a little as I do.

"Thank you for coming with me tonight," she says, leaning over and hugging me. "Even if it ended up being more fun for you than it was for me." She winks at me, and I flip her off as she climbs out of the car, laughing softly. Leaning down, she looks at me solemnly. "Drive safe, and please tell me once you're home. Any news on when Smithy is coming back yet?"

"He's due home on Monday," I tell her, beaming. I'm so ready for him to be back now.

"Good. I don't like you being there alone, not after everything that's happened. Are you sure you don't want to stay here tonight?"

I shake my head, my heart swelling at her obvious worry for me. "No, I'll be fine, I swear. Go to bed already. You have a big weekend ahead of you."

She rolls her eyes at me, but I know she's excited really. "Fucking camping in the middle of nowhere and likely no cell service."

"It's romantic," I tease, and she scoffs.

"If you say so. Right, I'm going. Night. Love you."

"Love you too," I call out as she closes the door, waving at me once she reaches her porch. Once she's inside, I put the car in gear and start the drive home.

The drive passes in the blink of an eye; but when I pull up to the gate and see police cars sitting there with lights flashing, dread floods my system.

What the fuck happened now?

I pull in through the gate, and one of the cars follows me up the drive. My heart sinks as ice cold fear squeezes my heart.

Please let Smithy be okay.

I put the car in the garage, making sure it's safely tucked away before hauling ass outside to the waiting police. "Evening, Officers, how can I help? What's wrong?"

"Miss Octavia Royal?" one of them asks, stepping forward.

I nod, clutching my arms around myself, praying to God this isn't as bad as my mind tells me it is.

"Miss Royal, you are under arrest for the assault and battery of Miss Blair Royal."

My jaw drops to the fucking floor at his words. "You have got to be kidding me."

The officer moves toward me, grabs me, and spins me around, pulling my wrists behind my back. The cold metal of the cuffs stings my skin, and once he secures them, they're way too fucking tight. "You have the right to remain silent. Anything you say can and will be used against you in a court of law. You have the right to an attorney. If you cannot afford an attorney, one will be provided for you. Do you understand the rights I have read to you? With these rights in mind, do you wish to speak to me?"

"What the fuck is going on here?" Lincoln appears, roaring at the officers as he storms across the front yard. The officer that has a hold of me manhandles me into the back of his police car while I watch another officer try to handle Lincoln.

I lean my head back on the headrest as the door slams on the car before the officer climbs in and starts the engine.

Just when I thought things couldn't get worse, my cousin fucking ups the stakes.

Fuck my actual life.

I sit in this holding cell for what feels like hours before an officer arrives to walk me to an interrogation room.

My shock must show on my face when the door opens and I find Lincoln standing inside waiting for me. The officer laughs under his breath. He walks me over to the chair and undoes the cuffs.

"Good luck, kid," is all he says before he walks away, leaving me in the room with Lincoln.

"What are you doing here?" I ask, looking nervously around the room. I've never been arrested before, and this is scary as fucking shit. I haven't even had my phone call yet. I have zero fucking idea what's going on or how the hell I get out of this.

He sits in the chair on the opposite side of the table, watching me closely. I can't tell which Lincoln Saint sits opposite me. The guy who crept through my window to help keep my nightmares at bay or the one who declared open war on me when I returned here. "I'm here to get you out."

"Then why am I still locked in here?" I fold my arms across my chest, trying to create some heat. The entire station is fucking freezing, and I'm in nothing more than my little denim cutoffs and tank top that I wore to fight night. I'm definitely regretting the outfit, given the circumstances. I likely still look like I was fucked within an inch of my life. Since I didn't get a chance to clean up, there's no way he can't tell.

Lincoln frowns at me before steepling his fingers beneath his chin. "There are stipulations."

I bark out a laugh at him and sit in the chair. "Of course there fucking are. Go on then."

"You need to leave Echoes Cove. Within twenty-four hours of your release. You can not have any contact with anyone here, and you can't ever return."

I laugh incredulously, but his expression hasn't changed. "You can't be serious?"

I watch his face as he waits for my answer, and I realize

he really is serious. This is fucking insane. So much for our truce.

"I'm not leaving, Lincoln. You might have your reasons for wanting me gone, but I have reasons keeping me here too. Yours are no more valid than mine." I huff and run a hand through my hair. What an asshole he is, using this against me. It occurs to me that the truce was a lie. That he could be working with Blair to manipulate me into this position, making it impossible for me not to accept his help.

"I won't ask you a third time, Octavia. Agree to leave, and I'll have you out of here in the next five minutes." He folds his arms over his chest, looking like the arrogant fuck that he is. He thinks he has me, that he's won. But he doesn't know me. Not anymore. Not really.

"Fuck you, Lincoln. I'll get myself out of here without your help." I let out a deep sigh, wondering if that's actually even possible, but I'll be fucked if I'm agreeing to his terms.

His hands shake as his jaw clenches, his rage on show for anyone to see. Except I'm the only one here to witness him unraveling. He stands to attention, the metal chair flying backward with the force of his movement, and he slams his hands down on the table, making me jump. "You're a fucking fool, Octavia."

"Better a fool than a puppet."

I quirk an eyebrow at him, and he growls before spinning and leaving the room. I guess he really isn't here to help me.

That's fine. I can totally save myself.

I think.

Twenty Five

To say a night in a holding cell is uncomfortable might be the understatement of my entire life. The upside is that I'm probably safer here than I've been at home since Smithy left town. No one can terrorize me in a jail cell.

Well, other than the officers, and they've been okay, despite still not allowing me to make a phone call.

Lying down and staring at the discolored ceiling while shivering is basically how I spent the night. I'm officially living the dream.

"Miss Royal, you are free to go." I look up and find an officer unlocking the door to the cell with a really fucking angry East looming over him. "The charges have been dropped."

I sit up, eyes wide as shock floods my system. I have no idea how that's possible, considering my cousin's the biggest asshole in the world, but I won't question it. At least not until I'm alone with East.

I stretch out before standing and exiting the small, cold cell. East wraps his jacket around my shoulders, all while wordlessly glaring at the officer. "Let's get you home."

I look up at him as he puts an arm over my shoulder and tucks me against his side. "Thank you."

The words are little more than a whisper, but he squeezes me tighter before leading me out of the station to his waiting car. He opens the door for me and helps me in before running around the front of the car.

I try to wait until he's in with the engine running to question him, but he beats me to it. "What happened?"

His knuckles turn white as he grips the steering wheel, his cheek twitching as he clamps his jaw shut.

I pick at the skin beside my thumbnail, hating how small I feel having been saved by him yet again. I never saw myself as the damsel in distress type, but I seem to keep ending up in situations where I need rescuing. Shame floods me at the thought as my stomach twists, making me feel like I might be sick. "I have no idea. I got home last night, and the cops were waiting for me. They said Blair had pressed charges for assault and then carted me away. Lincoln came and basically told me he wouldn't help me. So I figured I was on my own, but they wouldn't give me my phone call after he left."

"He's such a fucking asshole." His words are clipped, his rage obvious in the set of his shoulders as he maneuvers the car toward our homes. "He was supposed to get you out, not leave you in there. He told me it was handled, otherwise I'd have been here sooner."

He takes a deep breath as my eyes go wide. Here I was thinking Lincoln and I were making progress. I guess I was wrong. "So, how'd you get me out?"

He glances over at me, his gray eyes like a raging storm. The eyes are the one thing he and Lincoln have in common as far as looks go. Their eyes are the same liquid steel, and they're like an endless pool to get lost in. "I pulled a few strings. Let's just say that your family shouldn't be a problem again."

I gasp, my eyes wide. "Do I even want to know what that means?"

He shakes his head once, and I look down at my feet. I didn't think I'd end up caught in the web of crazy that is Echoes Cove while I was back here. It's only one year, but it feels like each day I stay here, the more entangled I get in the inner workings. Though, it feels like I have no idea what's actually going on around this place.

We spend the rest of the drive in silence, with the sound of his radio filling the space along with the black cloud of his rage. I mean, I'm the one who spent the night in a cell, but he's definitely more worked up about this than I am.

Am I pissed at Blair? Absolutely. But am I shocked that she did it? Absolutely not. I knew the second I hit her again that I'd regret it at some point. I hadn't considered this to exactly be *how* it would blow up in my face, but I knew something would happen. She's too spiteful and petty to just let shit go. Though I still have no idea why she attacked me in the first place.

I really should start working through all the bullshit swirling around me. Maybe I need a journal or a whiteboard or something. Just to try and work shit out.

That's a future me problem. For now, I'd like to get home, shower, and sleep for a few hours. Maybe then I can try to figure out what actually happened last night. With Maverick and with Blair.

I thought my life was a rollercoaster when I was out on tour with my dad. That shit has nothing on Echoes Cove. East puts in the code to the gate and drives up to my house. I jump out of the car and head for the front door, finding yellow tulips waiting for me again, with another blank envelope, red wax seal and embossed black card.

Yet another thing to add to the ever-growing list of mine.

East slams the door and stalks over to where I'm standing, flowers in hand. "What is that?"

"Flowers, they arrive here every now and then," I say with a shrug. He plucks the card from my fingers, and the blood drains from his face. My heart races because I'd put money on him understanding this more than I do. "What?"

"Do they always come with this card?"

He takes the flowers from me as I unlock the door and disable the alarm. Once we're inside, I put the flowers in a vase with some water, and he seems to be taking note of how many vases of flowers there are now. "What does the card mean? I figured it was a fan of Dad's, and since I love yellow tulips, I've kept them."

"I'm not sure what it means." His eyes flicker down to his feet, and I swallow down the disappointment I feel. I know he's lying to me.

What is it with these guys constantly lying to me?

I shrug and move to the refrigerator, pulling out one of the meals Mrs. Potts put together for me, shoving it in the microwave to heat since I haven't eaten since lunch yesterday. Lasagna for breakfast would probably send Smithy into a conniption fit, but he isn't here right now. "Fair enough. Well if that's all, I'm going to eat, shower, and head to bed. Thank you for dealing with Blair."

He opens and closes his mouth a few times before shaking his head. "Yeah, okay. I'll be at home if you need anything."

He comes over and kisses my forehead before turning and leaving out the back door, despite his car being on my driveway. I thought we'd come leaps and bounds, especially after our not-quite-date night earlier this week, but now I feel like we've taken about ten steps back.

One day I'll figure out what the fuck's going on around here, but today's not that day. Today calls for sleep, food, and not leaving my bed.

Absolute perfection.

I wake up to someone pounding on the front door, and I scramble from my bed, half asleep still. My feet clap against the hard wood of the stairs as I rush downstairs. My brain is hazy, but I have enough wits about me to wonder what the fuck is going on. I try to not care about my somewhat feral appearance as I catch a glimpse of my reflection in the window as I rush to the door.

I open the door ready to yell, and I find a stoney-faced Mac standing in front of me. Thank God I showered before I slept. "Uhm, hi?"

I blink a couple of times, and he stands there, silent, with his arms folded across his chest.

"What are you doing here?"

"Let me in, Octavia." His voice is low and rumbly, and I don't think I've ever heard my dad's old head of security sound so mad. I step aside without question and wave him in. That's when I notice a few paparazzi camped out by the gates.

Fucking awesome. This is just what I wanted.

I groan as I move to shut the door. I'm super tempted to flip them all the bird. A picture of me looking like this and acting like that, would be worth more money than I want any of them to have. So I resist the urge and lock the door once Mac's in the house.

"What the hell's going on around here, V?" Mac's voice booms through the entry hall, and I wince at the volume of his apparent anger. "Five years you were under my watch, and not once did anything like this happen. Less than three months away, and you've been in the media more times than I care to count. The latest being pictures of your arrest."

"Okay, look, I can see that you're mad, but how about you tone it down a little, and I'll explain. Coffee?" I walk toward the kitchen without waiting for a response from him. If I'm going to get a dressing down from a disappointed Mac, I need coffee to make it through. I pour myself a mug from the pot I brewed before my nap and pour him one too before sitting down and waiting for him to catch up.

What is it with all of the men in my life generating their big dick energy in my direction? I'm tired of being everyone's go-to to be pissed at.

"You had better start explaining, Octavia, otherwise I'm either pulling you from this place or moving in.

Because something isn't working." He leans against the wall, arms folded, and I sigh. I don't technically owe him an explanation, and he doesn't have the power to make me leave; but he helped raise me, so I understand some of his frustration.

I walk him through everything that's happened since I got home, and I wish I could say that it abates his anger, but at least it's redirected for the time being.

"These boys need to be taught a thing or two," he growls before finally sitting down and drinking the tepid coffee.

I bark out a laugh at the thought of him dealing with the four of them. "I'm not sure you'd do anything but give yourself high blood pressure and a potential heart attack. The four of them aren't really big on the whole authority figure thing."

He huffs a dry laugh and leans forward on the counter. "That sounds like they need a swift kick up the ass. But since I'm here, what can I do to help with this mess?"

"Honestly, I'm not sure there's much to do besides ride it out. Smithy's had the security increased on this place, and you're welcome to have a look around to make sure it's up to your liking. But beyond that, I'm kind of keeping myself on the down low as much as I can." I smile sadly at him and clutch the coffee cup in both my hands, hating how helpless it all sounds. I always thought I was a bad bitch, but being back in Echoes Cove is testing every single thing I ever thought to be true.

He stands, circling the island to wrap me up in those giant arms of his, making me feel like a little girl again. The fatherly comfort that radiates from him nearly makes me cry, and it hits me once again how alone I've really been without my dad around. There's nothing like being an orphan with literally no family left in the world—and my mom doesn't count because she left. She's never coming back, and I've made my peace with that.

"Let me take a look at your security system, and if anything's lacking, I'll sort it out. I wish there was more that I could do."

I squeeze him a little tighter before letting go. "You're here. That counts. But you have other people that need your special brand of protection now. I'm a big girl, and I have big walls here. I'll survive. It's not like I have a few thousand fans trying to break into my tour bus." I laugh at the memory of Mac trying to wrestle the door to the bus shut as a bunch of teenage girls tried to get to my dad. In the moment, it was terrifying, but looking back, it was kind of funny too.

He shakes his head, chuckling a little as he rubs a hand down his face. "Teenage girls are way more feral than anyone gives them credit for."

Mac left after checking my security. He upgraded the software so the cameras start recording ten seconds before the buzzer is pushed. He also installed an app on my phone so I can interact with people at my gate wherever I am out in the world. I had to give him more reassurances than I've ever given to anyone in my life that I'm okay. That was a few hours ago, and I've basked in the peace and quiet of the theatre room since.

I drop Indi a text to let her know I'm okay before I start the next movie, even though she has no cell service since she's camping. I can already tell she's going to be spitting feathers when she gets back to civilization and realizes what happened while she was gone.

I'm halfway through the action movie when my phone buzzes, telling me someone's at the gate. I pull up the app and see a guy who can't be much older than I am, standing with a giant box. "Hello?"

"Delivery for Octavia Royal," is all he says. I check out the van behind him, which looks legit enough, so I buzz him in.

I pause the movie and pad out to the front door, ready to meet him. It's a little late in the day for deliveries, but what do I know? I reach the entry hall as the knock echoes around the entryway, making everything seem far more sinister than it is.

Get a grip, Octavia. It's just a delivery.

I hope.

After the last few months, anything's fucking possible at this point.

I open the door and find the acne-ridden guy holding the box out to me. "Octavia Royal?"

"That's me. Who sent this?" I ask, skeptical as hell as I take the box from his outstretched hands. The black rectangular box is heavier than it looks, and I sag a little as I take its weight in my arms. Apparently I need to work out more.

He shrugs and thrusts his gadget thing in my face. "I have no idea, I just make the deliveries. I don't ask questions. Sign here, please."

I take the stylus from him and squiggle on the screen. He takes the gadget back with a nod before loping back to his van and driving down the lane to the still open gate. I wait until he's gone and close the gate, securing it once more before taking the box to the kitchen.

I contemplate calling East before opening it, but that seems way too dramatic. It's only a box. From an unknown source. With unknown contents.

Fun times.

I take a deep breath and undo the black ribbon that

secures the lid, practically holding my breath as my heart races like I'm waiting for a bomb to go off or something.

I really need to watch fewer thrillers. My mind is in hyperdrive right now.

As I pull the ribbons of the bow, a card falls to my feet.

It's the same black card that always comes with the flowers. Except this time, there's red lettering on the back.

For the Gala,
With Compliments
TKS

Well, that isn't creepy at all. I'm kind of glad I made the decision to not go to the gala.

I lift the lid and find black tissue paper inside.

Whoever this is needs a new color scheme.

I work my way through the tissue paper and gasp when I finally uncover the contents. I lift the soft material from the box, eyes going wide when I realize what it is.

The floor-length gown is breathtaking. The creamy champagne material is covered in white lace, and the neckline plunges down to the navel. It has a choker design with a high back and capped sleeves.

It really is stunning.

Creepy, but stunning.

I lay it over one of the barstools and rummage through

the rest of the tissue paper, but there isn't anything else in the box. No extra notes or anything.

I bite down on my bottom lip, trying to decide whether or not I should maybe tell someone about the dress when my back door swings open, and I find East standing there with Lincoln, Finley, and Maverick.

What a way to make this day better.

The alarm sounds, and East ducks to the keypad to turn it off. I keep forgetting he got the codes from Smithy.

"What is that?" Lincoln asks as he pushes past East into my kitchen.

I roll my eyes as they all enter the room, Finley closing the door behind them. "Hi, guys, yes, come on in why don't you. Make yourselves at home."

My sarcasm is met with mixed reactions.

Mav saunters over to the fridge behind me, grabbing a soda and slapping my ass as he does, making me yelp. Of course since we've fucked, he's overly touchy now, even if he was an asshole to me afterward. The tension as he looks at me is suffocating, so I glare at him, and he winks as he slides onto one of the stools at the counter. I wonder if the others know. Surely not. Finley leans against the wall with his arms crossed over his chest. East heads for the coffee pot, and Lincoln inspects the dress. Surely they'd say something if they knew. Lincoln huffs, and I turn my attention back to him and his earlier question.

"It was a gift," I say, finally answering him. I point toward the card, and he picks it up, scowling as he does before passing it around to the others, despite my frown. East is the only one who reacts, the same way he did when he saw the flowers.

East scowls at me, which seems to be his current default setting. I'm getting kind of sick of it. I don't know what's going on with him, but I'd like my chill, laid-back friend back. "I thought you weren't going to the gala."

I drop onto the stool as Lincoln folds the dress back into the box and sigh. "I'm not, not that it's any of your business. Can you stop looking at me like you hate me? I've had a day already, the last thing I need is all of this big dick energy pulling me down."

Maverick barks out a laugh, but East looks a little horrified.

"We wanted to stop by and make sure you were okay after yesterday," Finley finally pipes up, watching me intently. Maybe he does know, but if they're not outright saying it, I'm sure as hell not either.

I hold my hands out to my sides, lifting them in a sort of mock surrender. "Well, as you can see, I'm fine. So if that was all…"

"That was all," Lincoln says abruptly, pocketing the note that came with my dress. I'm too tired to argue with him about it. I'm officially learning to pick my battles when it comes to these guys.

I jump from the stool and glance at each of them in turn. It's hard to pinpoint exactly when I became more comfortable around them, considering everything that's happened since I returned to Echoes Cove. It's strange, but having them in my space doesn't make me want to light them on fire, so I guess we're making progress compared to just a few weeks ago. Maybe it's some weird Stockholm Syndrome type thing where I don't hate them despite all the shit they've put me through.

"I'm tired. If that's all, you guys can leave so I can sleep."

Mav jumps down so he's standing behind me, closely enough that I can feel his hard dick rub against my ass. "Sure you don't want me to stay?" he purrs in my ear, quietly enough that I'm sure no one else can hear. "I can make sure you have a real good time again."

A shiver runs down my back, but I shake my head. Last night was a mistake. I have no intention of repeating it. Even if the orgasm was so good my brain melted. His hands circle my waist, and it feels like an electric current passes through the room. I need to stop this before the others notice. Because if they don't know yet, it won't be long until they figure it out if he keeps this up.

"I'm sure," I say firmly, making Finley laugh while Mav looks a little disgruntled. That is firmly a *him* problem.

Lincoln's gaze zeroes in on me, and the heat of it is enough to scorch before his eyes land on Maverick. He definitely didn't know, but I'd put money on him knowing now. He's way too astute to miss Maverick being extra handsy with me.

"Am I missing something?" East pipes up, noticing the new tension in the room, and I step even further away from Maverick.

"Nope, not at all," I say, popping my p. "It's officially time for you all to go."

I usher them out of the house, despite their objections, and close the door behind them. I lean against the door once they're gone, finally feeling like I can breathe again.

All I wanted was a nice, simple year back in Echoes Cove.

I should really know better by now.

Twenty Six

It's been two weeks since the arrest, and life is somewhat back to normal.

Well, my version of normal anyway. After all of the bullshit with the guys and the media, I decided to put my head down and refocus my life. I've caught up on everything for school and managed to get ahead in most of my classes where I can.

I've become a model student and an upstanding citizen. I've also managed to avoid all four of the guys who have made my world tilt on its axis over the past couple of months.

I don't know what to think or feel when I'm around them anymore, so I've decided that avoidance is the key to keeping sanity firmly in place.

I grab my keys and phone from the counter and make

my way to the garage. Thank fuck this week's nearly over. Tomorrow is my dad's birthday, and to say I'm dreading it is an understatement.

Smithy ended up not coming back when we thought because his sister took a turn for the worse again. I can't be angry that he's looking after her when she's suffering so much, but I'm kind of sad that I'm going to be on my own for an unknown amount of time. Even if Mrs. Potts is looking after the basics. It's just not the same.

I shake my petulant pity party off and climb into the car. The dread I'd started to feel when heading to the unhallowed halls of ECP doesn't exist anymore. Even Blair has left me the fuck alone lately. I don't know what East did or said to my family when he got them to drop the charges, but I even got an apology note from my aunt about the 'misunderstanding.' It's been a very surreal few weeks.

I pull into what I've come to see as 'my spot' next to where Indi's already parked in the Wrangler. I grin up at her when she bounces around to my car door, two coffees in hand. I double check my hair in the mirror before climbing out of the car and taking the coffee she thrusts in my direction. "You, sweet cheeks, are a goddess."

"I know," she says with a weird little curtsy that makes us both laugh. We link arms and head into the school. I give Maverick a little finger wave as I pass by him, basically scaring the snot out of a freshman. He grins at me, and I shake my head as he drops the kid, who runs off the first chance he gets. "How are things going with the guys?"

I look at Indi, who has the audacity to look sweet and innocent, like she didn't just imply some sordid shit. "We've come to a mutual agreement of avoidance, I think."

"So no more public fuckery then?" She laughs, wagging her eyebrows, and I feel a blush coloring my cheeks.

"No, nothing like that. I told you, I'm not here for anything like that. I don't have time or the want for a guy in my life. Let alone multiples."

She pouts as she leans up against the locker beside me. "Spoilsport. How are we meant to do double dates if you won't date?"

"You think any of them would do a double date?" I bark out a laugh, and she shrugs. "Even if I was to date someone, it wouldn't be any of them. They've been so hot and cold that I have no idea where I stand with any of them anyway."

She rolls her eyes at me, and I sigh like we haven't had this conversation a few times over already. "I'm telling you, all four of them are chasing your kitty cat. They would all definitely do terrible things for a peek at the meow. Just sayin'."

I close my eyes, trying not to laugh at her absurdity. Who the fuck says shit like that? "Indi, it is a good thing I love you. Anyway, you don't need the comfort of double dates, right? I thought things were okay with you and Jackson."

She shrugs and clutches her books closer to her chest. I can't help but frown, apparently I've missed something. I've been so wrapped up in my own shit that I haven't noticed what's been going on with her. "Things have started fizzling out after the camping trip."

"Please tell me you didn't put out and now he's ghosting you. If you tell me that, I'll murder him. I'll have a straight up murder party and dance on his grave."

"I wasn't really ready to take that step with him; but he seemed so into it, I didn't know how to say anything since we were out in the middle of nowhere just the two of us." She shrugs, looking down at the floor, and I see red. That fucking asshole. I'm going to rip his dick off and then see how he feels. A tear slips down her cheek, and she wipes it away quickly. "I'm sure it's not that. Maybe I wasn't any good and that's why."

Her voice is so small, and I hate him for doing this to her, and I hate myself for not noticing something was off with her. I pull her into my arms and hug her tightly. "I'm going to kill him."

I let her go and look up and down the halls, searching for the jacked-up jock. And here I was thinking he was a half decent guy. I'll gut the motherfucker.

All of the weird emotions I've felt about my own shit, mixed with the looming sadness of tomorrow, are pushed into my well of rage toward Jackson.

Finley walks toward us, and his eyes go wide when he sees me. I'm seething, and I can't control how hard I'm shaking. "Who pissed in your Wheaties?"

"Uhm…" Indi starts to talk, but I spot the jock in question. She reaches for my arm, but I shake her off.

"You!" I hiss, moving toward the asshat that broke my friend's heart.

Finley doesn't even ask questions. He hauls Jackson up against the lockers, lifting him from his feet by his throat.

"What did you do?" he hisses, and Jackson coughs and splutters where he holds him.

The football player claws at Finley's hand, and Indi taps on my shoulder. "Please don't hurt him. Not here."

I look at Finley and nod. He drops Jackson, who crumples to the floor in a pile. Finley crouches down and talks to him so quietly that I almost miss the words that spill from his lips. "We are not done here, Jones. I'll be waiting."

He stands and nods at me before heading down the hall toward his class like nothing just happened. I turn to Indi, who's watching Jackson as he catches his breath. I move closer and press my foot against his balls, applying pressure before I lean forward to talk to him myself. "If I hear that you've done something like this before, you can expect to lose these." I push a little harder, and he squeaks like a pathetic fucking loser.

I lift my foot and turn to Indi, linking her arm in mine before dragging her down the hall.

"Thank you. No one has ever stood up for me like that before."

I give her a side hug, squeezing her as tightly as I can. "Ride or die, bitch. There isn't anything I wouldn't do for you."

She gives me a watery smile, and I want to turn around and step on Jackson's balls so hard they actually pop. I'll deal with him later. For now, my friend needs me, and that's all I'm going to focus on.

I wake up bleary-eyed from having cried myself to sleep last night. The room is shrouded in darkness, and I'm glad. Nothing about today makes it a happy or light day.

It's my dad's birthday.

The first since he died.

And I feel fucking hollow.

I wish I could say I cried myself out last night, but every time I woke up throughout the night, the tears started again. I look down at my phone and see that it's already ten in the morning.

I guess I'm skipping school. Honestly? Fuck everything today.

I keep my eyes open long enough to shoot off a message to Indi to let her know I won't be in and to not panic before putting my phone on silent and laying it face down.

The whole world can suck it today.

I curl up into a ball, trying to stop from feeling like my heart's bleeding out of my chest. Memories assault me of how we spent his birthday last year. We were half a world away from here, in London, doing all of the stupid things that made Dad happy. Like visiting the Queen's Guard and making fun of their unwavering stature. Wondering how many cake places we could hit up before someone was sick. Doing all the cheesy touristy stuff like riding the London Eye and visiting Big Ben.

And now... Now he's gone, and we'll never do any of that again.

I remember complaining about all the stupid stuff last year, taking for granted that it was just another birthday because we'd have plenty more of them together.

Sobs rack my body as the memories flood my mind, and there isn't anything I can do to stop them.

I miss him so fucking much.

I startle when the balcony door opens, and Lincoln walks in, his school shirt partially open. "What are you doing here?"

He kicks off his shoes and drops his blazer onto my dresser before climbing into my bed. "I remembered what day today is, and I didn't want you to be alone. You weren't at school, so here I am."

I try to wipe my face as he pulls me closer, until I'm lying on his chest. "Remember that one time, when we thought it would be fun to try to make a treehouse. Your dad ended up helping, but managed to nail-gun his shirt to the wall?"

I'm somewhere in the middle of laughing and crying at the visual. That day was so much fun. It was my eighth birthday, and the guys and I thought it would be a great idea if we could build the treehouse we'd been talking about for weeks. My dad was very much not a handy guy, but he loved me and wanted to help.

I sob on Lincoln's chest, and he strokes my hair, not saying a word about my tears staining his shirt or the fact that I've barely spoken to him in weeks.

He's here for me, exactly when I need him. Just like he was when we were kids. "Thank you," I murmur to him when my tears finally subside enough that I can form words.

He rests his chin on top of my head as he runs his hand up and down my spine. "You don't need to thank me, Octavia."

It occurs to me that he's the only one of them that hasn't called me 'V' since I returned. Not that I wanted them to call me the nickname, but it's like he's always known that we'll never be what we once were. Something about that realization hurts me more than it should, especially since he's right here, looking after me the way he did when my mom left.

Maybe it has something to do with me.

All my life, I thought it was everyone else, but maybe there's something wrong with me. My mom left. My dad killed himself. Even these four… They didn't want me around once I came back, so they left me in a roundabout sort of way too.

I let out a shuddery breath and pull away from Lincoln, refusing to get too caught up in the comfort of his embrace. I won't survive it if I get attached and he leaves me too.

I have to remember that.

People always leave.

"We should do something tonight," Indi says as we finish changing after Gym. "We haven't done anything in weeks, and it's Halloween. I freaking *love* Halloween."

I cannot believe it's Halloween already. This used to be my favorite holiday, but this year isn't the same. With that in mind, I realize that I desperately need to reclaim some joy. I've burrowed myself away, doing nothing but studying and starting my plans for the recording studio.

I've also written more songs than I have in my entire life.

It's been a weird few weeks.

I finish buttoning up my shirt and slide my blazer on before looking back at her. "Did you have anything in mind?"

She smiles up at me, her eyes full of hope. I haven't been able to say no to her since the whole Jackson thing. The sniveling little asshole hasn't said a word to her since that day either. I fucking hate cowards like that. "There's the house of horrors on the other side of town?"

I groan as I grab my bag and slide my feet into my Chucks. "Fine, fine. We can do it."

"Yes!" she exclaims, jumping to her feet. "At least we don't have to wear costumes, right?"

"I'll take the win."

She does a little jig on the spot, making me laugh. "You should because I was going to make us be Pippy Longstocking twins."

I laugh even harder at her as she grins. We head out of the school, ignoring everyone we pass, arm in arm, to where the cars are parked. "I'll pick you up at eight?"

I nod as I head to the driver's side of my car. "Sounds

perfect. I'll dress comfortably."

"Whoop! I'll see you in a bit." She bounces into her car, and I shake my head as I get my shit sorted out before starting the engine.

I feel eyes on me, so I look up and see the three boys who haven't been that far from me since my dad's birthday all watching me. They're kings surveying their kingdom, yet I'm their only focus. It's almost a heady feeling.

I shake it off because their attention isn't what I need right now. Or maybe even ever. I might have forgiven them for being assholes and taken refuge in each of them at one point or another since I returned to Echoes Cove, but we're not anything more than people who used to be friends.

I put the car in reverse and pull out of my spot, the weight of their gazes burning into me.

Sometimes I wish we'd never left here. I can't help but wonder how different life would be if I hadn't left with my dad all those years ago. But I can't really wish that I didn't have that time with Dad.

I drive home, unable to think about anything but the four boys who've had me twisted up in knots since I returned to Echoes Cove. One way or another, everything always seems to lead back to them.

I pull the car into the garage, spotting another delivery of yellow tulips on the steps.

I can't help but frown. No one should be able to get this

close to the house without me letting them in unless they're coming in via the Saints' property. I'm pretty positive the flowers aren't from Lincoln or East, and it's starting to feel a little creepy. Especially after how they both reacted to the cards that come along with them. So I leave the flowers where they are, spotting the plain white envelope and decide to head inside to get ready for tonight's house of horrors.

Fall is officially here, so I dig out a pair of jeans and the hoodie East wrapped me in the day he rescued me before grabbing a quick shower. He's definitely not getting the hoodie back, like, ever

It doesn't take me long to get ready, and I reheat some of the shrimp linguine Mrs. Potts prepared while I flick through the series I keep meaning to start on Netflix. I have way too many TV subscriptions for the amount of TV I don't watch, but fuck it.

I flick through the videos on the 'for me' page on my latest addiction of an app, glad that despite the shit I've dealt with, very few people even know about the account I have on here. The pictures of the football team preparing for their game make me scowl. What a fucking let down those guys ended up being. Indi has bounced back from the Jackson thing pretty well, but it's impossible to miss how she freezes up when he's near us at school.

I know she hasn't been to any games since their

camping trip too, which fucking sucks because she loves football.

Boys are so stupid. Who even needs them?

My phone buzzes in my hand, and I pull up the message thread.

Indi:

On my way

I put my dishes away in the dishwasher and pull my hair up into a messy bun. Screw hot girl summer, this is comfy girl fall.

I lock everywhere up and head down to the gate to wait for her, finding another bunch of tulips leaning against the railing.

This is getting to be a little much now, so I pull up my phone and snap a picture. I shoot a message to someone I totally didn't envision messaging anytime soon.

Me:

*Is this you? Because two bunches in one day is a lot *laughing emoji* also, if it's not you, can you check your security to see if someone's using your place to access mine because one set was left against my front door.*

Lincoln:

Wasn't me. I'll look into it

I check the post box while I'm waiting for Indi to arrive and flick through the junk mail. I find a manila envelope stashed in here. It has my name on it but no address, so it was hand delivered.

Weird.

I open it and the contents fall out.

There are so many photos of me in here. Photos of me with the guys, with Indi—all of their faces scratched out.

I think I'm going to be sick.

Then I see the note.

One day we'll be together. You won't have to be alone anymore. You won't have to run to them when you're sad.

One day isn't too far away.

This can not be happening.

Twenty Seven

After reporting the pictures to Smithy's friend at the FBI and actually having a meeting face-to-face with the guy Smithy sorted my security out with, I feel a bit better.

Needless to say, Halloween was fucked up, and I felt so bad for Indi. Which is exactly why I'm about to cave to her yet again.

"*Please.*" She gives me those puppy dog eyes of hers, and I about die.

I hate telling her no, especially after how shit these last few weeks have been, but I can't help but want to hide away in my house and never leave again. "This probably isn't a good idea. Not if I have a weird stalker out there."

"There's no way your stalker would dare to do anything to you at Ryker Donovan's party. The stalker seems like a total creep, but Ryker Donovan's a legitimate psychopath."

I swear, she almost sounds wistful when she talks about him like that. "I think I've had enough of psychopaths lately."

She bursts out laughing like I'm a fucking comedy genius, and I can't help but shake my head at her.

"Come on, we deserve some fun. We've been so good, and this is our senior year. One party won't hurt. We won't even drink if you're worried. I just want to dance and have fun. We could both use a night of that. I'm friends with Ryker's little sister, Scout, too, so if we hang out with her, Ryker will keep an eye on us anyway. Plus I have, uh… history with the twins. But that's a story for another day."

"Don't think we're not going to revisit that little tidbit." I bite my lip, indecision eating me. It would be really good to let loose for a night and live my life like an actual fucking teenager, but I can't help feel uneasy about it. Between the flowers, the dress, and the creepy-ass pictures, I want to hide in a hole somewhere that no one can find me.

We head to my locker so I can pick up my books before heading home for the weekend, and I consider going to the party. It's the moment I have all of my books gathered in my arms that I hear my name called.

"Octavia."

I look up to see Lincoln stalking toward me, looking just about ready to commit murder.

What the fuck did I do now?

Indi winces as he comes to a stop before us, and I put on my cheeriest smile. "Hey, what's up?"

"The flowers. Have you gotten any others?"

Ah yes, I almost forgot I asked him to look into that. The creepy stalker thing took over my every thought, and it only just occurred to me that the flowers could be from whoever that is too.

"A few different bunches since I came home, yeah. Some were also delivered when we were away on our spa trip… And there's the dress too, I guess." I pause, contemplating telling him about the photos. I ultimately decide it's probably better to tell him since he offered his help once already. "I, uh… also had to call the police last week because I seem to have a stalker."

He clenches his jaw and quirks an eyebrow at me, like he's waiting for me to continue. "Someone sent me a manila envelope full of pictures of me with Indi and you guys. Everyone else's faces were scratched out, and there was a creepy-ass note too."

"Why are you only just telling me about this now?" he asks, his fists clenching and unclenching at his sides.

I bite my lip, not afraid of him, but definitely afraid of how he'll react. "Honestly, I didn't even think about it. I only just called the police. It's the first envelope like this I've gotten."

His eyes flash, but he locks down his features in a heartbeat. "If you get any more shit, call me first."

That's all he says before he stalks off, joining Finley and Maverick where they're waiting for him at the main doors. I huff, trying to keep calm about him giving me orders, while trying not to overthink the weird protective thing he has going on. I let out a deep breath because I know Lincoln's like a dog with a bone. He'll find something out. He has ways of doing stuff that I don't. I'm not willing to ask what they are, or look at it too deeply; but if he can stop the flowers from showing up, I'd appreciate it.

"Dude, I'll never figure those guys out," Indi says, almost dreamily. "They're like your black knights or something. Can't call them white knights, but they're definitely always there watching out for you."

"Because that isn't creepy at all." I laugh. "Okay, let's hit this party, why the fuck not?"

She does a little dance as she bounces down the hall. "Hell yes!"

"Do you want me to drive, so you can have some fun at least?" I ask as we head out of the school.

She grins at me as we reach the cars and clasps her hands together in front of her. "Why don't we grab a cab? That way neither of us has to worry. Besides, I'm sure Ellis can give us a ride home if we need it."

"Ellis?"

She smiles dreamily, and I can't help but laugh. Okay, there's definitely some history there that she has to tell me about, pronto. "Ryker's twin brother."

"Of course," I say, rolling my eyes. "I'm good with whatever as long as we don't end up stranded or dead in a ditch somewhere."

"Deal! I'll text you when I'm on the way to your place."

I nod before climbing into the car. I'm almost looking forward to tonight if I'm being honest. Though there is a part of me that's dreading getting home to the possibility of more flowers or weird envelopes. My mood's a wash, I guess.

I cross my fingers and send up a thought to anyone who might be listening to let me have one night of normal, teenage fun.

That's all I want.

When Indi said these guys are the life of the party, she grossly downplayed how hard the ECH crowd likes to party. I've spoken to a few people I used to be friendly with, but for the most part, I keep to myself and dance the night away.

I'm not even sure whose house we're in, but the bodies are packed in here pretty tight. There have been more than a few wandering hands, but I've been able to fend off most of them and enjoy myself.

Indi has been whisked away into the arms of Ellis Donovan, and I get the feeling I'm missing a big chunk of their story. I'm not about to interrupt them to get more details. She deserves to be happy, and well... She definitely looks happy right now.

I push my way through the crowd. I desperately need some water and some fresh air. When I reach the kitchen, I freeze.

What the fuck is the ECP football team doing here? I thought there was some ridiculous school rivalry stemming from the two teams?

"Octavia!" Raleigh cheers my name like he hasn't been a giant asshat for the last month or so. He says it like I'm his favorite person in the world. He's obviously had more than a few too many beers.

I smile tightly at him and grab a bottle of water. "Come sit with us. Talk!"

"I'm good, thanks." I try to be as polite as I can considering no one knows where I am. Plus, he and his friends are all way stronger than I am, beer or not, and I do not want to have to throat punch anyone today.

I try to move past them, to escape out the back door and into the cold night air, but he loops his arms around my waist and yanks me back against him. He takes the water from my hands and puts it on the counter before spinning me round so the others can't see us as well. "I know you miss me. You were meant to be mine," he murmurs into my ear, and an icy shiver of dread runs down my spine. He sounds *way* too much like the creepy stalker's note.

It can't be him, right?

I shake off the thought and push at his hands until I manage to worm my way free of him. I grab my water from the counter and duck out before anyone can say anything else or grab me again. It's only seconds before I push out the back door and stumble onto the much less occupied patio out back, relieved to get some space for a moment.

This might be the 'bad' side of Echoes Cove, but the Donovans clearly aren't doing badly. I've heard a few rumors about them, but I'm not one to judge people based solely on rumors. I mean, that would definitely be the pot calling the kettle black.

I suck in lungfuls of the cool night air and chug the water back. It tastes weird, but it's been a minute since I had carbonated water. The cold liquid feels too good going down, so I sink the bottle and move to sit on one of the loungers out here.

I stare up at the dark night sky, and the scattered stars call to me, so I stay where I am, enjoying the quiet as the noises around me begin fading out.

"There you are." I look up, my head heavier than I

remember it being, and see Raleigh stalking toward me. "Did you miss me? Look at you finding us some privacy."

I try to sit up, but it feels like my body won't respond. He crouches beside me and brushes my hair away from my face. I try to speak, but my words come out slurred. My eyes dart around the space, but everything is fuzzy. Panic creeps in as the world seems to slow down.

What the hell is going on right now?

I try to sit up, but the world spins.

My heart races in my chest and I can't think straight, despite a thousand things racing through my mind. I try to suck in a breath, but it's like my body won't work right.

"Where are you going? This is our time." He pushes me against the lounger before he starts kissing my neck. My blood turns to ice in my veins as I try to push my hands against his chest but my arms are like jelly.

What is happening to me? Why can't I move properly? Fuck.

My skin feels like I'm rolling on a bed of needles, the pricking so bad it steals most of my attention.

I try to push him off, to tell him no as tears slip down my face. "You like that, baby? I knew you wanted me."

My eyes flutter closed, and when the world focuses again, my tank top is gone, and I don't know how. His lips move down my chest, and I scream out in my mind. No noise comes out of my mouth as he pulls the cups of my bra down, exposing me, before his tongue licks one nipple and then he sucks on the other.

I'm going to be sick.

I manage to lift my hands and place them on his chest as he lowers himself on top of me. "That's it, baby, fight me. I love it when they fight."

This can not be happening to me right now.

"No," I manage to murmur, but it seems to excite him, even as more tears slip down my cheeks.

His hand plunges into my jeans, and I manage a garbled scream as his fingers brush against my lace-covered pussy.

Please God, no.

"You motherfucker!" I hear Lincoln's voice in the seconds before Raleigh's body is ripped away from me. Indi's face appears in front of mine, and the sound of flesh against flesh fills the quiet space around us.

"V, are you okay?" Indi asks, tears running down her own face. She looks more angry than anything. She helps me sit up and grabs my tank top from the ground by my feet, helping me back into it so I'm no longer exposed. I look up and watch as Lincoln rains blow after blow down on Raleigh as a sob rips out of me.

I can't say anything as I rock in her arms.

"Ellis called Lincoln for me as soon as I saw you. They were already here. I didn't know what else to do. Let's get you out of here," she says, trying to help me stand, but my legs won't work. I can barely keep myself sitting up. Everything just feels wrong.

"Lincoln!" she yells, but he's lost to his rage. Seconds later, Finley and Maverick appear. Mav glances over at us, and then nods at Finley before heading straight for Lincoln, each of them practically vibrating with rage. Finley comes straight over to us, a sense of calm visibly washing over him despite his rage moments ago, and I swear I want to cry all over again.

I feel so fucking dirty.

I can still feel him on me.

God, I want to vomit.

"I got you," Finley murmurs quietly, lifting me into his arms like a rag doll. I hate being so compromised, but I know that while they're here, nothing else will happen to me. Even after everything we've been through, I know they'd never try to hurt me like that. Try to rape me.

I start to cry again just thinking about it.

Lincoln and Maverick appear before us, and Lincoln looks fucking feral as he growls at Finley. "Give her to me."

"Have you got yourself under control?" Finley asks him, and he nods once.

"Good, now I can show him what happens when he touches things that aren't his," Finley says quietly as he hands me over to Lincoln.

Maverick smiles softly down at me as he runs a finger down my face. "Don't worry, princess. You won't need to worry about him ever again."

I close my eyes at his touch, and Lincoln adjusts me on his chest so my face is tucked into his neck. "I'm going to get her home. Call me if you need any help with him."

"Oh, we won't need any help," Maverick says almost wistfully.

"I'm coming with you," Indi speaks up, and I see Ellis standing beside her.

Lincoln shakes his head. "You stay here, I've got her now. She's safe." His menacing growl is enough for Ellis to place a protective hand on Indi's waist and pull her against him.

She looks at me and nods. "You better have her, I'm not afraid of you, Lincoln Saint." Just then, Ryker joins her and his twin, looking just as protective as Ellis does.

He chuckles, his chest shaking where he holds me. "I don't think you are, and that makes you either very brave or very stupid. Thanks for the call, Ellis. We'll be seeing you both soon."

He starts to move, and my eyes flutter closed.

The next time they open, he's belting me into his car, being more gentle with me than he's possibly ever been. "Sleep, V. I got you."

Linc pulls me from the car and against his chest. I'm not sure what Raleigh drugged me with, but I'm starting to get control of my extremities back, and my brain doesn't feel quite as foggy as it did before. "I can walk," I murmur, but Lincoln holds me tighter.

"I'm sure you can, but I already told you I've got you."

"What the fuck happened?" East's voice reaches us, and Lincoln sighs. He gives him a brief rundown of the night's events, but that only seems to piss him off more. "Why didn't you call me?"

"You weren't with us. Would you have preferred we left her to be raped because we were busy getting you instead?" Lincoln argues, and a shiver runs down my spine.

"Let me down, please?" I ask him quietly, but his arms tighten around me. I place a hand on his cheek and bring his gaze back down to me. "Please?"

He watches me intently, but I see the moment in his eyes that he relents before nodding. He lets me down, catching me as I stumble while struggling to find my footing. "Thank you."

I *really* need to fucking shower.

I walk toward the front door slowly but pause when I see it.

A note on the doorstep.

I brace myself on the door to pick up the note, my heart racing as I do. I pull the black card it from the envelope and my heart fucking stops.

You're out of time, Miss Royal.

We're coming for you.

Ready or not.

Twenty Eight

LINCOLN
THEN

"What the fuck do you mean she's coming home?" Fear runs down my spine unlike any I've ever known.

She was supposed to be safe. That was the deal he made. Lose one, keep one. No matter how hard the decision was.

"Her dad's dead." Finley's words pack a punch, practically sitting me on my ass.

"How?" This can't be right. We did everything right.

"Suicide, apparently," Maverick grunts as he hits the punching bag in the corner of the room.

East drops onto the sofa and throws back his glass of whiskey. "You really think Stone Royal would commit suicide?"

This can't be fucking happening.

"You and I both know there's no way it was fucking suicide," I growl as I pull at my hair. "Stone Royal would have hung the fucking moon for Octavia. He would never have left her defenseless against them like that."

"You really think they'd do that?" Maverick asks, stilling the punching bag.

"You really think they wouldn't?" Finley asks, while I rack my brain trying to come up with a way to keep her safe and far, far away from here. "The real question is why? What could they possibly gain from his death and her submission?"

It hits me in an instant, of course. We've been blocking what they want for too long, and they know us too well. They know our weak spot.

It's always been her.

"Us... They fucking get us."

SIGN UP FOR MY NEWSLETTER TO HEAR ABOUT UPCOMING RELEASES

ABOUT THE AUTHOR

Lily is a writer, dreamer, fur mom and serial killer, crime documentary addict.

She loves to write dark, reverse harem romance and characters who will shatter your heart. Characters who enjoy stomping on the pieces and then laugh before putting you back together again. And she definitely doesn't enjoy readers tears. Nope. Not even a little.

Visit her website at http://www.lilywildhart.com to sign up for the newsletter or find her on social media through the links below.

ALSO BY LILY WILDHART

THE KNIGHTS OF ECHOES COVE
(Dark, Bully, High School Reverse Harem Romance)

Tormented Royal

Lost Royal

Caged Royal

Forever Royal

THE SAINTS OF SERENTIY FALLS
(Dark, Bully, Step Brother, College, Reverse Harem Romance)

A Burn so Deep

A Revenge So Sweet

A Taste of Forever

THE SECRETS WE KEEP
(Dark, Mafia, Reverse Harem Romance, Duet)

The Secrets We Keep

The Truths We Seek

Ingram Content Group UK Ltd.
Milton Keynes UK
UKHW010604040623
422833UK00001B/12

9 781915 473202